DENZEL THE ORPHAN DUCK

To

Rebecca.

Merry Christmas 2013

Godbless

S.J. Cart

Dedication

I'd like to dedicate this book to my Mum and Dad, my family as a whole, with special thanks to Ashley who inspired me to write this creative work.

Sidney James Carter

DENZEL THE ORPHAN DUCK

AUSTIN MACAULEY
PUBLISHERS LTD.

A CIP catalogue record for this title is
available from the British Library.

ISBN 978 184963 370 3

www.austinmacauley.com

First Published (2013)
Austin Macauley Publishers Ltd.
25 Canada Square
Canary Wharf
London
E14 5LB

Printed and bound in Great Britain

The Author was born in 1944 and was raised in St Pauls Cray, Orpington, Kent. He was one of ten children from William and Kath. Sidney's mother was of Irish Decent coming from quite a wealthy family. His father was originally from South London, coming from a not so fortunate background. The Author was born during the Second World War, being the middle child of ten and for unknown reasons became the lovable rogue of mother's brood. All the other siblings had chosen the right path whilst Sid became a notorious thief earning serious amounts of money over his criminal career, which enabled him to become a very eccentric character, through his generous ways and carryings on in and around the plot. The Author also became known as an infamous cat burglar, acquiring a respectable name in that genre. After a spell at her majesty's pleasure, during which time Denzel was born, he retired from his former life and now spends his time on his award winning garden, he came joint winner of London Borough of Bromley Environmental Awards 2012 for his back garden, complete with chickens and runner up in the front garden category. He also enjoys all types of wildlife, fishing and has a passion for good food and is an excellent cook.

Introduction

In the heart of the Kent countryside lies the small village of Horton Kirby, through which passes the river Darenth, which winds its way through sprawling hills, passing through such picturesque landscapes and other pretty villages, such as Otford, via Eynsford, which has its quaint ancient hump-back bridge, striding the river for the use of mankind. The river rolls on through the beautiful village of Farningham, and so to Horton Kirby, where, before passing, like many other rivers, it feeds the large expanse of lakes. These are huge holes that were left from the workings of old gravel pits in years gone by. In those days, man and his mechanical machines dug these gigantic holes for hogging, otherwise known as gravel. This was usually crushed to make ballast for the booming building industry. The great holes that were left began to fill with water from the rain, along with seepage through gravity from the water table below the earth's surface. At first, man and machine had left an ugly scar on the fabulous landscape but the very next spring, after man's departure, wonderful things started to occur, when? Old Mother Nature began to nurse that destructive onslaught, and springing forth from her bosom, such beauty appeared. The river ran through these lakes, bringing new life, such as seeds being carried by the fresh water and pond life of every description, from fish to insects, birds such as the magnificent swans, to the smallest warblers, ducks of every species, not forgetting the beauteous fabulous kingfisher. Also trees like the hanging willows, with many thousands upon thousands of wild plants, seeds and bulrushes. In other words, heaven here on earth, not only all the gorgeous wildlife, but a spectacle for the eyes of all men, that is second to none.

For nature's gift of the landscape is in truth the only real beauty, because none of what man calls money could ever buy such enriched genuine splendour. Man and his wealth are far too impatient to wait as Nature can, and does, to take its natural wondrous course.

Chapter 1

The Little One Survives

Well, it was in the vicinity of these lakes at Horton Kirby where our tale begins with the little fellow in question, (of thereabouts), a Master Denzel Duck. The time – early July 1964. Young Denzel was just coming up to three months old, and the poor little fella, had survived a massacre which left him the only one of the family of seven. One summer's evening, just before sunset, he, his mother and father, along with two brothers and sisters were crossing the big lake, making their way to their usual roosting place. Mother was the leader, followed by Denzel, then came his two brothers, Dennis and Dicky; close up behind paddled his two sisters, Delores and Delia. Bringing up the rear was their father whom Dicky was named after.

"Come along children," mother duck called to her following flock, "only a short way to our roost, then we can all have a good night's sleep."

"Goody," squeaked Delia, the tiniest of the family, "I'm really sleepy and worn out."

Suddenly, out of the night, without any warning, the most horrifying thunderous bang reached young Denzel's ears, and the little duck's head stooped back into his shoulders, at the most deafening sound he had ever heard in his young life. Alas, out of all of his family of seven, Denzel, on adjusting once again to the silence and peace of the lake and the now fading light to see in disbelief, his whole family, laying lifeless atop the now still water. For he, love his heart, was the only one to hear that dreadful sound. Crying in petrified silence, swimming this way and that, now hearing human voices, then the heavy splash, of a dog entering the water, Denzel losing all sense of direction, swam in desperation away from the pursuing canine. He eventually made his lonely terrified way to the safety of the nearest cover of dense reeds, and a makeshift roost on a floating log. Denzel, in total shock and confusion, clambered aboard and finally fell into a fitful nightmarish sleep. Denzel woke at daybreak to the dreadful memory of what had happened just a few hours before. Sitting on his log, lonely and terribly scared, and now wondering what to do; furthermore, where to go from where he was, knowing all the dangers that lay out there on the lakes and surroundings about which his parents had warned him, and his brothers and sisters of, since the day they had all hatched. One piece of luck was that the little duck was coming up to being one quarter of a year old and had managed to learn a few tips on life. He knew how to feed and preen himself, to keep his new feathers clean and tidy, so's to keep his nice shiny plumage in good condition. Sitting on his log in silence, the little Duck started plucking some unwanted duckling down from his breast, and wing tips. He had also learned not to take chances, by sitting sunning himself, on the banks of the lake, for "cunning foxes", as mum called them, "Would, given the chance, pounce and eat me all up", (he thought nervously to himself.) So he made sure that this was rule one, to be abided by at all times. This also applied to cats and dogs, he reminded himself, as the vivid warnings came back into his thoughts. His mother, and father both, had always told him, and the rest of the family.

"Keep away from open waters as much as possible, only cross the lake at dusk, or in the dark, or very early in the morning, as the sun pokes its head up in the east." Denzel knew even then it wasn't safe, for look what had happened to his family, but at least he knew he had a slight advantage by following these strict rules, making sure all dangers were at their least.

Denzel's little brain was ticking over, trying to remember as much as possible, everything his parents had told him of dangerous predators. He knew of dogs, and cats, because over his short life, he had seen such animals running about at the water's edge. This was when his mum or dad taught him the differences of each individual dangers that lurked in and about the waters they lived in.

"The Dog," his father would scold at them all at a very early age, "is a big hairy git, as your mother and I have shown you many times. Now he," his father would say " has got a long tail, big ears and a snout that can sniff you out, also other intended dinners!! They have long pointed faces, with teeth and jaws, that can rip you apart."

Denzel also recalled asking his dad, whilst he was telling them of all the dangers, and dogs,

"What are teeth and jaws?" So his father told him, and the rest of his flock.

"Teeth and jaws. Umm, well now, you see, us ducks," father went on, "we have our heads, right? And protruding from that, we have our bills, to quack and talk. Also to eat our food, so when we chew our food to break it up so it can be digested easily, right? Now on the other hand, animals such as dogs and cats, which are dangerous to us, as well as foxes, which are much the same as the Dog family, but they're more naturally wild, these have got their heads all shapes and sizes mind, but they have what we call jaws, instead of bills like us ducks, and fixed into these jaws, children, are very strong white stones that are very hard and sharp for chewing, just like we do. But! Why? Theirs are so razor sharp, unlike us where we only eat soft food, they eats meat, and I'm afraid, little ones, that is exactly what we are – their food supply." Denzel's father, went on to say that an old friend of his, a big old Tawny owl who lived in the highest craggiest willow tree, over on the far side of the lakes, had told him, many years ago, that these meat eating animals, were named Carnivores. He also told him that even humans were partial to a bit of duck, also other kinds of animal meats. "Now the Cat, he's another hunter altogether! Not at all like the Dog. He recalled his dad, at the time of telling the youngsters of such matters, had his brood of four half frightened to death, and found them all swallowing hard, and looking at one another terrified. "The Dog usually gives us prior warning, by crashing into the water, and puts us water folk on our guard. But! Old Tom Cat," their father nervously laughed, "he's sleek, and cunning, these furry creeps, as your mother and I have shown you, on many occasions. So I'll warn you kids, one and all, he'll just sit there all day, devious and crafty. He'll watch 'n' wait for you to turn your eyes, for just one moment, then he'll pounce so quickly, you'll be his dinner that day, as sure as our King 'n' Queen of the lakes are monarchs." As Denzel pondered on his father's words, "Be warned!" It led him to think of the most dangerous predator of all, Man.

He again recalled his old dad saying to them all, "Man has four legs, but as you have witnessed for yourselves, he only walks, or stands on the back two. The front ones..." Denzel recalled at this stage of their father's warnings that he and his brothers and sisters were shivering in anticipation of what was to come next, after all the other bad predators fore-mentioned. Leaving his own thoughts, back to his father's, "And the one carrying the firestick, that made that lightening flash, and the deafening bang!" As Denzel thought of his dad telling them of the man and the firestick, it all came to him so very clearly. That it was man who was responsible for the predicament he was now in. Because that thunderous frightening bang, shot through Denzel's head reminding him of the heartbreaking loss of his entire family, and the sounds, of drip dripping, was faintly heard, as real tears fell off his little sad face, into the water below his roosting sanctuary, in deep despair and loneliness.

At daybreak the heat from the rising sun woke Denzel, who was usually up and about at this time; but, because of unforeseen events, and hardly sleeping at all, he had over-slept with exhaustion. To Denzel's surprise on waking, he noticed, swimming towards him, the King and Queen of the Horton Kirby lakes and river. Within moments they had reached the poor little duck. Denzel watched from his resting place, as they approached. The little fella wasn't at all afraid. For these were friends of his mother and father, and they were the most beautiful pair of pure white Whooper Swans. He remembered Cyril the cob, and Grace the pen. Grace, as Denzel recalled his mother saying, acquired her name, because she swam so gracefully. God only knows how old Cyril got his. Denzel smiling to himself for the first time since his plight.

"Young Denzel isn't it?" hissed the lovely Grace.

"Er… er… yes." replied the duck.

"Well, my darling, never be afraid All of the residents of the lakes and rivers, have heard of your plight of losing your whole family to the firestick man. We have come here today to tell you we are all, here, on and about these waters, your friends. So go about your life as best you can. All the wild animals and birds feel so much for you. They have asked my husband and I to let you know that."

"Cheer up, son," said the old cob, "My name is Cyril, and this here is my good Queen Grace."

"Y… yes," replied the little duck sadly, "I know."

"Don't feel so unhappy, son; I know it hurts, laddie, but time heals, even the deepest of hurt feelings. Just you remember, son, any time you need someone for advice or just company, don't hesitate to come to us if you ever feel the need."

With this the two swans turned and swam away. Denzel was left pondering over what the kind elder swans had said, about all the other residents on, and in the vicinity of, the Horton Kirby Lakes. After they went, the young duck began to feel a little warmth come to life in his terribly broken heart. He never moved very far from the log he'd escaped to, just a yard or two, here and there, not feeling much like eating or sleeping, grieving over the terrible loss of his family. Once settled back on the log, he kept drifting back into slumber. He was dreaming of all the happy times he'd shared with his brothers and sisters; things like climbing to the tops of very steep banks on rainy days, sliding down on their little rumps on the muddy slopes, hitting the water causing a big splash, resulting in going under the water, then resurfacing some yards into the lake. Oh, such fun, he recalled; but the thoughts were just too painful for the little duck to bear. This went on for days, but on the fourth day, the swans had called round, to enquire about the young troubled duck's welfare, and to see how he was coping with his personal grief. To their amazement, they found young Denzel looking quite lively. He appeared to be shaping up very well indeed.

"Good morning, darling." Queen Grace called.

"My, you look much better, I must say son." Old Cyril said, as he caught sight of the smiling eyes of his beloved Grace, knowing it made her happy to see the young duck picking up a bit.

"Yes, I do feel a little better, thank you." replied Denzel, feeling much happier in himself. He had just woken from the best sleep he'd had since his loss, and terrifying experience, and he was feeling much better in himself altogether. He had, over the past miserable days, noticed a pair of ageing coots, who had swum near to where he sat on his log, never coming too close, calling and trying to coax the poor duck out of his dilemma, and to make sure he was alright. But Denzel, in his own self pity, couldn't even bring himself to reply, he just wanted to be left alone. Now feeling much better, and with a little more confidence, he thought he'd venture over. So stepping from the log that had been his sanctuary for the past four days and nights since the nightmare of what Man had bestowed upon him, he'd finally taken his first paddle into his orphaned future. The old pair of coots saw Denzel heading their way. At first the old couple made out they hadn't noticed, and went about their chores around the island, keeping one eye on the approaching duck, which, incidentally was Mrs Coot's idea.

"Let him come in his own good time, dear." she whispered to her doting husband.

"I think you're right, lass." exclaimed the old male coot.

As Denzel approached the pretending busy couple, he found himself not at all shy, in fact he felt quite cheerful, considering what he had been through of late.

"Good morning, Mr and Mrs Coot." Denzel said, copying what his parents would normally quack in passing the time of day.

"Well, good morning to you, lad." said Mrs Coot, bursting to get the first word in.

Mr Coot smiled, and softly said, "Would you care to take breakfast with us, little one?"

"Denzel!" he said "my name is Denzel."

"Well, isn't that a lovely name for such a sweet little duck dear," smiled the old hen, wiping some muddy water from her face with her wing tips. "And mine is Aunt Clara." She smiled, taking it upon herself, by adding Aunt, to make the little duck feel more at home. "So from now on you can drop that Mrs Coot business, my lad, and the old coot here is Clarence, my husband. From now on we are Uncle and Aunty, Ok?"

"Thank you kindly Aunt," replied the now much more cheerful duck, who, for the very first time since his trauma, had stopped thinking of it.

"How about that breakfast? It's only weed I'm afraid, but it's very nourishing for this time of morning, and helps your digestion, my lad," old Clarence explained to the young duck.

"You must eat your greens" Never forget that, lad, for greens are so good for your health." Clara fussed, as she sat on an old willow root that was poking from the water. The little duck nodded his yes, and smiled at the old girl, not fully understanding their kindness, after all that had happened of late.

Clara, at this time, was acting like a broody old hen, having the duckling around. Denzel had copied Clarence who had waded out from the island into the shallow water, where every few moments their heads submerged into the crystal clear water, to nibble on the fresh green weed below, surfacing in harmony to have a chew, and little friendly natter. Once he had eaten, Denzel, after about an hour of resting on the water's edge, sunning himself and chatting to this very kind couple, began to feel he'd come to life again for the very first time since his ordeal. On thinking this to himself, he asked Clarence and Clara if he could stay with them for the rest of the day and night.

"Of course," replied the two elder Coots, almost simultaneously. "You can stay, or come and go as you please," said the old boy.

"We'd love you to," said Clara sincerely. Clara then went on to say how she and Clarence had missed their own offspring, who had been paired off, the last being Claris, two summers ago. They both went on in their own way, and told of how they had reared a family of three, two boys and of course, young Claris. The eldest, Clarence Jr. "He married a lovely wife up at the lakes at the Crays, and they have a family of their own. We have never seen any of them, but grace and Cyril, the King and Queen, were that way in the spring, where Clarence Jr, told them of the joyful news."

"And the youngest boy?" enquired Denzel, really enjoying this conversation. With this, poor Clara's head bowed in sadness. Then old Clarence in a very painful voice immediately came to his beloved wife's aid, explaining,

"Like your family Lad, we lost him too. He was taken from us by the Firestick of what folk call around here, the Poacher Man." Denzel knew exactly how the lovely couple felt, and it brought pangs of hurt to his already broken heart. Not so much for his own loss, for he was beginning to mend, but to see this dear old couple deeply hurt was unbearable, after what he'd been through. "Time heals," said the old Coot "but as you can see by my dearest Clara, it never really goes away."

It was getting dusk by the time they had eaten, sunned themselves and chatted of this and that, and Denzel felt really tired. In fact, whilst listening to all the tales of this nice warm couple, the little lad did actually drop off once or twice, resulting in Clara telling him to find a more comfortable roosting perch, before he fell asleep where he sat, on the mossy grass of the island floor. Denzel didn't need telling a second time before he had found an ideal roost, on a low willow branch, and at last fell into a deep, and more contented slumber.

At dawn Denzel was wide awake and ready to face the world. He stepped from his roosting perch onto a lower branch, and pushed himself off into the fresh clear water. He then gave himself his morning's freshen up by dipping his head into the water and shaking it from side to side very quickly, shaking the moistness from his feathered face. On straightening himself up, he noticed that the old timer, Clarence, was entering the water, and doing a similar performance of cleaning and freshening up.

"Fancy a little swim, lad?" called Clarence on his entry.

"I'd like that very much," replied the now smiling duck.

Clara was woken up by the two males' conversation. "Thanks very much, you two noisy things," she exclaimed, " a woman can't even have five minutes beauty sleep these days," she sighed, but then smiled teasingly at the two of them, "Go on, you two, it'll do you both good, I'll clean myself up whilst you're gone. Don't be gone too long mind!" she called as Denzel and the old coot swam away to the edge of the Big Lake.

On arriving quite close to the water's edge, Clarence informed Denzel that over the top of this very steep bank, and a minute or two's waddle,

"There is the most wonderful sight you'll ever see my lad". and went on to explain all about the River Darenth. He then went on to tell Denzel how the river supplied all the fresh water that brought new life to all the lakes.

"Oh," said Denzel, "I've never seen the river. My father has mentioned such a place but told us at our age, it was by far too dangerous to attempt the journey. My father also said there are too many dangers lurking."

"Quite right, Lad," said Clarence, "but one day I will take you, I promise."

Clarence also began explaining "Without the river, our lakes would be sad, smelly places, for fresh running water, brings new life to the lakes; not only bringing fresh clear water, but also aerating it, and so fetch's new life to our beautiful waters."

"You know such a lot Uncle Clarence," smiled Denzel in pure admiration, not realising he'd made the old coot feel grand by hearing the lad call him Uncle for the first time.

"It's all part of the knowledge lad, but I must tell you that it only comes with age, and experience of living a long life." He then went on to tell Denzel, that he too would be knowledgeable on such matters. He also told him that one day he too would pass on his life's learnings, on to his own young ones.

Denzel loved listening to the old coot, who appeared to be even more of a story teller than his own father. (But he is soon to meet and even wiser old bird!) Together they swam the length of the big lake that ran parallel to the river, keeping close to the reeds, keeping themselves out of sight of a fisherman who they had seen earlier as they set off from the island. Denzel, who just like the old coot, was familiar with fishermen as they have been around even before old Clarence's day. In fact, according to Uncle Clarence, they have been a good food source, for they always seemed to throw food such as bread, and fruit of all kinds into the water. Sometimes they even bring food especially to feed the ducks and other birds and animals of the lakes. But as old Clarence had told Denzel,

"No matter how kind Man seems, always be cautious, never take for granted the ways of Man, for I have found through my lifetime, you never find two the same. So just remember, lad, never two the same," the old Coot repeated his warning.

"Yes," Denzel answered, but not really understanding fully his elder's experienced words.

On their return, Clara was sitting in the sun preening herself in the reflection of the still water of the puddle she used as her daily mirror. On seeing them round the bend into her view, she pulled her face away from the mirrored stillness, trying to hide her vanity.

"Have you eaten?" she called trying to hide her blushes.

"No!" came Clarence's answer, "Denzel and I thought we'd build up a nice appetite, and all have breakfast together, dear."

"How thoughtful you two are!" she smiled.

They all moved to the shallow feeding ground, where all three ate heartily till they nearly burst their bloated bellies. Denzel, being of the duck family, usually ate floating food, but being so young, the weed he was eating at this time, was quite sufficient, whilst he was on the mend.

"I'm bloated," said Clarence on raising his head from the water.

"I couldn't eat another morsel." chimed in Clara.

Denzel never heard a word that the two coots had spoken, for his little head was still down in the depths, nibbling on the juicy green weed.

"Ah, look at him, Clarence!" Clara smiled. "The way he's scoffing that weed, you'd never dream of the torment he's gone through, love his heart."

"Aye, I think he's on the mend, lass," said the old coot, smiling in joy as he spoke, for he and Clara both loved sharing the happiness the little duck had brought into their lives.

"You know, dear, he reminds me so much of our Clive." Clara choked, tears running down her soft feathered cheek.

"Aye lass, but don't go upsetting yourself now." Clarence comforted his loved one. "Let's be contented in what we have in our young friend."

"I am, dear," wiping her cheeks with her wing tips, "I am."

Once Denzel had his fill, all made for their respective sunning places back on the island, and settled down, and fell into a lovely warm comfortable sleep. Later that afternoon, after their nap, Denzel was feeling even more daring, and said to Aunty Clara and Uncle Clarence, that he'd like to go for a little swim on his own.

"Where do you think of going?" Clara asked, in a sudden loud moan.

Denzel said, "I've been looking out at that little cove over there, you see, just under those willows. My mother and father used to take us youngsters there quite a lot." He went on to tell them that the cove was a little trap for floating food, such as bread, that had been thrown away by the fisherman, and "although this weed is nice, I really could do with something solid, as I've barely eaten solids since the big bang."

"Oh! If you must, but do be careful mind, you being so young an' all, and so small too!" she reminded him.

"He'll be all right, lass", Clarence assured her, giving Denzel a wink behind the fussing female's back!

"But as she says lad, don't take any chances. I've told you, as your father did, these lakes hold many dangers."

"Yes, of course I will." assured the duck. Then off he swam, calling back to the watchful old couple, "See you both soon."

"Yes dear, and do be careful!" the old dear called.

"Will you please stop fussing, old girl, give the lad a chance; let him find his own way!" said Clarence, as he put his wing around her shoulder to comfort his adoring Clara. "I know you mean well lass," he patted her gently, "but the little lad will be alright you'll see."

The old coot could see the pain this lone trip was causing her, and showed the old girl a little more love and affection towards her.

Denzel had no sooner left the caring couple and was now swimming towards the Cove, which appeared to be another two hundred yards, or more, when, seemingly out of nowhere, a croaky little voice called,

"Oi!"

Denzel was not at all sure of what he'd heard. Then the sound came again.

"Oi, Ducky!" The little duck turned to his left, and there sitting on a piece of driftwood, was a big fat toad, with the most huge protruding eyes stuck out of the top of his craggy (to say the least) head. But what Denzel had noticed, even more strange, was the character's enormous extraordinary back feet. At first he could hardly make it out, for it was amongst a load of old bits of dried reeds. Then all of a sudden, it spoke!

"Are ya going over ta the uvver side ov the lake, me old china?" the cheeky toad croaked.

"Why do you ask?" replied the duck, shaking his feathers down from the back of his long neck, after being startled by Toadies sudden appearance so soon after leaving the two coots. "You made me jump!" retorted Denzel, and "I'm not your china, whatever that is supposed to be."

"China plate, Mate!" croaked his strange new acquaintance.

"What on earth is that kind of talk?"

"Slang," said the Toad, "yer couldn't giss a lift, could ya Ducky, as I'm not a very good swimmer; fact is I ain't too keen on water at the best of times," he chuckled.

"Well, for a start, I'm not your Ducky, and my name is Denzel!" he snapped sharply.

"I'm off to see me mates ya see, 'cause I'm getting hitched tomorra."

"Hitched?" asked Denzel completely puzzled. "I thought we scratched those."

"Na, ya feathered fool, wot it is, is when two ov us toads falls in love with each other, they gets tied togevver in marriage, ya see na, got it?" croaked the now smiling Toad.

"How long are you tied up for?" asked Denzel, not really understanding.

"Cor strewth, ya don't get tied up with rope! It's just an old London saying us Londoners use." croaked the stranger. "As I say, it's slang, London slang."

"London? What's London?" Denzel asked.

Toady burst out laughing. "You make me laugh you yokels, you ain't got a clue, have ya? Na! I'll tell ya wot I'll do! Denzel woz it?"

"Yes!" the very confused duck replied.

"Er... well... you just let me jump up on ya 'haystack', er... back". Toad thought he'd better drop his Cockney banter, on realising the young duck's brain, most definitely wasn't ready for his bunnying banter yet! For our friend Toad knew full well that he was by far too confusing for a duck of these parts.

"Let me climb on your back, and while you take me across, I'll fill you in, as we go, is that alright?" asked the toad.

"I... suppose so." sighed Denzel.

Toady leaped from his floating mess, and settled between Denzel's folded wings, nestling behind the duck's neck. "Well," he croaked "I need to get to the water's edge, cause I've got to meet me pals you know! Friends, as you yokels calls em. 'Coz tonight's, me stag night."

"Stag night?" asked Denzel, inquisitively.

"Yer mean ta tell me ya dunno what a stag night is?"

"No!" said Denzel, matter-of-factly.

"Well, when us toads gets married, which usually happens on a leap year, as you mob calls em, we haves a stag night!"

"I… I heard my mother say once, that all courting couples get married, and my parents got married after their courtship," smiled the duck on reflection, "But this stag night thing, I must say is all new to me."

Denzel thought… "What a queer toad I'm carrying on my back; and that lingo of his, he sure sounded a real rough customer, if ever I heard one!"

Although, strangely enough, Denzel liked the toad for the character he was.

"Now, how about this 'stag night'?" asked Denzel.

"Er… er, yers, as I say, even them humans have'sem! Wot it is? The very night ya's get married, ya have's ya last 'Hop Skip 'n' Jump, wiv ya pals, in uvver words, this is me last free night out wiv me pals. ''Cause once ya married, ya settles daan wiv ya gel, or lady like, then live happily ever after and have a few 'dustbin lids' of our own."

"Dustbin lids?" retorted Denzel, most confused, thinking that on his back he carried a total crackpot! Please, Mr Toad, will you speak properly, for Pete's sake!"

"Sorry, mate, I can't help the way I woz brought up nah, can I!" snapped the sharp talking toad. "Ya see-why I talks like I does, when I was a 'dustbin lid', I…"

"I thought you were a toad?" interrupted the duck.

"I am a blooming Toad, and will ya please shut your gob, for one minute!" Toad ranted, and raved on. "For the life of me, these country yokels, I da know, where I come from, the grown-ups call their kids, 'dustbin lids'. Get it? kids, lids. It sorter rhymes, if ya gets me meaning?"

Toad went on to tell the duck of how he came to be living in these parts, and the duck listened in awe, as he paddled his way towards the edge of the lake, to where Toad directed him.

"Ya see, as a kid, I woz hatched by the side of a little stream called the 'Quaggy' in an area where thousands of humans live, in big fings, made wiv funny shaped bits of mud. The name of the place I come from is 'Lewisham', south of

'London' which is the biggest human place of all! Anyway, last year our little stream got so filthy wiv Man's stinking waste. At that time, me old man 'n' me muvver had a hundred and twenty eight 'dustbin lids', hundred 'n' twenty seven of em were girls, me skin 'n' blisters, as us cockneys calls em, and I woz the only boy."

"Skin 'n' blisters?" laughed the Duck.

"Yers, Ducky, me sisters."

"Oh, I see, it's one of them 'sling things'."

"Slang" roared the Toad in laughter, and carried on with his tale of woe.

"One day, a load of them humans came wiv them big noisy moving fings, wiv them big shovels on, and started to clean up all the mess they made, in and abaat the 'Quaggy'. In doing so, it dug up our home at the water's edge, then we got lifted up, and tipped into one of them big moving fings, that goes along them big paths." He went on to say, "It was awful! me mother 'n' father, and me and one skin, got separated from all the others. Let me tell you, Ducky, it woz tellible, and a dodgy old turnout altogevver."

Denzel was listening to Toad, but he being so young, had no experience of life, and never had the slightest of inkling of this strange character's banterings. As Denzel paddled on towards their destination Toad filled him in, on part of his life story, and how he became part of life about the Horton Kirby Lakes.

"As I say, we were tipped into this big horrible moving fing, which brought us out 'ere in the sticks, and tipped us out in a field. I've been out this way ever since. Me mum 'n' dad, died of the cold in that tellible winter of 1963, and me only surviving skin, married a well-orf-toad, over Dartford way."

"Skin?" said the even more confused Denzel.

"'N' Blister. Sister," croaked the toad.

"Oh! You are confusing Toady." said the duck shaking his long neck in disbelief.

Nearing the water's edge after a slow ride, Denzel had realised after hearing part of Toad's life story, that some parts, were very much like his own. Also at this point, he again realised he didn't even know Toad's name.

"What is your name?" Denzel asked.

"Treadwell," croaked the joy-riding toad, who seemed to fall silent after mentioning his name.

"Treadwell? That's a funny old name for a toad, isn't it?" laughed Denzel jokingly, taking a glance at Toad's extremely large feet.

"Well yorn ain't too clever either, is it? Denzel! Ha, ha, Foreign ain't it?" Treadwell chucked a crafty croak, to himself.

"I... don't really know," the little duck answered, thinking to himself of all the traditional names his brothers and sisters had. But he distinctly remembered his mother telling him one day that she had met and befriended a lovely family of blackbirds, that had made a home at the side of the lake. Their youngest son was called 'Denzel', and seeing as she was running out of names that started with a 'D', "She liked the name and gave it to me, the last to be hatched."

As they reached the bank of the lake, Treadwell was still nattering, still snuggled up close to Denzel's feathers, enjoying his 'lift' as he called it!

Treadwell found he really liked this young duck, so much so, he asked Denzel if he would like to 'attend', or in Toad's words,

"Go to me wedding do, tommorra." He told Denzel all about it, and that it was being held on the banks of the river Darenth, under the bridge. The reason, according to Treadwell, was that some of the guests on her side, (meaning his intended) were arriving upstream from the Lakes, at Dartford. Also his skin, and her 'usband were flying in.

"Flying in?" asked Denzel, scratching his young confused head, with his wing tips, thinking by now that Toad was truly a raving lunatic.

Then Treadwell explained.

"Yer see Denz, my sister Tammy, 'n' her well-orf 'usband, Trevour, have a big Canada Goose as their friend. He lets 'em ride on his back, and flies 'em all around the Dartford Lakes, just like you are giving me a lift nah, get it!"

"I… I, suppose so," mused Denzel, toying with the thought that a goose would certainly have no trouble in carrying two small toads. "I would love to come to your 'Wedding', Treadwell, but I'm not old enough to travel on my own, the journey is far too dangerous."

"Never mind, Ducky, maybe we'll bump into each other on anuvver day," croaked the fat toad as he leaped from Denzel's 'Haystack' (as Toad called it), and landed with both enormous feet planted firmly on the bank of the lakeside.

"Yes, I'd like that very much, Toady."

"Yers, 'n' so would I, me old son," croaked the grinning Toad. "Er… before I goes pal, do ya live in this part of the lake?"

"Oh, I'll be easy to find. Just ask any of the birds, or animals of the lake. Not that I know many of them at the moment!" Denzel thought to himself.

"Fanks for the lift, Denz, I'll be orf nah, see ya, pal."

"Treadwell, before you go, what's her name?"

"Who?" replied the toad.

"Your intended."

"Er… Yers, well Tootsie," croaked Treadwell in a throaty laugh.

Then, without further ado, he had taken the mightiest of leaps, such as Denzel had ever seen from any toad, or frog either come to that. Springing up from his enormous feet, he disappeared over the heavily foliage bank and out of the little Ducks sight.

Denzel pondered for a moment, reflecting on this strange encounter. He smiled at the thought of his new-found friend. The little duck shook his head from side to side in wonder. Would he ever meet this Cockney character again? He certainly hoped so.

After his little reflection, it had occurred to Denzel that he had almost forgotten his original reason for being where he was, and immediately gazed in the direction of his intended trip to the small cove. He found himself a little way off the route he'd intended, but his meeting with the crazy toad seemed more worthwhile than fifty crusts of bread. In truth, he longed for the day when they would meet again. Denzel started to paddle towards the cove and hoped at least to find something solid, even if it was only a half-eaten sandwich, that some kind fisherman had tossed away. On his way to the cove, Denzel swam as taught by his elders, parallel to the bank which was covered in trees and shrubbery, of every description. He kept as close to the edge as possible, for he had learned from his parents, that by doing so he would keep out of sight of Man and other dangers. Not too close, he reminded himself, about twelve feet, he thought, just in case any foxes or dogs lurked in waiting!

It was late in the afternoon now, and Denzel was full of joy and happiness, because it seemed after the toad encounter, every few yards he swam, he was greeted by,

"Hello little Duck," or "Good day young fellow," from all manner of the residents that appeared in his path on or about the water's edge. Also by lots of their children, much the same age as himself, who were born in the spring of that year. Youngsters of so many different kinds of animals and birds. As a matter of fact, some he'd never ever seen, or even thought existed, come to that. But all the same, at this very moment in time, he was thoroughly enjoying his new found friends. Denzel never imagined that there was so much life on the lakes where he lived. Sure, he knew in his short life he'd seen, and met, many species of lake folk, but, what he was experiencing now had most certainly come as a surprise. "So many different creatures," he thought to himself. There were frogs, of all shapes 'n' sizes, some sitting with their mums and dads. As he paddled by on his way to the cove, he noticed some small frogs sitting on large round lily pads jumping for joy, and croaking their respective 'hellos' to the passing orphan. Some of the youngsters began to leap excitedly from pad, to pad, not far away from him. One small frog from out of nowhere asked his name. Denzel was chuffed at all this attention, and although he was really hungry, seeing that all he'd had was a breakfast of weed along with Aunt Clara and Uncle Clarence that morning, and the fact that in reality hadn't eaten anything substantial for days, yet he seemed for the moment to dismiss his hunger, due to his sudden popularity. So, forgetting all pangs at the thought of his aching belly, he swam up and stopped beside a single bloom, which was one of many of the most gorgeous water lilies, which sat beautifully on a lovely green floating pad. Denzel was smiling to himself as he watched at least half a dozen young frogs which he reckoned were about his own age.

"Please, Master Duck, tell us your name," a call came from one of many young frogs.

"You want to know my name do you?" replied Denzel, hardly being able to contain himself at all this attention.

"Denzel!" he answered, in his most sincere voice.

All the young frogs were still leaping from pad to pad calling his name as they leaped, making their way to where he floated.

"Denzel, Denzel, we like Denzel," they croaked, as they hopped to where he sat.

The duck was so overwhelmed that a big lump appeared to rise in his throat, and for a brief moment was stuck for words. But soon he pulled himself together and began to converse with what appeared to be a host of wonderful new found friends.

"What are all your names?" Denzel asked the excited leaping froglets, at the same time looking across at the parents of the little ones. Their faces showed a reassuring smile, then a sort of mimed silent hello, came from the mouths of the two proud, overseeing adults. Approving of him and the infants, who by now were all seated before him, wallowing in their new found friendship.

"Fanny, my name is Fanny," one little girl frog blurted out making sure she was the first to get her spoke in!

"Typical female," Denzel thought, only too pleased at her eagerness.

"Florence," croaked another, "but everybody calls me Flo."

Denzel was wearing, now, a smile you could see a mile off. He looked at her, and said "Then I shall call you Flo!"

"My name is Freda," another call came from a little chubby girl frog, who appeared to be half hidden through her shyness, behind the petals of a gorgeous white lily bloom.

"I don't know which is prettier, Freda; you, or that beautiful flower," replied Denzel, knowing it would help Freda's embarrassment. But the dear sweet girl, for reason of her own, wasn't expecting such a sudden gentlemanly answer, which made her blush even more, making the sweet little thing 'cherry up' all the more.

"Aren't girls silly things?" remarked the first of the little boy frogs to croak.

"I'm Fred, Denzel. And I'm very pleased to make your acquaintance." Then he dived into the water and swam out to where Denzel was treading water. The moment he surfaced, before the small chap caught his first breath, he had spoken without thought, or consideration.He said, "we are very sorry your family got murdered by humans."

"Hey, stop that Freddy!" yelled Mrs Frog.

"Yes," said Mr Frog, "don't you go upsetting young Denzel any longer with your chit chat and unwanted croakings."

At young Freddy's outburst, Denzel felt within a deep feeling of hurt, on thinking of his whole family being chewed up by humans. But he soon revived his feelings, knowing full well that little Freddy only meant to be nice, in his excited croakings.

"Oh that's all alright! Er…"

"Frances, 'n' Big Fred," chirped in Wally the Dartford Warbler, who happened to be watching all the goings on. When Denzel turned to see who, or what, had spoken, he noticed to his surprise, a tiny waif of a bird hanging sideways on a reed stem. The tiny little chap was about to introduce himself, when he was interrupted by two other voices that cried out at precisely the same time.

"I'm next," then both looked at each other, burst out laughing at their joint timing.

"Franky at your service," croaked a long gangly legged frog, who immediately started bragging of how he was the first to hatch. Also how he grew his legs from a tadpole the quickest.

"He may be oldest, but I'm the youngest," came a tiny, but very squeaky croak from the second.

"Oh!" said Denzel, "and what is your name?" Denzel, although speaking to the tiniest of the family of frogs, never once took his eyes from the cheeky little ball of feathers that clung to a reed stem, just a yard or so away.

"Findus," replied the squeakiest of all frogs.

Denzel couldn't help a laugh to himself at his sudden thought, "Findus, eh! Just like me, you ended up at the end of the queue, when it came to the naming department." Looking up at the proud parents as he said it! The two grown-up frogs, Big Fred and Frances, as informed by the little bird, were seated on the side of the lake, in the shade of some heavy foliage. Denzel began to thank them and their cheerful offspring, for the wonderful way they had made him welcome and made him feel at home in their territory, on and about the lily bed. Denzel, after thanking all the frogs for their kindness, now turned to face the cheekiest little bird he'd ever heard. "You were about to tell me your name." he said, looking directly into the small bird's beady round eyes.

"Who, me?" chirped the cheeky chappie.

"Ah, ah," mumbled Denzel, nodding his head, watching the expressions on some of the frog family's' faces as he said it!

"W… Wally," he said, in a stammering chirp.

"I've not seen the likes of you on the lakes before," commented the duck.

Wally explained to the duck, and all who were present, about himself, and indeed exactly to what species he belonged. "I'm a Dartford Warbler," he boldly told them, and went on to say, "the reason I'm hardly ever recognised is because, although there are other Warblers in the vicinity of the lakes, such as the Reed, Sedge, and the Garden Warblers, but us Dartford ones, are scarce. 'Rare' as them Humans call us."

Whilst all were listening to Wally's tale, Denzel came to like the little bird. But from what occurred in the few seconds after the ending of Wal's chirpings, the duck found he adored the little fella. No sooner had he finished, with a tiny flutter of wings, he flew up onto an elder branch and broke into a throaty burst of song. Denzel with his bill agape, was astounded at the sound of such a beautiful tune coming from such a waif. Just as the little crooner had chirped his last joyous note, all in attendance clapped or made their individual noises of appreciation.

Denzel, in all the excitement, hadn't realised just how late it was getting. He thanked everyone, and explained he had to go.

"It was lovely to meet you all, but I must be going, as it's getting late, and I must try and find something to eat," he called.

"You must come by again," Mr Frog croaked from his seat on the bank.

"Yes, yes," chimed in all the little frogs.

"Please do," came a sweet little croak from behind one of the Lily blooms.

"Of course I will, Freda." replied Denzel, as he saw her blushing face peer around the petals of the big bloom.

"Perhaps we will be able to play!" croaked young Findus excitedly.

"I'd love to, Findus," said Denzel laughing at the tiny frog's request, as he went to turn and go.

"Let the poor boy go for goodness sake!" said Mrs Frog, "he must be famished."

As Denzel moved off in the hope that at least he'd find an old crust of some description at the cove. He finally reached his destination, curiously being followed reed to reed by none other, than Wally the Dartford Warbler! Denzel's luck was in! As soon as he entered the mouth of the cove, there, bobbing up 'n' down in the now choppy water, was a discarded whole current bun, which he devoured in moments.

"Blow me!" chirped Wally, "you really were hungry; you didn't even chew it! The way you attacked that bun, anyone would think you hadn't eaten for a week."

"I haven't," retorted Denzel, now tucking into a piece of brown bread he'd also found.

"No wonder," chirped the little Warbler, at the same time asking Denzel to beg his pardon for his rude interruptions.

"Granted," said the duck, devouring another soggy slice. That will do for now, he thought to himself. He then turned in Wally's direction and said, "I must find a safe place to roost for the night, I'm not going back to that old log, and it's too late to get back to the island. As for going over to my family's usual roosting place, I really don't think I could handle the memories." he told Wally.

"I don't blame ya, mate," chirped Wally sympathetically.

"Excuse me, could you tell me if there are any decent roosting places up yonder, I've never ventured that far up the lake in my whole life!"

"As a matter of fact, there's just the place!" chirped the little bird. "But I'm not sure if any other birds have taken all the roosts," he chirped again. "Hang on, it'll only take me a minute! I'll fly up and check it out for you."

"Would you be so kind?" Denzel asked.

"'Course I will." With this, Wally took flight, and in no time at all, he reached some very stout old willows. But these were exceptionally old, and certainly very craggy. They were about fifteen feet high, with huge heavy trunks, and branches. Wally, whilst checking found that it was absolutely perfect, and very safe for his new found friend. All of a sudden, just as he was about to leave to report his glad findings, he'd heard what he thought was a sound coming from the hollow of one of the big craggy trunks.

"Can I help you?" came a deep intelligent voice.

"Er... y... yes, I s'pose you can," chirped Wally, not even knowing at this time where the noise came from.

Then a huge TawnyOwl appeared.

It was just getting dusk when tiny Wally caught his first glimpse at the meat-eating giant, who was sitting in the semi-darkness. At this sight Wally's spindly little legs started to knock together.

"What are you afraid of?" hooted the bird of prey.

"Who me?" Wally said in stark fright.

"Yes you! By the sound of your knees if I didn't know better, I'd have thought it was a woodpecker digging it's hole in a tree. Ha, ha!" The wise old bird laughed at his own joke.

"I'm looking for a roost for my friend," Wally stressed, his little knees still knocking ten to the dozen.

"Oh, and pray tell me who you're so-called friend is," asked the big tawny suspiciously.

"He's a young drake, a Mallard to be precise," chirped Wally.

"Well, he's not kipping in my tree," moaned the old codger, a name Wally had himself chosen for the moany old ird.

"Well, could he use one of the others then? 'Cause it's started to get real dark," pleaded the persistent Wal.

"I don't give two hoots where he kips, as long as it's not here, 'cause this is my place, and I don't share nothing." Almost immediately, after thinking very wisely, and of course, having second thoughts, Owl asked Wally, "This particular friend of yours wouldn't happen to be that duckling, I heard the king, and queen of the lakes talking about the other day, by any chance?"

"Yes, yes, the very same," chirped Wally having the feeling he was getting through to the owl's heart at last.

"You mean the one who lost his family? And before little Wally could answer, the old owl went on to say what a sad affair it was. "Dirty business," said the old bird, in one of his nastier hoots. After even more thinking, the owl had a change of heart.

"Oh, in that case then, your friend is most welcome to this row of willows."

"Thank you, Sir you're very kind," smiled the not-so-nervous Warbler.

"Yes, but he'd better not try roosting on my perch, got it?" hooted owl, still doing his moaning, as most very old owls do.

"Yes, I... er no", stammered Wally. "I... I'd better go and fetch him then, or it'll be too dark for him to climb up to this height. See you, then," chirped Wally, as he left the willow. He found out for the first time in his life that it was hard work trying to fly with knocking knees. "Phew, blow that!" he chortled to himself as he flew towards Denzel as fast as he could, and it wasn't easy seeing as it was in semi-darkness, trying to get Denzel settled in for the night.

When he arrived back to where he'd left the tired duck, poor Denzel was all-in, and so he'd perched on a fallen willow branch, almost asleep.

"Come... come quickly, I've found the perfect roosting place!" chirped the near frantic Wally.

Denzel really didn't want to move, or go anywhere. But knowing his new little friend had gone to so much trouble, the duck made the effort.

"Is it far?" enquired Denzel through a tired yawn, as he stepped down off the fallen branch into the water.

"Not at all, just a hundred yards, at most, come along Denzel, before we lose the light altogether," chirped the helpful little bird. "Just around this next bend." Wally informed the half asleep Mallard.

"Thank goodness for that! I'm pooped!" claimed Denzel, yawning again as he said it.

They reached the big stout craggy willows quicker than Denzel had anticipate, and there Denzel thanked Wally, and told him that he himself couldn't have found a more secure roost.... "Um," he thought, "very suitable indeed." Denzel half hopped, half flew up into the safety and cover of the huge tree, settling himself on a branch quite close to the heavily-barked trunk out of any sudden winds that might get up in the night.

Then, out of the night, came Wally's wee voice,

"D... D... Den, there's a small thing I've forgotten to tell you!" said Wally mockingly. "In fact, it's not really that, s... small."

"Oh?" said Denzel, looking straight into the Warbler's tiny beady eyes.

"No," said Wally, swallowing hard, "as a matter of fact, Den, it's a bit lumpy," the Warbler nervously chirped.

"Lumpy!" exclaimed Denzel, suddenly unsure, "what do you mean by lumpy?"

"Well, a bit on the large side, if you get my meaning," answered Wally.

"Like what? I'm sure it's not that bad; come on Wally, spit it out!"

"Er… er, well, there's an owl in the next tree the size of an eagle."

"What!" retorted Denzel, knowing owls were partial to a bit of feathered breakfast,dinner or tea, come to that!

"He's all right though!" said the little Warbler, trying not to sound so nervous.

"All… bloomin' right!" Denzel scoffed, "they're bloomin' cannibals!"

"Really, it's all right, I've asked permission and the old codger said he'd heard of your terrible trouble – you know, what the poacher man did to your family, and he said you can stay for the night, as long as you don't kip in his tree."

"Ha!" laughed Denzel, "as long as I don't kip in his tree, indeed. Ha," he laughed again, "so we've found ourselves an owl with a heart, have we? Most unusual!" thought Denzel, smiling to himself. Then, again going by Wally's description, he did sound a bit large for a Tawny. Denzel thinking aloud, "In any case, from what I remember my father telling me, they only like to eat small things, such as Bank Voles, mice 'n' small birds," he told Wally, hoping what he said was about right.

"S… small birds you say" enquired Wal half choking on his words.

"Well I'll take the chance," said Denzel "But I'd better keep one eye open just in case," he informed his new friend, Wally.

"So you'll stay?" asked Wally, yawning himself, "It's too late to go back to my roost, so I'll drop down to those reeds below, as I can't stand heights."

Denzel wished Wally pleasant dreams. They had decided to get up extra early, both agreeing on a brisk start. Also the pair of 'em not wanting to stay too long around the uncertainty of their sharp eyed neighbour. So the little warbler bade his new found friend good-night, with a last tiny tired chirp of,

"See you in the morning." He then fell away silently to the reeds below. Denzel did manage with his final breath, one last, "Good night."

But Wally was too tired to answer, he'd gone to sleep immediately on clinging onto the first reed he could feel for, in the darkness of night.

Chapter 2

Denzel

Very early the following morning, just as the sun's light appeared over the distant horizon, Denzel had been woken from a very deep sleep on hearing the fluttering wings of the returning Tawny Owl. Denzel, only a few weeks previously, had learned from his late father that owls were creatures of the night, and hunted for their food with huge round staring eyes. The wise old owl settled on a thick branch in the tree next to where the little duck was roosting. On landing the owl noticed that Denzel had woken.

"Good morning to you youngen!" hooted the old Tawny.

"Hello Mr Owl," said Denzel, very confidently on seeing with his own eyes the true identity of Wally's interpretation of an eagle, and immediately all Denzel's fears just went, for on hearing the manner of which the old owl had greeted him he began to feel easy in the big bird's company.

Owl, on first meeting Denzel, had noticed the worried look on the young duck's face.

"You have no need to be afraid of me!" Owl hooted again. "I don't like duck anyway, too strong for me!" he told Denzel.

"Strong!" Denzel shuddered and poked his little chest feathers out to their fullest, trying to look tough.

On seeing the little duck's brave attempt to look mean, with this show of bravado, the old owl had a little chuckle to himself, knowing the little duck had misunderstood his true meaning. "I didn't mean that kind of strong, youngen, I meant strong in taste."

"Er… Oh!" replied Denzel, with a cold shiver running through his whole body, on thinking at least, "this big old bird has tried us ducks! – or how else would he know?"

"Very sorry to hear the sad news of your family, umm, what's your name again?" asked the owl in his attempt to be friendly.

Denzel sensed this in the Owl's voice, and replied in a more relaxed and cheerful tone, "Denzel."

"Denzel eh," hooted the seemingly nice old fella, "Such a wise name too! Did you know youngen, that your father was an old friend of mine? Yes," he recalled, "we shared a few good tales over the years, had some laughs too." He chuckled to himself on his memories.

"Y... you knew my father!" exclaimed Denzel.

"Oh yes," chuckled the wise old bird, thoroughly enjoying telling the youngster of his dad. "Of course I knew him, in fact when I first met him he wasn't much older than you are now." He went on to say what a fine Mallard his father was. Owl was feeling quite cheerful in himself, knowing he was brightening up young Denzel's feelings. "I remember it well," he recalled. "All the young hens were always chasing ya father around these lakes."

"Really?" asked Denzel, marvelling at the old owl.

"Oh yes!" said the owl, who went on to say "He had the pick of the Mallard hens, and let me tell you, some of those girls were very pretty indeed!" remarked the wise old bird. "Though I must say, Denzel my boy, none were prettier than the one he chose to be your mother."

"My... my mother!" Denzel stammered in shock, and disbelief at this old owl's knowledge of his late parents.

"Ya mother originally wasn't from around these parts, no she actually was a Cray girl."

"A Cray girl?" asked the now very interested duck. "What's a Cray girl, Mr Owl?"

"Owen!" retorted the Owl, "Your father always called me that! So there's no reason why you shouldn't do the same ma boy." Owen said proudly.

"Thank you Owen, but you were saying that my mother was... a Cray girl?" the little duck asked inquisitively.

Old Owen went on to tell Denzel, "You see ma boy, not very far from here, there are lots of villages, just like here at Horton Kirby, but each have different sounding names, such as where ya mother came from It is called St Pauls Cray, then the next village upstream from that is, St Mary Cray, downstream there's Foots Cray, North Cray, and the last Crayford, which is the nearest to here. Now ma boy, just like here and the many villages surrounding these parts, have the glorious River Darenth running through them all before and after these lakes, the Crays have the River Cray running through them, just as ours", said Owl. "You see youngen just like us! There are lakes like ours in the Crays, and ya mother, bless her heart, as I say, came from a respected family of Mallards, from those Lakes at St Pauls Cray."

At this stage of Owen's story, not a single peep came out of Denzel's bill, he was mesmerised by this clever old owl who knew that he had his audience well and truly captivated. In seeing the little duck this way, he got himself settled more comfortably, revelling in his own wiseness, just as much as the young pupil who sat before him.

"I recall it well," he smiled on recollecting. The young happy listener was very eager,

"Please tell me more Mr Owl."

"Owen," retorted the Owl.

"Oh yes, I'm sorry, Owen, but please, please go on," the little Duck pleaded.

"Alright ma boy." Owen at this moment in time, and in truth, was getting just as excited. But of course he dare not show it, then the old owl continued his tale. "One summer's morning, your dad, and his brother along with a few pretty local hens, who as I've mentioned were always fanning their tails at ya father, where I must say, he had pick of any one of them."

"Yes, yes, so you said, but will you please go on," Denzel said, so eager now hardly being able to contain himself on listening to Owen's account of his folks.

"Y… es" hooted the owl, in a long drawn out drool. "They were showing off to these girls, by taking off from out of the water leaving all the giggling females afloat upon the water. Ya father, Dick and his brother, umm, what was his name?" the old owl was trying to recall, when young Denzel reminded him,

"Dennis."

"Oh yes! Dennis!" hooted Owen, he went on to say, "The pair of 'em would take off, fly all around the lakes, then fly right up the middle of the lake towards the ecstatic girls, the pair of young Mallard drakes would come skidding in on top of the water, spraying all the giggly girls. I watched it all from up here," Owen smiled in pride. "I must admit young Denzel, I used to feel quite jealous of them all enjoying themselves," Denzel at this time looked as though he was in a lovely daydream. He was dead silent, eyes closed with a smile on his little face, from ear to ear.

But old Owen went on. "Us owls live a quieter and more thinking life."

"You were saying about my father," Denzel reminded him again.

"Oh yes, yes," hooted the old Owl, trying to glean as much out of his story as possible, for it wasn't every day the old fella got a chance to express just how knowledgeable, and wise he really was.

"Right, your father! Now where was I?"

"Spraying the giggly girls!" Denzel said quickly, to get the old owl going again.

"That's right, so I was," smiled the old owl, "that's exactly right! Er… well…" Owen was about to commence when…

"Morning" interrupted Wally the Dartford Warbler, still wet from his morning's dip and preen.

"Shh," retorted Denzel.

"Sorry I chirped," said the very confused little bird. "I was only…"

"Shh Wally! Will you please try to be silent for one moment!" scowled the duck, behaving quite rudely to his new mate. "Please go on Owen," Denzel asked.

Poor little Wally felt quite hurt at Denzel's sudden outburst, but soon realised on hearing that what Owen was telling his very best mate was of such importance, that he fell silent; which wasn't at all easy for such a little live wire as Wally.

Owen continued his tale, which started off as a friendly passing of the morning but had now turned into a story of large proportion of the lakes and river folk.

"Ya father, as I remember, had just settled back on the water, after his third landing, where all the females were soaked to the skin, but all having the time of their young lives. When out of the blue sky four Mallards appeared, all were strangers to our lakes, they landed over there behind those bulrushes," Owl nodded in the direction of the rushes. Denzel and Wally both followed the old tawny's nod, the pair of them taking in every detail of Owen's wise words. He went on to tell them, "Your father and company had seen from a distance the strangers fly in, but never really paid much attention, being so wrapped up in what they were doing in their own fun and games, until he set his eyes on the daughter that is!"

The old bird could see that he had the two youngsters hooked, after listening to his cunning way of drawing his story out as long as possible. For if the truth was known, he too was enjoying it just as much as the two youngen's, as he referred to them.

"My... Mother!" Denzel said in excitement.

"Yes," Owen smiled. "It was love at first sight on both their parts," the old Owl smiling to himself yet again. "I had to laugh," said Owen. "Ya father was still showing off to the local girls, when all of a sudden, the four strangers had drifted out into view from behind the rushes, it appeared to be a family, mother, father, son and daughter. My... my the daughter, now She was so beautiful!"

At this stage of old Owen's story, both Denzel and Wally, were listening to their hearts' content, where Denzel's little heart was pounding frantically under his breast feathers.

"Was she really that beautiful?" smiled the little duck.

"Yup! She truly was ma boy!" he said in a very soft hoot, feeling a little choked on reflection.

As Owen said this to Denzel, Wally, who for the past five minutes or so had never been so still and quiet, was looking at his bestest friend with a small tear dropping from one of his tiny round eyes, too choked up himself to utter a single murmur, and as we all are getting to know, that is quite a miracle, coming from Wal's quarters.

"I'll never forget," Owen went on. "It was as if it were yesterday, there was ya father, and his brother Dennis, still the centre of attraction, both strutting their stuff. As I watched from up here, I saw he'd noticed that all the hens, and Dennis were agog and staring at something behind him. He turned slowly to see what everyone was gorking at! When your dad's eyes were, of a sudden, hanging over his bill as large as two lily pads, when his eyes met the most classiest chick he'd ever seen. She carried herself beautifully, head held high most proudly on her long slender neck, with feathers the shiniest I've ever encountered in all my years on these lakes."

"Really!" exclaimed Denzel, so full of happiness he found it difficult to even speak!

"Oh she really was," assured Owen.

"Did he chase after her? I would! Wouldn't you Den?" Wally blurted out, not being able to be silent any longer, falling over his own words, as they were coming out of his beak so fast.

"Well put it this way!" exclaimed Owen. "His dad never looked at another female, from that day on. As I've mentioned before, it was love at first sight!" the old tawny coughed with pride and said. "Also I'm proud to boast, youngens, that the following spring, yours truly here married 'em."

"You… married my parents!!" exclaimed Denzel, so overwhelmed he was almost reduced to tears.

Even Wally couldn't chirp a sound, through a lump in his tiny throat the size of that bun his best pal ate the evening before.

"Yes indeed boys, I surely did!" exclaimed the now very smiling old bird.

"So it was you!" Denzel interrupted. "My father used to tell my brothers, sisters and me, of an old tawny who lived across the lake." Now Denzel began to look more closely at his surroundings. "Old craggy willows?… this wise old tawny?" he questioned himself aloud. It was all quickly coming back to him. "It is you! Of course it's you, who told my father of the meat-eating carnivores and the humans. My dad said you told him!!" cried the excited little duck.

"Yes indeed I did." said the owl.

With this, Wally chirped, "What a sly old hypocrite!"

"Shh Wally!" retorted Denzel feeling quite embarrassed at Wally's sudden outburst, especially at a time the old owl was telling him of his parents.

"Well!" chirped Wally sharply. "His belly's full of Bank Vole, Den! I clung to my roosting reed in the night, and I watched the old codger catch and eat it! Tell you the truth Den, as tired as I was I woke at the slightest noise. Then after seeing the old codger munch on the bones of that tiny vole, sure there was no chance of me ever dropping off to sleep again!"

"Well now, I can't help my desires," said Owen meekly. "I'm afraid that's what nature has given me. None of us are to blame youngen, not even Man. You see," went on the old Owl, "we were all put on this earth for a purpose, it's just nature's way of survival."

"Ha! Blooming survival!" chirped Wally in a nervous laugh, "I don't call crunching the life out of that poor little creature survival!" ruffling his feathers on recollecting the funny goings on in the night. "In any case," Wal really laying into the tired old tawny at this stage, "it may be survival to them carnivals as you calls 'em", looking straight at the duck.

"Carnivores!" corrected Denzel.

"Well, whatever they are?" chirped a very flustered Wally.

"Now you listen to me Wally! And you Master Duck, and you listen real good!" hooted Owen with much authority in his powerful deep voice. Owen felt it was time to start to teach these two very uninformed youngsters. But as we can plainly see it was Denzel's trusty partner's sweet little gob that had got the old owl's back feathers up.

After hearing the tone in Owen's voice, Denzel was now glaring at Wally, not saying nothing, but Wally on seeing the duck's face knew that what he had chirped didn't at all go down too well.

"Now," said Owen. "If you want to learn from a wise old bird, you had better listen to what I have to say. Now Wally, pray tell me what you eat!" (Owen obviously knowing).

"Er... just teeny... weeny insects," Wal realising he too ate live things. "Er... only flies 'n' insects," chirped Wally, quite flustered, trying desperately to recover his faux pas. "But they're only pests, and them blimin flies they're horrible to you bigger birds, and animals and even them humans. "Yeah!" said Wal, "but it don't count see... cause flies and insects are pests, and in any case they're only small, not like them pretty little Bank Voles you eat so there...!"

"Ha! Ha!" hooted Owen. "So you are no different to me...!" the old Owl, who at this very moment in time was enjoying putting young Wally, more than Denzel, in his place, exclaimed. "So you eat living things also eh!" Owen said in one of his most sterner hoots. "It's rather like me seeing a Golden Eagle, when he takes a wild rabbit, or a young sheep for his dinner, and me saying to that eagle he's wrong in what he eats. Can you imagine what reply I'd get! Ha! Ha!" Owen laughed. "It's all part of natural life, and I can see the pair of you have got much to learn." Owen went on to tell the two youngsters all about the Food-Chain of Life. "No matter who, or what, you are in this world, whether you're a human, or the largest animal in the world, down to the smallest ant, there is always someone, or something that lives off the other. This is why it's called the Food-Chain of Life." Owen goes on to say, "It's nature that makes us all, and nature provides the rules of life. You see, youngens, it appears we all need one another to survive, I don't mean individually, what I mean is each species, or in other words, each kind of living thing."

The two young birds just sat in silence, trying to take in as much of Owen's teachings as they could take into their young heads.

"Now, you two! Let's say of everything in the living world was to live, and have offspring, and those offspring have babies, and so on! Since the beginning of time, and none were to die! There would be no room on our planet now, would there?"

After this very wise old bird had finished, Denzel, and Wally were nodding and shaking their heads in full agreement at his wise words, but in truth the old owl knew it would take a few more meetings yet, before they really knew the facts of life.

But it didn't stop Wally from enquiring "What's a planet?"

Owen, went on to tell them what he knew of the World and its ways, the two companions never understood most of what old Owen had been telling them, for the subject was too vast, and the two youngsters were having enough to learn about their own lives on the lakes, let alone world affairs. But Owen could tell the two boys loved their first day's listening 'n learning from this, most intelligent, tawny.

After Owen's lesson on life, it was way past his bedtime. He yawned, stretched his tired old wings then hooted. "One thing before I go to roost! Remember, all I have told you of life!"

With this the old tawny retired to a big hole in the thick craggy willow trunk, and, just before he disappeared, Denzel at the last moment, called to Owen to thank him for everything, especially the story of his own beloved parents. "Good roost!" he called again.

"I will!" came Owen's reply, yawning heavily as he said it.

"Sleep well," joined in Wally, "very pleased to have met you," the little fella chirped, thinking to himself, "What a nice old owl he turned out to be, and so clever too!"

Just as Owen was about to disappear, Denzel called once more, "We'll come and visit you again!"

"Any time, any time at all" said the old owl, "But please try and make it early evening as the sun is going down. For us owl's don't like having to get up out of the roost in the middle of the day, and I'm quite sure that you two wouldn't like it if I came a calling on you in the middle of the night." With this, Owen's big round eyes glared into little Wal's, knowing after Wally's minor outburst, about being kept awake during the night by his own eating habits. Owen did this just to let the little warbler know who the governor was, in the thinking department. Owen finally disappeared into his hole in the craggy barked tree. As the Owl went out of sight of the two youngsters' view, Denzel had made his mind up, that from this day on, just like his father in the past, he would visit this old friend to learn more on the way of life, especially from such a professor of the lakes and rivers.

"Wow!" Denzel spluttered, really taken in by all the things the old owl had told him, so much more he had learned of his parents, let alone life on the lakes and surroundings.

All of a sudden, the young duck appeared to have fallen into a silent world of his own, dreaming of such things as, "Will all the young females chase after him too?" But Denzel was soon put out of his daydream, on hearing Wally's sharp burst of joining the dawn chorus. When Denzel heard such a delightful sound coming from Wally, he looked up to the upper branches and was bemused by Wal's little throat puffing up and down to the different notes. Denzel was thinking what a joyful sound Wal was giving the world, as he watched his little mate chirp his little heart out. When Wally was through with his morning's blast, his best mate was most surprised at Wal's talent in the chirping 'n' chanting business. Whilst Wally was singing Denzel had been all ears, listening intently to his little friends performance.

"Do all warbler's sing as good as you do?" Denzel asked.

At Denzel's question Wally caught his breath, and said, "Well to be honest Den, you see, there are lots of other warblers, such as the Reed Warblers that are here! Also Sedge, and Garden Warblers, but us Dartford ones, for reasons I don't know, are very few, rare as them Humans call it! So to be honest I've only heard a couple chirping, and we all sound the same to me," Wal recalled.

"Oh," said Denzel, amazed at Wally's tale. Denzel went on to tell Wal. "Your singing really cheers me up!" and he asked Wally to sing more often, with a reassuring, "please", to his little pal.

"I most certainly will," exclaimed Wally, who had on request, broke into another sound of sweetness, that surely filled the air.

"Denzel!" chirped Wally. The duck gazed upwards to where Wal was perched. "Can I ask you something?"

"Of course you can you silly Warbler," laughed Denzel, wondering why Wally sounded so pitifully serious. "Come on Wal, what is it?" Denzel was getting very intrigued at what Wal was about to say.

"Ca... can ya be me best mate? 'Cause I ain't got no family, like you! Or any real friends I could call me own," said Wally so sadly. "I... really think you're a well nice duck. Honest I do Den!" said sad little Wally, and before the Duck could get a word in edgeways, Wally chirped, "Would ya Den? Would ya?" Wal was opening his little heart out to Denzel. This was the first time Denzel, although only young himself, knew that his tiny new found friend was very insecure indeed.

"Of course Wally! And I must say your company would be sadly missed, so it will be lovely to have you around especially as my very best friend," answered the duck smiling as he watched Wally's little face beaming all over.

"Oh goody," chirped Wally, now hopping madly from branch to branch, twig to twig, wallowing in his own happiness in finding Denzel as his very bestest mate.

Denzel at the same moment was just as cheerful in finding such a friend, as the little gentleman that Wally most certainly was.

"Where shall we go?" asked Wally very excitedly, still hopping too 'n' fro, around Denzel's head.

"Well first we must go up to the far end of the lake, to an island."

"Why there then?" chirped Wally in his wonderings.

"There's a pair of old coots that live thereabouts, and they are a very caring couple, and I'm sure that they will be worried about me." But before Denzel could finish, Wally piped up.

"So we must do the right thing and visit 'em so's to stop them worrying, eh Den?" chirped Wal, full of himself.

"Yes! That's correct," said the duck as quickly as he possibly could, for fear he himself would never get a word in if he let his erratic little buddy rave on.

With this, they both made their way down to the water, Wally flew, Denzel hopped down the odd couple of branches, and part flew the last few yards, causing quite a splash as he clumsily hit the water, where his young wings were not strong enough at this time of his young life. Floating down, Wally had caught onto and clung to a reed near by where he'd roosted was now looking at his best mate wash and preen up, and giving his young wings a few good strong flaps, testing for when he'll be ready to take his first upward thrusts to that sky above, and fly, fly, fly.

"You've a long way to go yet!" chirped Wally.

"I sure have, but there's going to be a lot of fun when I can fly, eh Mate!" emphasising mate, as he mimicked Wal's chattering. Denzel knew just how much Wally felt made-up and important to hear himself being called mate, by his new found buddy.

The two birds made their way across the lake heading towards Coot Island. Denzel was looking forward to seeing the lovely old coots, Clara and Clarence; he swam strongly, whilst Wally, flittering in short bursts above, began to chirp a little number, which brought harmony to young Denzel's ears. As they were approaching the two coots, Denzel had already filled Wally in on who and what this very loving, and kind aging couple had done for him, soon after his traumatic ordeal. By the time he had finished, little Wally was so excited he just couldn't wait to meet them.

Clara and Clarence both had their heads under the water, feeding on the lush green weed. Clara was the first to raise her dripping head from the shallow clear water, seemingly as usual enjoying her daily breakfast, when all of a sudden,

"Ah!" retorted the old girl, "You made me jump you little rascal!" She said it again, smiling like a Cheshire Cat in happiness, on seeing that the little lad had returned safely, not even noticing Wally perched on a willow branch. He was hanging upside down above her head breaking into yet another of Wal's variety of songs.

"Well now who have we got here Denzel!" asked old Clarence lifting his head out of the feeding grounds just below the waters surface, to hear Wally's beautiful notes bouncing on the morning breeze.

"Come along Denzel aren't you going to introduce your little friend," mused the old female coot. But before Denzel could open his bill to answer, Wal informed the weed feeding duo, that he was Denzel's very bestest of mates, even before he gave himself a name.

"Wally," he said finally.

"He's a very rare Dartford Warbler," broke in Denzel.

Clara and Clarence who had taken one look at Wally's antics, which appeared to be speeded up ten-fold, glanced at one another leaving Clara to say,

"Yes we can see that!" She and old Clarence eyed up Wal again, then each other resulting in the two old 'uns wearing a huge smile on their kind ageing faces. Wal was accepted immediately into the fold by them both.

Then Clara asked young Wally to tell them a little about himself, and where he originally came from. Wally was more than happy to tell them of his past.

"I've come along way!" He told his new friends in a cheeky little chirp. "Hampshire is where I'm from."

"Have you any family dear?" The old inquisitive hen enquired.

"Oh, yes, I've got a mum 'n' dad, five sisters, and a brother, Willy!" he chirpily told them, and stopped chirping immediately.

"And where are they all now?" Clara was beginning to think by the way she kept having to ask the little lad, she had thought it was like trying to squeeze blood out of a stone, and hoped he would open-up and talk more freely, about his life before he came to these lakes. It wasn't long before he went into a tale of his past. He went on to tell them, of how he was hatched into the world, in a nest in some thick gorse bushes on the chalk horse hills of Hampshire, and continued by telling them of his mother Winny, and Wilfred his dad, who, by all accounts was a bit of a character himself, the way the lad went on about him. Also five sisters, and his only brother Willy, who, according to Wally, was still that way when he left home early on in the year when he very first got the urge to travel. He went on to tell them that ever since he could remember, he always go these strange feelings to wander, and once he felt fit 'n' strong enough, he'd said his goodbyes and left. And when Clara, being the broody hen she was, asked if his mum got upset when he left. Oh the little lad reckoned there were plenty of tears in the family at the time, but his urge to travel over-rode his emotions, hence him being at the lakes on that perch he was now sat on.

"You see my friends, Dartford Warblers are the only members of the species who are resident. The unfortunate matter is, Dartford ones are entirely insect eaters, (Insectivorous) and where they cannot find ample food in the bitter months of winter, these particular warblers suffer many casualties, reducing the numbers of this rare species in England even more. than If any are to be found in numbers, it will usually be in the warmer parts of this country. They appear to flourish in Hampshire, also parts of Dorset, but every now and then, one of these small birds are hatched, and instead of an ordinary run of the mill warbler, you get a loner, a traveller, a gypsy, or just a plain wanderer. One who's not satisfied with his lot, in just flitting about those chalk horse hills of Hampshire, or delectable Dorset. No! It's flaps 'n' flitters, in short bursts out of it lively to search the wide open spaces. This my friends is exactly what associate Wally happens to be. Just you think, the last time a Dartford Warbler was seen on the plot at Dartford was 1773, and that was how they got their name, I mean this boy don't just flit on his own doorstep. He, Wal that is, he's a spritely bird of the world, well, Dartford that is. Yet! Still a tidy few flits 'n' burst from the old west country eh? Also, if and when Wally should find himself a little lady, he will in the coming spring start to build a number of nests all of which are poorly put together, but for reasons of the Dartford ones only, these are called Cocks Nests. Though it doesn't matter because it's all in vain, for the female builds the real family home, well thought out, then put together. The materials she will use are selected dried grasses, lined delicately with lush soft moss, usually if she's not a lazy nest-wife, and takes a fancy to a bit of nest comforts, the dear girl will drape the interior in a nice bit of soft comfortable silk, from a cocoon that can be supplied by Sidney the well spoken spider, and his long legged web weaving wife Winnie, whom unfortunately both unsportingly get eaten for their extensive labours. for Spider are one of the main food sources for the Warbler species. So Wally's family really rely on the creepy crawlies department for their everyday living. Just as Owen the wise had taught him and Denzel all about the food-chain of life.

"He's most certainly a lively little soul," Clara commented, ending in more laughter from all present.

"Yes," replied Denzel, "the cheeky chappy does tend to get carried away at times, but I'm sure you will get used to him." He was looking in Wal's direction as he said this, then at the two coots shaking his head, still smiling at his little mate's earlier performance.

"Have you two boys eaten?" called Clara.

"No," the young Duck replied. "we thought we'd share breakfast with you, and uncle Clarence."

"Well that's a nice thought lad." The old male coot spluttered, moments after raising his head yet again from the fresh cool water, weed and water still dripping from his bill.

With this, all three big birds on the water submerged their heads looking for the sweet green weed below. Wally at this time had dropped from his roosting branch, settling lower on a long slim reed stem where he'd found and pecked on some scrumptious little bugs 'n' flies. All ate heartily until they all had their quota. Wally had his blow out, and now had returned to a low overhanging bough, just above where the now three well fed birds were resting on the lush mossy grass, catching a few rays from the delightful warm sun.

When they had rested, and started to natter 'n' chatter among themselves, getting more than their fair share of interruptions from the tiny hanging ball of feathers, than from all the other life in the vicinity. Denzel lucky enough, managed to catch Wally off guard, in other words between breaths, and the proud young duckling went straight into his story of his very first day's events alone, since his terrible ordeal just a few days prior. He told aunty and uncle, of his meeting with Treadwell Toad, and briefly of the coming wedding, in which he reminded himself it was this very day. Also of the huge family of frogs, but rushed very quickly into his biggest bit of news, (before slippery Wal got his cheeky beak in first!), of their meeting with Owen, the big Tawny Owl.

"I've met a wonderful new friend," said Denzel proudly.

"Me 'n' all, eh Den," chirped in Wally not wanting to be left out of anything In fact, at this particular time, if Denzel was to tell aunt Clara and spouse, that Wal would put his head in a fox's mouth, he was quite sure that dear Wal would undoubtedly nod his little head in agreement, as he was tuned up in telling his side of yesterday's happenings. In truth all the little soldier wanted to do was spit out a lot of gobbledegook, but take nothing in, resulting in his babblings and erratic carryings on.

"Oh!" said Clarence, shifting his tired old eyes to meet Clara's, giving her a sly wink. "Then pray tell us!" the old Coot smiled interested in what the youngster had to say.

"Owen, he's a big Tawny Owl, he lives in an old craggy willow. Do you know him Clarence?" asked Denzel.

"Yes, yes, of course aunt Clara and I know him, we've known that old owl ever since we came here many years ago from up north."

"Up north!" asked Denzel, not fully understanding, that when uncle Clarence says this, he means Yorkshire.

Old Clarence explained to Denzel and Wally, of how they once lived up in the Yorkshire Dales, at a time when "Our Lass, and I!" as Clarence put it, "first got wed. The winter was so fierce that poor Clara couldn't stand the cold. Fact was, she suffering badly with her rheumatism, so one day I couldn't bear to see her in so much pain, another winter longer. So we decided no matter how long it took us, we'd move down south, for there was no way I could ever let her face another winter, knowing the way that dear Lady suffered."

"Aye Lad, and did you know he's the oldest bird on these waters, come to that, most probably the oldest creature around these parts for miles?" said Clara, who appeared to speak fondly of Owen.

"Aye Lass," agreed old Clarence. Then he went on to inform the two lads, "Apart from Claudia the Carp, and some of the other big fish under the surface, Owen is undoubtedly the oldest."

"So you must both know that it was Owen who married my parents," said Denzel interrupting.

"Aye lad, we knew that also! We were going to tell you all about that in time lad, but it appears that you have learned so much from the one who is far wiser than Aunty Clara and I, on such matters" said the old male coot. "So how did you come to meet Owen the wise?" Clarence asked again in wonder.

"Well!" Denzel gasped, not really knowing where to begin. Then it all started to come, "After my meeting with Treadwell, and then I had some wonderful fun with a family of frogs, time seemed to have passed so quickly, darkness fell before I gave a safe roosting place a thought. Lucky for me, I met Wally and fortunately he was kind enough to fly off to find me a suitable roost. This place that Wally had found, just happened to be old Owen's territory." Whilst Denzel was explaining, particularly when Wal's name got a mention, Clara and Clarence kept noticing Wally's little rib cage would on occasion expand, and his breast feathers puff up, and all the while smiling and nodding in agreement. Where on the odd occasion, whilst Denzel caught his breath during his tale, Wal would stick his little chirp in, with a,

"I did, didn't I Den?", trying to impress the two aging listeners, But the two old stagers, under their pretence of seriousness, in fact were in fits of laughter at the little fella's antics, and even over their short time of meeting Wally, the lovely old couple decided there and then that they loved him, as they did Denzel.

"Aunt," said Denzel, thinking to himself what he wanted to say, "Owen really was a nice, nice owl, and really, really wise too! Do you know Uncle, he's so clever he knows everything about the lakes and river? He even told Wally and me lots of things. Also about the Food-Chain of Life, and loads of other things."

"My word," said old Clarence. "You have perked up my lad! And I must say it's a joy to see you so happy, and in such fine spirit too."

"Yes," chirped Wally, "and we're going to have so much fun, ain't we Den?" Obviously Wally was equally in very fine form. "We are, eh Den?" he chirped again, before the duck had any form of a chance to even move, let alone utter a single syllable, Wally was looking back and forth at his company searching for his usual bit of reassurance, and ended by saying. "We are ya know!" But even then, Wal's little round searching eyes looking at the two elderly coots, and then back at Denzel, still searching for signs of reassurance.

"Yes Wally, we really, really are mate." said the duck, smiling in the pair of Coots direction.

Wal gave one agonizing sigh of relief, when at last hearing a bit of response coming from Denzel, to the relief in the insecurity Dept. Wal at last was more contented now, but he still won't keep his little trap shut at times he really should.

Before the duck had hardly finished, Wally burst out "Where we going to day, Den?" more than eager to learn of the coming days adventures. The two old coots appeared to be struggling to attain a straight face, at the very comical scene they witnessed.

"We'll swim to the opposite side of the lake to where we were yesterday'" answered Denzel, to Wal's question, and went on to say, "I've not been over <u>there</u>!" emphasising 'there', "since I... I, I... lost my family." All thoughts of his personal tragedy came flooding back into poor Denzel's head, transforming him from a cheerful smiling duck and all of a sudden his little face drooped in gloom and total sadness.

"Are you alright lad?" asked old Clarence, on seeing the drastic change of his little friend. "You'll be alright lad, you're bound to get your bad days, but time will heal your pain, you'll see lad, you'll see," said the old concerned coot reassuringly, but even Clarence felt a hurt feeling in his heart at the saddening sight of the little duck before him.

Clara, well she was so upset she made an excuse of saying she had chores to do, anything to hide what, and how, she felt at this particular sad time. Tears were streaming down her lovely soft face, as she shuffled off.

Wally, for the first time in his entire life, sat perched with not a sound or even the tiniest of movements, and for those few who knew him, could tell the little chappy was devastated seeing Denzel so distressed. Denzel after a short time, came out of his time of hurtfulness, and bad feelings which at the time broke the little duck's heart.

"I'm sorry" he said, I... er, was thinking of my family".

"I know Lad," said Clarence trying his utmost to comfort Denzel (which seemed to be working, for Denzel had regained his composure and was now much his old self once more).

"Now you two scallywags, go and find adventure, there's so much for you both to do and explore, at your tender years. I'll tell you now, these lakes hold much of that!" laughed Clarence.

"Yes I suppose there is!" exclaimed Denzel.

"Come on," chirped Wally, looking much livelier on seeing his best mate was over his unhappy half hour. "Come on Den, let's go eh, shall we mate eh." Wally just couldn't keep still, too-ing 'n fro-ing from twig to twig, it seemed that little bit of energy he'd saved, whilst keeping still and quiet during Denzel's sadness appeared to have doubled Wal's ability, in his nervous erratic ways. Lively Wal didn't know whether to sing, fly, hop or go to the toilet.

Denzel and Wally after saying their goodbyes for the day, started their journey to the other side of the big lake. On their way, Denzel remembered this also was the day of Treadwell Toads' wedding, and as they were on their travels, Denzel wondered just how it would feel to be married, (or 'itched as Toad called it!). The Duck smiled in fond memories of the character Toad, and wondered if and when he would next meet his cockney friend. Denzel had decided from their very first meeting that he liked and trusted him as he did Wally (and he thought the world of him) and at that very moment in time, Denzel had come to realise, that he'd most certainly be lost without his lively little pal Wal. Who incidentally, at this time was hovering above him chirping his little head off, fetching a bit of colour back into his bestest mate's cheek feathers as they went. The companions were about forty or so yards from the steep bank, when all of a sudden, Denzel was lifted in sheer panic and alarm, clear from the water, the duck had to flap his young wings to keep his balance. Looking down, he saw to his horror, a huge pointed head, with an enormous gaping mouth, full of the most terrifying jagged teeth.

"I'm going to eat you my friend," spoke the monster on snapping his jaws shut in a loud snap, almost catching Denzel's legs. Denzel flapped his wings frantically, just enough to lift him out of the beast's grasping jaws.

"Leave him alone, leave him alone!" Wally chirped in complete horror, and dive-bombed the monster, not even caring for his own safety. Each time Wal dived, he scratched with claws and flapped his tiny wings at the beasts eyes. Wally could tell from his overhead view point that his best buddy had flapped his wings and got himself free, but only managed to get a few yards before clumsily crashing into the water. Poor Denzel out of breath, and absolutely panic stricken, began to swim not away as he should, but around and around in never ending circles in total confusion. Wally at this time, and from his height of about twelve feet from the water's surface, could see the big fish swimming after Denzel.

"Fly Den fly! He's coming after you again!" Wal cried in sheer desperation as loud as he possibly could. Denzel by pure luck, managed after a few good strong flaps, to leave the water, just as the terrifying jaws snapped closed again. He did this in sheer fright, which forced him to use his young wings, and strength to the limits of pain, to get more distance from his immediate danger. Though Wally even after Denzel's brave attempt to escape, saw that this monstrous fish wasn't going to give up easily, and was once more darting towards Denzel, where Wally could plainly see that the duck was getting weaker and weaker, by his efforts at trying to escape. All of a sudden the huge Jack Pike struck up underneath the exhausted duck, tossing Denzel into the air The pike turned and diving deeper, turned again to make his final bite of the bedraggled duckling, when on his way up from the depths of the lake racing towards the surface, and the would be prize, when old Jack noticed, either side of the duck's form, two huge Swans looking down at the rising predator. On seeing them, the Pike knew he'd lost his catch, for he knew that he was no match for the king 'n' queen of the lakes, having much respect for his monarchs. Big Jack turned, and disappeared into the murky depths of the lake to hide.

Denzel was so shaken, he even had his eyes closed, and long neck sunken deep into his wings, then on realising all had gone quiet, then hearing old Cyril's welcomed voice, the duck just thought it was just another bad dream. Then, again he heard Cyril's friendly voice; he gradually came to open his eyes, not only noticing frantic Wally, who was now chirping,

"Oh my God! Oh my good gawd! I thought that big lout was going to swallow you all up! Oh Lord help us!" Wal was still nervously chirping, so silently now, even though the dear chap could see his best mate was safe, he still couldn't help mumbling things under his teeny breath, due to the terrible state he was in.

Also the regal pair were most concerned. "Are you hurt son?" the King enquired.

"Sure he's alright." said Grace softly, as she pushed Denzel's ruffled feathers back in place, with her long gentle yellow bill. "He's just shaken that's all."

Denzel, too shocked to utter anything, finally managed a very poor, "Yes." But never impressed the two elders.

"Look son," said the old Cob sympathetically, "What happened here today is a very rare occurrence, with a duckling of your size. But, this you must take as another lesson in life, and be aware of dangers, at all times, that lurk in, and out, of these waters."

Once Denzel had recovered from his terrible ordeal, and started to look his old self again, Cyril informed him and Wally,

"That, my boys, was the notorious Jack Pike, a nasty piece of work." Cyril went on to tell them. "It's quite unusual for him to attack a half grown Duck, but I must warn you, we lose a lot of young new hatched ducklings, by Jack's foul means, so always remember that in years to come."

"I do wish he'd stick to eating Fish, and smaller pond life," responded Grace, feeling quite upset by it all.

"Well he will not bother you now, for that rogue Jack knows full well he'd make me angry," said the King in a reassuring manner.

Gracious Grace was still, at this time, fussing, and tidying Denzel's feathers.

"Thank gawd, for that!" the little floating on air warbler chirped. Still trembling from the dreadful thought, of what may have easily been the end of poor Denzel, the thought of losing his best pal, really shook young Wally.

After a short time, where the Duck began to recover from his terrifying experience, Wally, out of sheer love and true friendship, chirped,

"Den!" in his sincerest of ways. "If you like, we'll forget today's adventures, and go back to Coot Island, and go another day, eh Den!"

Denzel felt the warmth of Wally's concern. He told Wal that he would be fine, even though he had cold shivers running down his spine. But there was no way, after what his brave little pal had done, that he could now spoil the day out that he and Wally were looking forward to so much.

"No, I'll be alright now Wal, I'm just a bit shaken that's all, but I'll be glad when I get my grown up wings, that is for sure." As Denzel said this, the slight beginnings of a smile came over the little soldier's face, so pleased that not only his best mate had survived an awful episode but still had the guts to go on, with that day's outing. On hearing such bravery of Denzel carrying on, Wally started chirping,

"That's it! Den, that's a boy, me old matey."

"Wally!" the duck broke in.

"Yes Den!" chirped Wal.

"I'd like to thank you." said Denzel.

"For what?" asked Wally.

"For saving my life, that's what for you silly sausage! You were so brave, and being the tiny thing you are, it makes you even more braver, especially the way you put your own life in danger, and I'll never, in all my future life, forget what you did out there on the Lake today."

"You'd have done the same for me, wouldn't ya Den?" But before the duck even had a chance to answer Wal's question. Wally burst in, "You would Den, wouldn't ya, eh Den!" (Wally of a sudden having a moment of insecurity, and second thoughts). But Denzel noticed Wal's split second thoughts, when he saw the sudden change.

"Of course my little soldier, you really were brave though," said Denzel, feeling even more closer to Wally.

"Absolutely chivalrous," exclaimed the King. "Denzel has every right to thank you. Good Queen Grace and I were just lucky enough to have swum around that bend when we did, to witness the whole incredible skirmish, and son," said the old swan. "You were like a knight in shining armour, and through your bravery, the queen and I personally will make sure that every living creature knows of how, "Wally the half ounce Warbler, took on and beat, the thirty pound villain, the notorious Jack Pike. Also you can be sure this tale will be told for generations to come."

Wally stuck his little chest out, trying to give it the big gun. But as he was so full of himself, the dear chap let himself down pretty badly, when a large lump filled his throat half choking him Tears of relief, and joy at the same time, poured down Wal's chops, not because he didn't have so many wonderful friends, but with what had just been said to him by the King himself.

Grace also agreed to everything that Cyril had said of Wally.

"My wings are really aching," stuttered Wally through his snivelling tears.

"Well," said Cyril, "why don't you settle on my head, and take a rest little one?" The King was about to go on, but Wal didn't need the invitation twice, oh no! Cyril had hardly got his offer out when Wally fell from the sky, and was now perched on the huge white swan's head, and now wearing the biggest smile you have ever seen.

"Where are you two off to anyway?" asked Grace.

"To explore the other side of the Lake!" replied the duck, grinning at the sight of Wal, with the huge smile on board, plotted up on the King's pure white head. Denzel could see that Wally was feeling quite the little chappy about the lakes, and he thought just how lucky he too was having so many faithful friends, in such a short space of time, let alone Wally.

"Jolly good idea," said Cyril, causing Wally to jump and making the little bird cling on to the feathers on old Cyril's head. "Grace and I will escort you both to there then, and we'll chat on the way, then you can go off together and enjoy the sights and meet even more new friends."

Through such terrible happenings earlier on, and although Cyril and Grace knew by now of Wally's name, Denzel had realised he had not officially introduced Wal to the regal pair. So he apologised, and on their way to lakeside Denzel did just that, and on their travels he had introduced them all formally. Whilst Denzel was saying his bit about Wal, the little Warbler was sitting up there on the king's head like a crown of feathers. He was wearing a grin now, where Denzel had thought to himself "If it got one millimetre wider, Denzel was positive Wal's face would most definitely have fallen in half, whilst listening of his own bravery. Once the duck had said his piece, Wally, now on a much calmer note, began to chirp in response to the earlier remarks about himself.

"That's alright Den, I'm only too pleased and happy to see you out of that big horrible pike's mouth. Oh my gawd." Wal chirped again under his breath, thinking how he'd never been so scared in all his short life.

"Lucky you arrived when you did," Denzel was saying, to the swans as they swam towards the far side of the Lake.

Wally, resting now, was snuggling against the soft pure white feathers. "A king's feathers at that!" he chirped to himself. Fact is, Wally felt really good in himself, and reflected back on so many happenings, and adventures he'd had since meeting Denzel, and so many new friends too. Wal was giving it the large now, in the smiling department, thinking to himself, "Even the King and Queen, of the lakes 'n' rivers, This left Wally feeling contentedly chuffed at his good fortune, in finding such regal friends. But soon our Wally will have his beak put out of joint, on meeting the Cockney Toad.

The companions reached their destination at the lakeside, which was situated on the opposite side to yesterday's events. After giving their thanks to the royal couple for their Majesty's help in saving Denzel from the clutches of Jack Pike, which Denzel and Wally would never forget in ten lifetimes, let alone one, and after a few more chattings 'n' chirpings, the company parted ways, Wal taking to the air from Cyril's head.

"Be careful, you two!" hissed the caring pen, from a parting distance.

"We will," Wally and Denzel answered together.

"Bye!" Wally chirped, as loud as his little lungs could muster.

This side of the lake had even more willows than where they ventured yesterday. Although they were tall and leafy, they were not ancient and craggy, like the ones where Owen the wise Tawny lived. No, this side seemed to be more open, and among all the greenery Denzel had noticed places all trodden down, and the odd Man thing's scattered about the spot, making it very untidy.

Denzel and Wally both knew it was a fisherman's place. As the pair came along, they kept as close to the bank as possible. As they rounded a small bend, they saw a fisherman standing on one of these Man places, between the greenery and all manner of trees. They also noticed, that he was throwing some bread into the water feeding a variety of water birds, when all of a sudden, one of the slices had escaped the clutches of the feeding fowl, and as luck would have it, was floating on a breezy ripple, in the companions' direction. Denzel, who was now hiding behind some bulrushes, keeping well out of sight, was listening intently to Wally's commentary.

"It's coming," chirped Wal, "a nice fat juicy bit of bread, for my best mate," he said, knowing all the time that his pal could do with something solid in his belly. "Cor en it a biggun!" chided Wally, pleased his buddy had found such a prize, and without having to look too hard either. As Denzel's bill closed around the thick crust, pulling it towards himself, just as he was about to start supping on the soft thick crust, all of a sudden, the crust was pulled from Denzel's bill, and there, on the opposite end of the crust, almost submerged, with a wrinkled face, and a bald head, was an old skinny waif of a Water Rat.

"Eh, give me that back!" retorted Denzel, and they both began a mini tug o' war over the tasty morsel. "There's enough for two", Denzel scowled, and with this the scrawny rodent gave way and agreed to share.

"Alright duck, that's fair enough", said the rat letting go of his end of the bread. Denzel then broke the bread into two halves and they both ate an equal amount of their findings.

"How come," asked Denzel mockingly, "you eat all that food, and you're no fatter than a gnat's knee cap?"

"Easy Ducksy," said the Rat, with a nervous laugh, displaying the most dodgy pair of front teeth.

"See me!" the Rat said, "that, what I ate there, was nothing." He then went on to say, "I eats that amount fifty times a day, and I never put an ounce on in weight."

"What!" retorted Denzel, "you can't eat fifty times what you have just devoured. For a start, you could never find that many crusts on all the lakes, let alone on this one!"

"I've got loads," the Rat replied, in fact I've got fousands."

"Thousands!" exclaimed Denzel, in true amazement, "and pray tell me why did you have to eat half of mine, you having so many?"

"That would be telling, wouldn't it!" said Ratty.

"In any case," said the duck, realising the rat appeared to be an out 'n' out fibber, but to what extent Denzel was yet to find out.

"Have you a name?" enquired Denzel, to the exaggerating Water Rat.

"Harry," the rodent replied, whistling through his dodgy pair of front gnashers.

"Do you live near here?" the duck asked rat.

"Yeah," said Ratty, "do you see that bank?"

"Yes," answered Denzel.

"Well" the rat went on, "well from right down the end there," nodding in the direction of the paper mill's chimney end of the Lakes, then a pointed nod up passed them where they were, to the opposite end of the lake, and claimed, "We own all that!"

"Who's we?" asked the duck in disbelief.

The Rat went on to tell Denzel, that he, and his family were very rich, owning homes all over the place.

"Oh," said Denzel. "So just how many are there in your family to need so many homes then!"

"A million of us," said Harry, without any conviction whatsoever.

"A million!" retorted Denzel, in utter dismay.

"Might even be two million," waffled Ratty, not even batting an eyelid. In the meantime, Wally, after seeing Denzel eating his easily found food, had flown off to the nearest reed bed to feed his tiny face. He returned at the precise moment to catch the rat mentioning the two million, and asked Denzel what it was all about. When the duck filled Wally in on his behaviour, they both burst into fits of laughter.

"What are you two laughing at? As it happens its nearer three!" said Harry.

Wally at this time, still in a state of hilarious laughter, was roaring his tiny breast off, but neither at this time, knew the full gist of the lying rodent, although what he'd heard so far was enough to make him realise that this was Harry the lying rat that he'd heard so much about from other manors of the lakes, where the rat was renowned for his uncontrollable porkies, and craftiness. Apparently, a little bird told me, that Harry being a little sick of mind, couldn't understand that every animal, or bird on the lakes saw through all his charade of lies and fantasies. Also, he never batted an eyelid at Denzel's and Wally's taunting and laughter, every time the wrinkled rat told his fabulous fibs, let alone his deceit and cunning. Ratty took his leave, and after saying cheerio, he clambered upon the bank, and disappeared under a huge dock leaf.

Denzel and Wally, decided to go further down this particular side of the lake, towards the old mill,s chimney end. This chimney is a landmark which could be seen for miles about the area standing erect rising out of the rural landscape. As Denzel and Wally went on their way they began to discuss the antics of the disturbed rat.

Denzel said, "so you have heard of Harry before then?" Wally at this time was hovering just above his head.

"Yeah Den, he's harmless enough, he's just in a world of his own," chirped Wally.

"So all this, to our left here that we are passing, isn't owned by Harry, and his three million strong family?" enquired the duck, giving Wal a sly wink.

"Ha ha," Wally roared again, "the poor creature has never owned a thing in his whole life, and as far as I can gather, he don't live anywhere in particular, he just drifts around the lake at will, and stops where and when he wants."

"Has he any family?" asked the Duck, feeling a bit sorry for the sad old rat.

"I suppose he must have," chirped Wally, "but like everyone else on and about these lakes, they more than likely got fed up with his nasty ways, and only talking of things he imagines in his own head."

After their encounter with the unreliable rat, they had begun to travel quite near to where a fisherman, whom they had seen earlier, still feeding what looked to the companions like a mixture of wild fowl, of at least thirty, or more of the lake's habitants, that all appeared to be ducking 'n' diving at the pieces of bread the kind fisherman was tossing into their midst. This from Denzel's view, was a whole loaf, seen when he had glanced earlier, just before his meeting with Harry. Some of the ducks and moorhens, also a few coots, he noticed, were quite close to the fisherman, as near as ten feet. Some of the bolder ones appeared to be showing off in front of the pretty females, by seeing who could get the nearest to the human being where the braver ones were getting lots of attention by the gathering of even more females of each species, who were cheering the boisterous game. Then seeing one of the young male coots actually being so brave, he was more than one yard away from his feeder. All the giggly screaming females, were so ecstatic at this point. Denzel with Wally, floated out just behind the spectacle, where Wal, was trying to prompt his best buddy into being even braver. As Wally put it to Denzel, to see just how brave his idol, and pucker pal was in such daring matters.

"Go on Den, you show 'em old mate," Wal was chirping as loud as he could, so's to draw attention. With this Wally was flying into the excited flock, in and out in short burst, and flitters, to the bravest of the bunch, informed him, "That's nothing Cooty, my best mate's braver than that!" chirped Wally confidently. However, Denzel who really and truthfully had no intentions of entering any of these bravery games. But when overhearing his very over excited mate dishing out all sorts of challenges the duck swallowed a big lump in his throat, knowing that Wally, who never realised his chirpings had put Denzel into a position, really couldn't back away from, for fear of letting his very confident Warbler mate down.

"If that's what Wally thinks I am?" Denzel thought to himself, "then I'll do my utmost to keep my little friend happy. I mean," Denzel thought again, "Wally did prove his worth, and undying loyalty when he helped him survive that ferocious attack, by the nasty Jack Pike."

"So you reckon your friend the duck is braver than me, eh!" retorted the brave coot, who appeared to be about Denzel and Wally's age. The coot now sizing, and eyeing up Denzel, and at the same time still goading Wally.

"Yes he jolly well is!" retorted a proud Wally, giving his bestest pal a sideways glance, and quickly giving one of Wal's craftier winks. This was to get Denzel to move in closer in among all the other feathered friends (who incidentally, all knew of Denzel's tragic past).

After a lot of prompting by wicked Wally's winkings, and now a few others from the flock had joined in, making their individual soundings, and flappings of excitement, cheering the young Duck on. Our not so brave Denzel, who at this time, had his poor heart beating ten to the dozen inside his rib cage, began to make his move towards the fisherman. All the other birds of all descriptions and ages, who'd been tucking into the fisherman's bread, all now had stopped feeding. Now all eyes were on Denzel. As he swam through the crowd of birds, they all parted. Denzel swam to about seven feet from the fisherman, who by now had noticed some funny goings on. As he looked, the fisherman witnessed the parting of the floating frantic feathered feeders, and saw before him Denzel, who appeared to be looking at him intensely.

"What a cheeky little blighter" smiled the kind human. At this time the fisherman had just one more whole slice left, in which he divide into two halves, but when he threw the first piece into the water, as usual he noticed most of the other birds nervously jostled, and scurried away to what they thought a safer distance. Not the duck. Oh no! Denzel floated, paddled his busy webbed feet towards the portion of bread. With this brave spectacle, all eyes were on Denzel's attempt of bravery (especially the mallard females). Even the brave coot had to give the duck his dues. So you can imagine the other merchant. He, Wal was so full of it all, and through sheer exhaustion from his erratic tauntings, and chirping his very best pal on, was hanging, clinging to a reed stem trying dramatically to recover his breath. But alas, it never lasted long.Soon the dear Wal, was back up in the air above the flustered fowl, chirping to everyone,

"I told you! I told you! And he's my very own bestest pal." All of a sudden, the fisherman on seeing how brave this young Mallard was, bent down holding out the very last piece of bread, holding it between his fingers, offering it to Denzel. All Denzel could hear above all else was the sound of Wally's reassuring support "Go on Den, go on Pal, you show em, buddy." On listening to Wally's come ons, the duck just couldn't bring himself to let Wally down in any way. When Denzel saw what the man was offering, and after devouring the first crust earlier, was in reality, not in the least bit hungry. But no way did he intend to embarrass Wal, especially now after the little rogue had taunted the others so much. Denzel moved in closer, he was only about a yard away from the fisherman, the young duck circled at this distance once, or twice and after even more encouragement from him above, Denzel made his final move. He swam without hesitation whatsoever into the waiting hands of the human. Denzel ate right out of the hand, and as he did this, the whole of the feeding birds present were cheering 'n' flapping their wings in pure joy of such a rare spectacle, which it truly was. But what made them all happier still, wasn't so much Denzel's bravery in taking the bread, but because all the birds in this company, from the youngest to the oldest, had known what it took for him to do as he did, knowing all the time, that it was humans who had taken his whole family from him. Whilst all the excitement was going on, Denzel listened, for Wally's racket, yet couldn't hear, over all the noisy commotion and cheering, any of excited Wally's chirps 'n' banter. But to Denzel's dismay, not a sound came from the little fella was to be heard from young Wal's quarters. Denzel a little concerned, swam through the noisy humdrum of the frantic flock in search of the missing Warbler.

Over by some reeds at the side of where he last saw Wally, Denzel and some of the others searched, and he couldn't be found anywhere. Denzel started to push his way through the reeds; as he moved in closer to the reeds, he peered into the thicket, and there lying on his back, little legs stuck up in the air, in a last season's bird's nest, was Wal. He was so worn out, after the long day out, even his lesser than matchstick like legs, had failed to support Wal's half ounce teeny body. Wally on hearing Denzel's approach, opened one of his tiny round eyes, trying to appear more livelier for his hero pal.

"You were great Den," the exhausted Wal managed to chirp. "Cor! Den when you took that bread out of the fisherman's hand eh! Ha, ha, you showed em! Eh Den," Wal chirped again, livening up a little. "Yeah, and you're my best friend, eh Den, not theirs eh? You are ain't ya Den?" chirped Wally, looking pitifully at his smiling partner, searching the duck's face for any signs of the slightest bit of reassurance.

"I am! And I will be your very bestest of friends, forever and a day. Also I shall tell not only the birds, and animals of these lakes, but everyone we meet in many seasons to come." said the duck, meaningfully. Wally on hearing what he dearly needed to hear, then of a sudden, became himself again.

"What did you think of that then!" chirped Wally, again goading the bravest of all the coots, and also all the other splashing spectators.

"Very, very brave," said the bravest of all coots, trying not to look at the waffling Wal's beady cocky eyes.

"Is he the bizz, or what?" chirped the over cheerful Wal.

"Yes, yes, I suppose he must be!" said the now very flustered Coot, who by now only wished the lake would open up, and swallow him, or better still that crafty little devil of a Warbler, he thought! Showing a false smile, trying to front Wally's fusillade of chirps. Denzel watching Wal in action, realising the brave coot's dilemma, and the duck could see the brave coot getting weary, and totally embarrassed with chirpy chappy's chattings.

"Will you please leave him alone, and stop pestering Wally," Denzel snapped, "and for goodness sake will you slow down a bit! Or you will make yourself ill." After seeing the brave coot a little more relaxed, Denzel made his way over to him.

"Please excuse my little friend," he said. With this Denzel looked to the sky above him, to watch his floating on air friend. "Wally," the duck snapped again.

"Er... er, ye...e...ss, Den!" chirped Wal, recognizing that tone in his buddy's voice, and of a sudden feelin a wee hint of the old insecurity coming over him. "Er, what!" Wal chirped, making out he never had a clue to what his pal was about to say.

"Now you say sorry," said the duck.

Wally took one look at Denzel, with his now sad beady eyes, swallowing as if he had a dried bulrush stuck in his throat. Facing the now smiling coot.

"Sorry" he said in one of Wal's meekest voices. Wally apologised for his far too over excited behaviour, and the brave coot accepted without further ado. But Wal just had to have the last chirp as usual whilst Denzel's attention was elsewhere, then chirpily managed a tiny whisper in Coot's direction, "He was the bizz though, eh Cooty" giving the brave coot a sly one for the road. Denzel did hear Wally's cheeky remarks, but took one look at the brave coot, and they both roared with laughter, fully understanding the excited little fella, also the dear chap's ways 'n' funny goings on. Whilst all this was happening, the fisherman packed, and left his post.

"What is your name?" came a quack from one of the female Mallards, who floated over by some bulrushes.

"Denzel," the Duck replied. "And what might yours be?"

(Denzel was reminded of the young hens that chased after his dad, of which Owen the Wise had told him and Wally back in the early summer.)

"Daryl," came her reply.

"That's a lovely name" said Denzel warmly.

"Have you any girlfriends?" asked another.

Wally listening to the flaunting females' familiarity, had started in his own little head, to see signs of danger a plenty, in losing his best mate to a silly girl duck, and was not at this particular time amused, and so put his spoke in, a bit sharpish.

"Er," chirped Wal, "he don't need girls 'cause he's got me eh Den!" Wally, taking a sly look at Denzel's reaction to what he'd said to the flaunting females. "I'm his very bestest pal ya know?" chirped Wal hoping it would deter the hussy hens off Denzel.

Denzel sensed Wally's jealousy, and soon answered his little friend. Telling Wal that he, can still have other friends, being it boys or girls, then tactfully assured the little fella, that they would still be best friends in themselves. For the Duck knew by now, that his tiny pal Wal was a very insecure little soul, but the Duck truly loved him like a brother. From that moment on, Denzel would always keep his buddy reassured through their future friendship.

"I'm very pleased, and proud to have met an heroic Mallard, such as yourself sir. If I may, I'd like to take the opportunity to introduce myself, Charley's the name, bravery's me game. But I must say young fellow, you most certainly took the cake this afternoon, Es... especially."

"Bread!" chirped Wally, in correcting Charlie's mistake. Well, so Wal thought.

"Yes, little bird. (coot really having to bite his beak now) Just a phrase of saying, my little friend," said Charlie, looking at Wally, with a look of strangulation in his eyes. Where cheeky chap just wouldn't stop having his tiny digs, in Cooty's direction. After windup Wal interrupted Charlie's introduction, the brave coot was about to mention the plight of Denzel's family, but just as he was beginning to speak he realised he didn't want to upset the duck by reminding him all over again. With this the brave coot fell silent in his tracks, and his head began to lower. "I'm so sorry!" said Charlie.

"Carry on!" Denzel, told the brave coot. Who knew inwardly of what the Coot was about to say.

Charlie at the duck's request, carried on. "A... after what the poacher man did to your family. I really am sorry," said the sincere Coot.

Denzel was taken aback by what the brave Coot had said, but he felt happy within himself at the thought that others around him cared. He thanked Charlie for his concern. Then, with all the others present, the demoted Charlie, was proud and honoured to hand over his reigning title of 'The bravest of all the Horton Kirby lakes 'n' rivers' over to Denzel.

"Yes!" a shout went up from the rest of the flock, with all their respective coos, quacks 'n' whistles, from the floating company; and a fair share of that noise was instigated by of course the little fella. Oh the happiness 'n' joy it brought young Denzel, and you should have seen the expression on Wally's little face. Him feeling part, if not the instigator of Denzel's success, this very day.

It was nearing sundown. Denzel and Wally, who had not realised it was time to leave, were so sorry to have to go as they had really enjoyed the meeting of such fine company, in fact they both felt a little sad. But deep down, Wal was glad to get his buddy far away as possible from those tail fanning females. Denzel and Wally said their goodbyes, and told his mixture of friends that they would meet up again another day.

"Bye!" came a lovely soft quack from Daryl, the gorgeous female Mallard. But before Denzel could take the chance to return his goodbyes, Wal was flitting up behind the duck, and those who witnessed saw with their own eyes that Wally was herding the duck away like a sheepdog, taking no chances whatsoever. Thus, they found a suitable roost, where Wally had made sure he wasn't too far away from Denzel, and what with having such an eventful day, the duo fell immediately into a deep slumber.

Chapter 3

The River

A few months had passed, where the summer emerged into autumn, bringing with it a crisp September chill each morning, and after a few hours of sunshine during the day, that same chilly coldness returned at night, where the landscape was beginning to take on its usual seasonal beauty that autumn brings. Where most of the trees, and foliage were changing from the many shades of greens and yellows, to all the browns, reds and golden splendour. Bulrushes were lying over, all bent and broken, and instead of all the healthy green, were now dead or dying, making way for the new growth in the following spring. Even the beautiful lily pads floating on the surface of the water, had lost their fabulous blooms, and the large circular pads were now going brown with decay. The steep banks surrounding the lakes were now covered in dying foliage, leaving animals like the rabbits and foxes more exposed to their own predators.

Denzel, now almost full grown, and although he had not quite attained his full grown adult plumage, had a slight hint of green showing through his mottled brown feathers, down his long proud neck and head. He was sitting in his usual roosting hole in a stout willow trunk, some twelve feet, or so from the water's surface below. It was just as the sun was rising, warming nature's life, also the bones of young Denzel. Dew from the rising warmth was causing tiny glistening diamond droplets of water to drip, drip, into the surface below, making miniature whirlpools. It was this dripping sound (to young Denzel's ears) that told the duck it was time to get up, for a new day had begun. Over the past summer months Denzel, and his very best of mates Wally the incorrigible Dartford Warbler, had shared a hundred 'n' one, new and exciting adventures in and about the lakes at Horton Kirby. Wally at this time was perched comfortably on his regular branch at the side of his little reed shelter which was situated in a thicket of reeds. His little abode was not a nest just a simple cluster of reed leaves that had died and fallen on top of one another, making a sort of thatched roof, which kept the wind 'n' rain off Wal's fragile body.

Wally too had grown, he was now togged up in his new rig out. His wintry attire was of dark chocolate, sporting a red rust waistcoat with a fine head of feathers of slate grey in colour. He looked a right proper Burlington Bertie! Only in the bird world, of course! But did he look smart! As Clara remarked to Clarence,

"That the little lad looked quite handsome, all done up in his winter nines." (Which he needed to be to survive the colder nights.) So now, all rigged out and almost fully grown, Wal was at his fighting weight of no less than that of a Field Mouse. Denzel and Wally some weeks earlier, had found these roosting places where Wal's reed shelter was only a yard or so from Denzel. Also only a matter of a few more yards, from the adorable coots, Clara and Clarence, who had taken it upon themselves to adopt the two lads. So the pair of old coots were contented in that. For they loved them both dearly, and as old Clarence, was heard telling King Cyril and good Queen Grace, just some weeks earlier, of their joy in having the two lads around, as it filled the loss they had of their own brood. Denzel's wings were almost ready now, to take him soaring into that long awaited sky, where he often, after a few attempts over the past weeks, kept dreaming of the day when he too could fly around the lakes, and come skidding in on top of the water, splashing all the giggly girls, just like his father, and uncle Dennis did. As old Owen the Wise had put it "showing off to the Mallard hens", as he told them both, on their first ever meeting. Denzel and Wally, over the past few months had visited Owen a couple of times, where they had listened for many hours and enjoyed his knowledgeable teachings, also stories the old Tawny had stored away in that huge round head of his. However, it seemed to put Wally on a calmer footing, he was still as erratic as he ever was, in his own little ways.

But all who knew the little fella loved and accepted his taunting and chirpings even more, knowing how insecure the cheek chappy was. So all of his and Denzel's ever-growing circle of friends made very sure they watched what they said, for fear of upsetting the little soul. In other words, they all knew Wal was alright dishing out the mickey-taking, or in Wal's case, cheeky chirping. However, when it came for him to be on the receiving end, Wally took everything to heart, and the little soldier just failed to cope. But our Wal did get his come-uppance, on being for the first time introduced to the cranky cockney, Treadwell Toad Esq. a little later. Wally left his perch and the tiny shelter of his thatched roost. He dropped down to the waters edge, hopping in and out of the shallow water, shaking 'n' shivering, giving himself a wash and a preen up.

"Brrrh, it's blooming cold" he chortled to himself, but Wally never realised just how cold it was going to be, once winter came. Old Clarence warned him and Denzel on such chilly matters, but never ever knowing the true extent of what Wally and his best pal were facing. "Brrrh", Wal chortled again on leaving the cold water, giving himself a last shiver 'n' shake. Once the little rascal was happy with himself, he flew up into a branch of an Elderberry Tree, where most of the leaves at this time were either dead or dying, ready to fall. The little fella braced himself with a deep, deep breath, then broke into the most beautiful burst of song.

"Hark at him," said Clara, to her loving spouse, "isn't he the most beautiful little singer!"

"Ha, ha," laughed the proud old coot, "Just listen to the little villain. You would never imagine that something so small could produce so much noise. But the lad makes a nice noise, mind," the old coot said, gazing up at cheeky chappy's chirping just ten feet above his head. On hearing Wal's performance in the chirping 'n' chanting department, this Denzel knew, was time to get up out of his roost and join his companion for their ritual breakfast. After Denzel too had spruced himself up, Wally flew to meet him, and they made their short way towards the caring coots.

"Good morning, Den," chirped Wally as he dropped down, hovering just above his best mate's head, as they both approached the two loveable coots.

"Here they are," said old Clarence, nodding his head to let aunty Clara see them coming into the edge of the island.

"They seem to be getting on well together, my dear," the loving Clara sighed.

"And very good for them both too, that is what I say lass," replied her spouse.

"I agree dear," she answered, feeling happiness in her heart.

Next moment the old coot got to his feet, spread his tired old wings, giving them a couple of sturdy flaps, readying himself for the morning breakfast.

"Ah! Just in time, you two!" he said, to the approaching lads, (which he called them).

"Yes," said the fussing hen, asking them if they were hungry yet.

"Yes please, aunty," they both managed together. "I'm starving, how about you Wal?" asked Denzel.

"I could eat all the blimin' insects in the lakes," chirped Wally, sounding very much like Harry the Rat, whom they had encountered some months before. After they had said their good mornings, Wally, not being able to wait any longer, flew to the biggest bed of reeds he could find, and got stuck into all the creepy crawlies he could eat. Needing of course, to stoke up with food as the little soldier burns himself out so quickly, through his erratic duckings 'n' divings.

In the meantime, Denzel found and ate the remains of a floating half eaten pear. The caring coots just pottered about eating what they could find. A fisherman from a distance, could see their heads bobbing in and out of the water partaking in their morning's blow out. After Clarence, Clara and the young Denzel had their fill, they all made their way back to the grass, and mossy comfort of the Island, and respectively took up their usual places to laze in the sun. For each of them knew that each day that passed, the warmth of the glorious sun was getting less and less as each day grew shorter. As they settled,

Clara couldn't help noticing Wal on his day perch, his little throat was so puffed up with his breakfast of insects, she told Denzel, and Clarence,

"It looked like the little lad has an abscess". An hour or so had elapsed, when the old male coot decided it was time for Denzel to venture further afield.

"Would you like me to take you, and show you *the giver of the lakes' life*?" he asked Denzel, giving Clara a glance, as he said it, catching her gaze of concern from her seated posture. The old girl was shaking her head from side to side, but saying nowt.

"Giver of Lakes' Life?" asked Denzel.

"Wot's that mean?" chirped Wally quickly, "Go on uncle Clarence, tell us! Eh Den!"

"The River!" declared Clarence, knowing full well what it meant to the two young lads. "You haven't been nowhere, until you have swum the River, and rode the ripples, of the Darenth," smiled the old coot.

"Very similar words" Denzel thought to himself, to what his late father had told him, and his brothers 'n' sisters almost one half year ago.

"Yes please, uncle! Did you hear that Wally?" Denzel called extremely excited. "We are going to the River!" the young duck cried again, with so much joy, and adrenalin running through his whole body.

"Er… yes!" Wally was giving it some thought. "We are, eh Den, just me, you, and Uncle Clarence, eh! (Wal obviously putting himself first of course) We don't want anybody else, eh Den! Do we eh?" chirped Wally, on and on.

"Wally, for goodness sake! Yes, just you, Uncle Clarence, and me, ok!" Denzel, tut-tutting, at Wally, at the same time, eying the now smiling Uncle Clarence, who at this time was grinning at the little fella's insecure chortlings.

"Yeah, just us, eh!" chirped Wal in a tiny whispered last word. With this reassurance from his two very best friends, Wal felt much better, and contented now that he knew for sure, he wasn't being left out of the biggest of all (past) adventures, to the famous River Darenth. It was mid-morning when old

Clarence and the two excited lads, were about to leave for the coming adventure of their lives. So to the water's edge, where Clarence had taken Denzel once before. But they didn't leave that island, until Aunty Clara had given poor old Clarence a terrible ear bashing. Telling the old bird,

"Be extra, extra careful" said the lovable old girl, knowing the many dangers of such a journey. As she nagged him, even with such a short way over land. "I still think it's too dangerous for a duck as young as Denzel" she fussed on.

"I know, I know lass," comforted the old male coot. "I just feel the time is right for the young lad. In any case, I've been watching the little lad of late," exclaimed the old Coot.

"Me… me," stammered Denzel seemingly surprised.

"Yes, you my lad, I've watched you these past few mornings, and I've noticed you testing your wings." Clarence went on to tell them all, "and from what I've seen, there is enough flap power in your wings to get you out of trouble, if need be, if an old sly fox, happened to be around."

"Do you really think I… I, could fly?" asked Denzel.

"Enough!" answered Clarence reassuringly, "that's why I said the time is right, lad."

They were at the lake's edge. Clarence had slowed down to let Denzel swim up along-side him, and Wally was floating above in the finest of form in the chirping 'n' chanting department. Feeling the happiest of little fellows, as they went. In front of them now was a very steep bank. Old Clarence found a most suitable spot for Denzel, and himself to climb. A little cover, but easy to clamber up to its top.

"Before we go," said the old boy, "I want you, Wally, to fly up over the top and make sure there are no dangers lurking."

"Yes, very important that is! Eh Den?"

"What is?" asked Denzel.

"Me going over the top to check there are no doggies, or slippery old foxes about," chirped Wal, "I mean it is, en it Den?" Wally so full of himself, yet again.

"Yes Wal, it really is," Denzel was now looking up towards the sky, sighing, "Yes, it surely is," he said again.

With a little interrupting cough Clarence said,

"Well are you going, or what Wally!" laughed the aging coot, full of smiles, knowing the little fella, just like Denzel, was ecstatic. Also, for the first time in the little scoundrel's life, he was asked to do something, so very important, as Wal put it. The old coot also admired the plucky little soul, especially on hearing from Grace and Cyril, the lake's monarchs, how Wally risked his own life in fighting with such courage, the notorious predator, Jack Pike. A loyalty to be admired by all life on, and about, the vicinity in which they resided. Wal, now feeling Mr Important, floated on a breeze up, up and flew over the top of the bank, scanning the trees, and leafy foliage for hidden predators, only to find peace 'n' harmony, where a dozen or so rabbits were feeding and pigeons were roosting in the trees. A good sign that all was safe and well. Wally flew in almost a straight line, keeping his watchful tiny eyes peeled for any unseen dangers, finding for them the straightest route he possibly could, finding it all up above the lake, clear of lurkers. Wally returned to the waiting expedition to give word on his findings.

"Come on, come quickly," chirped Wally, "It's all clear, and it's so beautiful up here, as peaceful as heaven," Sherpa Wal chortled. With this, old Clarence, told Denzel to climb out onto the lake's bank. Denzel started to clamber up the steep bank, gradually rising from the water's edge. He was feeling excited, but not so steady. Uncle Clarence saw Denzel struggling, and the old coot moved nearer towards the young duck, and gave a little help by putting his head and strong neck under Denzel's rump, giving him a wee shove in the right direction, into a world at this time unknown to him. Denzel after being helped forcibly, found himself losing his balance, and was sent crashing into a mass of stinging nettles, but soon found his webbed feet in a much sounder footing on the trail Clarence and the little scout, Wally, had chosen for his first ever trip abroad. They were both on the bank slope now, making their way up, when Clarence reassured Denzel that all would be well. Even though the young duck felt very strange having to climb, having never been on land, especially a steep bank, as this undoubtedly was. On occasions that he has, it had only ever been on the flat grass and mossy softness of Coot Island. After some effort, the two big birds progressed almost to the top of the bank. Denzel, not at all pleased with his struggled climb, was not very much looking forward to the downhill run, on the return trip. But it appeared that the adrenalin of this adventure, overrode the bad thoughts that ran through the little duck's brain. So (in his mind) he decided to worry about that, when the time arose, not wanting to spoil what was to come on such a special day. Wally was perched on a silver birch branch, chirping frantically for Denzel and uncle Clarence to follow.

"Come on, come along you two slow coaches," Wal chirped very excitedly.

"It's alright for you Wally, you can already fly," Denzel retorted to his floating little scout. Uncle Clarence, on hearing the two young lads, carryings on, smiled contentedly, knowing it was just the excitement of it all that caused the two of them, to waffle on at one another. Denzel and Uncle Clarence followed Wally's route, which both found most suitable. It was a well worn path, with ample cover from the most evil eyes. They followed, and reached the River Darenth without incident, good, or otherwise. All the company noticed was just a few wild rabbits grazing, who in fact never even seemed to notice their passing. When they first came to the water's edge, Denzel couldn't believe the sight laid out before him, a sight of beauty, from the silver rippling brilliance of the living river, let alone the gorgeous smell of fresh cool water that filled their nostrils and lungs.

"It's all, and more than I have ever dreamed of," Denzel sighed when taking in the full extent of this wondrous place.

"Well, what do you think, lads?" asked the old caring coot proudly, knowing all the time the two youngsters were alright in their own excitement.

"It's as good as my father had told us, and more," said Denzel, taking as much of it in as the little lad possibly could.

"More than you'll ever know, my lad. You mark my words," said the old boy laughing out loud, then being interrupted as usual by, of course, Wally.

"You going in, Den?" chirped bag 'o' nerves Wal. "Go on Den, go on in me old mate." Wally encouraged Denzel. But the water was very different from the calm on the big lakes. No! This was very rapid indeed, and ran too quickly, for Denzel's liking. But Wally still persisted in goading his best buddy.

"In you go Den, that's it, me old mucker." Wally was really laying it on now.

"All right!" retorted the very nervous duckling, "I'm going in right this minute." Denzel was still thinking twice about stepping into the rapid running water.

"Go on lad, it won't hurt you, and once you're in, you'll soon find your webbed feet," old Clarence assured him.

"Come on Denny boy, you show 'em what you're made of, matey."

"Wally, if you don't shut your little cakehole," retorted Denzel once more. Wally immediately bit his beak, then fell into silence. Eventually Denzel built up enough courage to enter the fast running water. He left the bank and gently slid down into the cold crystal clear water. Young Denzel found himself being carried away, off downstream by the strong current, just as Uncle Clarence, had told him. Denzel, now feeling quite chuffed with himself, turned and began to paddle his way upstream, to see Uncle Clarence entering the river. Also he'd noticed the old coot too was carried a little way down river.

"Yipee!" chirped Wally, on witnessing his two best pals as they fought with all their might, the rolling ripples of the rambling river. Clarence battled against the strong draw of the current to join Denzel upstream. Wally flew in bursts 'n' flitters, above the paddling pair, still chirping encouragement to the swimmers below. "That's it Den, you know… don't ya! Get them webbed feet going partner" Wal chirped merrily, as they went. Clarence by this time had joined Denzel in the river.

"Well," said Clarence, "it's entirely your choosing lad, up, or down!"

"Up, or down!" asked the duck, seemingly confused, at this sudden request from the old coot.

"Would you like to swim up or down the river a little way?" asked Clarence on seeing how confused the little duck appeared. But the old stager could plainly see it was through sheer excitement of the day's events that had put the two lads into a bit of a turmoil. So, when Denzel had decided to go up, old Clarence laughed to himself on watching Wally looking at Denzel, trying to make his mind up. Once Denzel had announced his decision, wee Wal immediately chirped,

"Yes, that's right Den, up! Eh!" But our Wal, as we all know, is not too clever in the 'O' level department, and speedily took off in the downstream direction, chirping, "Come along, let's get going!" Denzel and Clarence just couldn't stop laughing at Wal's comical capers of flying in the complete opposite direction. After Wally's sudden burst of speed the wrong way, and, as he turned to see, he was most surprised seeing the expedition retreating in the away direction. Wally turning, followed the two big birds. But Wal knew he'd let himself down badly, and realising that he'd be needing a few more lessons yet from that intelligent Tawny, Owen the Wise, before he put his little chirp in, in future. As they swam the old male coot was pleased the young lad had chosen up river, for there was something of much importance he wanted to show the lad. Swimming hard against the ripples, Clarence mumbled something to Denzel, of a surprise he had for him on the return trip. All the duck thought he heard was something about a ride back.

"A ride back!" exclaimed Denzel, thinking of his friend Treadwell's relations, flying in to his wedding by goose, and that was strange enough, thought Denzel shaking his head in amazement. But Clarence decided to leave the surprise to when the time came. Close on the old timer's treading heels, Denzel was thoroughly enjoying the trip and the lovely surroundings of over-hanging willows, bramble bushes, stinging nettles, with a few dock leaves, dandelions, and thistles scattered on the shady banks, leaving the Duck feeling quite safe with the river's natural cover. But, most of all, the education he was learning of life, on such a big adventure, with every paddle, of his aching webbed feet. At this time, Wally had gotten over his mistake of his dodgy misguidance, and now was plying his friends ears with a tasty tuneful sixties number, making the expedition a little extra special. Some time had elapsed when the trio had come to a clearing where the river forked off to the companions' right, on their upward swim. Old Clarence all of a sudden came to an abrupt standstill, where Denzel, in a daydream, and so full of everything he saw, swam straight into the halted Uncle Clarence, startling him, and sending the old boy off balance, just as he was about to leave the water.

"Woah, woah, woah, steady on there lad!" said the old coot.

Denzel, Clarence and wind-up Wally were all laughing at the comical capers 'n' carryings on. Wally however, on his own merit of intuition, had once again, without being told, scouted up over land for any undesirable lurkers. Seeing all was quiet, he returned to his companions, bringing good tidings that all was clear and safe. Just as the little Warbler flew over the top of the bank and down to where Clarence had settled, after clambering out of the water. This of course, was hardly as steep and awkward compared to the steepness at lake-side earlier. As he caught his breath, after the journey so far, Denzel, was just reaching the top and now getting more than his share of encouragement, from you know who, floating down from above. Denzel finally made it up and over, then came to rest alongside the ageing coot. The little duck, although a little tired, still had a spring in his waddling step. But suffering in complete silence the old male sat, putting on a brave face, though in truth he was in excruciating pain and discomfort, with a bit of trouble from his piles – Farmer Giles as spoken by Denzel's pal, the slang tongued Lasher of Lewisham, Treadwell Toad Esq. Clarence acquired his present condition due to having had to drag his poor old rump along the ground over a rough bit, when climbing the first major obstacle, the steep bank at lake-side.

"What's that noise?" exclaimed Denzel, on adjusting his ears to a strange thunderous sound he had never ever recalled hearing before throughout his whole life. It was a beautiful quiet sunny day, yet this noise Denzel was hearing now sounded very much like a heavy rainstorm, though much, much louder.

"That's the waterfall lad," said old Clarence. Wally had seen this place before, it was just prior to his meeting with Denzel. Being so young at the time, it had not made much impression on young Wal, because the dear chap had forgotten it ever existed. The river, just ten yards or so up from where the company had climbed out, had forked to their right, going upstream.

This is where the life giving river, branched off at this higher level, which poured over the steep bank in crashing torrents into the calm lake below, causing fierce crashing 'n' bashings to the water below, making the now bubbly water as white as snow, turning the immediate area below into a raging dangerous place. With currents that would suck and pull anything below that came in its path whilst the main body of the river Darenth rolled on its magnificent journey, where on its travels it brings new life to other lakes, and so to the deep blue sea. After they had rested all three of the expedition made their way towards the deafening roar that lay ahead of them. They came to a clearing, which brought them high above the raging waterfall.

"Look at that Den!" Wally chirped, gulping at the same time, in fear of the sight, and noisy sounds of a fearful but beautiful place.

"It's really wonderful," said Denzel in true amazement at the sight in front of him now.

"Aye, lad," agreed old Clarence, "But very, very, dangerous indeed," he sternly told them both.

"Dangerous?" enquired Denzel, catching Wally's tiny round eyes, the poor little scout, had his eyes popping out at the sight of this marvellous view.

"From up here," answered Clarence, "if you keep out of harm's way. No! But on the other hand, if you're below, and silly enough to swim near it, yes," he warned Denzel. Old Clarence, went on to tell them, "It will crush you, and drag you under. Even humans, who have been stupid enough, have fallen overboard, resulting in sudden death. So always remember for all time laddie: never, ever take chances by going anywhere near that dreadful place, when swimming below."

"He won't," chirped a particularly over-concerned Wally, already on hearing uncle C's words of warning, he was half worried to death at even the slightest thoughts of losing his very best pal, to this terrible dreadful place. "Will ya Den?" Wal asked a second time.

"Of course I wouldn't, Wal," answered the reassuring duck; Wally not noticing Denzel's winkings at the old coot, as he said it.

"I know you wouldn't Den, us being bestest mates, eh!" Wally still chirping, still not fully satisfied, or assured. Denzel and the old boy sensed this in Wal, and were still gazing at each other without a smile on their faces. But both had laughing eyes at Wal's insecure chirpings and unnecessary worrying.

"No Wal, I wouldn't want to go and do a thing like that, mate, would I now?" Denzel, making a little fun at Wal's expense. Wally, not seeing the tease, agreed whole-heartedly, by nodding his head, and at last the Warbler was feeling pretty well-assured, well for now, that is. All of a sudden, a flash of electric blue, and fabulous colour caught the eyes of the visiting company. And there, landing on a post beside the waterfall, with a minnow in its beak, was the most beautiful kingfisher, the little fish still struggling 'n' wriggling, trying desperately to escape its catcher's clutches.

"Lovely day for it!" exclaimed old Clarence passing the time of day with the delightfully coloured bird.

"Yes," answered the kingfisher, after he'd tossed the poor captured culprit into the air, catching it head first, and swallowing it all in one great gulp.

"Cor look at that poor little fishy," Wal chirped.

Denzel whispered for Wally to be quiet, hoping the cleverest fisher of all the lakes, and rivers, never heard Wally's rude remark.

"You just don't know when to keep quiet," the duck whispered again.

"Er... Den," Wally tried again.

"Shh, Wally, if you insist on not listening to your elders, you'll never learn anything at all. Got it!" said the whispering Duck. Whilst Denzel was attempting to get young Wally under some kind of manners, old Clarence, and an old friend, Kenny the clever Kingfisher, were catching up on much gossip of local matters, that had passed since their last meeting, back in the spring of that year. As they had finished one another's bit of news, plus the odd bit of scandal-mongering. Kenny flew from his post, dived into the water below, returning with yet another fat minnow. Again it was tossed into the air, being caught by its head first. Where the party of three witnessed the second devouring of a silver scaled tiddler, Denzel and Wally both looking at each other, and swallowing hard pulling the most horrid of faces, as the live fishy went slip sliding down Kenny's fat throat.

"Irk," was all poor Wal could muster. Then, "He's no better than that blimmin' old Owl, when it comes to a bit of grub," Wal still pulling his face of distaste at Kenny's frolics of flipping fat fish, for feasting. When out of nowhere, Wally told Denzel and Co, of how he understood and proudly went on to tell how Owen the Wise, had taught him and Denzel all about the "Foodrope" of life. Wally at this time, was smiling with pride, showing off his bit of knowledge 'n' learnings, to the three bemused onlookers.

"Chain," in a whisper Denzel reminded the little scholar.

"Eh?" Wally chirped, in sudden surprise, and now feeling a bit put out.

"Chain! Foodchain! Foodrope, you said," Denzel jokingly reminded the cocky little villain.

"Oh yeah, chain". Wally appeared slightly knocked off his perch at this time, at yet another bloomer of many.

But at least the wee chap's a trier. Surely we can't take that away from the little lad. I mean, as you well know, he hasn't done badly for a wandering West Country Boy, has he now?

"Umm, how very rude of me," declared the old, out-of-breath coot. "Kenny the Kingfisher, these are my very good friends, Denzel Duck Esq, and his trusty mate…" and, before Clarence had a chance to continue…

"Bestest," Wal retorted, a bit sharpish.

"Aye lad, er… umm, yes! That's right, bestest mate, Wally the Dartford Warbler," scoffed the interrupted Clarence. All present gave their individual nods of approval. Kenny once again left his post, where the travellers watched the skilful bird. Within seconds, the sleek multicoloured form struck the water's surface, just beyond the raging swirl of the furious waterfall, emerging yet again, with another silvery morsel. Fishy wriggled, and squirmed, just as before, in Kenny's powerful beak.

"Don't you ever get worried that one day one of them fishes will get stuck in your throat?" chirped Wally pulling another dodgy face, as the fishy slipped, sliding down Kenny's fat throat.

"G… nope," gurgled from the Kingfisher's throat.

"Well," chirped cheeky chappie, "Do they wriggle 'n' tiggle inside your fat belly then?" asked Wal in a pretty low chirp, thinking to himself that any moment he would be reprimanded as usual by his best mate. But, to Wal's surprise, nothing came, except from Kenny's answer.

"Once the fishy has gone all the way down in my belly, sometimes for a little while," Kenny told him. "But nothing much to bother me," said the kingfisher in a deep throaty chuckle at Wally's inquisitive questions.

"When they wriggle 'n' tiggle, do it make ya laugh?" asked Wally, feeling quite at ease being allowed his freedom of chirps without Deznel's usual interference. "I would!" chirped Wal, "I'd kill myself laughing, with all that wriggly, tiggly, goings on inside me, and so would you, eh Den? Ha, ha!" Wally was now in fits of laughter, trying to imagine all the funny feelings that were happening deep inside the clever kingfisher's belly. Getting loads 'n' loads, or wrigs 'n' tiggs. Just the thought made the little character roar up laughing. Denzel was thinking that Wally was most definitely over stepping his mark, but decided to let his little mate carry on, and after giving Wal his rein, in his cheeky chirpings. All present were enjoying such fun, and laughter, at the little fella's antics, and comical capers he cut, making fun at Kenny's way of eating, As you can imagine, by this time Wally was feeling quite the centre of attraction, so he took advantage of his freedom of chirps. But most of all, he was proud to add another to his ever-growing family of friends, even though he had to put up with Kenny's future swallowing, with followings, of wriggles 'n' tiggles, ending in giggles. Time was getting on, where old Clarence on checking the position of the sun in the sky, which told him that it was time to be heading off home, and to his worried ever caring Clara. For the old boy knew she would never be happy until the expedition arrived back safely on the island. It was mid afternoon, when Clarence told the two lads that they must set off home. After saying their goodbyes to Kenny, the companions headed for the river, but not before witnessing the kingfisher in all its fabulous beauty, diving for another juicy fish. On the way, Clarence told Denzel,

"Now's the time for the surprise! We're going to have a ride home," said the now smiling coot.

"Ride on home?" mimicked, a most confused uck.

"Aye, my lad," said Clarence, "for once you've ridden the ripples on the Darenth, you'll never want to swim ever again."

"Why?" asked Denzel, all excited.

They reached the river in good time, the old coot urged Denzel into the river,

"Just let the ripples take you on home lad." With this, they both waddled down the bank a short way, then slid easily into the water. The rapid water soon carried the two birds at a fast pace, where young Wally was flitting in very short bursts, causing him to lose his breath, where the dear chap was trying his utmost to keep up. Denzel was really enjoying the free ride, thinking earlier of the difficulty that Clarence, and he, had had fighting their way upstream through such rapid waters. Denzel soon found sheer pleasure in the ride back.

"Such a comfortable speedy trip home, don't you think lad?" Clarence called from a few feet behind, keeping a careful watch over the young duck's welfare and safety.

"Oh yes, yes," said Denzel, who by now was loving every moment of this new experience. Wally struggling to keep up, had over-heard his friends having the times of their life, felt very much left out of all the excitement, swooped low to Denzel's ears, and asked if he too could share in the ride. Old Clarence had overheard Wally's request, and told Denzel to pull in, at the next lay-by. Denzel immediately found a suitable inlet and stopped off. The old-timer slowed at the point where the duck had chosen, and the rushing water rolled on its path to the sea.

"Aye, this'll do nicely lad, now get on my back, Wally," said the kindly old Coot. "I'd be only too pleased, to share such fun with you lad." on hearing the old Coots offer, Wal was there perched between Clarence's wings. Now with Wal fully on board old Clarence's back, the trio embarked once more.

"Yipee!" chirped Wal as they all picked up speed.

Denzel was having the time of his life, although seemingly not half as much as Wally, who appeared to be having a field day, especially on such an important adventure. But Denzel, being a little reserved, was just as happy learning and taking in every detail of the day's events. He was still enjoying every moment, where many lake dwellers, from a fair distance, could hear the commotion of pure joy and happy sounds coming from the direction of the living river Darenth. On the homeward journey, which was far less tiring, Denzel began to relax a bit more, he also began laughing and joking along with Wally as they went on their way downstream.

"Go on Wal, you ride 'em matey" Denzel was excitedly cheering his little buddy on. Wal by now was clinging for dear life onto poor old Clarence's neck feathers, he was flapping his tiny wings, and hollering 'n' hooting, making himself almost breathless, when all of a sudden, Clarence began to back pedal his webbed feet, and started to slow down.

"Here we are lads, this is where we entered earlier," said the Coot in a very low voice, as he put the old brakes on lively. "Now," he whispered, "we've all had our fun, but, that was the good bit." This old bird knew exactly what this expedition had meant to Denzel and Wally. "But now's the time to be cautious." As Clarence spoke in this quiet tone, Wally lifted himself, and flew from the ageing coot's back, sailing up to a thick cover of brambles at the water's edge.

"Shall I go and see if it's all clear?" Wal chirped merrily, the tiny bird taking it upon his own initiative. Denzel, looked straight at Clarence in sudden surprise at the little scout's shrewdness.

"Aye," said the now smiling coot, still gazing in Denzel's direction, shaking his old tired head with pride. Since this trip, he had found the little warbler a blessing to have around. Clarence's attention was drawn elsewhere to the thoughts of the day's adventures, and so much to tell his loving Clara, whilst sunning themselves, the very next day. But then the old bird laughed to himself, and wondered exactly just how much of it all would be left to tell, once the two lads, had said their piece to Aunty Clara. Then Clarence, with another kind smile thought to himself, "Not a lot, if cheeky chappie, Wal, lives up to his usual chirpings." Again the old-timer smiled in his own thoughts, and felt quite contented, knowing at last he'd taken them on their first, decent outing. They crossed the stretch of land without any signs of danger, they even passed the time of day talking with old Rabbit Doe, who was keeping lookout over her multitude of baby bunnies, who were grazing. Finally they arrived back at the top of the bank that they had climbed up from earlier. Although Denzel had found it so difficult to climb on the outward trip, he was now petrified at the steepness going down. Wally at this time, seeing all to be safe and almost home, was so full to exploding point with news to tell Aunty Clara. So with no more thought for the others, he recklessly? abandoned his buddies and flew from the gorse bush where he was perched. Oh no! Crafty cod Wal shot at one hundred miles an hour, towards Coot Island, and the waiting ears of poor Aunty Clara, and believe me, as he flew, the little fella was absolutely bursting with news of the day's events.

"Aunt, aunt!" chirped the erratic Warbler, trying to get the whole day's happenings out in one continual breath, something Wally was, at this time very short of. His longish tail was cocked, and his head feathers in an untidy manner appeared ruffled like a crest on the top of his head, which is pretty normal for the lively little characters that these Dartford ones are "Oh Aunt," the little scout chirped. "We went up this big kingfisher, and we met this waterfall, who eats loads of fishes, and… and on the way back, I had a ride on uncle river's back, a… and," Wal gasped for air. "And I'm the most important Warbler, 'cause I helped scout over land, and made sure there were no lurkers in the bushes, an… and."

"Oh my God!" thought Clara. "Now you just slow down my lad! My, my, you are in a state of excitement little one." She was all ears, but for the life of her, the dear lady couldn't make head nor tail, out of Wally's jumbled mutterings. She desperately tried to calm the panting little soul, even though she knew Wally was attempting to steal the whole show. Well, let's put it this way, trying to. In the meantime, limelight stealing Wally, had missed out on something that would make this day even more spectacular. Denzel was just about to descend this horrid steep bank, when old Clarence, purposely bumped into the youngster, pretending it too be an accident, knocking him off his balance. With this, Denzel, let out a loud noise of desperation, and could do no more than to flap his wings to keep upright. But unbeknown to the duck, the sheer ferocity of his downward thrusts had lifted him out of the nettled area, into the bright blue sky. At first the young Mallard was in blind panic, he found himself gliding some fifty yards or so into the lake, flying past the back end of Coot Island, and came abruptly crashing 'n' bashing awkwardly, making a very big splash. When Denzel came to his senses, he'd realised his achievement, and all because of an accident, or so the sprite young duck thought. Once Denzel had gained his composure, he noticed Clarence leave the steep bank in flight. He watched the old male coot come gliding down and come skidding on the top of the water, to where Denzel sat floating on the surface. Clarence, once settled on the water, could plainly see that the youngster was a bit flustered, but he also detected signs of a smiling and a very happy Mallard.

"Well done lad," said the sincere old-timer.

"W… what happened Uncle? Did you slip or something?"

"Aye lad," replied the aging coot not in any way letting Denzel know what had really happened, and that Clarence, for Denzel's own good, had in fact pushed the dear duckling on purpose. This crafty old coot only did it to make Denzel, out of desperation, use his wings for the purpose God gave them.

"Did you see me fly?" young Denzel cried in happiness.

"Aye I did that lad, indeed I did." Clarence over the past few weeks had often wondered how he could get the young Duck to make his first attempts at flying. He again, had a sly little chuckle to himself knowing that his stumbling into Denzel was no accident at all, but was a perfect opportunity, one slippery old coot could hardly resist, in fact. When Clarence pondered on it, he couldn't have thought of a more appropriate place for such a beginner, being so high up 'n all. Clarence at this time decided not to let on, and keep the secret to himself, but he vowed that he would tell the duck, when he felt the time was right. As the two big birds swam the last few yards towards Coot Island, Clara watched Denzel and her loving old spouse approaching. She was sitting in her usual resting place, the dear lady's wings were spread over her ears, as Wally carried on his very speedy mixed up version of the day's outing. Clarence and Denzel were nearing the island, the old coot, wearing a big smile, called as he swam towards his beloved Clara. Clarence knew full well that what he was about to say was an understatement, if ever he'd heard one.

"Is there anything else left to tell?" he called, recognising the old girl's grin between the poor females wings. They were raised to the side of her head covering both ears, trying to ward off Wal's chirping onslaught. For the rest of the day, Wally had at last run out of steam. So Denzel and Clarence filled Clara in on the real happenings of that day's events. Clara was in a more relaxed state of mind than she was, after being almost sent deaf by the explosive chirping of the blabbering, Wal. She now sat nodding 'n' smiling at all the jabbering of the day trippers, but on a much, much calmer footing.

That night, as the family of four had said their blessings, they all settled down to roost, and dropped off to sleep almost immediately. At fifteen minutes past midnight, the residents in the vicinity of Horton Kirby were woken by the most terrifying thunder. Followed shortly after by lightning that lit the night sky, as it shot across the darkened night. As if from nowhere, a wind stirred from the east, and rain fell from the heavens in torrents. Denzel, whilst huddled snug and warm, in his hole in the tree began to realise that this storm was not an ordinary shower, and desperately thought of Wally and his ageing adopted parents. After giving the situation some thought, he decided that no matter how dangerous it would be, he must check that his loved ones were safe and well. Lightning flashed from the sky, and the treacherous east wind just blew 'n' blew. Wally in his little reed shelter at this time, was being tossed about like a falling leaf. In fact Wally was in dire straits, and the little soldier knew it. He flapped his tiny wings, and tried his utmost to cling to anything he could lay his claws into. He was trying to secure himself to keep from being blown away, which Wal knew could mean sudden death. Wally's reed shelter was, at the height of these winds, bending over so far, the little shelter was almost touching the rough choppy waves, which ebbed that much higher, only inches from Wal's only bit of safety. Denzel flew down from his roost, making his way, just a few yards to Coot Island, to make sure the pair of ageing Coots were safe, and well, only to find them sheltering inside the trunk of an old fallen elm tree, that had floated down to end its days stuck in the mud, just to the rear of their island. Over the past years this log had come in handy when such storms occurred. Clarence realised early that this was no ordinary storm. He had been shrewd enough to get his loving Clara and himself to safety.

"Where's Wally?" Clara cried painfully.

"Last I saw of him he was safe in his reed shelter." Denzel shouted through the blustery storm, so the worried coots could hear him.

"Are you sure lad?" enquired the uncertain northerner, from his and Clara's sanctuary. "I think we had better go find the poor little mite, don't you lad?" called a very worried Clarence.

"Yes, and I don't think you should lose another moment," screamed the absolutely petrified Clara, in thinking of poor little Wally, all alone out there, in such a terrible and dangerous storm. "Go, go," she moaned, for Clarence, and Denzel to make haste. As both males entered the water, they could still hear Clara's pleading and praying, for the little windswept Wal, out there in the darkness, and blustery night ahead. It had taken them less than one minute to reach Wally's quarters, but the inevitable, most drastic fears that entered the old coots head, had happened. All that was left of Wal's residence was four broken stilts, to which the small reed shelter was fixed, the rest was unfortunately gone. Denzel, and old Clarence, both with their hearts pounding out of their chests, suspecting the worst. They each decided to spread out, and comb the immediate area for any signs of Wally, or at least his little shelter. They searched and searched, calling as loud as they possibly could, the little fella's name, but alas, to no avail. Clara heard the devoted searchers' calls.

"Wally, Wally, where are you?" She heard Denzel's call to her left, then,

"Where are you lad? Uncle Clarence is here to help you, come on lad, answer, old Yorky? Please lad, please…" was the old coot's choking call. For he knew only too well that the chances of finding such as small bird, in this gale, were getting slimmer by the minute. Clara on hearing her life-long partner's saddened call in this way, realised the pain her old spouse was feeling at this very time. For this was the first time she had heard the old-stager use his pet name, in many a bright moons, in fact since their courting days, back up in the Dales, when Clara called him 'Yorkie' teasingly, during their months of courtship, and only on rare occasions these days, would Clara use it, with the exception of course, where she, like most other females of any other species, would use her charms to get her little wants in life. After searching through the night, and daybreak came, the three sad birds with wings sagged, head stooped in doom 'n' gloom, neither of them had the heart or strength, even to speak. But, at this very moment (in time), word was going round the lake long before the old 'current bun' appeared over the eastern horizon. Every living creature, that was old enough or capable enough, had its eyes peeled for Wally. All the frogs were searching their neck of the lakes. Every bird from water to land birds, such as Charley, the brave coot, was informed to tell his flock to keep a sharp lookout. There were finches of all colours helping in the search at lake-side. Even Cock Robin, in his very fine waistcoat, was skittering about his plot in the underbrush, not leaving a stone unturned in his bid to help recover the poor waif Wal. Owen, returned from his disastrous night's hunting, where the storm completely ruined any chances of supper. He knew he wouldn't have any luck, before he went.

"But owls have to eat, ya know!" he hooted to himself. Grace, on seeing the Owl return, called,

"My goodness, Owen, where have you been? I have been waiting for you such a long time," it was the way anxious Grace sounded that turned the hungry old Owl to being a bit grumpy, being startled at such an unearthly hour. But on seeing Grace without the king, he knew it was important business enough to be troubled at such an hour. Owen immediately flew down to where the Queen of Dartford floated. Grace told Owen of the sad tale of Wally's disappearance, and filled the old wizard in on what little she knew. She told him that she had left Cyril, to help organise the search party, also of the sad situation on Coot Island. As tired as a blustery nights hunting had left the old Tawny, he felt a sudden rush of adrenalin, as the power surged in the old bird's veins. For Owen knew full well, no matter how much he needed his long lost kip, the disappearance of his tiny friend and pupil was by far more important, and now he must go at once to join the search that was taking place whilst he and Grace spoke.

"Your highness, I must make haste, my big eyes, and most cleverest of knowledge is needed here!" exclaimed Owen, in a state of yawning whilst still in conversation.

"Go quickly," hissed Grace, "Use your skills, and wonderful knowledge, please Owen, please find that dear little soul."

Owen, with so much going on in that big brainy head of his, didn't even say goodbye, just left his temporary perch, flew upwards to gain some height, then dropped and glided in on the big lake, heading for Coot Island. He'd only gone a short distance, when his huge round eyes, so watchful, scanned the scenery, there wasn't much going on around these parts for miles that this old bird didn't know about. He was approaching the front side of Coot Island now, and was slowly descending to land. There didn't appear to be any of the inhabitants at home, when he heard Clara's heartbreaking cries. The old Owl immediately hopped, and partly flew, across the tops of the low gorse bushes and shrubbery, to see Clara at the back part of the island. Owen settled beside her.

"Clara, Clara" the old Owl hooted, "now what's all this then?" he comforted this heartbroken old hen.

"It's Wally!" cried the caring female.

"I know, I know old girl," Owen tried to pacify her as best he could. "Now listen my dear, where's your husband, and Denzel?" he asked, trying to get some sense out of the very upset Clara, who was still sobbing uncontrollably. Through her snivels 'n' sniffs, the old upset hen told Owen,

"They're, over there!" the old dear pointed her beak in the direction of the closest edge of the lake to where they sat, at the back of the island. Old Owen couldn't help feeling for poor Clara, he put his huge wing around the old girl, giving her a gentle pat to try and comfort her, he then took off in the direction of Denzel and Wally's roosting place. On arriving, Owen found the rescue party, almost an hour after the first alarm went out of the Warblers disappearance. As the big old Tawny settled on an old dead stump, Denzel, and Clarence both saw him arrive, Denzel part flapping, and paddling furiously across the water's surface, trying to reach Owen as quickly as possible, in the hope that the wise bird would have some news of Wally. Clarence made it to where Owen was sitting at about the same time as Denzel, but both their hopes were dashed, when Owen told them that he'd only heard of the situation a few minutes ago.

"Have you found any clues to what may have happened to him?" Owen asked the two distraught birds.

"No, there doesn't seem to be any trace of him, not even any signs of his reed shelter," said Denzel, not looking at all well.

Old Clarence showed Owen the four broken reed stilts that supported the cluster of dead reed leaves that acted as Wally's windbreaker.

"I see!" hooted Owen in his most deepest of thoughts, then the big owl started to calculate his sums and checked on the direction the wind came from. His big round eyes peered intensely along the bank of the lake, which was now still quite thick with all kinds of foliage in a state of greens, going brown with decay, mixed with entwining briers of the blackberry bushes. This particular part of the water's edge is where it swerves out into the lake at this point, about twenty or so yards, then bends round to the right, and carries on pretty straight right up to the chimney end of the lake. The worst of the weather had subsided now, the old Owl had drawn his own conclusions about where the search should concentrate, focusing on an area in a small corner, some twenty yards or so away from whence he came – Wal, that is. Owen fancied his wise decision, he had seen that if Wally was blown in that direction then the chances were he could have been blown into that thicket of brambles, that would have been springy enough to break Wal's speed. Maybe, just maybe, the boy will be alright, the old Owl thought to himself. Denzel, and the old coot, had fallen silent, whilst Owen was doing his thinking.

"Right!" hooted Owl. "Clarence, you go and get all the help you can muster. Denzel, you come with me, we haven't much time." Young Denzel watched the wise old Owl fly over the water to the bank, where it turns out into the lake. He watched him settle on a branch just above the thick density of the brambles, which he sincerely hoped was where Wally could have ended up. Denzel followed and swam over to the thick heavy bramble area. Owen hooted and told Denzel to look all around the edge of the brambles that hung out over the water's edge. Old Owen was scanning every inch, scrutinizing every section he glanced over. Within ten minutes, this area had more residents, so willing to help, there was hardly room to move. The search party was turning the place upside down, but still no sign of the dear Wal. Well, by this time you can imagine all the sad faces in that vicinity at this very moment in time, and tears! You've never in all your life witnessed tears like it! Without the slightest bit of exaggeration, there was so much water dripping from the resident rescue party, the lake was rising by the hour. Well, according to Harry the Rat, that is! They searched and searched, and the atmosphere, let me tell you, if there had been a fisherman, or a bailiff, on or about those lakes, he would have been able to cut the atmosphere with a knife, or at least, recognise the unusual amount of activity by the residents, in their searchings 'n' lookings for the missing warbler. The sun was at that place in the sky that told Owen that there were only five hours' daylight left. Old Owen stated that fact to Clarence, and when he looked down at the old Yorkie sitting there, just below, he could tell the old coot was completely worn out, not only from sheer exhaustion of hours of no sleep, but in the mind as well. In fact, the poor old geezer was out of his mind in worry, for you must realise the missing Wally was bad enough, but he had two lots. For Clarence was dreading going home without the little lad, because he knew the outcome regarding Clara, let alone Denzel. Clarence in truth was hurting very badly, and it wasn't doing his old heart any good either at his age. It's funny, old Yorkie never did mention his age, but going by the greying feathers upon his quaint old face, he was known to be what we call 'getting on a bit'. He managed to raise his head, still shaking from the dampness of the night's search that had chilled the old boy to the bone.

"Aye, Owen, I know," said the distraught old coot, "but I won't give up 'til then!" he said in a very depressed manner. "And nor will you, I'll wager!" said Clarence, knowing the big Tawny was just as hurt as he was.

"I'll search through the night if I have to. I've not eaten for ages, but I couldn't eat a morsel, right now. So I may as well keep on looking, for who's better adapted to see in the dark than me, eh, ma boy?" said Owen reassuring the tired old Coot, and there was no way he was giving up the search. At this time of conversation, the two elder statesmen, were resting a short while after a tiring fruitless search. Denzel was with them earlier, but decided to keep on with the search. He knew the two older birds needed a breather after hours of hazardous looking, but Denzel, through much determination, that was overriding the hurt within, never for one moment even dreamt of resting. He swam up and down the lake, organising other groups of searchers feathered, furry, also the leathery lot, the amphibians, in their hunt to find the tiny warbler. It was just as Denzel returned to meet Owen and Uncle Clarence that Maggie, the accomplice 'n' wife of Maurice the jewel-thieving magpie, was seen by the sharp-eyed Owen, heading in the companies' direction. As she dropped from the sky, the beautiful long necked bird landed on an old dead branch that was beside Owen. The dear girl was hopelessly out of wind but, as soon as she caught her breath, Maggie squawked, news of the missing Wally.

"Sir!" she was addressing Owen the Wise, "Me 'n' my old man were scratching about over by Crank's Hall, you know? That big old place, where them there humans lives, Well!" she squawked, then giving a crafty sniff, having to declare their bird burgling habits.

"Go on, my dear," hooted Owl, "I'm quite sure that all present have been at some time acquainted with you and your husbands, peepings 'n' creeping, ending in glittering gold, 'n' rings 'n' things. Maggie went on to tell them of how they were scratching about a large country house. She went on to say,... "We'd just finished our bit of grub, and flew up into the branches of a big fir tree. We wasn't up to anything dishonest, sir! (Maurice was in fact eyeing up a nice sized diamond ring that he'd spied on the dressing table through a slightly opened window) All of a sudden, a man came by, and my husband noticed he had something clasped between his paws, like. The man went inside, and Maurice, with his mischievous mind, thought by the way the man held his paws, it must be something, precious 'n' sparkling. Maurice flew from the tree down to a bush just outside to where the man was inside. But when Maurice looked, he saw with his own eyes, a little bird. When he crept close to the window, making sure he wouldn't be seen, Maurice recognised straight away that it was Wally. We'd only met him the once you see, back in the spring, but it was definitely Wally."

"Go on, Maggie! Please go on!" hooted Owen.

Maggie went on, "My husband sent me here to fetch you, he told me that he would stay there and keep an eye on things 'til you returned with me to Crank's Hall."

Owen immediately, took it upon himself to take full charge of the operation.

"Right!" he hooted sternly. "Clarence, you and Denzel head straight on home with what news we have! I think there's someone there who needs to hear of this bit of good news. She'll be needing all the comforting the dear sweet lady can get. Now go on back to Coot Island and get some rest yourselves, and leave this matter to me."

At first, Old Clarence, like Denzel, was not having any of it! Both insisted on going to Wally's aid, but as old Owen wisely told them, with them turning up in the grounds of Crank's Hall as well, they were more than likely to be shot, then fed to the hounds, even though it was out of shooting season. Clarence and Denzel both, never for one moment, liked the idea, though never argued any further, and began to turn to make their way home to the island and the waiting Aunt Clara. But at least they had the good news, of Maggie's, and her bird burglar husband's sightings at Crank's Hall. Owen and Maggie watched the two water birds on their way to Coot Island. Then they both took to the air, and as straight as a crow, flew speedily to Crank's Hall, a mile or so away. When they arrived, Maggie had taken Owen straight up into the big fir tree, to where she and Maurice had first spied the man carrying something. They both looked down and saw Maurice, doing his usual job of peering into windows. But on this occasion, it was of the honest kind, using his crafty mince pies in watching Wally's whereabouts. Whilst Maggie, had been gone, the black 'n' white bandit in the gems department never once took his keen eyes off the happenings of Wally inside. He had witnessed an elderly man looking and handling Wally (who incidentally had been battered about badly by the gale). But the finder, luckily for Wally, was an amateur ornithologist who, whilst out doing a spot of twitching, happened to stumble on a bird he couldn't even recognise, until he got home to Crank's Hall, that was. The country gent had taken Wally into his study and looked the shaken little bird up in his British Bird Book. He was most delighted at such a find, in fact, what he had brought home to his stately Crank's Hall was a very rare find indeed, for he, and only he, was the first person to record, not a measly sighting like that chap in 1773, but now in 1964, he had living proof that the Dartford ones were about again, in the Dartford area. He, the man that is, was so excited, he cleaned the little warbler up, and was pleased to see that all the little chap needed to be as right as a ninepence, was a good night's rest in the warm. Well, as we can all see for ourselves, it appears the bold Wal, under such circumstances as had a right touch! Not only was he lucky to be found by this kind man, who more or less saved the little fella's life, but Wal, now after this nice gentle man, who was at this very moment, after giving Wally a clean, and tidy up was now actually wrapping Wal in cotton wool! At first the cheeky chappie was very nervous, knowing he was in the hands of a human being. But Wal felt a bit more at ease at the kind Man's gentle care and treatment. Wally was beginning to calm down a little, snuggled in a bit of home comfort. In truth, Wal was lapping it up, especially after almost losing his life in that terrible gale that blasted the Horton Kirby lakes and surroundings! Whilst Wally was in this small temporary cage, which was actually a shoe box with a thin piece of netting over the top of it, placed on a desk, in the study, the outside onlookers had seen the man, who appeared to be talking to someone in his paw, which looked like a black bone. Owen raised his ears to the crack of the window, and this is what the old Owl heard…

"Yes! It's definitely a Dartford Warbler?"

"No! No! It really is! So you don't believe me! You don't? Well you'll just have to come round and see for yourself then."

Whilst all this was going on, the telephone receptionist had over-heard this conversation. By the strangest coincidence, this lady's husband just happened to be a bird fancier. In other words, a twitcher. She began to eavesdrop on the continued conversation.

"No, no, David, it really is a Dartford one! Well, if you don't believe me, you'll have to come down and see for yourself. My address? Yes that's right David, Crank's Hall, South Darenth, Dartford. Ok! Bye. Oh, by the way, don't let this get out or I'll have every twitcher in the country swarming over the place! Bye."

Owen had overheard this conversation, and smiled to himself. He turned to Maurice and his accomplice wife and said…

"At least the little beggar's alive." Then the owl asked Maurice if there was any way possible for them to get inside and get the little chappie out. Maurice thought for a while and remembered that the upstairs window that he'd been studying earlier, was open just enough for him to squeeze into, but the burglar felt a bit dodgy in declaring his reasons for being there at Crank's Hall in the first instance. Maurice gave a sly old cough and then said…

"Well, er… as me 'n' the missus 'ere woz passing overhead in flight, I sees master Wally there in the paws of this geezer. But honest gov, if I hadn't seen Wally, then we would surely have gorn straight past, ain't that right, gel?" squawked Maurice, winking at his cunning spouse.

"That's right; my husband is a good man, sir," squawked his accomplice. Owen sat for a while just listening. He knew all the time of sharp-eyed Maurice's crafty pickings 'n' nickings from the idle rich. But Owen let the masterly magpie tell it his way. As long as he could get Wally out, Owen wasn't interested in Maurice 'n' Maggie's dealings 'n' stealing from the likes of Crank's Hall.

"Go on!" hooted the very patient owl.

"Where was I? Oh yeah, we drops down on a branch to see where the Man woz taking Wally, when gawd help us! I just happened to notice an upstairs window open, just a wee bit mind! Not that I woz looking, like!"

"Never mind about that! Do you think you could find a way to get inside and help Wally to escape?"

"Well, guv, I'll have a bloomin' good try," exclaimed Maurice confidently.

"He'll get the little one out sir, you mark my words. My old man's the best there is, and he ain't frightened of dogs either," squawked Maggie, quite proud of her spouse's talents in the creeping department. In moments all three birds were back up in the big fir tree. Maurice pointed out the open bedroom window to Owen.

"There it is, Guv! See wot I mean, it's open just enough! Leave it to me," squawked the slippery jewel thief. With this Owen and Maggie, eyes peeled, witnessed this very cunning burglar at work. He was down and in, just as the old braggart had bragged, going out of sight of the tree top spectators. Once Owen, saw the endings of Maurice's long black tail disappear inside the window, he and Maggie flew down speedily and perched on a branch outside of the study window, where they were a few minutes before. The man was sitting in his chair in front of a huge desk, and appeared to be reading a book that had pictures in it of birds. Owen, from his position, aided by his enormous round eyes, was peering over the man's shoulder, and saw, as he flicked through the pages, there was a picture of himself on one of the pages. Owen, as he watched, had to chuckle to himself. But obviously him being so old 'n' wise, this wasn't the first time he'd seen things of the man's world.

Once inside, Maurice the much loved magpie hopped, skittered, and scurried out of the bedroom, along the huge hallway, until he came to a stairwell. Maurice knew he had to be very quiet, so to make minimal noise, the black 'n' white scallywag, hopped up onto the banisters, and silently slid all the way down to the bottom, making less noise then the local church mice, following his beak, along with a bit of knowledge of such great houses of taste. The burglar goes to work! Maurice made his way toward the room that was full of books, and the shoebox containing the worn out warbler. Owen, concentrating on looking into the study, had just caught a glimpse of a magpie's big black head appear and disappear behind the frame of a half opened door. Maurice never realised the man was still in the room where Wally was held, and he knew if he was to succeed, it would have to be before the fading light went out completely. Owen could see the antics of the mischievous magpie from time to time, when the brave burglar kept poking his long neck around the door frame. Maurice at this time was getting very worried that the man would never leave the room. The burglar was getting very impatient now, and decided that a plan of action must be taken. He left his post, which was just outside the study, on a highly polished parquet floor (which incidentally, at a later date he told listeners when doing his usual bragging, that if it had been a bit smaller "he'd a nicked that 'n' all!") All of a sudden an idea formed in the burgling bird's head. He flew, then scampered along the downstairs hall, and found a door ajar. Peering inside, he saw another beautiful room of antiquity. On entering, he noticed upon the mantelpiece a pair of pretty porcelain figurines. Maurice did no more. He flew up and flapped his strong wings at one of the figurines, until he knocked it off, causing it to tumble, making such crashing 'n' bashings. Immediately, even before that porcelain hit the floor, the cunning burglar, was back to his position outside the study door. He, the man that is, left his study to investigate the crashing noise in another part of the house. His thoughts, funnily enough, were of a likely burglar. The very moment the man had left that room, the burglar was inside and up to where Wally sat, in his cotton wool filled box, like a rat up a drainpipe. As the burglar tugged on the thin netting, one of

Wal's eyes opened, and then he came out of his exhausted sleep, but not knowing where he was.

"Wally!" whispered Maurice, "come along quickly, as fast as ya can! We ain't much time!" Wal never had the slightest of inklings where he was, or even what on earth was going on. Maurice, quickly explained the situation, but realised Wally was still in shock after being actually knocked out in the terrible storm. Fact was, Wal never knew of anything that Maurice had briefly told him. Wally had seen the netting was pulled away from the top of the temporary cage, and was up and out, then landed on the back of the man's chair.

"Quickly, let's get out of here sharpish!" squawked the burglar, and he rushed for the exit. When half way out, he realised Wally wasn't following. When the burglar looked back, Wal was in a queer old state, something not ever witnessed by the burglar, and I dare say he'd seen some sights on his travels. But when the dear chap went back to help Wally in the escaping routine, Wally was now on the man's desk, and appeared to be looking at the big thick book of birds. As the burglar settled on the desk beside the little fella to warn him that time was running out, Maurice noticed the reason. Wally, in his semi-delirium, was looking starry eyed at a pretty female Dartford one, and the little rascal in his haze had thought she was real. Did that Magpie have a job trying to get the love struck Wal away from that printed female? (As he told the company later... "It woz murder".) In the end Maurice had to show him Owen perched outside the study window on the window sill, prompting the burglar to get Wally himself out of there quickly. Wally, on seeing the owl, soon came out of his memory lapse and was now floating behind the fleeing burglar, who just like his accomplice, had squawked...

"Maurice had done a real professional job." When Wally and his rescuer, left that bedroom window, Owen, leaving Maggie perched outside the study window to watch the return of the man inside. The owl flew up to greet the escapees, meanwhile Maggie had left her post joining the others telling Owen the man had returned and was back at his desk continuing to look at the book, in her own lingo of course.

With this, all four birds took to the sky from Crank's Hall and flew in the direction of the Horton Kirby lakes, and the reception of Wally's return. Back at Crank's Hall, and the surrounding grounds, all manner of men in deer stalkers, caps and binoculars, were appearing by the lorry load. Inside the kind bird fancier was blind to all the goings on outside; all the twitchers, congregating in their dozens, all hunting for the first-ever sighting of a Dartford Warbler since 1773. As you can imagine, there was a lot of excitement in the camp among the twitching brigade. All of a sudden, the doorbell rang at Crank's Hall, and the man inside went to open it, as it was his butler's day off. He was greeted by the man who knew the one he was talking to earlier on the telephone.

"Ah, Mr Attenborough! And good day to you, sir! And I'm very pleased that you could come!"

"Thank you kindly, what was your name again?"

"Crank, sir, Peregrine Crank! Please would you come this way, sir!" Peregrine was ecstatic having such an authority on birds and wildlife coming to visit him at the hall. It wasn't every day you have such a famous gent come calling at the old property. "Oh no!" thought the laughing landowner, knowing his rare find would put his name in the record books.

"You are still satisfied, it's a Dartford Warbler?" the keen visitor asked.

"Oh yes, unmistakably!" said Peregrine Crank, rubbing his hands together in anticipation. "He's a Dartford one all right! Come along and I'll show you."

They entered the study. "Oh my God! It's gone!" screamed Peregrine in utter confusion.

"What!" exclaimed the furious visitor, thinking… "This idiot has brought me all the way from London on a wild warbler chase!"

"A Dartford one at that!" growled the infuriated visitor, "When it's oh so obviously plain to me that you have taken up bird watching a bit too seriously. After seeing this unique *Sylvia data* in your book, you decided to invent all of this charade to draw attention to your pathetic self! Or maybe a little prank. Eh! Mr Crank?" The visitor smirked at his own joke. "Bah!" muttered the visitor, "trying to get your name in the record books, eh my boy?" So embarrassed now, poor dishevelled Peregrine just couldn't believe his bad luck.

"Er... it appears that way. Yes!" said the most embarrassed Mr Crank.

"You mean to tell me you have brought me all the way out here to the sticks, for me to inspect a blooming empty boot box! You... you, blithering idiot!" shouted Mr Attenborough, the wound up wild-life lover.

"Honestly! It really was here! I found it battered and shaken over at our local lakes." But the poor man was just not believed.

"Good day to you sir! And my God! Goodbye!" The furious Mr. Attenborough snapped and turned to leave. As the disgruntled visitor left the study rapidly, prancing Peregrine was 'on 'is toes', pursuing the man who knows, who at this very moment in time, didn't even care anymore. Peregrine passed the fleeing frantic fancier.

"Allow me to get your warbler, Mr Attencoat!" said the confused Peregrine, winding old Attenborough up even more. He politely managed to open the front door of Crank's Hall, still very confused at what could possibly have happened to his prized find. Opening the huge oak door, Peregrine noticed the beautiful Rolls Royce, of the vintage kind, parked outside. After totally ignoring the owner of the Hall, the visitor left having already expressed just what he thought of poor Peregrine Crank. As he watched the vehicle disappear down his long drive, his eyes were suddenly attracted to a bit of movement in the shrubbery, to the left hand side of his drive. When the dear chap had taken proper stock, he saw to his amazement, there, sticking up out of a large bush of rhododendrons, was what appeared to be a deerstalker hat with a head underneath it, looking up into a tree, through binoculars. He was just about to shout at the half-hidden intruder, when even more to his surprise, he saw yet another gentleman in similar garb. Then a strange car turned into his huge gates, entering from Blackbird Lane. Peregrine stopped for a moment, to collect his thoughts, whilst giving his head a little question mark scratch. He watched the car crawl up the drive. He noticed three men inside, and a woman, who was driving. As they got closer, Peregrine could see every window of that car was wide open. Three heads appeared all holding field glasses to their eyes, hoping to catch a glimpse of a Dartford Warbler. The little flutter of feathers that had just drawn their sights was in fact a common house sparrow. As the car drew up, it skidded on the loose gravel chippings of Peregrine's forecourt.

"Can I help you?" called Peregrine.

"I say, old chap, have you seen it?" asked the man from the opened nearside window.

"Seen what?" retorted Peregrine.

"The Warbler! The Dartford Warbler," the front passenger asked enthusiastically.

"Oh, my good grief!" thought Peregrine. "How on earth has that leaked out?" The poor man was about to give these trespasser's their marching orders, when he was distracted. As Peregrine turned to look, there were more binoculars in the grounds of Crank's Hall than at Ascot on Ladies Day. Mr Crank was furious now, and began shouting "Get orf my land!" to all the twitching trespassers. Then another appeared, all rigged out in tweed regalia, doing his bit of twitching from the centre of Peregrine's rhubarb patch! Peregrine tried, and tried again, to convince the twitching twerps, that it had been a hoax. It was pitch black before the most ardent of the enthusiasts ceased trespassing, and at least, peace once again fell over Crank's Hall. Poor Peregrine, worn out mentally from all the unexpected goings on, returned inside the hall, slamming the heavy oak door closed. He walked back to his study to try and pick up from where it all went wrong.

"All I've done this day," he thought, "was find a real live rare little bird. I brought it home and gave it its life back. And all because I wanted to share my joy in what I'd found, I get Mr Attenborough, who does not believe me! My gardens here at the Hall, have been destroyed by what must have been every twitcher in the whole damn country I shouldn't wonder. My whole day has been one long nightmare. Attenborough almost bit my head off. My beautiful prized Dresden figurine mysteriously smashed to a thousand pieces, and when I went to see my guest out, I discovered there were more strange odd bods with bins than at an opticians' convention." Poor Peregrine, after all this was mentally drained. He returned to his study, and poured himself a stiff brandy, adding a dash of vintage port. He then collapsed into his deep red leather-bound chair, staring at the book in front of him, and the picture of a Wally lookalike. He sipped his drink, and whilst trying to fathom out how the warbler escaped, he also wondered where the little bird was now. Whilst searching his thoughts, Peregrine, fell into a deep exhausted slumber. He had been so mentally drained, it was daybreak when he awoke. For a few moments, whilst having his morning cup of tea, he gave the warbler another thought, and pondered over all of yesterday's events, wondering if it ever happened at all. "Am I going mad? Was it all in my imagination? How could this be?" he thought again, "there's the box I'd kept it in! And I did go to the lakes yesterday morning." Then he dismissed it as if it was a bad dream. It was seven thirty in the morning now, and soon time to catch the 8.35 a.m. train to the City, and his normal day at the office where all thoughts of yesterday's episode left Peregrine's mind.

Back at Coot Island, Denzel and the two caring Coots were waiting impatiently for news from Owen and the bird burgling duo, of Wally's whereabouts. There was a hour of daylight left for this long and arduous search when young Denzel caught a glimpse of something from out of the corner of his eye. When looking properly, he saw in the distance, Owen returning, along with the Magpies, heading towards the Island. Returning speedily, Denzel pointed the questers out to the rest of the company. But there was no sign of his best pal. He turned to the ageing couple of coots, who had both seen for themselves, the little warbler's absence from the three flying birds. Just as all the company were preparing themselves for the inevitable, to their shock, surprise and overwhelming joy, there, dangling from the neck feathers of the returning Tawny, was, yes, the dear Wal. Not in his usual, yarooing 'n' yippeeing mood, as he does on the odd occasion when the little fella gets excited. Though all present could tell at this time that the little lad wasn't his old self, but the mixed company of birds, did notice Wal's attempt in a few yelpings 'n' laughing. But Clara knew it was all a bit of a charade, 'cause Wal's usual personality just wasn't on board. Though now smiling, for the loving old girl also knew that she loved the little rascal, and with her bit of caring attention, in the fussing department, Wal would be the crow's toes in a day or two. After the dusk reunion, the Island residents were filled in on the rescue.

Owen had begun the story, but after rudely, and continuously being interrupted by Maggie, Owen in the end let her have her squawk of their part in "Operation Dartford One". Maggie was giving it the large, on how it was her 'n' her old man who found, and got Wally out of, Crank's Hall.

"How come you were at Crank's Hall in the first place?" Clara enquired. Maggie, who appeared to be squawking away, was still trying to cover her's and Maurice's tracks of the real reasons for being at the Hall. Maurice, who after twenty minutes since their landing, never opened his beak once, whilst Maggie never stopped squawking her and her old man's praise, which, as we all know, is allowed, and gladly excepted by not only the present company, but all the local residents on the plot of Horton Kirby. Not to mention how indebted they all were, to the two black 'n' white bird's sharp eyed spotting, resulting in Wally's escaping from Crank's Hall. In all the excitement, no one was more aware than the big old Tawny. It came to his attention that Maggie, since their return, appeared to be doing all the squawking, of how Maurice did this, and how she and Maurice did that. Owen considered both deserved some praise, then realised that ever since they had taken flight from Crank's Hall, the burglar hadn't squawked a note! Yet the old wise owl knew just what a braggart Maurice's character was. Owen found it strange, in fact very queer indeed. Owen's hoot cut through the rowdy excited company like a north wind.

"Maurice! Are you all right my boy?" hooted the Owl.

"Umm" A weird muffled sound came from the burglar's shut-tight beak.

"Are you ill then?" hooted Owen, getting even more than suspicious of the tight-beaked burglar.

"Umm!" came the muffled sound again; but this time Maurice was shaking his black old head from side to side in the 'No' movement. At this time, Maggie was silenced in her squawking, and was now getting a bit flustered, knowing the game was up.

"I see!" hooted the Owl, "Maurice! What have you inside your beak? Come along Maurice, spit it out 'ma boy!" With this, the crafty burglar went to say something, when out of his beak popped a sparkling diamond ring. It fell to the floor in front of the staring company, gasps of surprise sparked from the surrounding group, who now were all agog at the strange sparkling stone that was set in a beautiful golden ring.

"Oh dear!" squawked Maggie, giving a deep hard swallow, "You've gorn 'n' done it now! We're bang in trouble, and it's all your fault!" squawked Maggie. Yet after all she'd squawked, she was now cunningly trying to remove her part of Maurice's skulduggery of the missing tom-foolery that took place during the rescue.

"Ah! What have we here then?" hooted owl. "Been at your old tricks again have we, eh Maurice?" Owen stared piercingly into the old burglar's eyes.

"I... I'm sorry guv! I couldn't help it! Honest a God! To tell ya the truth, as me 'n' master Wallace here woz escaping out the window, as Wally flew past the dressing table, he accidentally knocked the ring down onto the floor. Course, I nipped down and picked it up to put it back where it woz, and gawd help us! the blimin' thing got stuck in me throat. I woz trying me hardest to cough it up! But then I hears this geezer coming up the stairs, and honest guv, if I'd tried another second, he would have fired that stick at me, on my old Maggie's life." At this stage of the tale, not only was the company unimpressed, but even the skulking Maggie wasn't too happy in having her life put on the line by the flying fibber. Maurice knew his burgling blarney might fool some of the younger company, but even he, with all his burgling talents, knew that this old owl was most definitely no fool. Owen flew down from his perch to inspect the ring with the shiny sparkling stone, even in the fading light, Owen was fascinated by its faceted glinting brilliance.

"Umm," the wise old owl mumbled as he inspected the pretty object before him. "It's getting dark! Let us all retire to roost, and we'll resume this matter after breakfast in the morning; your time that is!" on realising he, at this time, would actually just be getting up. Though he was still not hungry, after not eating for the past few days 'n' nights, since the storm. All present stayed in residence on the Island for the night, so that they could continue where they had left off, and of course, each and every one of them knew the place would be inundated with happy smiling well-wishers, all wanting to see the little lad, for whom they all shared in the searching.

When morning came, they weren't wrong! The whole of the surrounding area of this tiny island was inundated with all the animals and birds of all kinds from thereabouts. Willows, silver birch, and the many other shrubs, every reed stem and bramble, were packed with every species of bird. Even Kenny the clever kingfisher managed to make a showing between his funny swallowings of tiny fishes. Denzel was very proud to see so many new and old friends turned out to celebrate Wally's safe return. He also noticed Lou the shrew and his family were in attendance. Lou was locally known for his impeccable manners and shrewdness; in fact extremely shrewd indeed is our Lou. He never stood any old nonsense, always "knows what he wants and gets out of life." Yet still a good neighbour here at Horton Kirby, he and the wife Charlotte have been residing at lakeside for many years now, and very well respected by all on the plot, not forgetting their marauding infants, getting up to all kinds of mischief. Denzel also saw the frog family, Old Fred and his lovely plump wife, along with their almost grown up entourage of hopping happy froglets, whom he had met and befriended on his first ever trip from Coot Island. The duck took particular notice of one of the female frogs that appeared to be extremely pretty. Denzel couldn't believe that this was the shy little girl frog Freda, who had introduced herself half hidden behind a lily bloom, back in the spring of that year. Another member of the community, however appeared to have gone downhill a bit, since the wife flew off with another cock. This was Benny the broken hearted bullfinch. Ben's been about these lakes for many summers. Again, a very well respected member of the community, but that gorgeous bright orange waistcoat of his, since the wife went cockeyed, really has lost its sheen; in fact poor Benny was looking years older. Friends have tried and tried to make him pull out of his doom 'n' gloom, but hence the dear chap's name. He's ended up just moping 'n' moaning about the lakes, but being the local residents they are, they fully understood just how sad it was for this heart-broken bird. Denzel, also Wally, had met and befriended many of his neighbours. These are just a few of the many they had shared some good enjoyable times with. All at the gathering, were giving their individual noises of joy and happiness at the warbler's safe return. Grace and Cyril were spotted flying in, and all eyes raised to the heavens, to watch the pure white sculptured forms skimming the top of the water's surface, settling in the lake, and now swimming in the huge gathering's direction. On Coot Island that very day, Clarence 'n' Clara, along with their five lodgers, Denzel, Wally (who incidentally both will be moving to the Island for good, knowing at least the safety of that old dead hollowed log, if ever a nasty storm ever arose again.) Also Maurice 'n' Maggie, the breathtaking burglars, and of course, one very tired old owl, who at this time had lost all sense of his correct sleeping times and habits. Actually it had begun to show on the ageing wizard's face, his big sharp round eyes were showing signs of sleepless days, though it still didn't stop him keeping one eye on Maurice and the Crank's Hall diamond, but Owen of course was wise enough to enjoy the celebrations that were now surrounding them. Wally being the centre of attraction, which we all know he loves, was up in the highest of branches mustering a cheeky chirp or two. Wally was unable to get too excited, for his few cuts 'n' bruised bones needed a couple of more days yet. Denzel was waving and flapping his wings, and old Clarence was more like he was still a chick during the ecstatic goings-on, rather than his ageing years of many. Clara's eyes, whilst all the commotion was erupting, never left the sight of Wally up in that tree, but no matter how many times old Clarence has told her not to worry, yet it wasn't in the caring old hen's nature. She was staying staunch, and she was there to fuss Wal's every whim.

By 8 a.m., that morning, most of the revellers at the celebrations, had gone back to their daily routines. The company, all still exhausted, watched as the last few remaining stragglers drifted off in different directions to go about their daily dabbling in whatever they individually do! Back on Coot Island the seven companions, joined now by Grace and Cyril, who were chatting to Wally about his terrifying turn of events throughout the gales 'n' storm. Owen had filled the King 'n' Queen of Dartford in on the whole episode at Crank's Hall, leaving out Maurice's misdemeanour, of his dabbling in stolen precious stones. The regal pair left the Island at 9.15 a.m., just before Owen began to resume on the matter of the mysterious appearance of the Crank Diamond.

"Maurice," hooted Owen, "under normal circumstances, I would close my eyes to what you do, in your pickings 'n' nickings. But due to the fact that with our own eyes we saw that the human at Crank's Hall had undoubtedly saved Wally from near death, yourself and Maggie, did more than your share in locating Wally, ending in the rescue, so we all cannot thank you enough! Now ma boy, this diamond and golden ring, you say it got stuck in your throat?"

"Er... yus gov! Nearly bloomin choked I did," squawked the slippery old burglar.

"Did you indeed?" smiled the old owl, as he hooted. Denzel, Wally and the caring coots were all grinning at Maurice's deceit and porkies.

"Horrible it was, gov! Tell ya the truth, I never realised it was stuck until I woz trying to put it back. That's when the gent come tearing in with that big old firestick of his. I fink I nearly swallowed it! With all that choking, my gawd if I hadn't have got out of there lively, I'd a been captured, straight up, gov!"

Peregrine Crank, in a bid to chase 'orf' his land what must have been at least half the twitchers in England, also getting rid of the miserable Mr Attenborough, never even went up to the so-called bedroom that the misbehaved Magpie had mentioned. But even with this bit of old blarney, it never convinced the company.

"Now," hooted the wise old owl, "due to the man at Crank's Hall, Wally's here with us this very day!"

"What about my Maurice and me?" squawked Maggie, "We helped 'n' all Sir!" she squawked again.

"Well! Yes my dear, yourself and Maurice played your part, and very well I'll say that of you. However, I have decided the ring must be returned!" hooted Owen wisely.

"Returned!" squawked Maurice in utter dismay, thinking because of him and Maggie getting Wally out of Crank's Hall, maybe they would let them at least keep the diamond ring. But realising Owen's expectations, he craftily changed his tune. "Er... course, gov! I woz finking on them there lines meself! Why, only a minute ago I woz saying something on those lines to the missus there, right gel?" Maurice gave a sly wink in his spouse's direction.

"Yers, that's very true, that he did Sir!" squawked the fibbing female, without turning a feather.

"Well that's decided upon then! Now a plan, a plan to return the Crank's diamond" hooted a proud old owl. Wally had perked up a bit now, and he and Denzel, just like the old coots, were nodding in agreement with Owen's wise decision, though all were having a few internal chuckles at the two sick magpies, who at this particular time were not exactly pleased at their loss, especially after all the work that went into getting it. They all got comfortable, and Owen with the aid of the two magpies, pondered over how and when the diamond ring could be returned. But there was one thing that Owen was certain about, that it would be sooner, rather than later.

At five minutes past seven p.m., Mr Peregrine Crank arrived home from his City office after a long day's work. He was very tired and at this moment in time was feeling quite lonely. But, at this particular time of our tale, Peregrine's wife,

Prudence, was a journalist working out in Vietnam in jungle conditions for a well known daily linen *The Moon*. Also his two very beautiful daughters, were at boarding school, somewhere out Oxfordshire way. He entered the huge oak front door, which was opened, and greeted by Bertram the bald headed butler, who was head cook and bottle washer at the Hall. He was a smart old boy in his clawhammer coat and pin striped trouser. In other words, a Bert of all trades. He had removed his pleasant employer's topcoat, and then taken his Homburg hat, that his master acquired from Bates of Jermyn Street. Peregrine retired into his study, whilst Bertram poured a large measure of vintage port, then handed it to his master. Peregrine sat in his leather-bound chair, and between sips, he began to read the daily incoming mail.

"Ah, a letter from my dearest Prudence? And one from… that blasted tax man, does he never rest!" he spoke out loudly. Bertram took his leave, to fetch his master's dinner of liver 'n' bacon.

On Peregrine's desk was the book of birds. It was still opened at the page where he had left it. He was engrossed in his reading, when something twinkling in front of him caught his eye. There, as if being held by the beak of the little bird in the book, was the diamond ring, that he had reported missing in a recent burglary the day before when Peregrine had heard his beautiful bit of Dresden smash into a thousand 'n' one pieces. He peered in amazement, for it looked very much to him, that this Dartford Warbler in his book had returned the valuable gemstone. This really left poor Peregrine in a state of wonderings. To check on the time, Peregrine took his eighteen carat gold hunter watch from his waistcoat pocket, that dangled from its Albert chain. Peregrine was in deep thought now, then he said…

"Bertram!"

"Yes, my Lord!" replied the badger faced butler.

"Tell me," he said, "do you believe in fairies?"

Chapter 4

Toad Returns

It was the very next morning that Denzel, Wally, and the two caring coots were sunning themselves at their usual places on Coot Island, passing the time of day. Wally was practically his old self again after the experience a couple of nights before. It was just after breakfast, when all of a sudden a welcome voice reached Denzel's ears. All present had heard the sound, but only Denzel could understand the slang lingo of the cockney toad. And how pleasurable it was, thought the duck to himself, to hear the banter, and yes, even see that most incredible confusing sight , of this character Toad.

"Treadwell you adorable creature, how the chickens are you?" Denzel called, as he waddled excitedly to greet his old friend at the water's edge.

"Cushty!" replied Toad, with a grin that seemed to take up most of his face .

"Oh Toad, it's so good to see you!" said Denzel laughing in pure happiness at meeting his good friend again.

"Yers… and you, Ducky!" croaked Toad,

Whilst the two pals were doing and saying their respective hallos, the caring coots, Clarence and Clara, were smiling in contentment at the sight of all the goings-on in the reunion, and the old couple sat, absorbed in their silent sharing of the scene before them. Whilst all this was going on, Clarence just happened to glance up to where Wally was perched. Wal appeared to be engrossed in amazement at Toad and Denzel's happiness in finding one another once more. Wal had a big smile on his face, in seeing his very best of mates being cheered up with Toad's sudden appearance. But Clara, when looking up at the smiling Wal, could detect all wasn't too well behind the false smile that Wal wore like a mask. Clara also knew of the sensitive insecure ways and jealousy the dear little soul held within. Such a shame for the tiny waif, she painfully thought to herself, for she did love the little fella dearly. She then stepped in with a loud cough, to draw attention. Denzel, Clarence and the tricky toad all fell silent at the sound of Clara's cough, and gazed in the old female coot's direction. All the old girl did was raise her eyes upward, to where Wally sat, to make all three realise on looking up at Wally, who by now was very low, feeling left right out of it. But he soon revived confidence once Denzel had begun to make formal introductions. The duck introduced Clara and Clarence first, but not before telling Wal he'd be next (so's not to upset him any longer). Well, the tiny chap at this time was alight with excitement, toing 'n' throing from bough to twig, above his only family below. Just after the old couple of coots were fully acquainted, it was Wal's turn. Wally immediately flew to a convenient position, only inches from Denzel's ear. Wally hovered for a moment, and in one of his teeny weeniest of chirps, so's Toad couldn't hear,

"Is he sure about them feet, Den?" chortled Wal. On hearing Wally's dodgy whispers of joking 'n' poking of fun at Treadwell's expense, Denzel thought it best to ignore Wally's cunning chortling, but did manage, whilst Toad wasn't looking, to turn his dagger-like eyes in the little comedian's direction, just letting Wal know not to get too high on his perch, for Toad is not such a fool . Denzel knew only too well that Wally was certainly no match for the Leaping Loony from Lewisham let alone his sharp-tongued Cockney croakings. Unfortunately, Wal was so confident now, and for him in fine form, and totally ignored the duck's daggered warnings.

"At last it's my turn" chirped Wally to himself, who was now clinging onto a stem of water mint only inches from Treadwell, Denzel finally introduced his two very best pals to each other, apart from Clarence and Clara, whom he loved dearly and looked upon them as his new Mum 'n' Dad. He also knew that they regarded Wally and himself as family. Then it came! Wal's big moment.

"Toad, this is my very best, and most valued friend, Wally the Dartford Warbler!"

"Most pra'ad I am ta make your acquaintance," croaked the Toad, laughing at Wally's dodging 'n' dartings from mint stem to reeds, close by. "Lively little fella ain't he Denz?"

"More than you'll ever know," mused the now smiling duck.

"Er... umm," said Wal, clearing his little tonsils, "Very pleased to meet you," the tiny bird chirped, giving his best smile to his new found friend. Denzel then introduced Wal to Toad. "Wally, this is the one and only Treadwell Toad Esquire, originally from Lewisham, South London."

"Lewisham?" chirped Wal, "where's that then? And I've never heard of Donlon."

"Oh... not now Wally, plenty of time for that later. And it's London!" laughed Denzel.

"Very pleased indeed to meet you, Treadwell," chirped Wal again.

"Wally, eh?" croaked Toad, in a crafty croak to himself.

"Er... yes!" chirped the little warbler, and he went on to mention how Denzel had told him lots 'n' lots about him. Denzel had in fact over the past months, since his meeting with Wally, filled Wal in on the cockney character, whilst they were sunning themselves during the summer months.

"Is that so, my son?" croaked Treadwell.

"Yes!" chirped Wally full of himself. "Ss... on!" chirped Wal again, in thinking that Toad couldn't possibly be his dad.

Denzel, at this point in time, sensed the situation and immediately went to Wally's rescue, explaining that Treadwell's cockney banter was somewhat confusing.

"To say the least!" Cheeky Beak chirped. All of a sudden, Denzel's mind went into a drifting daydream, that left the duck with an enormous grin on his face and thinking to himself, "Oh, what have I done? I've just introduced the liveliest, cheeky chirpiest, most erratic warbler in the world to a toad that's got a pair of feet (plates as Toad calls them), without no exaggeration, very much like two maple leaves, with eyes so big and bulbus I'm quite certain Owen the Wise would be most proud of, and a mouth so big and wide everything the poor chap croaked only those of his own Cockney kind could really understand. Although I'm learning," thought the Duck. Wally and Treadwell had noticed Denzel's silence.

"Are ya ok me old China?" croaked Toad, bringing Denzel out of his haziness.

"Me old China?" Wal chirped up in laughter at Treadwell's funny lingo.

"Yers, Wal. It's me bit of London verbal ain't it? Ya see pal, it's a bit ov slang us Londoners use. It's called Rhyming Slang," croaked Treadwell, "Ya know Wal? China plate rhymes wiv mate, got it?"

"Er… to be terribly honest, Tread, no!" chirped Wally, winking at Denzel again.

"No?" croaked the Toad leaping into the air a great distance.

"No," chirped the cheeky little warbler again, at Toad's croaking. Then he slyly winked at Denzel, in his bid at winding the tricky toad up another cog. "Why go through all that nonsense, where instead of 'Are you Ok me old China?, when you can easily say? 'Are you alright mate, or Denzel'," Denzel now recovered from his thoughts, and now listening to his two best pals taunting one another, noticed Wal's tiny winkings in his direction, and was happy to see them both finding their feet. But Wally boy was really stronging it in his little games he was playing behind Treadwell's back. But Toad, unfortunately for the over-confident Wal, had caught sight of the teeny endings of Wal's wilful wink. This left the little chap, if you hadn't already guessed, completely sunk. The tricky toad had left the winking Wal nailed, so's to speak, and instead of Wally's pecking liberties (which Toad calls it) of Wal's chortles 'n' winkings, now dear Wal, was silent 'n' sinking. Toad eventually goes to work on Wally.

"Ere 'alf a mo," croaked the Toad, "you say, Denz, that this ere is Wally, the Dartford Warbler?"

"Y… Yes, that's right, Treadwell," answered the duck knowing full well this crafty Cockney was only waiting his chance to get even on Wal's tricky teasing. Denzel mused at Wally, knowing the wee fella never ever dreamt of expecting any form of comeuppance, and surely thought in his tiny head, that Toad would be too foolish to tag onto his friendly dabbling in such fun at his expense.

"Ere!" Toad croaked again, "Ya know what a Wally is in my London town talk?"

"No, I don't," retorted Wally, though Wal had the dreadful feeling come over his little half-ounce frame and a big lump came up in his throat the size of a full ripe blackberry. Even Denzel had never heard this expression before.

"It means a right proper plum!" croaked the now smiling toad.

"A plum! A bloomin' plum!" chirped the most frantic Wally.

"Yers, that's anuvver word in my lingo that means the same," Treadwell croaked again.

"Plums have got pips!" chirped Wally in wonderment.

Denzel now was utterly lost in the fray of taunting, but was soon to realise that whatever game he was playing on Wally, the slippery toad had Wal hopping on tender claws, in his bid to get his own back on the now sad faced Wal.

"Well come on widemouth!" chirped the wound up Wally, darting at one hundred miles an hour from twig to bough.

"Wally!" scowled Denzel "Don't you dare be so rude to Treadwell, now will you, please apologise to him at once!"

"Er... but Den? I... er only said wide, not big; and he started it, honest Den!" chirped the sad-faced Wal.

"No, Wally, you were fine when you were not on the receiving end of your cunning taunting 'n' chortlings," insisted Denzel.

"Yeah! But I was only playing! Really Den!" chirped Wally, not at all at this particular time feeling too secure in himself. "On one condition," the not-so-cheeky chappy chirped.

"Wot's that, then," croaked the toad, in sudden surprise at Wally's request.

"You tell me what my name is in cockney gerbil," retorted Wally.

"Ha! Verbal, you silly bird!" laughed the toad, at Wally adding yet another bloomer to what he was about to croak.

"An idiot! A dolt. A fool if ya like!" croaked Toad, going in for the finality of getting his own back.

"Well I never!" exclaimed Denzel amazed. "I've never seen you lose your erratic chirpings so quickly, Wally." Denzel, although smiling at Treadwell's hasty turnaround of Wal's comic capers, yet deep down began to feel a little sorry for his close friend. "Poor Wal," he thought. "He's really and truly done it now." The dear little chap was completely dumbstruck, in fact the tiny waif was chirpless for the first time in his life. Denzel and Toad really couldn't help laughing at the sight of their little friend's embarrassed face.

"Oh, come along Wally! You had your little joke on Treadwell, so he's just had his with you!" said Denzel warmly.

"Only jesting, Wal, and I'm praad to be yours 'n' Denzels proper pucker pal!" croaked Treadwell in one of his more comforting voices. Something not easy for such a hard case as Toad! Wally soon recovered his feelings, and realised all that it was, were two of Denzel's pals coming together, testing and sounding each other out, making sure things were as should be in a friendship. Treadwell was made welcome by all present, and it wasn't long before Denzel quacked the question, on how the Big Wedding went, and how it had gone so far, since their first-ever meeting.

"Please tell us about your marriage to Tootsy," Denzel asked in excited eagerness.

"Yers ov course I will," croaked Toad sporting one of his wider grins, Treadwell had found himself a comfortable damp mossy patch, in the shade under the hanging leaves of a bulrush bed at the edge of Coot Island. Once all settled, the leathery Londoner had positioned himself so he faced the happy listening company. He began as usual with plenty of the old gift of the gab, of how his life had been over the past summer months, since he and Denzel had first met.

"Yers, where woz I? Er... I dunno where ta bloomin begin!" He laughed, scratching his big fat belly with one of his front feet, which were somewhat smaller that his outrageous back ones.

"You can begin with the wedding!" Denzel burst in, a second, or maybe a third time.

"Yers, that's it, me old rubber," croaked Toad.

"R... rubber?" asked Denzel, dumfounded as ever by Treadwell's south of London lingo.

"Sorry, Denz mate! I can't help me rabbiting, can I na?"

"Rabbiting?" retorted the duck, looking at the other eager listeners, seeing all as confused as he.

"Yers, as I say?" croaked Treadwell. "I can't help me bunnying cause I woz brought up wiv it!"

"Oh, my God!" Denzel immediately thought that he'd better change the subject right away, in case whatever Toad had in his loony lingo maybe catching.

"Treadwell!" retorted Denzel, "will you please go on, and please Toady, do try leaving out all that slinging!"

"Slang," Treadwell reminded him.

"Yes, yes, quite!" replied the duck, whilst making himself more comfy. "Please, Toady, can we now hear of the wedding?"

"Well, I'll be blowed!" croaked Treadwell, who at long last was about to commence. At the word 'blowed', Denzel thought to himself, "Oh no, not more lingo? Then the teasing Toad began his tale of the events of Tootsy's and his big day.

"Well," he went on, "after I left you at Lakeside, I haves me last hop, leap 'n' jump with me pals that night, then me big day turns up!" croaked Toad with an air of proudness about him. "Course, next morning, I gets up a bit sharpish, gets meself all spruced up, polished me plates?"

"Cleaned his feet!" said Denzel, translating Toad's talk to the other listeners, who all looked at one another in bewilderment and total confusion. But all the same Clarence 'n' Clara were thoroughly enjoying the company, especially Toad's queer expressions in his banter 'n' comical ways. The loving old couple were more than happy in adding yet another to their ever-growing family. Strange as the little pack may seem, yet this character Toad was undoubtedly different from anyone that either of the ageing coots had ever encountered over their long years in this world of water. Wally was sitting on his usual day perch on a small patch of gorse bushes, looking and listening in amazement at Treadwell. But, little did he know, the lad from Lewisham hadn't even started, as Wal and Co. were soon to find out. Yet all were smiling, seemingly quite contented in their listening. Treadwell once again attempted to carry on,

"I ends up," he croaked, "on parade under one of them bridges, where the Darenth runs underneath. Well I arrives and I couldn't believe me blimmin' minces."

"Meaning eyes," said Denzel, taking it upon himself to translate any difficulties that the eager listeners may, or as far as Denzel was concerned, would encounter during Treadwell's cockney croaking.

Toad continued, "The whole place woz alive wiv weddin' guests, there were all manner of birds and animals, and of course us leathery lot, the amphibians, from both Tootsy's, and my side of the family.

"Amphibians" chirped Wally.

"Yers, Wal! That's wot all us lot is, and them there frogs 'n' newts 'n' all."

"Oh I see!" chirped Wal again. "So birds have got feathers and they fly, Animals like the rabbits and badgers have fur and move about on land, and you fibbers have leathery skin and leap about the lakes."

"Amphibians!" retorted Treadwell on hearing Wal's dodgy chortling. After Wally's few chirpy remarks he seemed quite pleased with himself in letting all present listen to more of his clever knowledge. He then rested contentedly on his day perch, getting impatient like all the rest, for Toad to carry on the very interesting but slow account of the wedding, even though it appears after hearing what the name Wally meant in cockney. Wal did get a bit upset inwardly and now was attempting to prove to Toad 'n' all just how smart and proper clever a little scholar he really was. The two aging Coots kept right out of all the croakings 'n' chirpings, leaving the three lads to themselves. But the lovely old couple were still eager to hear the bit of gossip of Toad's big day. (And going by the way it has gone so far, even the author's getting confused!)

Toad continued, "Yers," he croaked, "All in attendance woz a dancin' 'n' leapin' abaat, cutting loose to a bit of live music, that two Thrushes 'n' a Nightingale woz chanting at the tops ov their throaty voices. Yers! It woz proper swell it woz!" Toad was now showing a very smug smile on his fossil featured face. "It really woz tasty watchin' 'em all enjoying themselves 'n' mixing in, having the time of their lives. Praad I woz Denz, real praad! When all of a sudden, all the chirping 'n' chanting stopped dead, and silence fell all around, and ya know wot I mean, Denz?" Toad gave another emotional croak... "And all who woz there, looked up into that beautiful big blue sky and there, flying in our direction, woz a sight that brought tears to me dear minces."

"Mince pies, eyes," Denzel jovially informed the confused listeners. Clarence and Clara were nodding and smiling as if they understood, and appeared eager to get Toad moving again, to get his tale finished before it got dark. But the way it's going so far, all present were beginning to have doubts. Much as Treadwell tried to get his story out, a huge lump came up in his throat, and tears began to well up in the cockney's huge glassy eyes, when recalling his emotional tale. At this scene, Clara had to wipe her own tears from her old eyes with her useful wing tips. Denzel too got upset and a bit teary, Wally was hanging upside down from his perch, trying to hide a teeny tear that was drooping from his little cheek the size of a half carat pear-shaped diamond, which tricked down his tiny feathered face. It was Clarence, who was the only one who managed to control his emotions, but even he, if the truth was known wasn't too far from the old water works department, though he bravely managed to hold court. He then prompted Treadwell to continue with this by now epic saga, that in reality was a simple wedding. Yet it can only be told by Toad, in his own unbelievable words.

"And!" exclaimed old Clarence, looking for Toad to continue.

"And... when I looked up there in that big blue sky, woz a bird, a big Canada Goose, and as it came into land all the hundreds of guests from waters far 'n' wide woz cheerin' 'n' hoorayin', at the rare sight of me skin 'n' blister Trixy, and her 'usband Trevor flying in on the goose's back."

"Skin 'n' blister, sister! Do you get it?" put in Denzel, keeping the others informed on Toad's dodgy bits. All present gave their usual individual nods 'n' smiles showing the Duck and Treadwell all was understood so far... they thought!

Toad continued... "They floated in like a dream and settles on the water, the goose swam towards us at the river bank. My, they looked a pretty picture, sitting there behind the lovely folded wings of the big goose. The old current bun woz at its peak in the sky, which told me that any moment na me intended would be arrivin'. When all ov a sudden, I 'ears a whistle go up from one ov the feathered guests. It woz Stanley, the half starved starling, he woz whistlin' 'ere comes the Bride, which resulted in all manner of noises of cheerfulness for the arriving bride. Yeah, real cheerful it woz! And did she look tasty, Denz!" Toad recalled. "All the excited guests hopped, shuffled, and flew to gather all along the River bank ta see my gel Tootsy floating daan the centre ov the Darenth on an old log that woz decorated in the most gorgeous flowers, in every colour ya can fink ov. And there, sitting slap bang in the middle ov it all, woz me happy smiling gel. And Denz me old pal, the dear gel looked right proper!" (Meaning very, very nice, in Toad's lingo) The other listeners were so enthralled by Toads time-consuming tale they even forgot to have lunch, in fact it was getting well past noon, but the company were more than happy to let him carry on in the flow that appeared to be coming from him, and his Lewisham language. He croaked on... "Just a simple single white daisy bloom, had been fixed to the left hand side ov her forehead, sort ov just over one eye like. Ya know, to give that peek-a-boo effect, know wot I mean? Around her gregory..."

"Treadwell!" Denzel burst in, "Please try and leave the slang bits out of your story. And... what's a gregory?" the duck asked, still keen to learn Toads loony lingo.

"Gregory Peck, neck!"

"Who on Earth's Gregory Peck may I ask?" enquired Denzel.

"Ummm er, how do I bloomin' know? I only 'ears them there humans say it when they put gold fings round their necks. Yers many, a time I've heard 'em saying to others of their kind, 'That's a nice fing around your Gregory Peck!' So it rhymes wiv neck. See?"

After a bit more explaining still none of the listeners had the slightest idea, as yet, of what this potty toad was croaking about. Nevertheless the toad had them listening wholeheartedly, and the tricky character knew it. Denzel looked at the others and could only shrug his shoulders at his equally confused listeners. "Around her neck woz a load of willow catkins joined togevver, and fixed to each join, woz a bread 'n' cheese red berry from the horthorn bush. Cor! Did she look the biz, or what?" croaked Treadwell, smiling a huge contented grin. "And my Tootsy carried herself cushty," (meaning neat, smartly dressed, or even feeling well in Treadwell's talk). "Yers, blinkin' handsome she looked, wiv her lovely big smile on her gorgeous chubby chops…"

"Chubby chops?" chirped Wally, in fits of laughter at his very strange new friend's performance.

"Well… er plump face!" Toad corrected himself.

"Oh!" chirped Wal, none the wiser.

Toad croaked on and told them, "Her mum 'n' dad was praadly sitting either side ov their daughter, all done up to the nines they woz and looking real chuffed. There were no bridesmaids in attendance, for toads are a very proud lot and do not believe in those! Because they feel it takes all the attention off their respective brides, and really and truly they don't like the idea of lots of other pretty girl toads around on such a very important occasion. Well, all woz going ok, 'till I goes 'n' puts me blimmin' great plates of meat in it!" All of the captive audience looked on in surprise at what the Toad had croaked, wondering what catastrophe was to come next. "Well, just as Tootsy and Co were drifting into the side of the river bank, I gets so excited, I leaps into the air and Gawd help us, I jumps too far, 'n' Denz, it's the truth mate, I ends up, right in the drink. And course wiv these whopping feet ov mine hitting the water like they do, made a big splash that covered poor Tootsy and her muvver Tammy 'n' old Ted her Dad soaking wet. Course it caused all the happy guests to cheer 'n' laugh in such happiness. In the end, even my Tootsy, after a few daggers from her half-hiden eye, saw the funny side ov it fank God! Well, finally the time comes when my gel 'n' me get hitched. Er... married (Toad corrected himself). "Yers, we were married there 'n' then, by my great Uncle Treadlightly, and if ya's fink I've been blessed with big plates ov meat, ya wanna have a gander at his ones?" laughed Treadwell. "Fact is, whilst in the act ov the ceremony, my dear Uncle Treadlightly, when stepping forward to join Tootsy's 'n' my hand in wedlock the silly old geezer stepped so close, he trod on, and broke, one of my Toots toes. But, all jokes aside, he didn't put a foot wrong in the weddin' words, which woz real pucker, even if I have ta say it meself." Treadwell began to bring his story to a close regarding the wedding, apart from later when he told the happy smiling company of listeners the whereabouts of Tootsy and his place of living. Toad went on to tell them that they had set up home by the waterfall end of the lake, and that he wanted to introduce his new pals to his long-legged-leathery-looking Lolita, his tasty, tantalising, Tootsy. Toad finished his story by adding... "An' you know?" he paused for a little thought, "Ya know?" he croaked again, "The only fing that woz missing from the whole turnout, from wot I can see of it! Woz you lovely lot, me real pucker pals."

Wally loved the toad, especially Treadwell's strange antics in the leathery loons banter and comical croakings. Wal's little belly had lots of churnings 'n' turnings where Toad had kept his captive audience throughout his tale in stitches, with roarings of laughter one minute, and the next, all could be reduced to tears. For Toad, although coming from a rough 'n' ready family where he'd had it hard when he was a tadpole, yet the dear fellow was a master in his own right when it came to a bit of storytelling, which is told in such a way that only the toad and his cunning croaking can do. Treadwell had finished his tale at 1.55 p.m. in the afternoon, he started just after 8 a.m., when in actual fact the wedding on its day, started at 12 noon, and apart from old Uncle Treadlightly's mishap, was completed in twenty minutes. Not the festivities 'n' partying of course, that went on all day; but as we have all come to know, five hours of Treadwell's cockney banter, just to tell a twenty minute story, is nothing for such a clever croaker as the tale telling Toad. Apparently, later it was found out by his close friends, that this was one of Toad's shorter ones. However, it was loved and accepted by all members in the company, especially old Clarence, he just never stopped smiling and shaking his head from side to side in utter disbelief at this character before him. That not only made the old stager laugh, but the way Toad had him almost reduced to tears, particularly in the manner in which he told it. About half 'n' hour had passed since Treadwell's tale, when the Toad suggested that he, Denzel and Wally should visit Tootsy at home up by the waterfall.

"What a good idea!" Put in Denzel, full of the joys of autumn, and very much looking forward to being introduced to Toad's lovely lady. On hearing Treadwell's request, Wally flew immediately to Denzel's side. He clung to a twig of a fallen willow branch that was blown down in that terrible storm the night before last. The subject the two caring coots and the two lads were discussing the very moment before Treadwell's appearance.

"Oh goody good good!" chirped Wally doubly excited at Toad's suggestion. "Can we, please can we?" the little fella chortled.

"Of course we shall," smiled Denzel, winking at old Clarence, who was also grinning like a Cheshire Cat at Wal's waffling.

"Wot abaat Clara and Clarence?" Toad's manners were impeccable in putting the lady first, and it didn't go without recognition. The two elders, from that first encounter had drawn their own conclusion; that one thing was for sure, Toad was a true gentleman, especially after taking the dear chap's upbringing into consideration. Although Toad at times sounds as if he were a bit of a ruffian, when in fact underneath all of his old bunny, he was a thorough gentleman at heart. Clarence could tell what Toad was about to croak was an invite on the journey to visit Tootsy. But he declined the offer, saying that he and his ageing Clara, would only slow the trio down. Then he reminded the three lads, that if they were going, they'd better depart soon, as there wouldn't be many daylight hours left for such a lengthy trip. Denzel, and his two best pals left the island after saying their farewells to the lovely ageing coots, and what a sight they were. Treadwell took up position plotted on Denzel's back, Toad had taken full advantage of the ride. There were no flies on the slippery lad from Lewisham, Oh, no! He, Toad, that is, was lying back there, as cool as cucumber, resting his craggy head in his leathery hands against the Duck's long neck, with his right leg over his left one. Wally was flitting in short bursts on the much warmer breeze, rather than those terrible winds a couple of nights before. The little Warbler as usual was having the time of his life, but as they rounded the bend, they were confronted by two strangers on the lake. They could plainly see that they were a colourful pair of Great Crested Grebes. As Toad spotted them, he got up from his comfortable feathery bed, and was now on all four feet in the normal toad position, staring with those enormous eyes at the strangers. All of a sudden, the male grebe when seeing the approaching companions, spoke to Denzel.

"I say, old chap! What extraordinary company you keep!" The grebe was now eyeing up the trio, especially given Treadwell's big back feet a momentarily fixed stare, as Toad was plotted there on the duck's back. "And goodness me" exclaimed the male grebe, "Just look at those huge feet!"

"Ere… Wot's wrong wiv me plates then?" croaked Treadwell, not liking these poshens with stuck-up attitudes and behaviour one bit. The male grebe coughed,

"Your plates, old bean?" asked the totally flummoxed male grebe, "What on God's earth, 'as plates got to do with those, those huge things on the ends of your back legs, surely they're not normal?" enquired the stranger again.

"Oh my God, Gerald, just look at that dreadful creature!"cried the posh lady grebe, also staring at the laid back toad.

"I see exactly what you mean, Duchess," replied the very stuck-up male.

"Me plates of meat!" croaked Treadwell quite angrily.

"Plates of meat!" retorted the posh grebe again.

"Yers, don't ya see, plates of meat, feet! Oh, oh, oh!" croaked Toad in laughter, knowing he'd confused the most intelligent Gerald.

"Ah! I see, you're one of those cockney chaps, I gather?"

"Yers, that's right gov, an I'm bloomin' praad ov it!" croaked Treadwell.

"Oh, darling! Wasn't that grubby old coot we had as our errand boy one of those cockney types, ya," she smarmily uttered so matter-of-factly, and posh.

"If you're so clever and posh, were do you come from then?" chirped Wally, not very happy at these two at all.

"We reside at the water's edge, at Henley on Thames, and most of our friends are swan!" the duchess said, lowering her eyes in snootiness.

"And where do you three live, may I ask?"

Wally replied, and explained about Coot Island, and about the lovable old coots.

"I thought as much!" said the duchess, still down treading the three lads.

"Well, if you're so high and mighty, and think that we are not good enough for you, why come to our lakes in the first place?" retorted Denzel.

"You see, master Duck, early yesterday morning my wife and I, had thought the storm had ended. So we decided to visit some of our friends up on the lakes at Windsor, but we were unfortunately blown completely off course by those terrible winds, and because of the dark drawing in. The Duchess and I, had no alternative than to land, and take temporary roost."

"What d'ya bloomin' mean!" croaked Treadwell, very furious at being even more down-trodden by this Lord 'n' Lady Muck. "Who ever do they fink they are?" he croaked to his best pals. "Ain't we good enough for ya, me Ladyship?" Toad was about to put these two snobs in their rightful places.

"I fink the pair of ya's is pie 'n' mash!" croaked Treadwell.

"Excuse me!" cried the duchess. "What was that again?"

"Pie 'n' mash, trash!" roared the cunning South Londoner. Whilst listening, Denzel and Wally were pulling a few funny faces, knowing what Toad had just said must have been funny, 'cause Toad was now on Denzel's back, holding his rather fat belly, with tears of laughter streaming down his craggy face.

"As it happens, you bolt-eyed flat-footed leaping lunatic, you're absolutely right! And may I say, I cannot stay here on this common lake one moment longer!" the duchess snapped back. "I mean, darling, just look at these surroundings, and as for that monstrosity of a chimney sticking up in the beautiful blue sky, it's a disgrace, that's what it is, a downright eyesore!" she raved. "Well my three, ah umm! What shall I call you? Ah a mixed bag! Yes that's it, a right mixed bag," said the duchess aloud in a nervous laugh. "We!" she boasted "live in an area of exquisite beauty," lowering her eyes to the three onlookers, as she said it.

"Yes, and each year, one of course goes to our local Regatta, doesn't one, darling Gerald," she put in, and went on to brag... "the scraps that get thrown to us on such an occasion are of smoked salmon and caviar!" she boasted further.

"Not like here, at this dump! The duchess and I thought we would find something tasty to nibble on before we started back on course, but all we managed to find earlier were a couple of skinny stickleback's, and we could hardly bring ourselves to eat such filthy rubbish!" interrupted Gerald.

"Why?" chirped Wally sharply.

"Because for one, it was far too small and horrible, you twittering twirp! And two, there happened to be a bald headed rat! clinging to its other end!" cried the duchess almost hysterical.

"Good Gawd, it sounds like 'arry's been abaat!" croaked Treadwell, to his two muckers.

"My God!" screamed the Duchess. "This place is so degrading. Gerald, I want to leave here! And I want to leave right this very minute, do you hear me?"

"Y... Yes, of course, my darling?" answered the toff grebe. "I too have taken all I can from the three stooges here?"

"Three stooges, eh?" retorted the now very angry Toad. "Well ya know wot I fink don't ya's?" croaked Treadwell, who like Denzel, and Wally, was indeed furious at this pair of imitation grebes, with their ignorance of life attitudes. "I fink the pair of ya's had better clear orf aat of it! And a bit bloomin'sharpish, before I does a tap dance on ya nuts! Wiv these here plates of mine, an ya's wouldn't want that nah, would ya's?" croaked Toad, who was at that very moment in time, feeling extremely enraged at these two stuffy-nosed interlopers, who had turned up at the company's part of the world, acting as though they were more royal than the Royals themselves.

"That's it, Tread, you tell 'em, eh Den?" chirped Wal.

"Look at that funny bit on the tops of their heads!" commented Denzel, laughing whilst he said it.

"Yeah!" chirped Wal. "They look like a couple of bulrushes, eh, Den!" Wal, and Denzel, and the tricky Toad, were now in absolute fits of giggles at their taunting of the two harlots from Henley.

"And what, may I ask, are you three smirking about?" retorted the now furious Gerald.

"Your barnet!" croaked Toad, with even more laughter coming from the taunting trio.

"And pray tell me... exactly, what a barnet is!" shrilled the two flustered Grebes together, both baffled and unsure about this strange lingo used by the crafty Cockney.

"Barnet Fair! Hair, got it?" croaks Toad, after more giggles coming from the three lads. Toad then explained that this turn of phrase was used by humans, cockney ones that is! This bit of slang was derived from the Barnet Fair, that was held each year in North London for the hair that grows on their heads. "A bit like that mop on your bonces!" croaked Toad "but yorn are made wiv fevers!"

Well, this just about did it! Poor Wal was laughing so much he had to take a breather, and had to join Treadwell on Denzel's back. As he did so, he knocked the cockney, who at the time was rubbing his big fat belly where it was aching so much, he lost his balance, causing him to fall off the duck's back, and disappear under the surface of choppy water. The two grebes were watching the performance, and both had the beginnings of a smirk on their faces themselves. But they were soon to lose it! For the Toad, although he could have done without another wash that day, thought he'd use his unfortunate tumble to teach these two Henley dwellers a lesson well deserved. Gerald and the Duchess, as well as the other two lads, were waiting to see Toad's reappearance, when out of the water the Duchess gave an almighty shriek, flapping 'n' thrashing wildly, as the dear female left the water, which was only a few inches. But this was enough for Denzel and Wally to see the tricky Toad dangling from the left leg of the frantic female. Toad knew he'd done the trick, in giving the ungrateful grebes a bit of their own back. He let go of the Duchess's leg... (Scotch egg, in Toad's cockney lingo)... Treadwell swam over leisurely and rejoined Wally, on Denzel's feathery back. But to his amazement, the two grebes were still there, a little bit flustered, but they still managed to hold their own. Even though poor Gerald was absolutely fuming at Toads bit of skulduggery toward his beloved Duchess, and shrilled... "Well of course my Duchess, these three idiots! Being of such low intellect, with all their brains put together, wouldn't recognise a Royal Crest, when they see one, or even begin to know the meaning, come to that!"

"A Royal Crest!" chirped Wally, "more like a bloomin' nest!" he chirped again, making the soaking wet toad, who as we have become to know from earlier experiences, is not too keen on the swimming department, crease up with laughter, at Wal's bit of comical verbal.

All visitors who should happen to arrive on these lakes, or would like to set up home, as long as they are respectable, they are most welcome, and treated with the same respect they deserve. Just as all members and residents on and about the Horton Kirby lakes 'n' rivers. But these two toffee nosed Tatler reading toffs, had most certainly over stayed their welcome.

"Yers going then!" croaked the Toad, feeling very pleased in seeing the back, (haystack) in his lingo, of such 'snobbish rubbish'. Denzel and Wally had heard the Toad's croak under his breath.

"How dare you croak at us like that, you young leathery leaping layabout!" sobbed the duchess, who obviously was not getting her usual doting attention from her spouse Gerald the gullible grebe, who fussed over her ladyship's every whim. Now being confronted by this 'mixed bag', as she addressed them earlier, was just too much for the disgruntled duchess.

"Now, now, what's going on here then?" came the familiar voice of Cyril the king, and at his side the beautiful snow white form of Grace. "Now what seems to be the problem?" asked the King.

"Thank God... you came!" cried the cunning duchess, swimming or so she thought, to enlist the king's aid. "Your Majesty! During our flight from Henley on Thames up to the lakes at Windsor, my husband and I were completely blown off course, so yesterday morning we had no alternative but to take refuge here on these water's." She blurted so craftily 'n' sly. Gerald at this time had let the duchess do all the talking, in the hope that her female charm would work. Before the king spoke again, he thought he'd be the gentleman he happens to be, and let the pretty female have her say.

"Carry on my dear!" hissed a most intrigued king, catching the eye of Grace as he'd finished. When the duchess went blabbing on in her attempt to get the three lads in worse trouble, than they thought they were already in. The duchess said, "Then, as my Gerald and I were searching for something to eat, these three here, accosted us! Especially that one!" complained the duchess, now pointing her beak at the cockney toad.

"Accosted you, did they, madam?" asked Cyril, knowing all along what had really occurred earlier.

"Oh yes, your Highness. Especially that nasty specimen, and his villainous ways!" She really had it in for poor Treadwell.

"And… your Worship!" broke in Gerald, "going by that cockney croak of his, it would not surprise me at all if he were a right proper scallywag! And the duchess, and myself demand, in your regal presence, an apology this very instant!"

"You do, do you?" said the King, after the three lads, along with the two swans, had heard such utter rubbish. The boy from Lewisham had just about all his towny temper could hold.

"Nah listen 'ere, bulrush bonce!" croaked the very wound-up Toad, deciding there 'n' then, he much preferred redstarts to upstarts. The king made his presence felt, with a deafening authoritative voice.

"Enough!" he hissed. "Now!" said the King, "where did you two say you came from, my dear?" he asked the Duchess.

"Oh! Henley on Thames, your gracious ruler!" She was going a bit overboard now, still attempting to impress the two royals. But unfortunately for them, the King of Dartford was soon to put the lakes to rights.

"I see!" he said. Then he began to tell the two social climbers that he and his good Queen Grace had been taking lunch just a few yards away, when they were interrupted by raised voices, "We, the Queen and myself, also heard something about your friends being of royal blood? Is this correct, as I do believe I'm not mistaken?" said Cyril, winking at the three lads, and all three in turn looked to the king and his meaningful wink, resulting in them all looking at one another, and beginning to see whose side the King was really on. And rightly so, all three had thought to themselves, in a silent nodded agreement.

"Well, yes, your Highness!" Gerald dashing to the duchess's aid, to answer the king's question. "Well, not exactly on speaking terms. But…!"

"But what, my dear fellow?" asked the King, turning the tables on these two imposters. "I thought as much!" said Cyril, tut-tutting at the two social climbing fraudsters, who in reality never knew any birds, who were any bird of such high esteem, as far as birds go, that is; royal crest, or not. "Yes…!" said the smiling to herself. Before Treadwell had left home that very morning, he had told his pretty wife where, and for whom he was going to search. Ever since their wedding Toad had never let a day go by without mentioning his meeting with the young troubled Duck. In actual fact, it was her own idea, knowing her spouse's feelings of friendship towards Denzel, that prompted the toad to go and find his pal, whom she'd never met, and in reality hardly knew. But now she could see for herself, he'd not only found, but had brought his "Ducky", as Toad calls him, home to meet her at long last. And very pleased at the sight she was. As she watched them getting closer, it dawned on her,

"Denzel!" She croaked aloud. "Oh my Gawd!" She mumbled to herself, the dear flustered gel using a bit of her hubby's cockney verbal, which, obviously through living with such banter, the sweet girl from Chislehurst had found it quite impossible not to pick up an odd dodgy word or two of her old man's crazy croakings. Tootsy, of course, came from quite a well-to-do family, who reside at a pond on Chislehurst Common. She was a friend of his sister Trixy, and Treadwell had came to meet her through his sister's well off husband Trevor. She had lived with her mother and father, Tammy and Ted, who were a prominent family from a line of toads who had lived there long before man had begun to destroy the world for selfish greed. This family, eighteen months before, had befriended a large Canada Goose who had arrived one day on the plot and for some reason had stayed. You see, Trevor is Tootsy's brother, who before he'd moved to Dartford had lived at Chislehurst with his family and was very successful at anything he turned his hands to. It was through this determination he never felt satisfied with just leaping about Chislehurst, for he, like Wally wanted to get out and see the world. So one day all that time ago, he'd asked Mac to fly him to other parts, hence him now being a respected resident at the Dartford Lakes.It was when Mac had taken him to Horton Kirby one day that he met Toads sister Trixy. And when they married and settled down at Dartford, Mac used to visit them at least once a week. It was when the goose had visited them

king, in a long drawn out hiss. "I personally think an apology is quite in order here."

"Oh, thank you, your Divineness!" shrilled the duchess, in her false smiles 'n' stuffiness. Well, until the king's next words that is.

"Yes!" he said, "I'm satisfied that an apology would most definitely be in order, so Madam, Sir! Please do your duty, and apologise to these three upstanding, most honest trusted friends of all life on, or about these parts!"

"Hooray!" chirped Wally, full of smiles.

"Bloomin' right too!" croaked the now smiling Treadwell.

"Be quiet, you two!" scowled Cyril in one of his more sterner hisses.

"Er... sorry, gov!" croaked the Toad.

"Oh my goodness!" thought Denzel, thinking. "As if we weren't in enough trouble without Toady calling the King of Dartford gov!" He, incidentally, hadn't even been formally introduced to the lakes monarchs. Yet here the Toad was, plying such banter to the King 'n' Queen of Dartford, calling him gov!

"It will not do at all," Denzel thought to himself, too terrified even to raise his eyes, in case they met Cyril's.

"D... do you mean my husband and I, apologise to these... these hooligans!" The duchess practically choked on it.

"Yes I do, Madam, and this very moment!" demanded the king, who by now was getting very mad at the two jumped-up grebes. And he stated a fact, "There were too many of your sort in the world, and it just won't do!"

After this shock decision, Gerald and the Duchess realised that their fakery in the snobbery department, had been well and truly rumbled, and knew full well they both had to resign themselves to this fact of apologising to the three lads in the presence of the royal pair. After both grebes gave their hard swallowing of pride, they gave a sorrowful apology. Gerald took it upon himself to speak on the duchess's behalf, knowing the stuffing had been knocked right out of her charade of dreaming. Gerald collected his thoughts, gathered what little pride he had left. He turned to address the trio, then spoke...

"My wife and I are both terribly, terribly, terribly sorry!" With this, the pathetic Gerald bowed his head in shame. Can you imagine what this did to the disillusioned duchess, who at this time had her snooty head bowed so low with embarrassment she could see the snails on the bottom of the lake, hoping in all honesty that it would open up and swallow them both, anything as long as they were long gone from this predicament they were facing now. But before Gerald could utter one more note, Cyril stopped him dead in his tracks…

"Enough!" hissed the king in his most authoritative voice.

"Yes…!" Answered the two embarrassed grebes simultaneously.

"Now be gone with you!" demanded the king. With this the two downgraded grebes swam a little way, then both took to the sky, not even daring to look back at what they thought was an absolute nightmare. As the two delightfully coloured birds were just dots in the sky, heading in the direction of Henley on Thames, or was it the lakes by Dagenham Gas Works? Well wherever! But one thing was made quite clear that day: it will be the last they'll ever see of those two compulsive dreamers. Once out of sight, which all present witnessed, Denzel, took it upon himself to utter the first words.

"We are very, very sorry, Sir!" said the duck, in a saddened tone.

"Oh, they asked for it!" laughed the King of Dartford.

"Yeah! And did you see her face! When you er…?" Wally bursting in as per usual, but now realising he'd opened his mouth before his little brain told it to. The King went into a deep belly laugh at Wal's erratic bursting interruption. Grace who had been silent through the whole of the sordid business, just sat floating on the water's surface looking as usual most regal, with her beautiful smiling eyes, that peered from her pure white angelic face.

"Go on!" she said, in her softest hisses. "Swim along now, you still have plenty of the afternoon ahead of you, to enjoy your young selves!" Then she just smiled at the lads, and then at Cyril, who was still rolled up in laughter, not only at Wal's remarks, but the whole ridiculous turnout.

"Oh, thank you!" said Denzel and Wally, almost toget[...]

"Gawd bless ya, Gracie Gel!" croaked the Cockney. B[...] Denzel, and Master Wally's surprise, the regal pair[...] understood all the different languages 'n' lingo's of their [...] fortunate subjects, and that includes that bloke with the cr[...] none other than the Cockney Toad himself.

"And to you all!" the king replied with deep feeling. Af[...] saying their farewells, the company of three went on their w[...] towards the waterfall, that was now in view to them, som[...] sixty or so yards ahead.

Dozing in the afternoon sun was Treadwell's belove[...] Tootsy. She was woken by the squeaking excitement of one o[...] their neighbours, Neddy. "Nuthouse Neddy" as Toad refers to[...] him, was also of the amphibian family, a newt to be precise, a[...] Great Crested Newt! But this particular candidate, who's most[...] definitely lacking in the old grey matter department, and[...] known in these parts as "Neddy the nutty newt, happens to be a[...] character in his own right! But so harmless! In fact he was well[...] liked and loved on the Manor by all that came into contact[...] with him. Neddy at this time was resting on the large stem of a[...] huge dock leaf, which was drooping down over the water from[...] the bank, not quite touching it. Along with the sight of the[...] approaching Duck, who had just appeared around some reeds,[...] Neddy caught a glimpse of his pal and neighbour, Treadwell,[...] being chauffeured between his shoulders. As the Duck swam[...] nearer to the bank, the excited crackpot newt lept into the air,[...] and in his squeaky little voice squealed,

"Weeeee!" in a long drawn out, tiny sound. Then landed[...] further down the huge sloping leaf and sliding down into the[...] water, making even more of his squeaky noises, before his[...] skinny handbag handle frame plopped into the cool water[...] hardly making a splash. Neddy plopped into the Lake[...] squealing 'n' splashing, trying to attract attention to himself. It[...] was this sound that brought Tootsy out of her afternoon siesta,[...] but now she was hopping excitedly to the water's edge, to[...] watch the approaching scene of her husband being carried on[...] the back of a gorgeous young Mallard. Tootsy didn't had to be[...] told twice who the stranger might be. "Denzel!" she thought[...]

one day and had brought Tootsy along, when Trevour had suggested they take Trixy and Tootsy to the Horton Kirby Lakes to meet her brother Treadwell. So, if it wasn't for Mac none of them ever would have met at all. It was a funny old turnout really. The moment they set eyes on each other, it was love at first sight on both their parts. And funnily enough, it was mentioned at a later date, that it was Toad's huge feet that actually attracted Tootsy, to Treadwell, on their very first meeting. As one can imagine, with them coming from such posh parts, when her mum and dad, Tammy and old Ted first came into contact with his 'common', as the stuck up grebes had put it, 'cockney verbal', it had not gone down well. In fact for the first few months were not happy at all in their daughter's choice of husband. But time proved on this account, that their estimations of the lad from Lewisham, and his loony lingo, soon proved himself a deserving catch, even for those frightfully well off Chislehurst pond dwellers. And to this very day, both of Tootsy's parents will readily admit that Treadwell Toad was a gent, and would never have a bad word said about their loveable son-in-law. Especially by that Chislehurst lot!

Whilst all this was going on, Neddy swam out to greet the duo, for as yet he had not seen the already perched Wally, high in the trees above. The weird little newt was still squealing 'n' screeching with excitement at the top of his tiny voice, which seemed to attract at least one half of all dwellers in the vicinity of about half a metre. In other words, through his smallness, anyone in that range could see Neddy's actions, but unless he was close to your ear, you'd have thought he was deaf 'n' dumb, or at least miming, a sort of amphibian Marcel Marceux type creature; but the silly thing really and truly thought he could be heard, just the same as anyone else on the plot. Though he still carried on with these performances not really understanding that unless he was only inches away he could not be heard, or understood. Hence his name, that the cockney toad had given him. In fact Denzel, despite all Neddy's squealing 'n' screeching, and arm waving in the Newt's bid, to draw attention to himself, had almost bumped into him before the cockney toad managed, with his superb vision, to catch sight of poor Neddy, who was near exhaustion, and even more silent through his nutty antics. Denzel came to an abrupt halt at Toad's request, for this was the first glimpse Denzel had caught of the little pip squeak!

"What the...?" Denzel paused for a moment to find words. Toad introduced Neddy to the Duck.

"Pleased to meet you, Neddy!" said Denzel, smiling at the quaint crinkly creature. The little newt clambered aboard the Duck's back, not only to join Toad, but to get up nearer, so Denzel could hear his tiny squeaky voice.

"Hello," was all the tired newt could bring himself to say, and even that was difficult for Denzel to understand. During their final approach Tootsy realised she had better check to see that her personal appearance was in order. She leaped immediately to her natural mirror, this being a crystal clear puddle, much the same as Aunt Clara's back on Coot Island. Tootsy peered in at her reflection and thought to herself that she didn't look too bad, so she just touched up her chubby face in the clear fresh water that was freshly filled by the rain a couple of nights before. Feeling quite satisfied with her appearance, she immediately leaped back to the water's edge to greet the approaching company. Tootsy had not noticed Wally in all the excitement, who had himself already landed in the higher branches completely out of breath, with wings aching, just above her. At that precise moment he was by far too breathless to utter a single chirp, not that the little rascal didn't want to; fact is he was greatly annoyed at himself, if the little lad was to be truthful in admitting it. For this sole purpose he had flown quickly toward Tootsy; to do his usual in blurting 'n' blabbering the whole day's episodes out before any other poor creature ever got the chance, as we noticed on a previous occasion, when returning from their first trip to the River Darenth, some months before.

On the last leg of the journey, now moving into Lakeside, Treadwell had informed Denzel about his new passenger and his crazy performances.

"He's a funny little thing, isn't he!" laughed Denzel.

"Yers!" croaked Toad "Fing is, Denz, he finks that everyone abaat the plot can 'ear 'im, that's why I calls him Neddy the Nutty newt, our neighbour!" Toad went on to say… "Fact is, Denny boy, it woz Neddy, love his heart, who found our new home up 'ere by the Waterfall, yers!" Toad recalls. "Just before Tootsy 'n' me got married, we'd been home hunting all over the lakes, daan there by the chimney end of it. Then we searched up by the River itself, but all to no avail, so one morning my Toots 'n' me, thought we'd have a peep up 'ere by the big Waterfall, when we happened to bump into…"

"Bumps?" Denzel interrupted Toad.

"E… er sorry pal, not exactly! Er… met!" croaked Toad, who was swallowing hard.

"Oh!" said the Duck, prompting Treadwell to continue with his story.

"As I sez," croaked Toad, about to carry on… "We meets Neddy 'ere, and after telling him wot we were doing in his part of the Weld (world), and roughly wot we woz looking for, he then told us he knew of just the place we were searching for.As you'll see for ya-self in a mo, our Neddy wasn't wrong!" croaked the now very smiling Toad, who at this particular time was as pleased as punch about what Nuthouse had found them.

"Ooooh sweetheart!" croaked Toad, on seeing his titillating Tootsy waiting at the water's edge "Lookin' a picture," he informed his best pal. "Well!" he croaked on, "Is she the bizz Denz, likes I told ya, or wot?"

"Very, very sweet!" replied the Duck. Tootsy had overheard her husband's remarks, and began to move in such an alluring way; she was acting as most cunning females, doing her crafty bit of posing, even giving a few extra blinks. Of course girlie toads are not born with eyelashes, though Treadwell, even Denzel had tumbled the little games she was having with her equally in-love Toad. Treadwell was giving it the large, trying to hide a bit of embarrassment, but Denzel could tell the slippery Cockney was loving every bloomin' minute of it. Treadwell laughed again, when out of the corner of his extremely wide mouth,

"Don't ya fink she's a beauty Denz?" Then, before the Duck could answer… "An do ya fink she's got a tasty pair of scotches?"

"S…scotches!" retorted Denzel.

"Yers, her Pins!" croaked Toad. Before the Duck could ask what were scotches, he had realised Treadwell was beginning to confuse him even more. Then Toad explained his question he knew the Duck was about to ask. "Yus, scotch eggs, legs!" croaked the crazy Toad. Denzel now knew it meant legs, but decided he wasn't going to go into it at this particular time, because he was more interested in meeting the lovely Tootsy, who at this moment was giving her hubby one great big smacker on his slim wide lips (fish 'n' chips, which Toad was to call them at a later date). Treadwell, in reality, never knew much of his banter or even how it came about, yet being born a Cockney who originally lived at Lewisham South London, when the dear chap was a tadpole, right up to when he grew his own scotches, as Toad calls legs. And although he'd been in the Dartford area for much of his one-and-a-half year life, he still couldn't shake off his cockney verbal, not that the proud old chap wanted to mind. Oh no, he made it quite plain from the start, especially to Tootsy's mob, who had at first tried to change him. But as he tells 'em in his own words,

"I'm praad to be wot I am, and that's a real proper Londoner who, not through choice, had been forcibly moved out to the sticks as a youngster. If they don't like me for wot I am, then you can blow the lot of 'em, that's wot I says, and mean it!" He croaked in a none caring way to others' attitudes in the posh department. After all the kissing 'n' cuddling, Treadwell got down to more serious stuff of introducing Denzel to his loving Toots. Since this meeting, Denzel had noticed Toad had dropped the Y from his usual banter. Tootsy was overwhelmed in real tears, as she met the Duck that verbally had become part of their life ever since first hearing of him on their wedding day, when Treadwell mentioned their most memorable meeting. Yet she was even more surprised, when Wally, who had now regained his strength and breath, burst in from a few feet above her head.

"Hello Tootsy!" Wal chirped.

The female Toad was totally taken by surprise, looked up to see the now smiling Wally, she then looked straight back at her spouse in sudden wonder.

"Ho! Ho! Ho!" laughed Treadwell, on realising he'd almost forgotten Wally in all the excitement. "Cor, blow me daan wiv a fevver!" croaked the Toad. "Sorry Wal me son, I'm a bloomin' handy merchant ain' I, wiv all the goings on, I forgot you woz up there, me old pal." Wally understood the situation fully, and knew that Toad's forgetfulness wasn't meant. Once all were acquainted, Treadwell and Tootsy, faced each other, rose up on their back legs threw their arms around each other in a long embrace. Denzel and Wally witnessed the huge smile that had spread across Treadwell's face, as he planted the biggest smacker of a kiss on his eager Tootsy's lips. The two lads along with Nuthouse Neddy, all looked on at the loving scene, then at one another, and were all now smiling at the happiness of the contented couple. After their moment of tenderness, Treadwell and Tootsy decided it was time to show their new home off, that Neddy had found them. Both Toads leaped up the steep bank, where Neddy scooted along after them. Wally clung to a low elder branch, now waiting for his best pal to clamber out of the water, and followed the short way to the two Love-Toad's home. After Denzel and Wally, had spent a leisurely afternoon viewing the toads'' home and surroundings realised that it was getting late, and decided it was time to part company. Whilst the two birds were exchanging their respective goodbyes, Neddy the nutty newt thought he'd say his farewells at water's edge. So at this thought, Neddy scurried off down the bank, knowing he'd never be able to keep up if leaving together. As the four friends came to the water's edge, Neddy was there to greet them. The duck had taken note of Neddy's eagerness to say his own personal goodbyes, so s Denzel made a point of thanking the newt for his hospitality, and for finding his friend's marital home.

"My pleasure, sir!"squeaked Neddy. "And I wish yourself, and Wally, a most pleasurable journey home to the Island!" he squealed again, grinning at the duck and Wally, who was perched on a low bramble briar, that hung just to the right of Denzel's head. Denzel couldn't help laughing at Neddy, though he felt he did like the little amphibian. In fact the young Mallard liked him a lot and showed his feeling when promising the newt that he and Wally, would visit every day whilst the sun lasted. Neddy jumped for joy, Treadwell and his luscious leathery lady at his side, on hearing Denzel's promise, and seeing Nuthouse Neddy overjoyed, and now leaping with excitement, caused Toad to look at his Tootsy. But that girl could see as plain as day, her beloved husband had found his pal he'd so long missed. Though Tootsy, as in love with him as she was, had a sense of feeling and happiness in knowing her chubby hubby's longing was over.

"Yes!" she thought to herself, "perhaps now he'll pay a bit more attention to me!" as her private thoughts ran through her mind.

The two birds finally set off; Wally not saying too much, for he was very tired, and after this day of events since Toad's arrival on Coot Island, what with Toad's tale of the ever-lasting wedding then attempting to understand this Craggy from the Quaggy. Also the meeting of the ungrateful grebes, and finally all the excitement of meeting Tootsy, and of course Wal reminded himself of the unforgettable Nuthouse Neddy.

"Ha!" laughed Wally to himself, "What a blimmin' name that crafty Toad has given him." Wally hovered above the duck's head as they returned home to Coot Island, yet Denzel couldn't see the now wide crack of a smile that filled the little devil's face, that was from ear to ear, whilst pondering on the wonderful memories Wal and his best friend had shared this very day.

Following a respectable night's sleep, the residents of Coot Island were up at the crack of dawn. There were two reasons, one being the two lads were excited to bursting point to tell of the afternoon's happenings. And two, Aunty 'n' Uncle were barely able to contain themselves in waiting another moment longer to hear of it! After some time of listening to such riveting goings on, which had left the caring Coots, staring directly into each other's eyes in awe at what they had been told, especially those horrid grebes, Clara 'n' Clarence just shook their heads in disgust, when that bit was being told to them. But all ended well once they were filled in on Tootsy and the incredible Nuthouse Neddy. During the next couple of days, the two lads had visited Toad's every day as promised, and the happy times they'd shared were priceless. On the third day, all three males had decided to return to the River. When Denzel first mentioned this to Toad, he leaped at the chance.

"From now on, Denz, me son, let's always be togevver, wad'ya say? Eh, me old mucker? We'll be like them there three Musk Rats Ears, all for one 'n' one for all!" Toad, croaked in laughter. Soon after, Treadwell gave Tootsy her farewell smacker on her luscious lips. The trio set off to the same spot along the bank as before, where Clarence had taken the lads for the first time. Denzel found it just as hard on his second attempt at this slippery slope. Toad, leaped and leaped, yet even with those feet of his, it still took him a good few leaps 'n' bounds to reach the top of this awkward climb. Both had reached the summit, and were now half way down this path, the same run Wally had chosen. They were merrily going on their journey, when to the company's surprise, that terrible remembered sound of a firestick, rang in Denzel's ears. The duck and toad crouched at the deafening noise. The caring toad immediately looked at the duck, knowing the memories his pal must be going through. Denzel at this time was so scared, all he wanted to do was disappear. Wally, on adjusting himself, flew to another much higher branch to scout from whence it came. Instantly Wally, caught a glimpse of something now gone out of sight, behind some dense thicket of brambles. Wally sat concentrating on the danger that lay ahead. In moments a man carrying a firestick, appeared in Wally's view. The man was heading down the same run, to where Denzel and Toad, sat terrified. Wally, saw the danger, and quickly flitting down to his best mates, to fill them in on what was occurring. Denzel and Toad had already dived for cover in the thick density of nettles, at the side of the path. The man's footsteps came closer, and when he reached the exact same spot where the terrified two were, he stopped for a moment, then moved off further down the run toward the river. Wally had taken refuge back up in the highest branches, hidden behind a huge cluster of mauve ripened elderberries, his little heart beating furiously. He watched the man stop exactly at the same spot where his two pals were hidden. Wally kept his beady little eyes on every move the intruder made. The man walked on at a slow pace, then suddenly Wally saw him stop, bend down as if to pick something up. But the mans lowered arms went out of Wally's vision. The tiny warbler quickly flew in one flittering burst to land on a twig directly above the Poacher Man, who once again brought fear to the panic stricken residents. This total idiot was murdering as he did before, not to mention the shooting out of season. The beauty of the Horton Kirby Lakes and surroundings didn't need this sort of atrocious behaviour. The sad sight that Wally witnessed made him turn away in a gagging choke. There, before his eyes, was an old Doe, this being the same Rabbit that he and Denzel had passed on their maiden trip with Uncle Clarence, earlier that year. The duck and toad had both their heads protruding from the scrub, out into the path, trying to see what the man had again stopped for. Wally speedily flew to, and landed beside, a cascading cluster of blackberries, that hung from a thick prickly briar, just above the long-necked lookers, ending their neck stretching curiosity by telling them (between gasps) the sad news of Mother Rabbit's fatal outcome. Denzel was too upset even to talk; the cockney toad turned and leaped back into the thick scrub, uttering words of anger under his breath, too devastated to even face his two close pals. A few moments had passed when Wally took it upon himself to fly up into the highest branches. Once perched, Wal saw the man walking away in the distance. He could also see the mutilated body of old Mother Rabbit, swinging head down over the man's shoulder. Afterwards Wally, pulling yet another face of distaste, returned to the camouflaged company, giving a sure signal of all's clear. The three lads each made their respective ways to the place of the evil carnage, to be confronted with the sight of much blood. Denzel managed a little prayer, which he recalled his mother had on occasions quacked to him, and his brothers and sisters, before they retired to roost! As they silently stood, sat or perched, an old Buck Rabbit appeared from a hole at the root of a tree. He hopped down the run towards the company, hoping in vain what was inevitable wasn't true. On reaching the saddened spot, old Mother Rabbit's husband, of numerous years found that his hopes were sorrowfully dashed. Although he'd known when she hadn't returned to the warren with the rest of the family. But what confronted this old buck now, was just too heart-breaking to bear. His gracious old face seemed to age, as he sat on his hind legs, beating his chest furiously in agonising pain, at the loss of his lifelong friend and loving wife, of many moons. Whilst this show of frustrated anger flowed, many other rabbits of all ages and shapes (well, rabbit-shaped) began to form a small circle around the old Buck. Denzel, the cockney toad, and Wally at this time were in position, Wal on a low listening perch just inches above the gathering. His two buddies, were now seated among the distraught family of Rabbits. wal, was holding his own in the teardrop department, for he knew, sad as it all was, in finding everything he'd learned about the Foodchain of Life was coming perfectly true. Wal had begun to realise this, there and then that he'd be seeing a lot worse before his met his maker. A little shiver ran through the whole of Wal's feather frame at the thought. Wally could hear all the Rabbit's bunnying their thanks to Denzel and Toad for their concern. One very old Buck, crept up on Denzel's earhole and whispered'

"My Mum used to tell me that one too." He then hopped away towards his hole nearby. Everyone present began to disperse, leaving the company flummoxed, trying to decide whether to go on or return, due to their upsetting (to say the least) day. Their decision was made in no time at all; they decided after what had occurred to give up the idea of going on any further and began to make their way back along the trail. Wally once again went into his role of keeping scout, and in no time at all the gloomy faced trio were at the top of the bank. Wal, who on such occasions would normally be in full chirp, was plotted up hardly breathing, let alone blasting his bonce off as usual. But no, not in the mood at all was Wal, or was the little devil being crafty, by saving all his strength? For on Denzel's command of 'Let's go!' Wally would normally flitter off as before to blast the poor caring coot's ears off, giving dear Aunty Clara a second helping of Wal's mixed up chattering 'n' chirpings of much happenings, that were so much further from the truth. The little scallywag can't help it of course. It's his erratic way, but some would have it that Wally was also partial to spreading a wee bit of gossip. ('Who, our Wally? Never!') Denzel, as he looked up at Wal, at first, for just one teeny second, was expecting Wally to do his usual. But, he, and Treadwell were shocked even more, for it appeared to them that Wal wasn't interested today. Denzel could tell at a peek that much like himself and Toad, Wally was genuinely upset at the day's sordid happenings. Treadwell croaked up at Wal,

"Go on Wal, me son! You go back to the island! We're coming nah! There's nuffin' we can do, mate! Go on, pal!" With this Wally left his post, flittering in short bursts. But unlike before, he just flew casually in flits 'n' bursts back to Coot Island, leaving Denzel and Toad to decide on their choice of going down this very steep slope.

The main reason for this trip (though for reasons of their own they were keeping it a wee bit of a secret from Wally, and the adorable coots). Now! Right this very moment in time, Denzel is about to make his very first attempt at flying at will! Not with the aid of the ageing coot, who accidentally happened to trip, stumbling into Denzel, on their first journey over-land to the River. This resulted in the young duck, out of sheer desperation, taking to the sky. No! This was it! Denzel stood there contemplating his wing movements. Treadwell, as usual, gave his old mucker a bit of South London support. Verbally, that is!

"Go on nah, Denz, me boy, flap them old wings, me son!" croaked Denzel's pucker pal, Toad.

"I'm trying!" retorted the stirring Duck, feeling uncertain now the time had come, why he was there. He stretched himself to full height, chest out, then began to thrash a few good sturdy flaps to get warmed up. Then he was up from the ground and into the air, as natural as life itself. His powerful young wings had become an extension of himself, a feeling he had never ever felt before in his whole life, filled his heart to bursting point! Denzel's very own wings had brought him up out of the decaying shrubbery, into the air as cleanly and beautifully as if he'd always flown. (He did admit to Treadwell, a bit later on, that he was a bit frightened at first! Though once Denzel did arise, he soon found all the confidence in the world. Even more important, he knew that from this day on, he could stay up without fear. The duck also knew he was at last on his way; Denzel Duck Esq. could fly.

"Go on, Denz, give 'em some, me son, keep them old flappers going, me old 'China'!" croaked Treadwell, as he witnessed with his own minces, his Mallard mucker rise up from the earth into the air. The scatty Toad cheered his pal on and leaped ecstatically as he watched his very own buddy flying at long last. All of a sudden Treadwell was thinking crafty thoughts to himself. The slippery Londoner, who's a bit too lively 'n' sharp for these country yokels, happened to be pondering awhile. Then, with an enormous grin, Toad chuckled to himself, in thinking… "Now, he too, just like his sister, and her well orf 'usband Trevor, had transport in the flying stakes." Chuckling again, he then croaked out loud,

"Cor, will ya have-a-gander at that? I've gorn 'n' got meself, a bloomin' chauffeured flying quaxi! Ha, ha," he croaked in glee. After Toad had had his private bit of fun he was now watching his best pal not only flying very strongly for a beginner, but to Toad's surprise and disbelief, the duck wasn't struggling and was now gliding in a wide half circle on his way back, landing without incident, and was on his way back towards Treadwell. Toad in all honesty, expected Denzel to leave the steep bank and just fly straight down into the water at best. But, as we have read in Toad's earlier thoughts, the leathery Londoner has his own ideas. Denzel, now swimming on his way back to the bank where Treadwell was making his way down the very wet and slippery slope. It was the duck's turn for a wee chuckle now, for he too was in thought. But

Denzel was thinking more on the lines of which was the most slippery; Toad, or the slopes he was tackling? Denzel, without even blinking, knew what his choice would be, and I've got to say it, the slope came second. The duck watched Treadwell's descent whilst still making his way back to him; he saw the Toad making his way down. It was very difficult for a Toad with back feet the size of the Lewisham Leapers, which were in fact much more adapted on going up, rather than down. Then alas! The inevitable happened! Toad, was still watching Denzel in the distance swimming to meet him, got a bit carried away. Whilst Treadwell was in a state of jumping for joy, the cranky Cockney's bottom heavy feet became top heavy, resulting in his huge plates of meat (as he calls 'em) catapulting over his own head, causing the confused Cockney to go head-over-heels for the remainder of his descent, making the trip very very bumpy indeed. Yelping 'n' hollering, oohing 'n' arring, the Toad was making a right old nonsensical performance. But he got down much 'quacker', according to Seamus, the Shoveler's, recollection, when in the throes of one of his story telling, told a gathering of the most earnest listeners. Just one group of many he'd told, as time went by, of his witnessing of Toad's terrible tumblings. Treadwell Toad, was very lucky, because of the weight of his huge back feet, which wasn't to the dear chaps advantage in the first place, when hitting the bottom. Yet, as per usual this tricky toad had landed right on his feet, disturbing a resting Shoveler, who had stopped off at the Lakes to feed and rest, before heading deeper into Kent, on his way to visit his tater-eating relations on the Isle of Sheppey.

"Be-jasus! You'll be scarin' the living daylights out of me!" spoke Seamus the Shoveler, a strange bird to the lakes. Treadwell, who was just as startled as he on landing, and although a bit shaken, at least had his 'bigguns' planted firmly on the ground.

"Jee's!… Holy Mother of Mercy, Toady! Oi tought ya was a flying Frog, oi, did, oi did! Be-Jasus, oi did, to be sure!" scoffed a bird who, going by his strange tongue, was almost as confusing as Toad. (Then again, on reflection, no! There couldn't possibly be, could there?) Seamus could feel his ruffled feathers standing up on the back of his neck, when the tripped over Toad's croak was heard,

"Cor, bloomin' eck! I fink I've gorn 'n' done me haystack in nah!" Treadwell moaned, as he was straightening himself up.

"Ya haystack is it!" retorted the Shoveler. "Well, I tink ya's e'll be having a result ta be sure Toady, it'll be takin' me a fortnoight ta get this 'knot! out of me neck, of the fright of it all at all!" He rambled on.

"Gawd help us! Sorry Mick, me son! I... er slipped didn't I?" croaked a very embarrassed toad. Seamus, during all the to-do, never heard any more. His eyes were fixed rigid, staring at the 'tings that were extended from Toad's ankles, in utter disbelief. Even the brightest scholars in the land, with all their brains still, after years of research into Treadwell's family line of extraordinary whopping feet, still haven't been successful in finding the reason why.

"Now will ya's be takin a look at the 'dabs' on the quare fella!" Seamus exclaimed! Well, oi've never seen the likes in me loif! How on God's earth did the feet, fit de egg....? Let alone the wee fat fella dat's fixed to em!" chuckled the lad from leprechaun land. Denzel had seen it all, and now had stopped swimming to watch the shenanigans going on at lakeside. He could tell Toad; and the stranger's performance, soon after Treadwell's miscalculated summersault, were well worth watching. So for more entertainment, the Duck moved in closer to the fray of queer spoken words. The Shoveler, when first taking Treadwell into his sight, was a bit wary, but, in moments he sensed no danger at all, he soon realised that it was only a genuine accident. Fact was, the stranger was just thinking... "The quarens a foin character, oi can be sure of dat, now!" Denzel was now floating no more than a yard or two from the Toad and the strange bird. Denzel was laughing to himself at the Shoveler's sharp character and still smiling to himself in thinking...

"One's hard enough, but trying to understand both of them. Impossible!" He laughingly thought to himself. The two lads and the stranger, after such an extraordinary introduction, found they had things in common, apart from Toad and Seamus's gift of the gab, that is. Soon after their first encounter, and some very queer discussion, Seamus told the two lads that his family had originally come from waters in and around County Wicklow, at a far-away place called Southern Ireland.

"Oi've never ventured out to leprechaun land meself! But oi've heard me delations telling me mater 'n' pater, not a year back, dat it's a foin place ta live! Oi'll be tinking of retiring out there, to be sure!" As Seamus finished filling the lads in on the incidentals the Paddy, who does the shovelling, went straight into a little Irish jig, and sung a few verses, if you please, of the 'Blaydon Races' whilst in the throes of his handy bit of footwork in the mud at the bottom of the muddy slopes. Denzel and Toad were looking at one another, thoroughly enjoying their new friend and his strange carryings-on, so different from any other bird the two lads had ever seen. Seamus settled down after the private little performance, then sat telling Denzel and the toad, who at this time appeared to be mesmerised at the Paddy's magic mumblings. Seamus continued his tale, and told them how he happened to be stopping off at these particular lakes just as he'd been stopping at different relations, and friends on his way back from the yearly Gold Cup festival. He explained his song, then continued,

"Every year, in the month of March, during the week celebrating St Patrick's Day, hundreds, and thousands of us Irish birds go to this Cheltenham festival. Seamus, told them that it was a man's thing, where the humans ride on the backs of big horses in a game called racing. This is where once all the Irish bird's and dem-dare humans of Irish descent, were gathered as spectators to watch the famous race, the Cheltenham Gold Cup, which (to the Irish) is equivalent to what the Derby is to the English. Seamus, continued... "Be Jasus! It's a foin tree day meeten; ya's can hear de noise of excitement at it all for moils around! I did hears dat de winner of dat dare big race gets presented with a golden cup! Oi did, oi troly did! Oh... oi've watched dem humans all roight, a betting on who'll win de race, and ja's know? Some of the stupid egits, oi've seen em lose the shirts off their backs! Dem very tings, day cover demselves wid!" Then cunningly, he laughed to himself as he slyly took a shufty at his two engrossed happy listeners. He continued... "Ta's be honest wid ja's now...! Oi've been known to have a little flutter meself, I have, I have ta be sure!" He laughed again, enjoying himself in knowing he had hogged all the limelight! Not that Denzel and Toad minded, they were more than content in listening of the ways of others.

"A flutter! Mick, wot's that then, me old sunshine?" enquired the inquisitive Toad.

"Well, oi'll be! Ya's be meaning ta tell me you've never heard of the gamblin'!" The sly paddy laughed again, as he began to explain to the two lads about the procedure of the human's gambling habits, and all the odds 'n' sods about the game. Seamus ended his story by telling the lads of how he and a few other friends from his native Ireland used to gamble their food on horses, that each one had-had a fancy for. Seamus also recalled, and again roared up laughing to himself, when telling the lads... "Fact is, one of dem flew orf wid me winnings! But oi've caught up wiv the scoundrel since, and I tumped him on the beak, for the cheek of it all, at all!" The Shoveler had finished his tales and after saying his goodbye, he departed on the last leg of his long journey to the coast.

Back on Coot Island Wally and the ageing coots were waiting for the two lads to arrive. All three were wondering what had been holding them up for they should have returned soon after Wally; although I must admit Wal did want to go back and try and find out what possibly could be keeping them. But Old Clarence, even before Clara, put his webbed foot down. Each was telling him that Denzel and Toad would be along shortly. It must have been a good whole hour, when they first sighted them heading toward the island. Treadwell was plotted on Denzel's back, they were discussing not only the exploits of the 'jigging Mick' as Toad called him in conversation. But they kept their secret from Wally and the caring coots as far as Denzel's flying was concerned. Denzel had told Toad how he wanted to give the biggest of surprises to his family in the not-too-distant future. But little did the crafty Londoner know, that under all of the duck's charade of keeping his flying a surprise from Wal, and the caring coots, yet couldn't wait to see the surprise on the faces of the rest of the company but will, in fact, suddenly have the tables turned on himself. Once settled after their return, Denzel and his two best pals were filling the two coots in on the parts that Wal had obviously missed during his usual erratic chirpings. It had turned out weather-wise a very sunny day, so after such a bad start they all decided to catch a few rays before the sun went down altogether. All of a sudden Toad said,

"Giss a song, Wal!" Treadwell explained that they all needed cheering up, after such a terrible start to their supposedly happy day's outing. Wally, on hearing the Toad's request, followed by his two companions' conversation with his own vocal contribution. Wal just sat up there, chest out, with a little smile on his chops that even the cheekiest of chappies would be proud of. Then the little soldier breathed in the biggest breath of fresh air he possibly could, until his half ounce frame could take no more, before the rascal blew himself up altogether. But you can be sure as there are fairies at the bottom of your garden, as it appears there are at Cranks Hall, going by what its owner told Harry the Bowls player in the saloon bar of the village pub, which was owned and superbly run by his mother Alice for nigh on sixty years. And if you were one of the lucky ones, who might just happen to be within a quarter of a mile, of where that boy was perched, then you know, don't ya? The moment that little bird exhaled on single note, both Denzel and the toad stopped dead in their tracks, looked up, looked back at one another, and neither uttered a sound. Some fair distance away, an ageing female coot was busying herself in the preening 'n' cleaning department. She stopped what she was doing, on hearing notes on a single breeze tenderly come to her ears. A smile fell upon her kind old face in contentment and joy.

"Can you hear the little villain, lass?" called Clarence, whilst having a little dip to cool down, where he'd been sweating a bit whilst sun bathing.

"Yes dear! Who could mistake him? God bless his little feathered throat!" said Clara, as she listened to Wally's wonderful performance. The dear old lady was almost reduced to tears, and at this time was feeling more contented now than she had been in years. But old Clarence was no fool; he could plainly see that she, like he, was overwhelmed at the sound of music, a sound to compliment the rising of the Sun, bringing cheerfulness to those near at hand. It was only said last week, by one of Treadwell's relations, who had over-heard Lou the Shrew, telling Mrs Sparrow how the little lad livens the place up, when he's got his tiny lungs going. When the little songster had chirped his last note, the atmosphere about those lakes was completely silent; you could have heard a tear drop. It seemed that every single bird, animal and insect stopped still for a moment in time. Treadwell broke the silence leaping in sheer joy, and as he sailed through the air, he called...

"Good on ya Wal!" When he landed safely a couple of feet away. "A proper little wind-bag, ain' he Denz!" Denzel at the same time was flapping his wings, and cheered his little wind-bag, as Toad put it. Wally just sat there feeling very happy and cheerful in himself, knowing his music was appreciated, not only by his two best pals, but by all the other residents about this place. Wal flew down to perch and settled on a gorse bush. Then...

"Well, I thank you! Thank you!" chirped Wally. He raised his tiny wings gesticulating for his two buddies' attention. Once Wal had got their undivided attention he thanked them again, and continued to say, "Den...! And you, Tread! I'm really glad we're the bestest of mates, are you Den, eh! What about you, Tread, are you 'n' all, eh?" chirped Wally, searching his two pals' eyes for any signs of a yes. His two pals, both assured the little bird, but their quick response was no match for Wal, who continued to chirp..."I don't know what I'd do if I hadn't met you!" he chirped in a sad sort of way... "And Aunty and Uncle," he sadly waffled on. Course

Toad takes no prisoner when it comes to a giggle, and even though poor Wal was under pressure in the sympathy department, and Toad couldn't resist the tease,

"You hum it Wal, and I'll tap it wiv these 'ere plates of mine." The company fell about the island in uncontrollable laughter. But the reality was that Denzel and Toad could plainly see that Wally, after his wonderful performance, all of a sudden seemed to have fallen into one of his low periods. The duck and Toad had a good old chinwag with the little warbler, and explained to him that they would always be the best of friends, and would always be together, (strange as the little pack was). Wal appeared to perk up a bit, and with one of his nicer smiles coming across his feathered face, now looked reasonably assured.

The time came when Tootsy was to visit the caring coots, which as we know would be her first time, so you can imagine her excitement as she and Treadwell waited for his two pals to pick them up at water's edge just below the happy newlyweds' residential spread, half-way up the steep bank. Denzel and Wally had left their island at day-break to fetch Treadwell and Tootsy, who were waiting in great anticipation to meet the loving old coots, that Tootsy has heard so much about in recent days. As they waited patiently, Toad's two muckers showed up on time as it should be; if there's one thing Treadwell hates it's unpunctuality (bods being late in the London town talk).

"'Ere they come, gel! Wot did I tell ya!" croaked the grinning Cockney.

"Oooh… I'm getting butterflies in me belly!" giggled the young female in a sweet girlie croak.

"You'll be all right gel! You'll just love 'em, sweetheart, I just knows ya will." Toad was referring to Clarence and Clara, of course. "Morning, chaps!" croaked Treadwell, as he and the wife watched his two pals approaching close by. Wally flew in and landed on an old dead bulrush stalk, whilst Denzel swam into where the Toads sat in the shade, eagerly waiting for the coming day, even though Tootsy wasn't exactly too keen when it actually got down to the riding on a duck's back. The dear girl expressed this to her hubby earlier, but he assured her that it woz a doddle (easy in Toad's dodgy bit of verbal). Denzel swam in very close to where they were, Treadwell immediately got Tootsy in a good position so's to get the dear girl safely on board, but before the Toad had a chance, the duck for reasons of his own told them to stay where they were. Denzel unbeknown to the others, had got a surprise of his own, and although he and Treadwell were the only ones who knew of his ability to fly, yet the duck at this time was feeling so happy in the way his life had turned out since his sad beginning, he now very much wanted to give all the lakes dwellers something really worth talking about, and what this young duck has got in mind, would keep the residents in gossip for months.

"Treadwell!" exclaimed the duck.

"Yers, Ducky, me son!" croaked the toad wondering what his pal was about to say.

"Now listen, I want you both to come with me to the top of the bank, at the rear of your home. Is that all right?" Denzel asked. This threw the tricky Toad, and the Cockney couldn't see for the life of himself why his mucker wanted him and Tootsy, to traipse all the way to the top of this extremely steep slope. Especially after his performance in trying to get down the last one, when suddenly meeting Seamus the Shoveler.

"Er... why's that then, Denz? Er... I mean, it's a fair old trot up there ain't it? Yer know wot bloomin' happened last time me son, don't ya's nah?" Treadwell was a most confused Toad. "Why of course, if yer like," he answered, still intrigued at Denzel's queer request. Wally too, couldn't for the life of him understand why Denzel wanted to climb to the top of this bank.

"And an exceedingly steep one at that!" thought Wal, who was also in a fine old state of wondering at his best pal's sudden ambitious suggestion. The duck and the two toads began to make their way up to the half way mark, which happened to pass the front entrance of the Toad's moss and ivy-clad home; when as if from nowhere, Nuthouse Neddy suddenly appeared. Neddy was very happy to see his friends return, then casually asked in his usual squeaking where the little band was going.

"Well, after we've gorn up to the top ov this 'ere 'ill 'n' gorn daan agin, we're orf ta Coot Island ta visit Clarence 'n' Clara, so's me Toots there, can meet the two oldens!" When Treadwell told this to Neddy, Neddy too wished so much that he could go further afield to visit and meet new friends, especially the ageing coots he'd heard so much about from his neighbour, and best friend, Treadwell Toad.

"C... can I come?" asked Neddy coyly.

"Well, it's up to Denzel!" croaked Toad, knowing the duck as he did, would be only too pleased to let the lively little newt come along and share in the excitement.

"Of course you can come, Neddy!" called Denzel from a little further down the bank to where Neddy and the two leaping toads were trying desperately to reach the top of this steep steep climb. All reached the top of the bank, with a very pleased Neddy in tow. Wally was flitting about agitatedly from bush to shrub, just feet above the resting foursome. He was still restless and baffled by Denzel's sudden decision about climbing this horrid steep bank. But what puzzled Wally was he knew just how much Denzel hated the very thing that the duck and the others had done minutes ago. After the little band had taken ample rest, Denzel rose from his seat, turned, waddled over to the edge of the raised outlook over the best part of the Horton Kirby Lakes. Denzel with his keen young eyes looked out over the beautiful landscape and for the first time in his life saw it all in a new perspective and realised as never before, that the world was far greater than that of the lakes in which he lived and loved. As the duck looked down, the vast expanse of water loomed far below. Not thinking another thought, Denzel told the two toads to climb on his back, Treadwell looked at Wally, then back at Denzel shrugging his huge craggy shoulders. He then motioned for his beloved Tootsy to hop on board, but the dear lass from Chislehurst started to flap, and I don't mean in the way that the duck was about to, Oh no, she felt very nervous indeed. As the Toads made their way finding themselves a suitable position in the centre of Denzel's back, Tootsy was lost in her own thoughts at this precise moment whilst sitting there on the back of the duck. She was thinking of how easy it was for Mac the Canada Goose, looking now at Denzel's size compared with Mac's. (Though even I have to admit, the dear sweet girl did say at a later date, that she was terrified.) Once the Toads were on board, Denzel looked around to see where Neddy was. Well, to be truthful, the duck felt quite choked at the sight of poor Neddy's face, who'd obviously thought he was about to be left out. Denzel noticed Neddy's skinny lips were all a-quiver as if he were very upset and about to cry.

"Come along Neddy!" called the duck, "are you coming or not?" Hearing this coming from Denzel himself, Neddy's sad face brightened up, and he was up on the duck's back so fast it appeared that he had arrived before he'd even left. Wally, as you can imagine, had never once seen Denzel in flight. That had been a well-kept secret that Toad and he were keeping from Wal as a surprise. As we all know, Uncle Clarence had taken part in the young duck's dealings in the taking off and landing stakes. Yet the duck and Toad even kept the coots in the dark, but old Uncle Clarence was no fool, he knew in his cagey old head that Denzel and the cockney, had been up to a bit of skulduggery, that time they were almost an hour late after Wally's return the day the old doe Rabbit was killed. Can you imagine Wal's face at the moment his best pal started ordering the Toads and Nuthouse Neddy, to climb on board? Without a chirp, he watched in satisfied amazement, shaking 'n' nodding his little cocked head. Wally was now watching all three amphibians securely on board. The Duck began to test his wings. He gave a couple of powerful flaps, but those were only a warm up.

"Here we go! Hold on tightly!" Faster and getting even more powerful by the second, in fact at that moment Denzel was flapping so strongly he at last began to rise up and go forth, then down, down and out into the lake heading in the direction of Coot Island.

"Gawd help us!" croaked the tongue-tied Toad.

"Wheeeee!" squeaked Neddy as he clung on for dear life with his crinkled fingers. Tootsy wasn't too sure at first, but knew that Denzel was far too educated to even think of quaxying them about, if he knew it wouldn't be safe. No she, just like her chubby hubby and the miming-mouthed Newt was enjoying the flight tremendously. On his perch Wally was absolutely stunned chirpless, one moment he was so engrossed in his watching; the next, Denzel was up and gone leaving Wal agawk. Surprised at his best mate not only flying, but fully laden too, he realised he had been left behind, but instead of the silly little lad taking to the air himself, and follow on Denzel's tail, he started like he does, to feel that Denzel was paying more attention to the others. He decided to fly back on his own, but Wal was in a sorry old state of flits 'n' bursts, his tiny mouth and beak area was drooped low, and the return trip for Wal was a life-time. Clarence and Clara were at the water's edge looking out over the lake in the direction of the waterfall. The two northerners knew that very soon the lads would be returning with Tootsy, whom they could hardly wait to meet; they were both sitting at the front end of their island which faces out over most of the lake, keeping their keen eyes peeled on the water for any sightings of the floating company en-route towards them. During their wait the ageing couple were reminiscing about when they were at the lad's ages, and the good times they had shared in the lakes back up in the Dales, with all their friends and relations. Their thoughts still, even after all these summers past, left the pair of 'em a little homesick, although each admitted that these days it was getting easier but, both knew that it had to be the way it was for the sake of Clara's condition. Clarence, was just about to end his verballed fancying of something he'd not eaten in years, which was that of a real proper Yorkshire pudding that the fisherman used to feed the birds on a Sunday afternoon back in the times he was dreaming of.

"Aye, lass, it was grand!" He was about to ramble on, when their attention was soon back scanning the water for any signs of the returning company. To his and Clara's surprise and total disbelief in what they were witnessing in the young duck doings, the old couple had come to realise, that the duckling had at last become a duck.

"A fine young mallard at that!" thought Clara smiling to herself. Whilst the old couple were in conversation, and at the same time focusing their eyes on the lake, something caught their attention and even before either of them could grasp their vision, to the old couple's surprise, Denzel came gliding in to land some twenty or so yards before the front edge of the Island, then began to swim home smiling proudly, like he'd never smiled before. The coots were so full of Denzel's coming of age and getting his wings at last they had momentarily forgotten everything else. As Denzel was swimming the last fifteen or so yards Clarence, had spotted some sort of movement behind the duck's shoulders. It was only then, Uncle and Aunty saw Treadwell come into their view.

"Watcha, Clara gel, every fing all right darlin'," croaked a very happy Toad, so near to bursting point in dearly wanting the caring coots to meet his tasty Toots. Clarence and his lovely lady were hardly able to contain themselves in what they were seeing, but what they did take note of was that the duckling that had left them that morning at sun-up, had returned to them a duck. Not that the ever loving Clara liked the idea of losing one of her babies, yet the old dear smiled in thinking to herself,

"But what a fine Mallard drake he had grown up to be," and both coots agreed whole-heartedly to that in smiling satisfaction. As Denzel came into the edge of the Island, Treadwell and Tootsy were so excited, they both held hands and leaped from the duck's back, and landed directly on the moss 'n' grassy floor infront of their just-as-excited hosts. During the preliminaries, and jovial introductions of Tootsy to the ageing Coots, Neddy on the other hand decided to hitch a ride all the way onto land, not that the narrow chappy was scared or anything, he was just a bit shy that's all. Clarence and his wife in all the excitement never expected or even dreamt Neddy was on board hidden among the folds of

Denzel's wings. Wally was seen by the ever watchful female coot, Wal was heading in the company's direction.

"Oh dearie me!" exclaimed Clara. The others had heard her expression and turned to witness the returning Warbler, where all could plainly see that Wal wasn't the happiest of birds, going by the look of his drooping beak area. The quick thinking Cockney leaped to meet Wally as he landed close by, but his face was as long as a kite. Toad was the first to greet Wally, because he saw the way the small bird was sauntering along on the wing in the weakest of flits 'n' bursts. Yet the Toad was there at Wal's side in full cheering up banter...

"Come on Wal! Cheer up, me son, ya's can't keep flying abaat the plot wiv ya mooey (face) looking like it does! Ya's see, me old pal, Denzel just wanted to give you, Aunty Clara and Clarence 'ere a blimmin' surprise that's all; honestly mate, that's all it woz, straight up!" Wally listened to Toad, but he was still a bit reluctant, but after seeing all the happy goings on, and big smiles everywhere especially on Aunty 'n' Uncles faces, just that sight alone cheered and livened the little rascal up, and once he was satisfied, he too partook in the afternoon's gathering and was now as contented as the rest. Treadwell, because of his Tootsy being present, began to show orf a bit of his collective knowledge of life in general. He told the company some of the expressions he'd come across over his life, and once he got started, the others of course couldn't get a word in at all. But I must say another listeners told me shortly after the incident that there were no complaints coming from their quarter and they were more than happy; and no, not even as much as a whisper came from Wal. For as we all know, there's no-one, but no-one can and does keep a captivated audience in the same league as this south London character. Fact was, the contented listeners were actually egging him on, would you please. Even Tootsy, the dear girl, after hearing her hubby's stories for the thousandth time, just sighed 'n' swooned at the sound of her Toad's every word. Oh yes, Wal may be the crow's toes in the chirping 'n' chanting department, but when it comes to a bit of story telling then Treadwell would have undoubtedly have out shone even the most ardent tale teller. All of the company were plotted comfortably when in the throes of listening to Toad at work. He was now in full flow, and the cheeky Londoner was waving his arms about whilst conveying his tale. At one point, he even leaped up onto an old mole hill that hadn't been used in yonks, long before the ageing coots were on the scene. Whilst he was up there Toad carried on conducting his grand performance like a true actor, and I've got to say it; that day the boy was bang on form.

"Ya's know, gang!" he went on... "My old Uncle Treadlightly's been abaat ya know! He told me a-while back that he knows two villainous Ravens, at a place called the Tower ov London!"

"Tower of London?" enquired Denzel.

"Yers, by all accounts it's a great big human place, even bigger than Cranks Hall like! Me Uncle says it's a real important place where loads ov them there humans go to have a gander at the craan jools." (The dear chap of course means the Crown Jewels). The company were enthralled, and didn't seem too concerned even if the talking Toad took a fortnight to finish as they were enjoying themselves so much, and now all were looking for the Toad's London verbal to begin again.

"Well ya know that sparkling fing that, that Maurice nicked from Cranks Hall?" The company all gave their nods of agreement, letting Toad know they wanted him to carry on.

"Well, jools is wot them diamond 'n' fings is and accordin' to Treadlightly, this Tower gaff looks after that there human Queen's big parcel of tom-foolery!"

"Tom-foolery!" laughed Wal.

"Yus! Course Wal, me son, come on nah, wot does it rhyme wiv!" Ha, ha, ha, Toad was waiting. Wally giving it loads 'n' loads of thought when all of a sudden the little lad sparked up a bit lively, as if he knew the answer, and then said... "Cats clevery!"

With Wal's weird answer Toad absolutely collapsed in a heap on the top of that old mole-hill. Still holding the belly area where the dear chap was in fits of laughter. The listeners all appeared to be finding the whole show very confusing, but whatever, they just couldn't help grinning their heads off just at his antics, let alone at the most confusing talker in the world, well, Horton Kirby at any rate.

"Nah, ya Wally, oops, beg ya pardon Wal, no offence meant mate, honest," croaked the toad. And before Wal could even chirp, the slippery toad shot back with a… "Tom foolery, joolery! Ok, me son!" The toad caught a glimpse from the corner of his eye, and saw Denzel glaring at him for winding Wal up. But the tricky customer covered himself immediately.

"Well, he's got a learn ain' 'e, else he'll end up fick!" Toad went on to tell them… "Anyway, my Uncle told me that there are some raven twin brothers up there called Ron 'n' Reg, and according to Treadlightly, they rule the roost up there on that manor. A right couple of tearaways by all accounts, but my old uncle reckons if they don't watch aat, cause of the way they've been shaping up ov late, 'e said 'e can see 'em being put into a cage for a very long time. Cor, 'e went on… They must have been scary, cause my uncle told me that at the Tower of London, there was a big bullying feline that woz tooled right up wiv long sharp claws and teeth, who's name woz Jack the Cat, and Treadlightly swears they even seen 'im orf!" Whilst Treadwell was in the throes of telling his tales, he was keeping his minces on the happy harkening band, making sure he had 'em a listening. The dear chap never had a worry in the world on that score, for his audience were absolutely entranced, let alone captivated. So this crafty customer run past them with yet another one of his cockney capers…. "And ov course," he went on… "Yers ago, someone even named human tracks after us leathery lot!" (The amphibians).

"They did?" enquired the duck, prompting Treadwell to carry on croaking.

"Ya's no Denz! Where I come from, ya know, South ov the River, Lewisham like, well them their folks who live up there, calls roads, Frogs 'n' Toads!"

"Ha, ha, ha," laughed the ear straining company, not able to get enough of this Bow Bell banter. Even though he was a South-side boy, he sure knew how to keep 'em hooked.

"I don't get it," chirped Wall, after laughing with the others, but not really understanding the slightest thing the toad was talking about. Treadwell was just trying to educate his pals with a bit of street knowledge, and began to explain a little more clearly, and then he continued... "Well, er... as I woz sayin' I've sat plotted up by the banks ov the Quaggy, and I've orften heard 'em, humans that is! They walk daan them big man paths, saying to one another, "I'm orf daan the Frog 'n' Toad!" meaning...!"

"Road!" Wal chirped before he even knew he'd said it.

"Very good, me son!" Toad croaked on picking up on the Warbler's little brain-wave. The others present also caught on to Wally's speedy response, and all were looking at one another pleasingly realising that with all of Wal's erratic insecure moments, it did appear he had a tiny bit of the old grey matter on board somewhere, and just think he remembered that from one of Toad's other tales from way back. Even Aunt Clara was in her element, listening to Wal's intelligent conclusion, of what he made out of Toad's tellable talkings, and during her recollection she brought to mind an earlier experience of Wally's blunders in the brain department. Ever since their first encounter the old dear had, within just a short time of meeting him, expressed to Clarence,

"What can you expect from the dear little mite; just look at that sweet little head, and the most dearest of faces. I mean, my love," she said, "it doesn't leave much space for you know what, does it?" But listening to him now, Wal had gone up in all the company's estimation, yet all knew Wal the little Warbler, was well worth his lot in these parts. Treadwell explained that roads, as them humans calls 'em, were just tracks, much the same as animal tracks to go about their business, only much much bigger. Toad whilst on this subject, felt it a good opportunity to fill the eager band of listeners in on the way of the humans (from his point of view that is).

"Nah, them there humans, wot a queer old lot they are; they walks abaat on them two back legs ov theirs as stiff as bulrushes, how the bloomin' 'ell they don't get the back-ache, I'll never know! They wrap a load ov funny joined-up leaves around 'em, to keep 'em warm in the winter. I've even seen some ov 'em galloping past wiv fire 'n' smoke coming from their mouths. Yers as I say, queer old mob altogevver!" he trailed off....

"Fire and smoke!" exclaimed Clarence, knowing exactly what Toad was saying, for he had seem what fire is, and what it can do if mis-used. The male coot began to scratch his tired old head in wonder of man and his mysterious ways and goings-on. But he wasn't so silly, for he knew he'd never begin to understand, how greed had made Man stray from God's intended path. Clara and the lads never really grasped much of Toad's attempt to tell them the ways of the unpredictable human. She also could never understand, and shuddered everytime that humans were brought up in their chirpings 'n' chattings, and if she had her way, it would never be at all. Though she was pleased that Treadwell had said his piece, and it was then she took the initiative in suggesting a little siesta, or in Toads words,

"A good afternoon's kip!" All agreed, and as Clara suggested this, Clarence, Wally and Denzel started to yawn, not realising that when the Cockney tells a tale, it drains your strength just trying to comprehend the leathery loon's lingo, let alone get half a chance of getting the true drift of whichever story the tale telling Toad had croaked. As they all went in their different places, Clara took full charge of Tootsy. She told the males to get on with what-ever they were about to do and leave the ladies to themselves. Clara, unbeknown to the company, had been keeping an eye on Tootsy, and on the odd occasion their eyes would meet, especially when her hubby got to the good bits of his stories. But there was one thing Clara was satisfied with, and that was she knew for sure that Tootsy was in love. And so is he, she mused to herself.

Chapter 5

A Taste Of Winter

During the few weeks that led up to winter Denzel, Wally and Treadwell Toad were inseperable, and on many occasions Tootsy, Nuthouse Neddy, even Uncle Clarence would sometimes tag along and go out and about, whether on business or just plain fooling around. However the company continued to have the most fabulous times. Even Aunty Clara was heard telling her neighbour Mini, an old moorhen spinster of how Clarence of late had been traipsing about the place with the youngsters a -giggling and a-flapping; anyone would think he was a spring-chick all over again.

"Who does he think he is? The silly old fool?" she was heard to say during one of her gossiping turnouts; but make no mistake the loveable old female in truth loved every minute of all the excitement that was all about her, in her new ever growing family. Oh, she had had her little moans 'n' groans, but all in all, she was a very contented lady at this present time. Clara, for the past couple of years, had rarely left the island, except for feeding, and even then it was only a matter of a few yards. In fact the very day she and Clarence had first seen the little orphan sitting on that log a few months before, was the furthest the old dear had been in yonks, and even that was only fifty yards at most. It was late September when the Toad and his adorable Tootsy, along with all the species of the amphibian family, went into hibernation. Once asleep underneath their ivy-clad home they wouldn't awake until the spring. When first hearing that this was what Toads did though the winter months. Denzel and Wal couldn't understand why their best pal had to leave them for such a long time, but little did the pair of 'em know that Wal would soon be on his way to a foreign land, or would he?

It was a very mild day for October, Denzel and Wally were out having their last trip around their plot before winter set in completely. They had decided to go flying, something that was natural for both at their ages, although everywhere they flew Denzel got there first leaving Wally to bring up the rear; though the duck did try to fly a bit slower so that Wal could catch up, but this proved too difficult. So wherever they went from now on, they would always make arrangements: in other words, if they were going quite a distance Wal would cadge a lift, but if only on the manor, the little Warbler would make his own way. On this particular outing the two birds had decided to fly over in the direction of Cranks Hall, they both wished very much that Treadwell could have been with them, but as we know Tread and spouse were tucked up in the kip until the old currant bun made its spring showing. Nevertheless, although there was a nip in the air, there was no stopping the two lads in their adventures. Denzel now able to fly at will, didn't need to go clambering up steep banks anymore, when wanting to take to the air, oh, no! They took off from the island together, Wal, on this trip being so far 'n' all decided to ride on Denzel's back. The reasons: one, because of the lengthy journey; two, so that Wally could give the duck directions, as Denzel had never in his life seen such a place, and the sole purpose for this trip was because Denzel just couldn't wait till the following spring to see the mysterious home of man. Whilst going over some marsh-land heading for the Hall, Denzel thought he'd land on the marsh and have a chat with some local mallards that he'd occasionally met over the previous months. As they came in to land, Denzel had noticed a shallow crystal clear puddle, just like the one Aunty Clara used back on Coot Island, but this was three times bigger. Denzel couldn't help noticing it was inhabited by a multitude of water beetles. He and Wally were watching them going about their own lives, when out of nowhere…

"Fascinating aren't they?" came an even smaller chirp than Wally's. Both birds turned, then looked up to see the tiniest of birds the pair had ever encountered: a tiny round reddish brown shaded bird with a short, stubby tail. Denzel smiled at what he saw perched in front of him.

"Do you have a name, and please little one, tell us what kind of bird you are," he asked, smiling as he said it.

"I am a wren, the smallest of all birds in these parts and a lot more come to that! However, my name is Jennifer, although folks around here call me Jenny!" said the feminine fluffy female.

"And do you live here alone?" Wally asked, admiring the very small wren.

"Oh no!" laughed Jenny... "Regards my own family, yes!"

Then the friendly female told them of how her parents had a clutch of eight eggs, and how her mother had told her and her brothers and sisters, of how the hand of a human had stolen the first three eggs that she had laid. She continued... "And when mother had laid another five, she told us that her and my father, were always frightened that the bad man would return and steal the rest of us and, as you can see for yourselves, I survived, and so did the rest of the brood!" The little wren went on to tell them wrens were territorial birds, that's why her brothers and sisters had moved on to find their own domains around the area.

"I see!" answered Denzel "And what were their names?"

"Very similar, really!" she said smiling at the two strangers. "My eldest sister's name is Penny, she hatched the first, then there's Benny, he's a comical little fella; then comes Lenny the second eldest, and the youngest is, how should I say? The brainiest I guess!"

"Er... what's his name then?" enquired Wal, getting his spoke in for the first time.

"Christopher!" she said.

"Ha!" laughed the duck, "Christopher Wren eh? I see, and I suppose he builds all the best nests around here, does he?"

"He does, actually. How on earth, and water do you know that?" exclaimed Jenny.

"Let's just say a big bird told me!" answered the duck laughing (meaning of course Owen). Wally was lost in the fray of words, leaving all the talking to the others. Although Jenny at this time was most intrigued by the way this duck carried himself, she realised there was something about his manner that seemed to make her feel differently about him, compared to any other bird on the lakes. She then asked politely about Denzel's upbringing. The Duck never got a sentence out, when Jenny cut him short.

"I'm terribly sorry! So you're that duck, the one who lost all of your family to man's ill ways! You have no need to continue, for I was hatched last spring as yourself, and as far back as I can recall, it was the talk of all of this lake and many more, I've also heard that yours was a very respected family and I must say how pleased I am to have made your acquaintance this very day." Denzel felt quite choked at the little bird's concern and thanked her. They said their goodbyes, and as he and Wal were about to leave, the duck called to Jenny...

"I say, aren't there a lot of beetles in this pool!"

"Yes...! A busy little band aren't they?" replied Jenny Wren... "The beetles have been quite popular since the early sixties, though lots of their friends died from taking too many bugs, but they appear to have made a come-back going by the millions they've made to date."

Afterward they stopped and chatted to the Mallard drakes, and then returned home when they met with Charlie the brave coot whom, as you'll remember, they had met under strange circumstances on the day of Denzel's extreme bravery, by pipping Cooty to the post and by feeding right out of the fisherman's hand. Cooty told the duck and warbler that he'd been searching the whole Lake for them. He told them he had even been to their island in his bid to find them. Denzel wondered why the brave coot needed to see them so urgently. He told them that he had been passing by over near the old graggy willows at day-light, and was just about to have a wash and preen up, when out of the shadows came an old Tawny Owl. He told me, if I was to see you about the lake to tell you that he wanted to see you both urgently.

"Apparently it's got something to do with Wally."

They cancelled their intended trip to Cranks Hall for it wasn't that important, and the two lads thought there would always be another time in the spring; and in any case they both felt it wouldn't be the same without Treadwell. It was a shame really, 'cause since Denzel had heard so much about the place where Wally was rescued, he just thought he'd like to see the exciting man place for himself before winter closed in. It was getting on for midday so they decided to nip back to have lunch with their adopted mum 'n' dad, until it was late afternoon. Both birds did just that, and by late afternoon it was time to visit the old Owl. They made their way towards Owen's territory. Denzel swam leisurely, and Wal flew in short flits 'n' bursts above his partner's head. There was no singing, or even talking come to that; no, Wal didn't feel too clever at all, not after what Charlie had told them, especially his saying Owen wanted to see him urgently. They arrived at the Craggies, Owen's residence, at 6.15 p.m. just in time to catch the old fella getting up out of his roost deep inside the thick ancient willow.

"Good afternoon, Owen." called Denzel, looking up at the old wise one from the water below, as he spotted the old codger coming out onto his roosting perch.

"Ah! Just the two I wanted to see." called the brains of the lake to the approaching lads. Wally, in one flitter 'n' burst, flew up and settled on a branch beside the big Tawny Owl, Denzel, on the other hand, was in the throes of half-flapping and skittering up into the branches to where his two close friends were perched. Owen had got himself comfortable, whilst the two youngens, as he calls 'em, were adjusting their perching arrangements; and he could tell they were both looking very sheepish, wondering what he could possibly want to see them about that was so important. The whizz-kid of the willows knew the pair of 'em could hardly wait to hear exactly what was so very, very urgent. Denzel couldn't hold out any longer, and eagerly asked Owen why he wanted to see them. The very wise old Owl was now comfortable enough to say what he intended to say. Owen gave a little cough, then he began to tell the lads why he had summoned them at this particular time of the year

"What I have called you here today for is for me to give you, Wally, some very wise advice! And my sound warning to you, youngen, is that you must migrate to a more suitable climate, preferably the South of France, where you can be sure to survive our bleakest of winter months. Owen had barely gotten the words out of his mouth, when Wally threw a panic stricken fit…

"I ain't going, I ain't goin!" insisted Wally. "I'm not leaving Denzel, and Aunty 'n' Uncle. Never, never, never…!" screeched Wal in an awful little temper 'n' tantrum. (And I've got to tell ya, the boy was adamant!)

"Now you listen to me, you cheeky whipper-snapper!" Owen having to put his foot down, for he knew exactly how close the little warbler had become to all of the friends he'd made about the area. Owen knew even before Wal had arrived, that he was going to have a hell of a job to get the little bird to migrate to the safety of the sun. As old, and as wise a bird Owen was, at the sight of his little friends heartbreaking pleas, he found it most difficult for a moment to swallow. Once he had found his throat he tried again; he went on to tell Wally of the coming harsh winter weather, and of snow and ice, and he told him… "If you think that storm was bad, ma boy, you had better think again! And always remember youngen, if it wasn't for that kind human at Cranks Hall, you ma boy, wouldn't be here with us this day. Just look at you…! There's more meat on the bones of that bloomin' anorexic Stanley, the half starved starling. And he wouldn't ever have survived the winters as he do, if it wasn't for…" Something that the Owl was about to say had given him an idea, but this would only act as plan two if, and I say if, he couldn't get the little Warbler to go abroad for the winter.

"Ah… um!" Owen stopped dead in his hootings, not finishing what he had intended to say, leaving the old Wizard to try a bit more coaxing. Well, coaxing he tried, in fact he was running out of stories of terrifying ordeals that had occurred about the lakes during winter weather. Whilst Owen was trying his damnedest to think up something even more scary, well, in the end he was more of less trying to frighten poor Wally off the plot. The old Owl knew he wasn't getting anywhere, and even tried to conjure up an odd dodgy story, anything to scare Wal off to the safety of a warmer climate. Denzel, had not said an interrupting word, knowing as much that it was hurting him too, everything that Owen was saying was perfectly true. But he was wondering why Owen had deliberately shied away from the Stanley story. Even Wally, as you can imagine, was feeling so dejected 'n' low; fact was, he couldn't have been much lower else the poor waif would have been under the branch he was sitting on. Yet as the dodgy old Owl spoke, each of them twigged a wee crack of a smile running from one corner of the intelligent Tawny's hooked beak.

"If it's going to be as hard a winter for Wally as you say Owen, then why are you smiling now!" asked the duck.

"Wha... What! Me, smiling? Never!" spluttered the caught-out Wizard, not feeling too clever himself at being rumbled by a couple of his own pupils "It won't do at all," he internally chuckled to himself, and then had a second thought that made him smile even more... "Why, oh why didn't I think? Cor, if only I'd got Harry the Rat to tell Wal one of his winter stories; 'cause knowing the Rat as I do, and his ferocious fibs, Wal would already be flying round the Cap-Farrat with a beret on his bonce, stinking of garlic-flavoured flies. Yet, alas, it will never be. Well the winter of '64 at any rate. Wally, still not a happy little solider, was sulking and mumbling things under his breath, not even able to raise his teeny head. Denzel had been keeping his eyes fixed on Owen's, in the hope he had come up with an answer to solve the problem that Wally faced. He had been watching Owen ever since the crafty old Owl had deliberately stopped during the middle of the Stanley story. Yet the old codger still wouldn't let on, in the hope that in the next few days Clara, if not Clarence, could talk young Wallace out of the country. Well the meeting ended much the same as it started, with the dear Wal staying put. Before the two lads had left to go home, Owen spoke,

"All right, master Wally, for the moment ma boy, you win, and I'll do everything in my power to help you survive. But, I must warn you again son, it's gonna get rough, and I mean rough!" Owen was still trying to keep a stern face in the hope that Wally might take his good advice, even though he knew in his heart that there would be no chance, he chuckled to himself and thought… "Ever!"

"Hooray!" shouted Denzel excited, because he was so pleased, though not half as pleased as for Wally, who was now a bit chirpier but still too frightened to trust a living soul, even though in the little lad's heart, he knew that his best friends and family would only want to help him for the best.

Once the two youngsters had left, Owen, after giving the subject a little more thought, realised that what he had to do: he would do it in the morning before returning to roost from feeding.

The very next morning the Big Tawny was on his way home from a successful nights hunting, but instead of him going straight home to his hole at the craggies, the residence his father before him had bequeathed to him back in the real olden days, but instead he headed in a funny old direction indeed; as a matter of fact to the Horton Kirby paper mill at the far bottom end of the Lake. (Well, way past H's three million family residence that is) Owen once in flight was down from his perch across, and out of the lakes, heading for the old paper mill. He approached the mill by flying over the roof-tops of the village pub, down through a huge viaduct that carries the trains that deliver the Perigrine Cranks of this world to the city of London and many other destinations. As he flew under the archway, he flapped a couple of good thrusts and up he spiralled and came to rest on a very unhealthy man-made asbestos roof, where an old bedraggled down 'n' out pigeon was stooped sorrowfully. Owen knew this poor pathetic pigeon, and knew the cause of his downfall. Apparently the story that went around the lake, was that he was quite a prominent figure in the vicinity, with a cracking looking wife, and father to many children; he was a bird of many properties, having homes scattered all over the continent, the best of them of course was his penthouse loft in Kensington above the Duke of Westminster. Before his downfall he used to readily admit that he never actually rubbed shoulders with any of that lot, as living where he do, he felt they were a little beneath him. Also there was his Marbella treetop retreat, which over-looked the valley out over the sprawling hills. His Monte Carlo love-nest, where the sly old rascal was said to have kept a young chick, said in those times to have been half his age; and there was a whisper that it even sported its own bird-bath. And finally his other penthouse loft at Rheims, in the old Champagne country; but this establishment unfortunately became the beginning of the end for what was sitting in front of Owen now. Because it was here, at a time in 1963 when the human world was mourning President John F Kennedy. His trouble started when he innocently was hunting the grounds and vineyards, of the sixteenth century chateau for some food 'n' drink when he came upon lots of old oak wine casks. Apparently he was just mooching about and came across a sweet nectar-like substance. He was wary at first, but on his third taster he found he liked this new flavour; in fact the dear chap liked it very much indeed. But his boozing began to affect not only his own life, but those whoever came in contact with him; not to mention what he'd put his family through with his inconsiderate carryings-on, and intolerable behaviour. It got so bad that, in the end, after countless attempts to get him back to sobriety, he never had a single friend left, and his very comfortable world fell about him. Even the hussy chick at the Monte Carlo penthouse had cleared it out and fled the nest, and it was mentioned that the girl even left the bath dirty. Tut, tut, I don't know, do you? Anyway for the past eighteen months he's been hanging about at the back of the local pub just grabbing a drink when he could out of all the empties that got stacked at the rear of the ale house. Of course the landlady Alice knew the old pigeon who in fact wasn't old at all, but through the demon drink he had let himself go to rock bottom, and instead of all his past fine residences, he now lived in a rundown roost, where instead of all the home comforts, he's now shacked up in the eaves of the dusty old mill, plotted in a nest of cardboard.

"Walter, ma boy! How the devil are you old chap!" asked Owen, with a friendly tone in his hoot.

"Oh it's you, Owen? Coo, I could desperately do with a drink, old Bean. You wouldn't happen to have a wee tipple about your person, old boy, would you now?" answered the down 'n' out. After exchanging words for a while, Owen was making a last plea trying to talk Walter out of his nonsensical way of life; the wise bird knew full well he might just as well have been talking to himself. But once their little chat was over Owen then asked him where Stanley's roost could be found. The down-on-his luck pigeon told Owen that he'd find half-starved Stanley in a hole facing South, a third of the way up the huge chimney. Owen thanked him and just as he was about to head off in Stanley's direction, he noticed Walter's eyes when looking down almost sprang from their eye holes, upon spotting the old horse-drawn brewers drey pull up outside the back gates of the pub. And whilst the dreyman were unloading their delivery of mixed ales, the village drunk had spotted Alice appear from the back door carrying a couple of pints of ale for the delivery men, placing the ale on a stack of empties. Owen, who as I have mentioned was just about to leave to find the anorexic starling, couldn't help lingering for a moment to watch the ways of Walter and his sad alcoholic condition. He watched with wide eyes as the bedraggled bird fell from his roost, then glided in to where the dreymen's drinks were put. As the old Tawny looked on he saw the smelly pigeon perched on the crates sampling the dreymen's beer, and before Owen took his leave to go and find Stanley, he could have sworn he'd heard cheeky Walter, even in the state he got himself into of late, complain that the beer was a bit cloudy.

Sad as it all was, Owen knew that there was nothing he or anyone else could have done for him, for he was too far over the hill even to begin to think otherwise, so he left poor Walter to go his own heartbreaking way.

"What a waste of a good life," the old Owl thought to himself as he flew up onto the gables, then up even higher to the south facing side of the tall stack and immediately found the hole where the starling was residing. As Stanley appeared from his hole in the red brick stack, Owen landed on a narrow ledge at the side of the chimney, though Stanley must have heard him because as the owl settled, the pathetic excuse for a bird showed his skinny head at the hole's entrance and enquired what nature as brought him to his territory. Owen was slightly startled by the starling's sudden showing, and Stanley, just as surprised, then wondered what on earth had brought his old friend here to the mill. But it wasn't too many seconds before he would know.

"What can I do for you Owen?" asked the hungry-looking bird, wondering what the wise old Owl wanted in his part of the world. Once Owen had got his breath back he asked Stanley how his health had been of late, and was he getting any decent grub down himself; but the big Tawny only had to look at the dear chap to see that Stan was still bang in trouble in the lean cuisine department. In fact Stan wasn't only skinny, the dear chap was narrow-minded as well, making him a target for some of the local yokels, who always made fun out of his unfortunate predicament of this terrible slimmers' disease that he'd got himself into for not eating regularly enough; yet you'd never find a more decent fellow, even though he was a very sick, sick, bird.

"Stanley, ma boy! How the devil are you these days?" hooted Owen.

"Not... too bad, Owen, not too bad at all!" exclaimed the shrunken-faced bird. He then asked Owen if there was anything he could do to help.

"As a matter of fact there is!" smiled the wisest of all birds. "Tell me," he said, "is this the hole where you spend the cold winter months; and if so, does the heat of the chimney keep you nice and snug in the deepest of winter?" After Owen's question he sat and listened in hope that the answer he was searching for would spill from Stanley's beak.

"Absolutely! This high rise home of mine is the warmest on the plot, and apart from those sparrows, I'm about the only one around here that's got central heating. You see, Squire, there's not a lot of flesh on my old bones, so I had to hunt high and low to find a place suitable. Ok, as you can see for yourself, it's built to last, and it's as warm as toast on cold winter nights. Why do you ask?" enquired Stanley, who felt most honoured to have such an important guest come visiting at the stack. Owen went on to tell the starling about Wally, and how the little warbler was risking his own life because he blatantly refused to migrate abroad. And although the black rainbow-speckled bird had never met Wally before, he'd most certainly heard of him. And do you know? Even with his wasting illness, he was so concerned for Wally at the time he went missing, it was Stanley who had organised his very own search party to go looking for a little bird he didn't even known. And apparently his efforts didn't go un-noticed, although poor Stan after the long search, found he was too ill to attend the celebrations along with all the other good residents, when they all congregated on Coot Island the day after the warbler was found. The reason why Owen had arrived here at the Mill was because of the idea that came to him whilst trying to convince Wally to leave the country. The ageing Wizard had, during the time of giving Wal his marching orders, had recalled to his memory Stanley's fragile state, and wondered how he'd survived the cold during winters past. Owen then asked the starling if it were possible that if the winter got too severe, could Wally come up here and share the hole until spring came. Well, Wally's luck was in; at Owen's request Stanley appeared to perk up a bit and whistled, "Why, of course he can! And I'd only be too pleased, old timer!" The starving starling smiled and said again… "It's boring though, but it won't be, from what I've heard of the little character… Tell you the truth, Owen old boy, the little lad will be a god-send, and will be good company throughout the bleak mid-winter."

"Thank God for that!" exclaimed Owen with a sigh of relief, knowing now he could go back to Coot Island with some good news which had solved the erratic warbler's winter problem. Once Stanley had agreed whole-heartedly, Owen thanked him, and after another hour or so discussion on other local matters, the two birds said their goodbyes; then Owen dropped from the ledge and glided down into the mill grounds, then up over the asbestos roof to where he'd first met his potless pal Walter. He did have to laugh to himself though, as he flew past the spot where they'd chatted, his eyes were distracted below. When he looked down into the pub's yard, he saw the two dreyman chasing and aiming sticks 'n' stones at the half sozzled fleeing thief, when finding their ale glasses had been tastily tampered with. Well, although Owen might be pleased with his plan so far, yet he knew only too well that a roof over Wally's head was just half the problem. You see, just as birds of all walks, or flights, of life, unfortunately have problems in finding food during winter but, insect eaters like Wally, who refuse to go abroad, don't realise that when winter finally does arrive, there will be nothing for him to eat.

So this was the wise teacher's only problem now, though the old owl was pleased at his day's achievement. And for now Owen was more than happy in getting this first obstacle out of the way, and decided to think on it more when he got back home. Whilst Owen was on his flight back to the lakes, it had begun to get dark and he knew that most of his friends would be in their roosts at this time. He had realised there wasn't any rush back, for what he had to tell could wait until morning, so he decided he might as well hunt for his supper whilst travelling back to the lake. At day-break, when Clarence, and the two lads were awake and now emerging from their comfortable secure log Owen was there to greet them.

"Morning!" he hooted whilst perched on an old dead willow stump, that protruded from the water some yard or two form the family home. All three exchanged pleasantries, whilst at the same time the duck and Wal were looking at Owen for signs of his findings, especially Wal, who, was still terrified of being sent away to a far-off land.

"Have you any news?" asked Denzel, in the hope that Owen with his exceedingly sharp brain had come up with a solution to Wally's unwanted holiday. The duck, even without Owen opening his beak, sensed by the way the proud old codger was sitting there smiling between yawns, they could tell that he'd definitely got news of something, "Else why should he be smiling?" the duck was thinking to himself. It was a bitter, cold morning. Denzel and Clarence were having a quick wash 'n' preen up in and around the log, whilst they chatted with Owen. But the old owl had his eyes on Wally, who, wasn't making his usual attempt to wash and tidy himself up a bit. No, Wal was already feeling the difference in the dropping temperature, and this morning appeared to be a bit shy in the old washing department. The old wizard, whilst in conversation with the two bigger birds, never once took his eyes from the shivering warbler. Once the two islanders had cleaned 'n' preened, along with Wal's very sad attempt, the Owl was about to hoot, then just as he was about to start, Clara had made a show as she exited from the log's entrance, and she was just in time to hear of Owen's findings.

"Now listen to me, youngen!" he hooted to Wally, "I have been to see Stanley at the mill, and I'm very pleased to report that as long as we can find enough food to store away to support you through winter, then you, my lad, can stay here with us!" Before the old wizard had got his few words out, Wal and the rest of the company were ecstatic at the wonderful news!

"Now, before you all get too carried away, let me tell you how this will be made possible!" Owen then went on to tell them of his trip to the old mill and his meeting with Walter, he then went straight into telling them of the arrangements he'd made with the very narrow Stanley. All present apart from Wally, were quite pleased with the coming situation and were nodding 'n' chatting in full agreement, but Wal, he wasn't too sure at all, Oh, he was overjoyed at the thought of being able to stay on at the lakes all right. Yet he still wasn't very happy in having to sleep with more or less a stranger; but at least he'd heard of the starling, especially after Wal hearing of Stanley's contribution to the searching for himself throughout that dreadful storm. Wally, feeling the way he did at this particular time, was at the stage where he couldn't argue, the little lads beak had begun to click as he shivered 'n' shook, and the poor little chap still hadn't even tested the water with his tiny claws, and going by the way he was shaping up the rascal wasn't going to either. The company now including Clara, who hadn't been up and out of the roost long, could see for themselves that Wal's winter sleeping quarters hadn't come too soon, because looking at his tiny shivering body now was a very sad sight indeed, and winter hadn't properly arrived yet; but you try telling that to Wal! As it happens, Wally, after feeling his first real cold day, had realised he had made a big mistake, and knowing in his heart what lengths the Owl had gone through in trying to help him, decided at last to admit he was wrong, and chirped,

"I... I'm sorry Owen, I... just didn't want to leave Denzel, and Aunty 'n' Uncle for such a long time,, and anyway, I was scared I wouldn't find my way home in the spring! Please... Owen, please don't be angry with me!" All the while Wally was doing his best to apologise, his little head was lower than any of the company had seen in all their togetherness, and they knew that Wally was going through one of his bad turns again. Denzel, who had been looking on and listening to the Owl's and Wally's hootings 'n' chirpings, was glad now that Wally had accepted what Owen had found him (a winter roost at the old mill). It was Aunty Clara that spoke first.

"Owen, I think the sooner he's in the warm the better." As the old girl sat, folding and unfolding her wings in her worrying about Wally's welfare.

"Yes!" chimed in Denzel and Uncle Clarence almost together, nodding their heads in agreement when looking upon the shivering waif. On hearing Clara's suggestion, and seeing Denzel's and Clarence's noddings, the old Tawny spoke,

"Well it's all agreed then!"

Wally looked at them all one at a time, he was a little down, but for him he didn't seem too bad; in fact it most certainly seemed in his family's eyes, that after all his stubborn performance the little lad had come to accept it, and was now looking forward to meeting the anorexic Stanley. ('course we think the cold had a lot to do with it).

"Well, it looks like I'm going to lose another day's sleep," smiled the Owl, quite chuffed with himself. It had been easier than he expected getting Wally to go anywhere other than where he was now with his loved ones.

"So you'll go to the mill then?" asked Owen confidently.

"Er… yes," chirped Wal without any hesitation whatsoever, but he did ask… "Den, ya's will come and visit me won't ya?" And even before Wal got upset Denzel had made sure he answered first, knowing it would help Wal, before he drifted into one of his dodgy doom 'n' gloom moods.

"Ha!" laughed Clarence… "You silly thing! On mild days, there is no reason why you and Denzel, can't see one another, even if it's only for a few hours!" The male coot laughed again, then all of the company joined old Yorky in laughter, and believe it or not, so did the Dartford dodger, even though it was through his clicking beak. Owen then asked Wally… "Would you like to go and see Stanley at the mill?"

"Only… if Denzel can come with us too!" the little warbler chirped.

"You just let anyone try and stop me!" said the duck joking about, for now he could tell by Wal's change of attitude, that his bestest little mate had realised his big mistake, though now appeared to be more than grateful for what his caring family and friends had done.

"Yeah! Ok then, I'll go! But you promise you'll come and get me on milder days then, eh, Den?" chirped Wal. The caring coots couldn't believe that this was the same warbler. No, Clara, even Clarence, kept glancing at one another, so happy in themselves knowing that everything would be all right. Knowing Wal as they did, the old couple were quite surprised at the warbler's change of heart. Each of the remaining company had noticed the sudden change which seemed to have come over Wally, because instead of being in one of his low periods, because under such circumstances, he'd normally be well down in the dumps by now. But no, the whole company could most definitely detect a big change in the little Warbler, and it seemed as if, it had told them all; that Wally had at last matured. Wally had shocked the company into disbelief; they had each had visions of the most dreadful tantrums coming from Wal's quarters, and all were so relieved that not only was he going to stay with Stanley, but the little lad was going of his own free will. Denzel waddled away from the log, and the three elders headed towards the front part of their island. Wally had taken flight, and in a quick burst was at the Duck's side, perched on a low bough next to his best pal's head. He and Denzel were reminiscing over their past bird months together, (which of course are more like our years to most animals and birds) and he could even be heard by the oldens laughing 'n' joking whilst going over some of their more comical carryings-on, during the summer past.

"Hark at 'em, dear, anyone would think they were going out for one of their usual fun days, the way they're behaving at the moment!" Clara smiled.

"Aye, lass, it's far from what all of us had ever expected of the little lad that's for sure," answered her doting spouse.

The old wizard gave an interrupting cough, then hooted... "Well I think it's time, don't you?" The lovely old ageing Coots nodded their heads in agreement, but Owen, being so sharp-eyed 'n' all, had just caught sight of Clara's tears as she turned and waddled over towards their log home. Owen was about to say something to her, in the hope that it would cheer the old dear up. Then Clarence sadly spoke.

"Let her go Owen, she'll be fine in an hour or two; I do wish the lady wasn't so sensitive." Owen never answered, and decided to call the two lads, for it was time to leave for the mill. Just as Owen was about to call them, Clarence gestured with his head, then turned, and went over to the log where Clara was now sitting, just outside the entrance, brushing the few tears away from her feathered cheeks, that were beginning to dry. The wise old owl understood the situation and used an excuse, then hooted to them that he had to attend to other matters. But of course, this understanding intelligent Tawny had realised that his close friends needed some time to themselves before Wally was to leave. Clarence left him to go to Clara's aid to try and comfort her, when Owen hooted to them.

"I'll be back at noon," then took flight and left the island without further ado. It was 10 a.m. now, which gave the island family three hours to say what had to be said, before Wally headed for Stanley's stack at the old mill. Clarence had reached his lovely lady, and the pair of them were now having a little cuddle, Denzel and Wally, had had their private little beakwag, and were now coming back towards the coots. The Duck waddled and Wally flitted above him, they could both see that Aunty Clara was being comforted by Uncle Clarence. On seeing this Wally, (who incidentally would you believe was now actually looking forward to meeting this character Stanley) darted from above the duck's head, straight as ya like, to the log where his loved ones huddled 'n' cuddled. Immediately after he had landed, the little Warbler chirped...

"I'll be alright, Aunty, it's only a short way to the mill, and on fine days, Denzel can come and fetch me here to see you and Uncle Clarence at the Island!" It was Wally's confidence that helped the old dear to perk up a bit, and made her smile at the little rascal she loved so much.

"Aye, lad, but I'll miss you all the same!" she sniffed back.

"The time 'ill pass, my dear, you'll see!" comforted Clarence. Denzel was just as upset at the whole to-do but he just looked on at the scene in front of him; then an idea came to him, that he felt at the time would break the ice, as it were, then called.

"I know it's a bit late, but does anyone fancy a nice breakfast!"

"Aye, what a good idea!" exclaimed Clarence. "Come now lass," he said as he escorted her into the cold choppy water. Denzel and Wally, had earlier decided to go across the short stretch of water to the cove, where they had very first encountered the unreliable rat, Harry. It was Wal's idea, telling the duck that it would be nice just to have one last trip before he went. As they were leaving to go, they just called to let their adopted parents know where, and what, they were up to. Clara had heard their calls, but the old fella had his head well beneath the waves in search of a tasty nibble. Clara acknowledged the two lads, and carried on eating the morsel that she'd found, leaving the two of them on their own. When they reached the cove, Denzel's luck was in again; in fact there was a whole un-cut loaf of bread floating very close to the water's edge, so he made a dash for it. Wal, on the other hand, saw that his best mate was in luck, so he flew and landed at the water's edge. But instead of Wally nipping lively to one of the reed beds, or anywhere that insects were clustered in their multitudes, was now struggling to find his food. He watched Denzel approach the huge crusty loaf with caution, and seeing the duck happy he began to skitter about the dead leaves and foliage, not leaving a leaf unturned, finding the odd chrysalis, or larva that helped fill his little belly up. He'd only been hunting and feeding a minute or two, when he heard the Duck's surprised quacks.

"Agh…!" As Wal looked up he saw the bald-headed rat prancing about on top of the crusty bread that Denzel had found. He saw that Denzel had calmed down now he knew exactly what had made him jump.

"Harry, y… you, frightened the flipping life out of me, I do wish you wouldn't keep doing that!" he retorted.

"Well, I was here first!" snapped the rat through his even dodgier pair of yellow front teeth.

"Well I can't argue with that," agreed the duck, "though I must say, there's enough food here to feed the whole lake!" What the Duck had said couldn't have given Harry a better cue for his following statement.

"See ya's didn't believe me, did ya's! You and that Dartfordite, Wally, when I told ya's I own loads 'n' loads of grub!" bragged the skinny rodent.

"Yes!" said Denzel, "but you told us that you had thousands of crusts, so if what you say is true, where on water are they?"

"Some of 'em I'm sitting on right now!" boasted the rat.

"But this is a whole loaf of bread!" retorted the duck, "and in any case you said you had crusts only!" Denzel stared at the rat questioningly, thinking that would stop Harry's brags 'n' boasts, when old H came back with a blinder.

"Yeah, well… I stuck 'em all together, didn't I!" retorted the Rat, with one of his little white ones. Denzel, after a few moments of swimming round and round the crusty loaf, had seen where the scrawny rat had come from. He had noticed that Harry had eaten his way through to the inside of the bread, but little did the duck know that H had used his loaf all right. He'd eaten the entire contents leaving just the surrounding crust, so when the Duck tried to sink his bill into the huge loaf, to his surprise it went straight through. Leaving Harry, who was still balancing on the bread, to have a little giggle at Denzel's expense. Until the Duck's bill got stuck in the loaf, that is. Denzel tried to pull his bill from the bread, and Harry unexpectedly was sent into the air in a double somersault, shutting him up altogether.

Whilst all this was happening Wally had met with Victor, the three legged vole. They were passing the time of day, when the Vole told Wal he was for the high-jump when he got home, because he hadn't been home all night. Whilst in conversation, both had witnessed the plight of the wrinkled rat, who had gone overboard and was now attempting to climb back on his bread raft, and the two witnesses were in a state of extreme laughter. Denzel was laughing too, especially when the rat had first surfaced all spluttering and out of breath, only to hear them all in uncontrollable roars of laughter. He was so embarrassed he clambered back up onto the shell that was left, and disappeared inside the entrance he'd made.

Denzel, after looking about the cove, had found ample food and had now joined Wal and the vole for a natter. The two lads had met Victor in passing way back in the early summer. He had asked about the two lads' welfare, and they told him how this was Wally's last day of the season, and that he was going to stay with Stanley over at the mill. Victor knew Stanley quite well and told them that he was a real genuine character. He also told them that he was too good-hearted, and the real reason he's so skinny was because the silly fool kept giving everything away. Whilst Vic was saying his piece, Denzel couldn't take his eyes off the Vole's missing left front leg. Then out of the blue he asked the question.

"Victor, how did you manage to lose your left leg?" The Vole went on to tell them that one day, back in the early summer of 1963, he had been out hunting for food when he came across a fish that was jumping and wriggling on the bank of the lakes.

"Talk about a fish out of water, it was thrashing and bashing, and then came crashing to the water's edge, and that's when I went to investigate. It happened so suddenly! Just as I was about to get to grips with the monster fish to try and roll it back in the water, the bleeder struck!"

"Who did?" chirped Wally, in anticipation.

"Cornelius the Cormorant. The blighter came from nowhere. I was only going to help, when I found myself roughly handled by the huge bill that had come from behind, and before I realised what had happened, my front leg got ripped off; and what made it even worse, when Connie realised what he'd done, he'd dropped me leg in the lake, and still flew off with the fish! Course it left me three-standing, and one away, and that was bloomin' floating on the water's choppy waves."

"Cor, it must have half hurt!" chirped Wal. Whilst he and Denzel were listening to Victor's tale, each of them was pulling all sorts of faces at some of the dodgy sounding bits.

"Ooh!" Denzel shuddered, "It really must have hurt you when it first happened!"

"Hurt?" retorted the Vole... "It flippin' nigh killed me! I was hobbling all about the place for near on three months, but I've got used to it now, and sometimes when folk around here make fun in asking what I do for kicks, I just tell 'em straight, I use the other three." He chuckled. "Oh it don't stop me enjoying my life at all!" I don't suppose it does, because Victor the Vole, had his voluptuous lady Doll who was extremely plump, or well-rounded as some might say, but all in all, a good-natured soul, but very volatile, yet the girl had a heart of gold, and her amputee husband absolutely idolised her.

It's funny how it turned out; Victor, when first ever meeting Doll, wasn't really interested in females at all, but once Doll scurried into his life, poor Victor never had a leg to stand on. The dear chap was roped 'n' tied, even before he could shake his long whiskers; but now of course Victor and the love of his life, his sweet plump wife, whom he calls his dumpling Doll were inseparable. You see what had really happened regarding his missing leg. Apparently according to Owen the wise, what had really occurred was this; Connie had caught the fish, and had taken flight with his catch in his bill, when the fish had wriggled free and fallen from the sky landing on a piece of ground at the water's edge, just at the precise moment when Victor was passing in search of food. The Vole didn't even like fish, but he went to investigate the fallen still wriggling creature, and that was when the Cormerant struck. Yet to see this handicapped Vole's scurrys 'n' hurrys about the place these days, you would never know he was disabled. However, he and his family got on very nicely with the rest of the Horton Kirby dwellers. Yet for a while after his misfortune in losing his leg, he always kept an eye out for the Cormerant, but on second thoughts put it away in case the greedy thing came by and ate that an' all. Now this three legged Vole and his plump wife Doll, had a litter that was three months old. She had loved him at first sight, even with her choice's plight, when first meeting in a deep dark hole. They had settled down nicely living in their hole under the bank for the last couple of lake-years, this last litter being the third. Oh yes-even with Victor's stump the old chap was still active, and went about the Lakes accordingly, doing his bits 'n' bobs, anything just to make ends meet. Cornelius on the otherhand, according to that very wise Owl, was a bit of a liberty taker when it came to partaking in a bit of tucker. Because Cormerants, when it comes to a bit of grub, would eat huge amounts of food as long as it was fish shaped. Even Denzel recalled, after witnessing one of his divings 'n' dippings in his bid to secure a daily dish of wriggling fish, which at times were as big as himself. In some cases this greedy long black necked fish-nabber would emerge from the water with a fish as big as his own head, and the best part of the glutton's long lean neck, which reminded the Duck of what Owen had taught Wally and himself of the food-chain of life. But Denzel, after watching Connie's gulping 'n' pulping in the old eating department, took umbrage at this greedy big bird who was taking far more food than nature intended. He recalled the wizard's wise words: 'That nature's way is for all of us to only take what's needed, no more. That way there will be enough for us all'. Time had passed and Denzel informed Wally that it was time to return to Coot Island because it was nearing the time for Wally to leave for Stanley's residence over at the mill. After saying their respective goodbyes, Victor excused himself and ambled his way along the bank on his way home to get a volley from Dolly for staying out all night.

The two lads had been back on the land about twenty minutes when Owen at last returned. He smiled a pleasing smile when seeing Wally happy enough saying his farewells to his adopted parents. Ever since Owen said Wally could stay here at the lake, the little fella appeared to forget all his earlier shivering, and was now full of himself, and to all the company's amazement he seemed quite keen to go.

"Are you ready to go to the mill?" hooted Owen.

"I suppose so!" chirped Wally, his eyes darting to each of his loved ones in turn. At any moment now, the three grown-ups, and most certainly Denzel, were expecting the little chap to fall into one of his dodgy turns, but no, to the company's surprise Wal still held himself together marvellously, and Clara whispered to her hubby how Wal had definitely got his act together in the growing-up stakes. Well it was time to leave. Denzel had made himself ready to go, Wal was just receiving a last peck on the cheek from Aunty Clara, and old Owen hooted,

"Come along, young Wally, let's get you to the mill and the warmth of Stanley's stack!" Denzel was just about to tell Wally to get on his back ready for the short journey to the mill when all of a sudden, a loud bang made all the company stoop their necks in shock at the sound of a firestick that came from part of the mainland that is the nearest to their island, quite close to the place where Owen miscalculated the lost warbler the morning after the storm. Owen immediately flew up to the higher branch to investigate further. He had just settled when he began to shake his old head in disgust, for only a week or two ago, a similar shot rang out leaving a cock Corncrake heartbroken at losing his lovely wife to the ill ways of man.

But alas, now he too had been taken by the same means. In the few moments he watched, the old Owl pondered on his thoughts. He remembered only too well that whilst comforting him when his wife was killed, just what the sad old bird had sobbed to him, saying, 'Now that she was dead, he had nothing to live for anymore!' And here, only a matter of days later, Owen was watching a recurrence in the male Corncrake's death. Owen who was now joined by Wally in the highest branches on the Island to see what was going on, leaving Denzel and the caring Coots on the ground.

"Is anyone hurt?" chirped Wal as he settled beside the Owl, but he never needed to be told, for now he could see for himself of the Corncrake's outcome. "He's nothing but a rotten murderer!" he retorted "That's two he's killed in as many weeks!"

"Yes…! He's what folk around here call a serial killer!"

"A serial killer," Wal said "Why do they call him that, then?"

"Well, it appears our murderer eats corncrakes for breakfast."

Soon after this heartbreaking incident, all cheerios had been done and the three birds had reached the grounds of the Horton Kirby paper mill, where they had seen Stanley just picking at his food out of one of the humans dustbins. Stanley had seen the trio land on some grass just below the bin where he was sat, and joined them immediately not wanting another second to pass before meeting the new flat-mate he'd heard so much about, and of course he was pleased to meet Denzel for the second time, after the first meeting to organise the starlings search party on that awful stormy night a few months earlier.

"So you made it then!" whistled the half starved Starling.

Owen winked before he hooted, letting Stanley know Wal was as sound as a pound, as far as moving in was concerned.

"Yes, and Wally here cannot wait to meet you, isn't that so, young Wally?"

"Er… yes," chirped Wally sharply, but feeling a little agitated at having to live with some bird he'd never met before, even though he knew he was as safe with Stanley as he would be with any of his closest friends.

The introductions were made there and then on that lawn below the dustbin, where Wal, on first seeing Stanley, told Owen and Denzel that he liked what he saw in his new flat-mate, and could tell straight away that they would get on like a stack on fire.

"Smoke 'n' all, I shouldn't wonder, knowing these two like I do!" thought the Owl to himself. Once they had made each other's acquaintance and a few laughs were had by all, it was time not only for Stanley to show Wally his winter saviour; his heated home, or stately stack, which the Starling prefers to call it. It was also time for Owen and Stanley to get their heads together and think of a way to find the little Warbler's food supply throughout the severest of winter months. Stanley told them that when Owen had first gone to the stack to see him about Wally's plight, as soon as the old Tawny had left to return to the Lakes, the half starved Starling, had also realised and wondered what Wal could possibly find to eat once the big freeze came.

So Stanley never wasted a moment; his sharp thinking told him to go out and search for any possibilities that may prove fruitful, to keep the small bird alive. That's our Stanley for you although he can't be bothered searching for food, or eating much himself yet, it seems he'll go out of his way to help others. So when Owen mentioned it first, Stanley's face had a big grin come over it, and then he broke the wonderful news that made Wal's stay more probable, and more importantly, he had even more chance of survival. Stanley went on to say,

"When you left me the other day, Owen, when I agreed to let young Wally there stay at the stack I, like yourself, gave the matter a lot of thought, and realising that the shelter side of it was only half of your problem Well, hopefully we needn't worry too much on that score, because I have checked out every building around here from loft to cellar, and there's enough larvae and things to keep you in winter that's for sure! In any case," smiled Stanley, "there's a herd of gipsy horses in a field up aways, and when I used to have a proper appetite, me and me pals used to peck the fleas from behind the horse's ears, so he won't go short of grub; oh no, not all the while I'm about, at any rate!" he proudly boasted; not that Stanley was a boastful sort of chap mind, he was just kind of pleased with his contribution that's all. Denzel, Owen and Wally listened to the starling not wanting to interrupt, for so far everything Stanley had spoken about sounded more than good, and the happy listeners were smiling and shaking their heads and nodding at all of Stanley's conversation regarding Wal's food supply for the coming winter; and Stanley could tell by all the cheerful smiling faces just how pleased they all were.

"Well, Stanley ma boy, we are all thankful for the help you have given, but my advice to you, is whilst you're about helping young Wally here, that you force if you have to, a nibble or two down that scrag-end of a neck of yours, or else you won't be helping anyone. And if last year's weather is anything to go by, we'll all be lucky to survive!" hooted Owen the wise, just letting Wally know that it still wouldn't all be rosy in the months to come.

"Shall we go and see your new home, Wal?" asked Denzel.

"Hold on now, young Denzel! looking at you, my son, there is not a chance, no chance at all!" whistled Stanley.

Denzel for a moment had thought, going by the way the starling sounded, that he had said something wrong, but Stanley soon put the duck at ease. It was then the skinny starling spoke.

"As Owen will confirm, there is no place up there for a bird of your size, especially with webbed feet, it just isn't possible!"

"Oh," said Denzel, "I guess we'll have to say our goodbyes here then!" The duck was beginning to get butterflies in his belly at the thought of leaving Wally behind, and he could tell Wal felt the same. Yet the duck, as well as Owen, could plainly see that Wal wasn't too bad at all under the strain, and seemed reasonably happy in the situation he now faced. Wally in fact told his two pals quite cheerfully,

"I'll be all right, Den, and thank you Owen for helping me find a warm place to live. Give my love to Aunty and Uncle, and tell 'em I'll be seeing them soon when the weather gets milder!" In the last few words that Wally chirped, Denzel and the two older males had noticed Wal's little beak start to quiver, so Owen quickly put his hoot in.

"Well we'll be going now youngen!" said Owen, giving Denzel and the half-starved Stan a sly wink. "Come along, Denzel."

And the owl took to the sky and flew in the direction of the lakes. As the two pals went out of sight, Stanley had taken charge immediately.

"Well I reckon it's time to have a look at your new abode, Wally me boy, don't you, eh?" Wally of a sudden had gone a little quiet, but did manage with lowered eyes to nod a 'yes'. The pair of them took to the air and flew upwards and off in the direction of the mills huge chimney stack some fifty yards away. When they had reached it Wally followed Stanley around the south facing side, where the Starling came to rest on the same narrow ledge that the Owl found difficult to get comfortable on when speaking to the anorexic Stanley outside his hole just a few days previously. Wally was now perched on the brick-work right outside the hole when Stanley disappeared inside the hole, and in a flash his head was protruding again

"Well, come on then, Wal, don't be frightened of me, young fella!" With this invite Wally thought to himself,

"Oh well, in for spider, in for a bug!" and the little chappie hopped inside. He swallowed as he followed his flat-mate, skittering close on the starling's spurs, around and around they went until they came to the Starling's very untidy nest, but although it was pitch black, after a while Wal could make out a piece of twig had been wedged from the cavity wall across to the outer skin, just a few inches from Stanley's nest area. Wally hopped up onto the perch that the starling had put in for him, and Stanley asked Wally if it was suitable for his needs, and with the warmth that Wal could now feel all about him he nodded a silent 'yes'. Although Stanley told the islanders when next meeting them, that Wal never chirped at all for the first half 'n' hour but,

"Gawd help us, I haven't been able to get a word in edgeways since." But the bird with the narrow nut, openly admitted that the little fella did cheer him up.

Wally, as we can all see, appeared to have settled down at Stanley's stack for the cold season. It was late October now, and following an unusually chilly night's sleep, Denzel clambered out of the old log that he had been sharing with their ageing adopted parents ever since the night of the storm, which had almost robbed the little warbler of his life. The moment Denzel's eyes opened to the day outside the youngster could hardly believe what he saw; his eyes seemed to spring from their sockets. The lake had a thick layer of ice over it. The duck hadn't realised when he left the log to go outside, that he hadn't noticed Uncle Clarence, who'd been out and about, twenty five minutes earlier, appeared to be standing on water. The young Duck was dumbfounded, for in his short life he had never ever seen such a shimmering sight, and couldn't wait another moment to get over to where the old coot was standing.

"What is it, Uncle? What has happened?" asked the confused Duck in a total state of shock, as he stepped from the log's end to the icy surface below.

"Oopsy-a-daisy, lad!" called the old boy as the duck's legs slid from beneath him causing him to topple onto his rump. He was trying to find his feet, but kept on slipping back down again.

"I... c... can't get up Uncle," he said extremely puzzled at the whole to-do. The old stager, on seeing Denzel's mishap, half walked, half slid, to Denzel's aid. He was laughing as he slid and skidded. Clarence put his old head and neck under the duck's rump, so's to help get Denzel to stand on his own two feet, much the same as he did on their first-ever trip to the river. Once the duck had found his feet, he and Clarence made their way just a yard or so onto the land of Coot Island. As they were stood on the ice talking, Clarence was about to tell Denzel of nature's weather ways. The Yorkshire coot began to explain all about the four seasons, and of the different temperatures and how extreme cold had turned the water into the state it was now in. He then carried on telling him of the coming snow, and how Owen was right in giving Wally a dressing-down when the little rascal had earlier refused to migrate in the first instance. Denzel had never seen the old Owl lose his temper so swiftly on hearing Wal's stupid decision. For Clarence knew the old wizard, some weeks earlier, had already tried to persuade the little lad by telling him of the harsh conditions, which each and every year brought death to a multitude of frail-built birds, which are not adapted for such severe temperatures. The duck was shivering just listening to Uncle's grim warning, let alone the funny frozen water that he and Clarence were staring at now. Well, until their eyes were distracted that is. After the two birds had taken second sight, they saw a female stork that was passing by, striding on her long spindly legs. The dear girl accidentally did the splits, causing the rest of her to come crashing to the ice in a loud painful bump, knocking the wind right out of her. Both males immediately attempted to race to the poor unfortunate lady's aid, but as they did, they slipped 'n' slid, till they reached the well spread stork. She was splayed on the ice and they saw in a trice that the poor girl couldn't talk, for the stuffing had been knocked right out of her as she lay there with her well-spread pins; but as she raised her head to greet their help, she noticed the two wide grins. Now, the two big birds, gentlebirds as they were, went over and began to help the long lady to her feet, which took some doing, I mean, do you know how far that girl's feet were from her body? Well, going by the rat's account it was six feet, but I doubt that very much, knowing him as we do. As the two helpers were helping longshanks to her feet, the dear girl couldn't thank them enough, and after much effort they finally managed to get the stork on a firmer footing. And once they had got her up, Denzel had introduced Clarence and himself, and then asked her name, and what part of the world she came from.

"Marge!" spoke the female, adjusting her stance.

"Ha, ha, ha!" laughed Denzel, now making his way back to the warmth of their log home, the very same one that Clara was still squatting in, (though the sweet lady didn't like the winters at all, only venturing out to feed, for her old bones couldn't take it, any more) Denzel couldn't help laughing at the stork's name, when first hearing it moments before.

"Aye, lass, with a name like that, no wonder you slipped!" Clarence the comedian appeared to be trying to butter Marge up with his slippery bit of Yorkshire humour at the same time. Yet as far as Denzel was concerned ice, or not, he much preferred on such chilly days, to be tucked up in the old log, listening to one of Aunty's fairy stories; and after making sure that Marge was ok, that's exactly what he and Clarence did, and on such a cold 'n' frosty day the ageing female happily obliged.

Well, due to the time of year there wasn't much activity going on around the lakes, but sometime in early November, something that recurs at the same time each year, happened soon after dark, and most of the residents on the plot were in a state of turmoil. For once it had got dark, every few minutes the sky would light up and the bangs 'n' flashes were seen and heard, leaving every living creature terrified. That made them believe it had something to do with the firestick of man, that had caused so much devastation. Even Treadwell, who knew quite a lot of man's ways, couldn't explain it, for the dear chap was always asleep at this time of year. And when you think of all the knowledge that the old Owl had stored up in his big round head of his, yet even he was clueless about the spectacle that man appeared to have each and every year. Of course to the human's it's Guy Fawkes night, which is loved by the youngsters of man. Yet to the animal world it's an absolute nightmare, especially the huge fire that raged at Crank's Hall where Peregrine's daughters were home from boarding school and were sharing with friends a celebration in the grounds of the Hall, although the youngest, Leah Marie, was much like the animals and didn't really care for all the rockets zooming 'n' booming in the night sky. Yet Catherine-oh she loved all the excitement, and when they were asked by their father if they were ready to join their friends down at the roaring bonfire, Leah told him.

"I don't want to go to the fire, Daddy," then added... "But Catherine will!"

Denzel, old Clarence and Aunty Clara, whilst sitting inside their log home, had heard the first fireworks exploding, and the inevitable question was nervously asked by the youngster.

"W... what is that noise, Uncle?" The duck was ruffling his feathers as he said it.

"To be very truthful with ya, lad, we just don't know a thing. All we can tell you is that it's one of man's strange carryings-on, and that's all we know lad. Whilst the old male was telling Denzel the little he knew on the matter, Clara just sat listening to her hubby's advice, and was shaking and nodding her head at Denzel at what her spouse was saying until old Clarence's next words... "Would you like to go out and see for yourself?"

"Oh yes please, Uncle, could we, please?" answered the coming-of-age duck, who was so willing to learn as much as he possibly could of the ways of the world.

"That's it!" I knew it, Clara wasn't too happy at all, and she started to cuss 'n' fuss at her old spouse's ridiculous suggestion, and as usual tried to put her big lobbed foot down. But even with all her moanings 'n' groaning Clarence wasn't having any of it, and after calming her down, the two males left her in the safety and warmth of their old hollowed log. Once outside in the pitch black night, the two birds sat on top of their home and stared into the darkened sky. It was only a matter of moments before Denzel had got his first glimpse at the distant coloured display that was erupting everywhere they looked.

"Well, laddie, do you like what you see?" They were looking at a huge bonfire, over in the direction of Crank's Hall.

"It looks quite pretty from a distance, but I most certainly don't like those big bangs. It reminds me too much of all the slaughtering that's gone on around here!" As Denzel expressed this he and Clarence witnessed something known to man as a rocket blaze through the blackened night sky resulting in the most wonderful display of colour, then an explosive loud bang, which was enough to send Denzel and the old boy running for cover.

At the very same instant over at the mill, Stanley was doing likewise, showing Wally the same spectacle, which was by far a better view than that of Clarence and Denzel; but once the dear Wal heard that biggest of bangs, which rang out from the village close by, he was back in that hole like a shot, and if you mob think he's had knee knocking trouble before, then you had better read on, for our Wal was in and up on his perch treble lively, absolutely flitting himself. And when the subject was brought up at a later date, it was said that Stanley the half-starved starling, had had an 'elluva job to calm the warbler down. The following morning Stanley was up and out of his roost at the crack of dawn. He had woken up early by the smell of the day outside; he knew by what he'd smelt that it was going to be another gorgeous mild day for the time of year. He sat on his usual place on the ledge for a few moments when he heard a small muffled sound coming from his hole by his side. All of a sudden Wal's tiny nut poked out from the hole. As Stanley sat silently watching the little fella's head, he noticed it turn right, then a sharp left staring straight into the eyes of his anorexic landlord.

"Is it all right to come out?" chirped Wally. "There isn't going to be any more of them big bangs, is there?"

"Not until the same time next year, that's for sure!" exclaimed the Starling. "You can come out now, Wally boy, it's a lovely morning, and you've nothing to be afraid of!"

"Yeah... it's nice, innit!" the little lodger chirped, as he popped out double lively to join Stanley on the ledge.

"Do you fancy nipping over to the island to see your family?" suggested Stanley.

"Oh, can we, please, can we!" insisted Wally.

"Of course, Wally me boy, as long as we get going soon, so's we're back by sundown!"

"Come on then, let's go!" chirped Wal excitedly.

"But what about breakfast?" Stanley asked.

"Er… well, we'll eat it when we get back!" chirped cheeky chappy, so eager now at the starling's suggestion. Wally obviously didn't realise he'd be needing to stoke up to go on an even short journey, especially at that time of year.

"No Wally, you must always eat before a journey, no matter how far it may be. Now, I'll tell you what we'll do; if you eat just a couple of those crispy chrysalises that I found you yesterday, ok. Then we can fly to the island to get Denzel, and old Clarence if he fancies a day out, and we can all nip up to that pasture up aways, to where those gipsy horses graze. Oh, oh…!" the Starling laughed… "And I'll knick a few nits from behind the bugger's earhole!" As the starling spoke, Wally was a-nodding away 'n' smiling; he was agreeing and hanging on every word that Stanley whistled.

"What, live food? Cor, lovely lovely!" chirped Wal savouring his tiny taste buds whilst munching on a few encased creepy crawlies that Stanley had plundered for him the day before. The little warbler, now that it was mentioned, was looking forward to eating a bit of live grub. (I suppose in human terms, it would be like eating a hot meal gone cold. I mean it's not the same is it?) Back on Coot Island, the residents were out 'n' about, making the most of and enjoying the much milder weather. Most mornings Denzel would talk to his adopted mum 'n' dad, and the topic was mostly of how he was bored, or how he couldn't wait for the coming spring; but mostly, a hour never went by when he didn't wish he could go and see the little pal he missed so much; just as he did at this very moment… when out of nowhere the little chappy, and of course Stanley, appeared in the treetops above the Islander's heads. It was Clarence who first spotted the pair of 'em.

"Well, I'll be blowed!" the old boy spoke aloud, which attracted both Clara's and Denzel's attention, Denzel really and truly couldn't believe his own eyes.

"It's Wally!" cried out a very cheered-up lady, satisfying herself at the sight of the little one; and it was plain to see that Stanley, true to his word, had surely kept his promise in keeping the little one in food.

"I don't believe it, I just can't believe it!" exclaimed the duck in startled surprise at the sight of his best mate perched up there as real as ya like; and at his side was a good, but very pathetic-looking Starling. Well, was this a reunion! Everyone was so happy enjoying themselves, in sharing one another's stories and odd bits of local gossip, about all the funny-goings on about the place. Muchmerry making was had by them all before the two lads and Stanley left the island to make their way overland to the pastures further afield, where a dozen or so gypsy's horses were kept for grazing, when not doing their usual task of pulling the homes of their owners along the roads that man had built. Stanley and the two lads left the Island at 12.30 p.m. on their way to the pasture that the starling had told them about. They followed him and flew out of the lake area across a couple of fields, and as they approached the next, there were some shabby-looking horses grazing. Denzel, on descent, glided in and landed a few yards away from the nearest, which was a small black 'n' white (piedbald) pony. Wally had found and settled close by on a fat chestnut fence post next to his landlord Stanley, who had taken up position on the barbed wire that was stretched from post to post, and enclosed the whole field.

"There they are, Wally me boy, you stay here and I'll nip over and have a word with Levy, he's that big stallion over there." Stanley pointed his sharp beak in the direction of a huge black horse... "He's the boss out of this lot!" he whispered. When the three birds arrived it attracted the attention of the whole herd, who were now with heads turned, looking at their visitors and talking among themselves in their own tongue.

These horses were good friends with the starling, for he had given them service in the delousing department for the past two years.

It all began the very first day they were put into that field. Apparently what had occurred, was one day Stanley was out and about on the plot, when he had come across these horses playing and fooling around excitedly. Why they were like this was because they had just been put out to rest and graze at their own leisure, after spending months on the road, slogging their guts out pulling the heavy homes of their human gypsy masters. It was a couple of summers back when they first arrived, and that was when the starling, who incidentally had a bit more meat on his frame then, had flown up onto Levy's haunches, marched straight up the horse's spine till he reached his right ear, when out of the blue the horse spoke to him and asked if he could do him and his pals a big favour. And when he asked what this favour was, the stallion went on to tell him about the fleas had been creating havoc behind his earhole, and were running amok, which was driving him and the rest of his pony pals crackers, and that's when he asked Stanley if he would peck 'em out to ease the itch that drove them mad. Ever since that day Stanley had obliged, and had been delousing the lot of 'em regularly.

"Dickeye (look) it's our nit-pickin' Stanley, and it looks like he's brought a couple ov chavvies wiv im!" exclaimed Nelson, the retired one eyed pit pony, who had just gone through a bad patch. The starling left Denzel and Wally's side and flew up onto Levy's back, and whistled in the big black horse's ear.

"Watcher, mate, how's it going then!"

"Not too bad, moosh; 'n' how's ya-self, and who's the couple ov mooches wiv ya then?" replied the tall handsome Levy, almost in one breath.

"Oh, I'm fine thank you, Levy, and as for my two associates, they're as sweet as a nut," whistled Stanley as he walked up onto the horse's long lean neck, coming to rest just behind his left ear. The starling began to explain about the little warbler's situation, and the reason he was here at an unusual time of the year, because usually he only did the delousing during the summer months when the nits, like most living things, thrive, causing much itching among the friendly grys. (Horse's in gypsy lingo.) These horses got on every well with Stanley, for he did a great job in getting rid of the dreaded itch that made life very uncomfortable if left on board to multiply.

"Have as many as ya like, my old bruvver," whinnied Levy smiling, and Stanley got stuck in without being told twice, and the starling pecked away, sending Levy into seventh heaven. Whilst Stan was in the throes of scratching that annoying itch, Denzel and Wal, couldn't believe the way Stanley was so high up on his horse, and was getting away with it. 'Course the two lads didn't realise that their buddy not only had full permission to do what he was doing, but was adored by them all for doing it. Stan in seconds found a right cluster of lively lice and immediately began to peck away at the fleeing fleas, and in no time at all had filled his beak with enough food for a little starter for Wal. He flew to where Denzel and Wally waited for him at the foot of an old oak tree some twenty feet away. He gave them to his little friend and returned to Levy's other ear and began to peck again.

"Oh, that's cushty, bruv!" Then he asked Stanley to move his beak up half inch… "Ooh, that's it, umm, just to the left a bit Stan; ooh, lovely that is, my old chavvie!" Watching this performance, apart from Denzel and Wally were of course the rest of the herd; when all of a sudden, some of the other horses started complaining that Levy was getting all the treatment, and that they wanted a bit of attention also.

"Lordy, dordy, my dear Levy, ain' it time you let one of us have a go?" said Bubbles the bay gelding, a retired trotting horse that it's owners loved and never had the heart of sending him to the knackers yard so he could end his day peacefully.

"Your turn 'ill come, fella," said the stallion, and then whispering, "Up a little bit!" to Stanley's scratchings 'n' scratchings. "Um… That's it my old moosh, lovely, that is!"

Whilst Wal was eating his fill of fat fleas, Denzel was watching and listening to Stanley and the stallion. He just couldn't even begin to understand the queer lingo coming from the old age traveller, let alone their enjoying letting the startling nibble at the rear of his ear. He had also noticed the other gipsy nags were saying things to the big black horse, but Denzel for the life of him couldn't understand this strange tongue. Whoever the horses were, he could tell that they were good hard working folk who at this time were enjoying a rest from the road (especially after pulling heavy waggons all over the country during the summer months).

"Levy, don't be greedy bruv, let one of us have a go, my old chavvie!" exclaimed Sammy the retired circus horse, who was put out to graze for the rest of his days; and although he was getting on in years, he could still manage to run rings around the rest of the herd, except for one that is; this being the horse Denzel had noticed alone at the far end of the paddock. When asking Stanley the reason, he told the duck, that he preferred to keep his own counsel.

Now the horse in question was the most pitiful sight you'd ever seen; bones sticking out everywhere, a dip in the middle of his back, so low, that it made him look like it was a reversed camel's hump, sagging between his leg; half of his teeth missing. His two back legs had hooves so worn down at the outsides, that the village blacksmith hadn't been able to nail a set of shoes on him for a decade. So, what with his bowed legs, dipped back, and dodgy Hampsteads (teeth in toad's cockney lingo) no wonder the old chap was down on his hooves. Stanley had collected enough fleas to fill the little warbler's belly, and when the little fella had eaten his fill, Denzel asked Stanley to take him and Wally down to the bottom of the paddock to see the sad looking nag. Stanley had only been too pleased to introduce the two lads to the horses, and whilst Denzel was asking, the starling glanced up to look at the old horse at the bottom end of the field.

"Well, to tell you two the honest truth, they tell me he don't like visitors much, that's why he's always on his own. Apparently the trouble started when he first came to these parts, he kept wanting to be treated better than all the rest, saying that he was a star. If you asked me, I'd say he's off his head."

"A blimin' star! So he's fell out of the sky then!" chirped Wal, not understanding which kind of star Stanley meant. No one laughed because none of 'em did, neither. Nelson had overheard the duck's earlier request, and said to Stanley...

"Bruv, let me take the two minors down ta see the old gry. Be fair moosh, I mean ta say, I am used to 'em, more 'n' any ov us here."

"Can I have a ride on your big back then?" chirped Wally to the parading pit pony coming towards him and Denzel. Nelson laughed at the little fella's antics, and told him to fly up on board and they made their way down to where the old nag was standing. Denzel made their own way, and at a much closer range the two youngens could see for themselves that the poor thing was in an even worse state than they had first thought; he had lumps poking out everywhere. In fact it was a toss-up who was bang in trouble the most; him, or the nit-picking anorexic Stanley. The old nag saw the three of them; when all of a sudden…

"Hello, is it all right if we come over for a chat?" called Denzel. The nag lifted his head, and raised his eyes in their direction, so's they could see his drawn haggard face. Not even Nelson in all the time he'd been in that field had ever really looked upon the old horse as close as he was now, and said to his little friends…

"Have a gander at 'im, there's ever a tidy-looking mooey on the poor old chavvy. It's enough to trash a ghost to death!"

"That was a bit below the shalves, wasn't it Nelson? No need for any of that, around here!" interrupted Bunkhouse Bill, an ex-guards horse. Bill, a few years ago, had been purchase by its gipsy owner. When retiring from his duty on Horse Guards Parade up at the Palace. Although over the past five years, since joining the gipsy contingent, he had managed to keep up appearances, after five years on the road as an old age traveller, it was inevitable that, living with the Romanies, he was bound to pick up the odd bit of their lingo.

"I was only joking wiv 'im, Billy Boy…" Nelson was, of course, fibbing, cause Bunkhouse was no fool and he knew the old forty niner was making fun at the old bang-in-trouble nag's expense. What had happened once Nelson and the two lads had made their way down to the field to the nag, Stanley and the rest of the herd had sauntered down and were now in a group close by. It was when they got within earshot of Nelson's harsh words and mickey-taking, that Bunkhouse was prompted to intervene. You see, if Bill hadn't been proper shrewd when he first came to this pasture, he too could have been sent to Coventry like the old nag, but he kept his past life at the Palace mainly to himself, because he just knew that these gipsies, who never really understood his old way of life, just wouldn't believe a word he said, unlike the nag, who'd made the mistake of boasting that he was a star, and found himself laughed out of the company. I mean, it wouldn't have gone down well if the old chap had started banding it about that his best pal was Sefton, now would it? (Sefton being of course Queen Elizabeth's favourite horse.)

After Denzel had spoken, the old nag nodded yes, so the duck and friends moved a bit closer, Denzel asked the sagging nag, what he meant by saying he was a star. All of a sudden, the old nag raised his head proudly, well, as proudly as he could, and went into a right old acting performance…

"Friends, Romans, and Countrymen… I have come to bury Caesar, not to praise him!" Then the old nag fell silent for a brief moment, then raised his head again and chanted… "I was an ac… tor, my dear, dear, child, and none of this lot have the intelligence really to understand just how important I was, even to them there human. Now they… used to love my performance, oh yes, they really know a born actor when they saw one!"

"Actor? What is an actor?" asked Denzel, who was just as confused as anyone of the remaining company. As the duck had asked his questions, he began to look at the nag for an answer first, then looked at each individual in turn, but none showed any signs of knowing. It was obvious that the old nag could have tried to explain, but in his own mind knew it would be a pointless trying to explain his past trade. He told Denzel, "It'll be easier trying to take a drink with a feed bag over me chops, than it would trying to make this ignorant lot understand my importance in the acting world I have retired from!"

"More like the back half ov a pantomime horse!" chuckled Nelson, causing the rest of the gypsies' horses to roar with laughter. But again, they didn't have a clue to what even Nelson had comically said. Of course they didn't know, although they knew that the pit pony had for years, since retiring from going down the deep dark coal mines, in recent years, been on the rounds delivering coal to the human homes around Canterbury; and most days it was nothing for the pony to pull two tons of coal from the Bettshanger colliery. It was at this point in his life that, one day, his owner had driven him to the side of a Canterbury theatre where he was tied up outside, and whilst he was there he peered into a side window, where he happened to see some rehearsals in progress of a coming pantomime. Apparently it was whilst being nosey he had seen a horse prancing about on stage. That was when, the dear old chap told the others, the first and only time, he'd actually fallen in love. Well, until two days later that is, according to the story told to me by an old retired coalman, the very same one, who had originally sold Nelson to a gypsy horse dealer. The story goes that when he came by a rubbish tip, there, on the scrap heap, was the pantomime horse in two sad halves. Of course, as you can imagine, he was a very confused gg, and it was mentioned later that he was a bit broken-up over the whole affair. But after being told what it really was, he put it down to being down the coal-mine in total darkness for too many years, which makes his eyes go the way they do.

"So what is your name, then?" Wally asked the old nag. The old run-down horse, who was still insisting that he was some kind of star, at last answered the little warbler's question. The old actor lifted his head, looked straight at the two lads and said,

"You lot mean to tell me... that you've never heard of Champion, the wonder horse? Well, that was me, you know; but unfortunately now that I am old, no one around these parts believe a word I say, and honestly I can't for the life of me, think of the slightest reason why; I'm still good at doing bit parts. Oh, how I miss hearing my name being sung by that sweet voice of my good pal, Frankie Lane, and I'll bet none of you have heard of him either!" muttered the ageing starstruck nag, who looked even more knackered than the yard he'd end up in.

"Ha, hark at the old moosh!" whinnied Bubbles. "More like Champion the blunder horse, going by the state ov ya, you silly old gaffer!"

"No need to be nasty, Bubbles my dear chap!" retorted Bunkhouse Bill, who was still trying to protect the old nag from the fusillade of gypsy verbal, that he was getting from the tormenting travellers.

"The old gry's dinlow (mad), chavvie, dik at him, the old moosh's head's gorn! Bruvver, just have a dik at his mooey, will ya's!" The bay gelding still wouldn't let up on the old actor, and he repeatedly insulted the long-forgotten Champion; but the actor didn't bat an eyelid, for he was used to big crowds, especially when attending the yearly Oscar-winning awards ceremony. It was mentioned by an old English actor some time back that the old actor horse was the only performer he'd seen walking up the red carpet on Oscar night that had a stable hand in tow with a bucket and spade.

It was time for the three visitors to leave. Denzel, seeing that time was running along, had decided to go back to Coot Island alone, so that Stanley could get Wally back to the stack before the sun went down any further. They said their goodbyes to Levy and the rest of his gang, but before they went Stanley told his clients that their next delousing appointment would be sooner than they thought, seeing as he's got to feed Wal daily. As you can imagine, there were big, big smiles coming from the relieved, not-so-thorough bred horses.

Just after this episode Champion got on famously with Bunkhouse Bill, and from that day on they became good friends, both being able to express themselves, only talking shop when the others were not within hearing distance; though one day Levy had got close enough to hear the old nag telling Bunkhouse,

"I never actually won an Oscar, but I knew plenty of stars who did!" And although the ex-Royal Guards' horse believed what he said, especially hearing him mentioning Trigger and Roy in first-name terms. I mean, Bunkhouse ain't silly, but the old royal minder of course not knowing, wasn't having any of the old stagers cobblers, as he put it to the others.

Time had passed, and Wally had been at Stanley's stack now for over two months. The human population was celebrating Christmas, and snow had fallen for the first time that winter on the morning of New Year's Eve, which covered the landscape in a beautiful blanket of whiteness, a sight that the two lads had only heard of, but had never seen in their young lives. The snow had covered the land as far as the eye could see, it was still a bright sunny morning, which caused the whiteness to thaw. Denzel left his log home to go outside at sunrise. Immediately he saw the snow glistening beneath the clear blue sky, and there was hardly a breeze in the air. The young duck had been wisely told, not only by his adopted parents, but Owen had also given the two lads insight into the ways of winter. Some of the stories he'd heard sounded very harsh indeed, but as Denzel sat there admiring the picturesque landscape, he could tell at a glance that this was most definitely one of winter's nicer days, even if there were four inches of snow covering his world. Clara and Clarence had emerged into the open, where they had noticed Denzel just sitting there on top of the log taking in the sight of his life, so far.

"Good morning, lad! Well, what do you think?" asked Clarence. Clara at this time hadn't spoken, she was too busy getting her old body warmed up, getting used to the fresh morning air. Once she had got herself together in the cleaning 'n' preening department, she spoke,

"Are you warm enough out here, ducks; and what do you think of the snow now that it has finally arrived at the lakes?"

"It's so pretty, Aunty! Can I go and play in it for a while?" the inquisitive duck asked.

"Of course you can, lad!" answered the old male Coot, "but don't venture too far from the log, so Clara and I can keep an eye on you, and one for the poacher man, for this is the time of year where we tend on lose a few ducks to that awful firestick, and the meat eating humans!" Denzel promised he would stay near, and as he stepped from the log the two lovable coots sat by and watched him swim, and then waddle onto their island, pushing his way through the pure white softness of the fluffy unspoilt whiteness.

Once he felt the cold snow, the pureness reminded him so much of the two swans, so beautiful and fresh in their appearance. He also couldn't help thinking of how he would have loved Wally and Treadwell to have been there to share this fabulous experience with him, although he knew that was impossible, for both would never be able to survive if the temperature were to drop suddenly. Though at that moment it wasn't far off being a lovely spring day, apart from the snow and that didn't feel all that cold with the sun now shining on it. Oh, he thrashed 'n' bashed, yelped 'n' yarooed to his heart's content, and whilst he played the fool, the caring couple watched over him lovingly; and as the old couple looked on, they were more like hawks, than the ageing Coots they most certainly were. Meanwhile the warmth of the sun melted the snow making a million droplets fall to earth and water from the branches that were covered with snow on Coot Island. Well, Denzel's first day's experience of snow had given him a feeling that this stuff he'd heard so much about wasn't as bad as he had been told. His second was as mild as the day before, was most unusually for the time of year which was now New Year's Day 1965. Denzel in all the excitement didn't realise that the weather he was now experiencing was no-where near it's usual severity, and the little lad had taken it for granted that this was how snowy weather was all the time. Oh, he'd suffered the bleak frosty weather of ice and freezing winds, but just because the sun had been shining for the past two days, he had automatically thought it was the norm, when it snowed.

It was the very last day of the year, and over at the mill Stanley had risen very early and was out clearing the snow from his ledge so's he could sit and take in the full extent of nature's wonderful whiteness. As Stanley sat there admiring the scenery, he heard Wal stirring inside. He was wondering what the little warbler would think of this sudden change of scenery, when Wally appeared at the hole's entrance.

"Er, what's all that funny white stuff then? 'N' cor, innit a nice sunny day!"

"It's not too bad, I mean it is the last day of the year, you know, and it's bloomin' January tomorrow and a fresh new year for us all, and I just can't believe how mild it is for this time of year. If it's like this tomorrow, do ya fancy we nip over to the island and wish them all a happy new year. What d'ya say, eh Wal?"

"Yeah…" chirped Wally, "but will I be all right landing with all this stuff about?"

"Of course you will, mate. The sun's melting it off all the branches this very minute, and it's only early yet. It'll get even warmer by the time we get there anyway!" Stanley could see that the little bird wanted very much to go and wish his family a happy new year, but the bit of cold white stuff was making Wal think otherwise. Although it was a wonderful sunny day, Stanley thought it wise not to take any chances by taking Wally too far from the stack, as he knew how nature can play its own little tricks by its ever-changing ways. No, he and Wally just sat and enjoyed a natter whilst catching the odd ray or two, from the old currant bun (sun). By mid afternoon it began to get colder, so the two birds decided to go back inside the stack in the warm. They were quite compatible in their sharings of company, and both got on famously together, where both of the chaps were a bit partial to a giggle or two, when the time arose of course.

It was the morning of New Year's Day. Stanley as usual was the first to rise, yet on this particular morning Wal wasn't too far behind his landlord. He was hoping in his little heart that the weather was going to be similar to yesterday's. Well, he wasn't to be disappointed; it was much the same as yesterday, but most of the snow that had fallen previously had almost melted away.

"Oh, goody good good!" chirped Wal. "Are we still going then?"

"We sure are, Wally me boy! Did you eat your breakfast I left for you?" (meaning a couple of nice juicy chrysalises, that Stanley had collected from the eaves of the old mill).

"Yes, thank you Stanley, they were so gorgeous 'n' tasty I swallowed 'em hasty," chirped Wally, who was now smiling in happy contentment knowing just how lucky he really was, not only in his winter arrangements, but also being lucky enough not having to go abroad for the winter.

The landlord and his cheeky little lodger, set off for the island at approximately 8.25a.m. on that mild winter's morning. When passing Walter's run down roost, the two day trippers, on passing the old down 'n' out, attempted to pass the time of day, but they saw the heartbreaking state he had gotten himself into, where neither of them could get one ounce of sense out of him. Unfortunately, just like most other mornings, poor Walter was suffering badly from a terrible hangover; but, of course, being the time of year it was, the king of cardboard nests had been getting more than his usual share of the old mother's ruin, and was now suffering badly.

From there they flew directly to the Island. Only a matter of minutes had elapsed since leaving Walter's run-down residence, and they were now approaching the island, and the two of them began to make their descent ready to land and surprise the Duck and the caring coots. But it was they who were surprised, not only to see Denzel, and the two elderly coots out 'n' about, but to see Owen, still up at this unearthly hour, also good Queen Grace, unescorted by the King; it caused them to feel concerned. Owen's sharp intelligent eyes spotted them arriving from the direction of the mill end of the lake, and as they came into land, they both chirped 'n' whistled to the company of valued friends a,

"Happy New Year.

But although the niceties were returned, it wasn't in the usual jovial way; no, something told them both that there was something terribly amiss. Once settled properly, Owen and Grace between them explained the very serious position of the king's health, telling them of how a fisherman's hook had got caught in his royal throat, and he was now lying very sick indeed in their royal residence, 'Gracelands'. Owen the wise had also told the two surprise visitors that they had just caught them in time, as they were about to leave to go to the king's aid. Wally and the Starling, without any hesitation whatsoever, agreed wholeheartedly to go with them. The company of seven set off from the island.

Owen, Denzel, and the two visitors made haste by flying straight to the king, who at this time was in a very serious condition, and was nearing death's door with every second that passed. Grace and the caring coots took to the water, for Clara's benefit. As we all know, the elderly lady's health in the past had always stopped her from venturing too far, but this being the King of the Dartford, and the old dear hearing just how serious it all sounded, the loving lady made her mind up to go and see, not only the king, but her very close long-time friend and neighbour.

The four flying birds approached the royal roost, which was constructed at the far tip of a small piece of land that came out into the lake, very similar to a small peninsular jutting out almost to a point into the lake. This was not the same one where Denzel and co, lived; no, this was the next lake over, which sat directly behind the bigger main stretch of water. As they came into land they could see that the ailing king was in a far worse condition than all had ever imagined. On landing, the look on each member of the visiting company's faces was of devastation and deep sadness at the sight before their eyes. They saw the powerful ruler that Cyril most certainly was but no sign was there of his usual regalness, in fact dead the opposite. The poor bird was lying there at the water's edge, pitiful and helpless. Grace had arrived, she had left by water, along with Clara and Clarence; but once they were on their way she had told them to take their time in getting to Gracelands, and that she was to go on ahead at a much faster pace. She did this knowing that this trip, that Clara was making, was out of sheer respect for her own husband, and she admired Clara's courage, whilst travelling so far 'n' all, especially with the old condition 'n' complaints department.

At Gracelands, the scene was heartbreaking. Denzel and the others rushed to the king's side, Grace left the water in a manner that wasn't very graceful at all, in her endeavour to join the others at her beloved husband's side. The sick middle-

Well, it was a sad day when it started, but it ended on a much happier note, and after much chattings 'n' lots of farewells 'n' thank yous, the company left the king to get all the rest he could get, and don't worry, his beautiful pen will see he does. Denzel and the caring coots returned to Coot Island along with Stanley and Wal, and after a bit of chit-chat 'n' gossip, they had to leave to get back to the stack in time before the sun went down, and the coldness returned.

Well, all turned out fine for the king, and within a couple of weeks of the operation, and Grace's loving care and treatment, Cyril was feeling much better, though he didn't exactly feel like doing somersaults around the lake's at this particular time; but, I must say, he was getting out 'n' about, and appeared to be getting stronger by the day.

January 'n' February, came and went, and the freezing old winds of March were blowing chillingly from the north. Denzel, along with most of the residents, apart from those who, like Treadwell, were hibernating or on migration, also had hardly been out of his log home, except to feed and exercise, which the ever caring coots made sure he did daily. He was most thankful that Aunty Clara never seemed to tire when, not only telling the duck hundreds of stories, but even repeating some of them several times over the months that had passed, at the request of a very bored Mallard.

Stanley and Wal, even with the freezing temperatures, never stopped having a giggle whilst telling each other's tales of each one's past adventures during this very first winter. The two lads had witnessed freezing rain 'n' sleet, snow 'n' ice, winds that would cut you in half if anyone was silly enough to stay out longer than he had to.

When spring finally arrived, the two youngsters had gained quite a lot from their life's experiences, which meant they were still young but had now reached adulthood; but the pair of 'em would never have realised how their lives would change so dramatically in the months to come.

It was the first real mild sunny day for at least three months, so you can imagine all the excitement and buzzing going on about the place, not only by Beatrice the busy bumble

aged King had seen them coming and could barely raise his head through the weight of his long neck, and even that had seemed to have taken his life's breath away. No matter which way he tried to turn or make the slightest movement to get himself comfortable, the pain was too much to bear, and all the poor old chap could muster through all of his pain, was a very weak half smile. He couldn't even talk because the sharp barbed-steel hook was imbedded in the back of his throat.

It had been a couple of hours since it had happened, and when Cyril opened his mouth at Grace's request, for all to peer inside and observe more of mans' handiwork, each one stood back aghast. Once inspected it was not Owen, who was about to take charge on such matters, but Denzel's young brain sprang into action. An idea had instantly come into his mind after seeing exactly where the hook was hooked.

"But it could work?" he thought aloud. Denzel taking it upon himself then waddled closer to where the King lay, his royal head hung low on the ground from his now drooping neck, that lay on the snow scattered floor. Denzel bent his own neck down and whispered softly into the king's lughole, and asked him to open his bill as wide as he possibly could, Cyril nodded in co-operation, then opened his bill so wide that it ached from the start, adding even more agony to the pain already caused.

"Wally!" Denzel spoke in a most authoritative of voices.

"Who, me?" chirped the little fella in blind panic, wondering what on earth and water, would the duck be calling his name out for at such an important time.

"Yes… you, Wally, there is no time to waste!"

"Er… what then?" chirped Wal.

"Come here quickly please!" said the duck. Wally never hesitated for one moment, he was there like a shot, settling on a thick stem of grass just at the side of his best mate, who was only inches from Cyril's opened bill. As the two pals peered inside they saw, to their dismay, the deadly hook and line that were choking the king to death; and make no mistake, if it wasn't removed very quickly the king would most certainly die. Denzel explained to Wal that he, and only he, was small enough to attempt to withdraw the implement from the King's throat. Without as much as a blink, Wally, although feeling very brave, did recall the same knocking sound that his knees were making when very first meeting the ancient Tawny, was in fact suffering from a bit of the old nerves complaint, or as the tricky Toad would call it in his slang lingo, the old (Hors d'oeuvres, trouble)

"Y… You mean me, go in there?" Wal's little knee-caps started to play an even clickier tune, as the sound of a little trumpet fly flew between his knocking knees.

"Yes, Wally, for it's His Majesty's only chance," the duck insisted. Without any hesitation the little Warbler hopped on to Cyril's bill and moved closer to the task at hand. On close inspection he could see the damage caused. He weighed up the situation as he saw it, he grasped the dreadful hook by its barbed end, and began to wriggle 'n' tug, wriggle 'n' tug, as hard as he could with his tiny beak, gradually loosening the destructive implement. Whilst Wally was doing his utmost to extract the hook, poor Cyril had almost fainted from even the slightest movement of Wal's efforts inside his very sore throat. But Cyril knew full well it had to be done, if ever he wanted to end his days in old age with his lovely Grace, who at this time was at his side gently preening and caressing the underside of her husband's long white neck, whilst Wally was at work inside.

After a few moments of the little bird's attempt, unfortunately causing much pain to the old cob , the hook, to Wally's surprise, after his third, or was it the fourth wriggle 'n' tug, came cleanly away, and was now being held in the beak of the tiny bird. Wal was concentrating so much on his very important task, the little physician hadn't even realised. Then it finally sank in, Wally smiled to himself, then thought aloud to himself.

"I've done it!" Then it really sunk in… "I've done it, I've done it!" he chirped again. But, still not fully absorbing the true extent of just what he had done. It hadn't occurred to him or even registered, that he, single-handedly, without any form of doubt, had saved the life of not a paltry earl, or a measly

duke, but the King of Dartford himself! A confused moment of triumph, he had realised ex had done. Wally turned and before he could op beak the company cheered 'n' jumped with glee had witnessed.

At this time Grace's head was still undern her husband's feathery pain-stricken throat. She cheers, but couldn't see what was going on abov efforts. She was feeling exceptionally low at thought how dreadful it would be to lose her lif and believe me it showed on the lady's unsmili all of a sudden she heard the cheers and commo happiness, which brought her lowered eyes sh then she knew in an instant what had miraculo from those sounds coming from her wonder neighbours. Grace took her support gently awa cob's neck to find out what had exactly happen came up she poked her long neck forward, and standing on the lower half of the King's b wicked-looking implement in his beak; and a released it, it fell to the ground, and a huge smi little chops. At a later date, Grace was heard t she was positive it went all the way around his head. All the company were amazed at how q bird had done the job, especially after the v seen, with their own eyes, the way Wall knocking when first entering the king's bill. I what has been performed this very da unrewarded. Relief came almost immediate although the swan was still very ill; but at lea over, and with Grace's loving care, he'd be n health in a month or two. His lovely queen on seeing her husband relieved, and not the from hours of his being in agony. She coul enough, for he had instigated the whole ope Wal's performance, the job was so professio little physician that the little Warbler has turr aged King had seen them coming and could barely raise his head through the weight of his long neck, and even that had seemed to have taken his life's breath away. No matter which way he tried to turn or make the slightest movement to get himself comfortable, the pain was too much to bear, and all the poor old chap could muster through all of his pain, was a very weak half smile. He couldn't even talk because the sharp barbed-steel hook was imbedded in the back of his throat.

It had been a couple of hours since it had happened, and when Cyril opened his mouth at Grace's request, for all to peer inside and observe more of mans' handiwork, each one stood back aghast. Once inspected it was not Owen, who was about to take charge on such matters, but Denzel's young brain sprang into action. An idea had instantly come into his mind after seeing exactly where the hook was hooked.

"But it could work?" he thought aloud. Denzel taking it upon himself then waddled closer to where the King lay, his royal head hung low on the ground from his now drooping neck, that lay on the snow scattered floor. Denzel bent his own neck down and whispered softly into the king's lughole, and asked him to open his bill as wide as he possibly could, Cyril nodded in co-operation, then opened his bill so wide that it ached from the start, adding even more agony to the pain already caused.

"Wally!" Denzel spoke in a most authoritative of voices.

"Who, me?" chirped the little fella in blind panic, wondering what on earth and water, would the duck be calling his name out for at such an important time.

"Yes… you, Wally, there is no time to waste!"

"Er… what then?" chirped Wal.

"Come here quickly please!" said the duck. Wally never hesitated for one moment, he was there like a shot, settling on a thick stem of grass just at the side of his best mate, who was only inches from Cyril's opened bill. As the two pals peered inside they saw, to their dismay, the deadly hook and line that were choking the king to death; and make no mistake, if it wasn't removed very quickly the king would most certainly die. Denzel explained to Wal that he, and only he, was small enough to attempt to withdraw the implement from the King's throat. Without as much as a blink, Wally, although feeling very brave, did recall the same knocking sound that his knees were making when very first meeting the ancient Tawny, was in fact suffering from a bit of the old nerves complaint, or as the tricky Toad would call it in his slang lingo, the old (Hors d'oeuvres, trouble)

"Y... You mean me, go in there?" Wal's little knee-caps started to play an even clickier tune, as the sound of a little trumpet fly flew between his knocking knees.

"Yes, Wally, for it's His Majesty's only chance," the duck insisted. Without any hesitation the little Warbler hopped on to Cyril's bill and moved closer to the task at hand. On close inspection he could see the damage caused. He weighed up the situation as he saw it, he grasped the dreadful hook by its barbed end, and began to wriggle 'n' tug, wriggle 'n' tug, as hard as he could with his tiny beak, gradually loosening the destructive implement. Whilst Wally was doing his utmost to extract the hook, poor Cyril had almost fainted from even the slightest movement of Wal's efforts inside his very sore throat. But Cyril knew full well it had to be done, if ever he wanted to end his days in old age with his lovely Grace, who at this time was at his side gently preening and caressing the underside of her husband's long white neck, whilst Wally was at work inside.

After a few moments of the little bird's attempt, unfortunately causing much pain to the old cob , the hook, to Wally's surprise, after his third, or was it the fourth wriggle 'n' tug, came cleanly away, and was now being held in the beak of the tiny bird. Wal was concentrating so much on his very important task, the little physician hadn't even realised. Then it finally sank in, Wally smiled to himself, then thought aloud to himself.

"I've done it!" Then it really sunk in... "I've done it, I've done it!" he chirped again. But, still not fully absorbing the true extent of just what he had done. It hadn't occurred to him or even registered, that he, single-handedly, without any form of doubt, had saved the life of not a paltry earl, or a measly duke, but the King of Dartford himself! After Wally's confused moment of triumph, he had realised exactly what he had done. Wally turned and before he could open his cheeky beak the company cheered 'n' jumped with glee at what they had witnessed.

At this time Grace's head was still underneath, stroking her husband's feathery pain-stricken throat. She had heard the cheers, but couldn't see what was going on above her calming efforts. She was feeling exceptionally low at this time, and thought how dreadful it would be to lose her life-long spouse, and believe me it showed on the lady's unsmiling face. When all of a sudden she heard the cheers and commotion of excited happiness, which brought her lowered eyes sharply upwards; then she knew in an instant what had miraculously happened, from those sounds coming from her wonderful friends 'n' neighbours. Grace took her support gently away from the old cob's neck to find out what had exactly happened. As her head came up she poked her long neck forward, and she saw Wally standing on the lower half of the King's bill holding the wicked-looking implement in his beak; and as the little fella released it, it fell to the ground, and a huge smile came over his little chops. At a later date, Grace was heard telling Clara that she was positive it went all the way around his handsome little head. All the company were amazed at how quickly the small bird had done the job, especially after the way they had all seen, with their own eyes, the way Wally's knees were knocking when first entering the king's bill. But all knew that what has been performed this very day wouldn't go unrewarded. Relief came almost immediately, to the king, although the swan was still very ill; but at least the danger was over, and with Grace's loving care, he'd be nursed back to full health in a month or two. His lovely queen was so full of joy on seeing her husband relieved, and not the pain-racked face, from hours of his being in agony. She couldn't thank Denzel enough, for he had instigated the whole operation; and as for Wal's performance, the job was so professionally done by the little physician that the little Warbler has turned out to be.

Well, it was a sad day when it started, but it ended on a much happier note, and after much chattings 'n' lots of farewells 'n' thank yous, the company left the king to get all the rest he could get, and don't worry, his beautiful pen will see he does. Denzel and the caring coots returned to Coot Island along with Stanley and Wal, and after a bit of chit-chat 'n' gossip, they had to leave to get back to the stack in time before the sun went down, and the coldness returned.

Well, all turned out fine for the king, and within a couple of weeks of the operation, and Grace's loving care and treatment, Cyril was feeling much better, though he didn't exactly feel like doing somersaults around the lake's at this particular time; but, I must say, he was getting out 'n' about, and appeared to be getting stronger by the day.

January 'n' February, came and went, and the freezing cold winds of March were blowing chillingly from the north. Denzel, along with most of the residents, apart from those who, like Treadwell, were hibernating or on migration, also had hardly been out of his log home, except to feed and exercise, which the ever caring coots made sure he did daily. He was most thankful that Aunty Clara never seemed to tire when, not only telling the duck hundreds of stories, but even repeating some of them several times over the months that had passed, at the request of a very bored Mallard.

Stanley and Wal, even with the freezing temperatures, never stopped having a giggle whilst telling each other's tales of each one's past adventures during this very first winter. The two lads had witnessed freezing rain 'n' sleet, snow 'n' ice, winds that would cut you in half if anyone was silly enough to stay out longer than he had to.

When spring finally arrived, the two youngsters had gained quite a lot from their life's experiences, which meant they were still young but had now reached adulthood; but the pair of 'em would never have realised how their lives would change so dramatically in the months to come.

It was the first real mild sunny day for at least three months, so you can imagine all the excitement and buzzing going on about the place, not only by Beatrice the busy bumble bee, buzzing from blossom to blossom tasting the first sweetness of nature's nectar. Denzel and the ageing coots were up at the crack of dawn and were out on the much warmer water enjoying the first of the sun's spring warmth on their feathery backs. Clarence and Clara both remarked on how handsomely the youngster had grown, also pointing out how the sheen of his plumage on his long proud neck, had turned into such beautiful shades of green, rising up from his strong mottled shoulders. All three were enjoying the sun's rays on their backs for the first time in months, and it felt so good to be able to meet, and converse with the many other residents who, like them were only too pleased the cold winter weather was finally over.

Wally and Stanley, had become as thick as thieves, over the period he'd stayed at the stack, and if the starling was to be honest, he had grown very attached to his little lodger, and his comical capers they had shared over the bitter months that had passed. On Wal's first day of spring he and the starling thought, seeing it was his last day before returning to Coot Island, they would spend the whole morning together going about the mill saying cheerio to the friends he'd made whilst residing there.

They were up very early, and to Wal's surprise it wasn't hard finding some early insects that were once again out in their multitudes.

Chapter Six

There was no mistaking that spring had arrived at the Horton Kirby Lakes. It was nearing the end of both March, and of the dull grey skies and quietness. Throughout cold winter days movement of the residents about the place, was far less than on these lovely fine sunny days. This was mainly because most of the summer visitors migrate abroad, leaving the lakes 'n' rivers to the more hardy species, who are the real residents here, and are more adapted to our typically chilling British winters. Also absent was the whole of the amphibian world, who hibernate at the same time, along with many many of the wee furry folk, who bury themselves deep beneath the banks of the waterways; not forgetting the insect population with its magnificent infrastructure of the complex world they have built for themselves. Yet although they are tiny creatures, all of them play their part on the plot as active members. Even though many get eaten, thus unknowingly playing their role by being a link in the food chain of life. Well, the lakes were showing signs of much activity, where birds of many different kinds were returning from their migratory grounds in the warmer continental climates. Of course they loved a nice change when going abroad, especially following the old currant bun, so's they are warm all year round, (I mean, have you ever met a bird that didn't like going abroad?).

Why, only a matter of days ago my informant, who has enabled me to tell of such-goings on in the past that were taking place right under the noses of the human population, at the Horton Kirby Lakes, has, at last he's given me full permission to disclose his existence in those parts. Since our first ever meeting, back in the spring of 1964, he made me swear not to tell a soul; and once I agreed, and parted with the half sovereign he'd taken a fancy to, which was hanging on my watch chain; only then did he start his revelation. I was so astounded by some of the things he said, I just ripped the golden coin from its Albert chain, and gave it to him gladly. It was then that he let me in to his wonderful secret. He was a very small man of Irish descent who was, if my eyes 'n' ears didn't deceive me, was no more than eleven inches tall, and without any exaggeration, an at least two hundred-year-old leprechaun. But, when I asked his age, he laughed and said "One hundred 'n' ninety-nine." I personally never doubted the little character, and if he was fibbing about his age, what's a year, in the life of a leprechaun anyway, eh? I found him to be good-natured, and must confess he most certainly had a way with the old words.

In his own Irish tongue he told me the most outrageous tales of extraordinary proportions during the dozen or so times we'd met on the banks of those lakes. In fact almost a year ago, the very first time I had met him, his stories sounded so remarkable, they prompted me to venture to those lakes. I took his advice by visiting them before dusk, concealing myself in a temporary hide, wishing not to disturb what I hoped to see. As I was concealed in my hide, daylight came, and I witnessed the waters come alive; and as one can tell by this written account, it was all happening just as the little man had said. Thus enabling me to collect enough material to write my observations, adding to the many tales he'd told. As I say, it was only the day before yesterday I bumped into him again, whilst I was strolling the lakes with my little dog Sam. I asked if he would sit a while and take some bread 'n' cheese with me. Accepting my offer, he sat on a toadstool close to me, and we both ate heartily, even though to us larger folk, he never ate enough to keep a sparrow alive. After our feast, he began telling me about a young hussy Reed Warbler chick he'd recently heard telling some hens from her own species whom, she had met up with and of how she had met up with and of how she had just returned from St Tropez.

My informant also tells me that she was a-flapping 'n' a-giggling, whilst telling her excited companions of how she had flown from the mainland to one of those big man-made floating things which had lots of humans on. Some were pouring bubbly water from funny-looking green things that popped like a firestick, which they drank, and it turned them all silly. There had been human females lying all over the place, not looking at all like they do when on land.

"They all had funny lumps 'n' bumps sticking out of the queer shaped bodies," she was heard saying… "And some were dancing and singing to some right funny old noise that was coming from an odd looking bit of wood. But whatever it was, girls, it sure got that strange lot of humans a-partying!"

According to my informant, she had met up with some other warbler chicks who were also on migration and were having the time of their lives with some French male warblers of similar ages, and whilst enjoying themselves, they had seen a beautiful yacht that was anchored just off shore of this millionaire playground. So being the young pretty bird she was, and on her holidays too she decided to accept the invitation, and flew out to a big yacht. There they had spent the rest of the day lazing about on their chosen perches, high up on the yardarm of some very rich human's boat, enjoying the sun on their backs, and the fresh mild breeze that kept them cool. She was also heard to say that one of the French chirping warblers had taken a drink from one of those things that was full up with the funny water with the bubbles in it, and afterwards he flew back up to where the rest were all sunning themselves, and joined his company. And by all accounts, all he kept doing, apart from breathing the old garlic over 'em, was singing the girls love songs, between the couple of times he'd drunkenly fallen off his perch.

So you see folks, all that going abroad on migration wasn't half as bad as the terrified Wally had imagined. In fact, if only the little character had known it, and not been so terrified; he could have learned a lot more from life by going; but no because of his little temper 'n' tantrums he had missed out. But then again, by living with Stanley at the stack, he'd not done too badly in his life's learnings, and he had most certainly picked up a few tips during his winter stay at the old mill, plus new friends a-plenty.

Denzel and the caring coots were out and about on their island, and had been staying outside the log a lot more since the brighter weather had arrived. Over the past day or two, since the warm spring weather came, the three of them traipsed the whole perimeter of the island to make quite sure that all was as it should be. As they waddled along doing the rounds of the island's grounds, they nattered 'n' chattered, and gave the time of day to many other varieties of life around them. Whilst they were talking it didn't take long before Denzel wondered, and asked, why Wally hadn't returned. The old couple told him not to worry, and they assured him, the little lad would show up at any moment. As the day went on, they sat at their usual places at the front of the island. It was a happy time of year for all concerned. As they watched, along with many of their neighbours, they saw many other different kinds of birds returning from far-off lands, to their breeding grounds about the lakes. As they watched, they saw a formation of Brent Geese fly directly over them, heading north to their breeding grounds on the tundras of the USSR. Many smaller migratory birds were returning in their flocks; and all the time the company watched, as did other residents who had stayed at home. All were glad to see and hear again those wonderful, most joyous sounds of every kind of birdsong, which brought harmony and love to the hearts of everyone who dwelt in this wonderful place. No wonder this was the time of year for love 'n' mating, I shouldn't be surprised, after listening to all those different love songs, that were drifting through the air coming from a multitude of lovestruck males, when strutting their stuff during their ceremonial courtship.

It was late afternoon, and there still wasn't any sign of Wally at all, and by this time of the day, it began to show, not only on Denzel, who was looking rather sad, but on Clara 'n' Clarence too. As the day went on, by 4 p.m. it was starting to get quite nippy, when suddenly Clara began to get restless, and cried out in a worrying moan, so she tried to make it sound as if the cold was affecting her, but there was no fooling her life-long spouse oh, he knew deep down that his old dear was worrying herself silly. She'd been smiling a false smile all day, and on one occasion during that time, she had almost leapt from her seat in thinking that a glimpse of a passing stonechat was the Dartford dodger returning. That was when old Yorkie first realised she was getting upset at Wal's late return.

"Don't you go worrying your lovely old self, ducks, the little lad's as safe as a nest, all the while he's with Stanley; you mark my words, lass!" said the old boy, trying to comfort her. That night they all went to roost thinking of Wally, and hoping in their hearts that he would return the very next day. Well they didn't have to wait long, Clarence was up at the crack of dawn, and was scanning the early morning sky. It was a beautiful sunny day, and the old boy was in the throes of rubbing 'n' scrubbing in the cleaning 'n' preening department, when Wally's little voice was heard.

"Mornin' Uncle!" said cheeky beak with a smile on his saucy little chops. At first it startled Clarence, but was he glad at seeing Wal and Stanley, sitting on a willow branch that hung above his head! The old bird was overcome with emotions at the sight of them.

"Welcome home, lad, am I glad to see you two!" Old Yorky sounded relieved as he said it. "My, you look real grand, lad!"

Denzel and Clara were woken up by the sound of voices coming from outside the log. They could make out Clarence's voice, but even after straining their ears, neither of them could make out who the devil it was he was talking to at such an early hour; yet whoever it was, they could tell by the muffled voices that there was more than one visitor. Well, curiosity in this case, never killed the cat, but it was enough to get them up and out of the roost lively. Denzel, being young and sprightly was the first to leave the log, and appeared out in the glorious sunshine.

It took him a while to adjust his eyes to the brightness of the outside world, but when he did, and spotted Wal, with his respected landlord, having a laugh 'n' a joke with Clarence, he was the happiest duck alive. I must say, from what I've seen 'n' heard, the reunion was so magical it almost had 'em all in tears, with the exception of Aunty Clara of course, but that was expected anyway.

Owen arrived soon after the appearance of the landlord 'n' lodger. He happened to be returning home from his usual night's hunting and realised that now the warmer weather was here, he'd better fly over to the island, and check if the tiny chap had returned home safely. Well, even in flight and approaching the island, he could see for himself the little group of birds having a good old chuckle 'n' chin-wag. He smiled to himself contentedly at what he saw in this close-knit family, and was more than glad that Wal had not only survived the wicked winter, but had safely returned. Not that he had any doubts whatsoever of Stanley's ability in the minding department, even in his half-starved anorexic condition. Owen landed on a thick old stump that was poking out of the ground just at the water's edge, near to where the company sat at the back of the island, not too far from the old log. The company had seen him approach and settle, and as he was getting himself more comfortable cheers went up from them all,

"Hooray...!" they sang to their hearts delight.

"Why, good morning one and all!" he hooted. "You're back, I see, Master Wally?"

"Yes, Owen, thanks to you and my good friend Stanley!" Owen and the Warbler's adopted parents could tell by Wal's answer that he had matured from the little character had been into a young-adult bird, leaving the three olduns to raise their eyes to each other approvingly at the lad's coming of age (whereas, before he went to live with the starling, they never in a million years thought it possible.) Whilst they were all enjoying themselves in catching up on their different stories 'n' carryings-on, of the encounters that each had had throughout the cold winter, Owen sat listening. But as he sat there a huge smile came across his big round face, at something he'd noticed, that made him a very happy owl indeed.

"Stanley, I do believe, having young Wallace at the stack with you, has done you the world of good, ma boy! And are my old eyes playing tricks, or do I detect a little bit more meat on those bones of yours?"

"Aye up, lad, you've filled out a treat; don't you think so, lass?" asked the old boy. Clara nodded yes, between her wings, whilst wiping away tears from her flustered feathered face. As for Stanley, he just sat there taking in all the compliments, that anyone would like to give. You see, Stanley at this very time in his life, well, since he was struck down by his awful illness, never even dreamed that one day he would get his appetite back; but since he'd taken his lively little lodger in he had for some unknown reason, regained his normal eating habits, and was showing sure signs of fattening up. Of course, the rest of the company had seen with their own eyes the change in the Starling's stature and a more get-up-and-go look about him, which was a far cry from the anorexic state he was in.

It was so obvious that it was Wal's gift of character 'n' comical carryings-on, which had brought new life and willpower back into the starling's heart. They could also see that Stanley was as happy as a sand martin sitting up there next to Wally, lapping up all that was being said about his person.

"Yes, I feel much better thanks to you all!" he whistled, "I feel like a bird again, and do you know, before young Wally-boy, there, come to live at my place, I wasn't able to get a morsel of food down my neck, and I've got to be honest (he was choking back his words now) I... I was losing my will to live, and I knew that this past winter could have been my last. Yet since the boy came, I've never felt so good in all my life!" Once the surprise of their return subsided, Denzel and Wally couldn't wait a moment longer to get together. Leaving the four elder birds to chat, they went off a little ways towards the front of the island, so they could share their winter stories, and speak of what was to come. It had been a couple of hours since the warbler's return, and whilst the two lads were out of earshot, the four older birds were discussing how marvellously he had conducted himself whilst staying at the stack.

"Well, I must confess, the boy's utterly surprised me! Especially after that little temper 'n' tantrum, he'd performed at the beginning!" the old night hunter was heard saying. Owen was feeling very tired now, and after seeing with his own eyes that all was well and back to normal on Coot Island, he decided to leave. He said his farewells to all and took his leave, heading as the crow flies towards The Craggies, in the hope of catching up on the sleep he had lost. Stanley, on the other hand, stayed for the rest of the day enjoying his new-found company; not only having some fun with the two lads, but also adored having a natter with Clara 'n' Clarence. You should have seen old Clara's face light up on hearing some of the gossip that Stanley was telling. Clarence at one stage had to stop himself from smiling, for he could tell by the way she'd been acting, whilst listening, she was getting more excited at every word the not-so-narrow bird had spoken. He was having a crafty little smile to himself for he knew what he'd heard so far would undoubtedly be retold by Clara to Mini the moorhen at the very next gossiping-session. Clarence knew her old game by the way she had been tut-tutting, a-nodding 'n' agreeing, folding and unfolding her wings, especially each and every time the starling mentioned some of the juicy bits. You see, ever since he'd fallen prey to this heartbreaking slimmer's complaint, he had basically lived the life of a recluse, as far as his own flock were concerned. He really only had the odd chat with Walter Pigeon, and he couldn't get a lot of sense out of him most days, and as for his gypsy pal's lingo, it didn't leave much regarding an intelligent conversation (with the exception of Bunkhouse Billy of course), but after the excitement and chatting he'd done today, even he knew he was on the road to recovery. So much so, he asked if he could stay on the Island for the night so's he could spend his last night with Wal. Soon after retiring, Wal and Stanley were perched together gazing up at the moon and twinkling stars, then both drifted off to sleep.

In the morning, just after breakfast, Stanley was about to leave for the mill when Clara asked him to stay on a little while and share some food before he went. The starling decided to take the offer and perched for a little longer with his company. Denzel and the ageing coots had taken up their seats at the front of the island, while Wally, and his ex-landlord Stanley perched above. They got themselves settled to rest 'n' digest and catch a few rays from the sun; they had just got comfortable, when Wal came out with a blinder...

"Cor, Den, you should have seen the stars last night, there were millions of 'em, wasn't there Stanley?" reported the little fella.

"How... many?" Denzel asked, smiling at the others.

"Millions, wasn't there, Stan?" chirped Wal. The starling knew Wally was telling the truth, and backed him all the way. The duck had only been jesting, for after hearing Wally mention of millions, he couldn't help thinking of Harry the Rat; then wondering if the pathetic fibber survived the winter cold.

"I know what them stars are!" chirped Wally, and everyone looked straight at him in amazement.

"What are they then, ducks?" asked Clara.

"Them's are flying horses!" he said. The whole of the company began laughing at Wally's dodgy bit of knowledge in the flying horse department. Then Clarence stepped in...

"Nay...lad, they're the lights of heaven, that's what they are, laddie!" Clarence's answer was just as silly as Wal's but it sure sounded a bit better than the little fella's account.

"They ain't!" chirped Wal quite adamantly, "'cause I know one of 'em, and you 'n' Stanley, eh Den?" No one was more surprised that the duck at this time, and he sat flummoxed; even the Starling couldn't believe what the little bird had said. Clarence broke the ice by asking the little lad what he meant.

"He's an old horse, up at the pasture, and he told us he was a star, eh, Den?" chirped Wally.

The company started to laugh at Wally's beliefs; Denzel and Stanley knew the little bird was talking about the retired Champion, but after explaining to the old couple, neither of them had any ideas of what was really up in the sky. But one thing they knew for sure: the particular horse the little lad was talking about had a job to walk, let alone be up there, galloping about the galaxy.

Meanwhile, over at Toad's terrace, there was the awakening of Treadwell and wife; they had been stirring for a few hours, but weren't fully awake, for it's not easy leaping about when one has to sleep in the same position for nigh on half-a-year, without eating a morsel, too.

"Cor, strewth, my haystack's killin' me, Toots, ah's yorn?" croaked the cockney, having a good stretch 'n' yawn.

"Oh, I'm all right! A little stiff, but I'll be ok!" she croaked, looking at her hubby lovingly. "And did you miss me, when we was asleep, darling?" she asked .

"Yers, ov course I did; tell ya the troof gel, I... er, woz finkin' abaat you lots, sweetheart!" he answered as usual, without thinking.

"You lying Toad!" she goaded him. "You were snoring, even before we got into bed, let alone having sweet dreams of me, you fibber!"

"Yers... well, I... er, woke up a couple ov times, and I finked ov ya then, honest gel, I luv ya ta death, you know that, don't ya, nah?" As Treadwell made his recovery, Tootsy and he looked at one another and burst out laughing, for both knew full well that once toads go to sleep they are practically dead to the world about them. Well, in this toad's case, he was more dead than the huge log that housed them. However they're up and about now, with lots to do. Before anything else, they both had to tuck into bundles of grub, for during their long kipping period they lost their body fat, which had built up through the previous summer months. And looking at them now, you would hardly recognise the pair of 'em. But knowing them as we do, they'll be fit 'n' well, in a week or two.

On the third day of Wally's return, and all the excitement of being together again had settled down, the two lads decided they couldn't wait another day to go and see if their best pal Treadwell Toad was up, out of his winter's sleep. After saying cheerio to their adopted parents, they set off for the waterfall end of the lake and the location of Toad's Terrace. Denzel and Wal were in no hurry, and took a leisurely journey across the lake to where the cockney lived. Denzel could have flown the short distance but thought it would have been much nicer going over water, where he and Wally could pass the time of day with other residents, hoping to pick up a bit of news of far-away places.

On their way, they met Charley the brave coot who told Denzel that he had spoken to Treadwell and wife, a few days ago at the water's edge, just below their home. Denzel looked at Wally, to see him with a big smile, just like he had himself. For now they both knew for sure that their bosom pal had risen from his bed, and was actually about the plot, something both were uncertain of when setting out. After a brief chat with the coot and saying goodbye, the two lads were so pleased at what they had heard the pair of 'em forgot all about the leisurely bit, and took off double lively towards their destination. Reaching lakeside, and just twenty feet below their cockney pal's residence (Toad's Terrace) the two lads couldn't see any movement in the camp, which made them feel unsure, then...

"Oi, oi!" came a loud croak from the toad. They looked up, and there, squatting on the old patio in the warm sunshine, was the Londoner himself, accompanied by the trouble 'n' strife, Toots. Denzel and Wal, were in the throes of a bit of cheerings 'n yarooings, when both at the same time stopped dead in stark shock at the sight of the dear friends they loved. Not so much Tootsy, for what they saw quite suited her, but as for the other bloke well, they were immediately attracted to the feet department, for that was the only part about him that hadn't changed. If anything the old chap's dabs looked even bigger, but the character attached to 'em was not at all like the cockney pal they knew. And thus thought to themselves if he had been any thinner, he could have been mistaken for his handbag handle neighbour, Nuthouse Neddy. Although the loss of weight didn't suit the Toad one bit, yet I must say that Tootsy's, new found slenderness suited her down to the ground, and oh, how she knew it! Treadwell was heard telling the caring coots one morning a day or so later.\

"Clara, gel, she was prancin' abaat 'n' singin' and she never stopped standing on her back legs, with her hands on her slim waist a-smilin' and a-hummin' in that mirror puddle ov hers!" And then he went on to tell them of how he had to practically drag her away; and that, I hear, wasn't until the sunlight had completely left the mirror... tut, tut! (Well, I don't know about you lot, but the way that girl's been acting of late, I don't for one minute think it will be long before the sound of tiny Toads will be heard on the slopes, if I'm not mistaken.)

"Goodness gracious me!" spluttered Denzel. "Treadwell, what on earth and water has happened to you? You're so thin." Denzel turned to Wally, and could tell by Wal's little eyes that he too was shocked at the toad's weight loss.

"Gawd helpus, wot the 'ell d'ya expect? We ain't had any grub for six months!" croaked the toad, not liking his present stature at all. In fact he likes being a bit of a lump, as he's known on the manor, but hates being the skinny figure of a toad who sat on his terrace this day.

"Yes, I can see that!" said the duck, "But... but, you just don't look the same!"

"Well, nor would you, if you was in the roost for six moons, would ya's, nah? Anyway, don't you wully me, son, I'll soon put a bit ov puddin' on!" croaked a toad who, going by the sight of him, had definitely taken over from where the half-starved starling had left off. But soon after their initial shock, they were all more than glad that the gang were back together again. Whilst in conversation, Tootsy nudged her hubby's side and mimed a little go-on, meaning for Treadwell to say something to his two pukka pals. Well the cockney huffed 'n' puffed before the news broke from his lips'

"I... I'm going to be a Dad!" he piped up.

The two lads' eyes went as wide as ya like, and...

"You mean you're going to have some little toadies?" chirped Wally, who one could plainly see was loving every bloomin' minute of it all.

"Yers, Wal, me son! Another few weeks 'n' the gaff will be running alive wiv sproggs!" chuckled the daddy-to-be.

"Er... I know what them are!" exclaimed the little scholar. "They're sparrows 'n' frogs mixed together!" This left the company, even Wally, in uncontrollabe laughter. Poor Wal had done it again.

"Nah, ya w... warbler!" Treadwell almost called Wal, that dodgy name for idiots 'n' fools, but cunningly realized and changed his tune from not wanting to upset his little pal, especially after meeting the little character for the first time since the autumn. Toad went on and put Wally wise by telling him what sproggs really were;

"Dustbin lids,!" the Londoner blurted out, confusing the warbler even more, but it didn't take him too long to know what they really meant.

"You mean, you're... you're going to have tadpoles?" asked Denzel after being in happy shock since his pals had broken the news. It had taken a bit of time to sink in, but when it did they were as chuffed as anything, and could hardly wait for the toads to break their good news to Aunt Clara 'n' Uncle Clarence, who they knew would be thrilled to bits. The two lads spent most of the daylight hours with their friends, and were about to leave in good time to get back to the island before dark, but just as they were about to make arrangements to meet the very next day, the cockney had the shock of his life 'cause Tootsy for the very first time had put her foot down.

"On no you don't, Treadwell Toad! You, my lad, have now got responsibilities!" she croaked. Toad's body shook, for that tone in her voice was all too new to him. Swallowing hard, the boy from Lewisham was no more; he was an adult now, or so she tried telling him.

"You made your bed, Mr Toad, and now you must lie in it!" winking at his two pals as she said it. Toad hadn't seen Tootsy's winkings, and was absolutely dumbfounded. Then looking at his two pals he shrugged his shoulders and said,

"Well, that's put the block on that!" Then... "Ain't it!" he croaked, not looking too happy in himself at all. Denzel and Wal knew it was a tease, but never let on, and sat watching their best pal stew in his own juice, thinking his gallivanting around the plot with the chaps had come to a standstill; and now the old cockney was on a bit of a downer... "Cor, is it worth it? I can't even knock abaat wiv me china plates 'n' all for the sake of having a few dustbin lids on board. Gutted I am! Bloomin' 'ell, it's a bit strong en it!" he sadly croaked. After putting her old man through a couple of minutes of hell, Tootsy looked, then smiling at Denzel and Wal from behind her unhappy hubby's back,

"Of course you can, diddums, I was only having some fun with you, wasn't I, boys?" A huge grin automatically appeared on Treadwell's face.

"Gawd love a duck, d'y mean it, Toots darlin'?"

"Yes, of course, my lovely little cherub chops!" she was really rubbing it in now, letting his pals know that the hard-case from Lewisham was in fact a big old softy when alone with his stunning cunning Tootsy.

"Leave it aat gel, you've gorn 'n' made me go all red nah!" Tootsy, being a Chislehurst girl, was well clued up on a bit of lake knowledge, and although her hubby was brought up the hard way in a rough neighbourhood, that girl could do what she liked with the loveable scallywag.

Denzel and Wal looked at one another, and together mimicked Tootsy's lovey dovey words;

"Diddums.... cherub chops!" as loud as they could. This was just about the end of the cockney's hard-case image for good. But in truth, and especially since hearing it was all a joke, the father-to-be was lapping it all up and couldn't, and I mean couldn't, wait for the day to arrive; but at this very moment the old Londoner was definitely under a bit of embarrassing pressure. There was only an hour of daylight left, and after being asked to stay the night, the two lads decided they must go home so's not to worry Aunty Clara, especially so soon after getting back together again. But before they left, Tootsy made the two lads promise not to say a word to anyone, about her condition especially Aunty, or Clarence because it was obvious the dear girl wanted to break the joyous news to them herself. Well, the promise they made, and if ever there was a test of will-power for the erratic Warbler, then this was surely it.

A couple of days had passed and life on and about the lakes were getting back to normal for this time of year. It was a wonderful place to be in spring-time, and if we humans think the sound from these modern day music machines can make a half decent sound, then you'd better grab yourselves a cotton bud 'n' clean your lugholes out. Because if you happened by this neck of the woods, then maybe you could be fortunate enough to hear the love songs coming from the multitude of courting couples, that, I'm sure it would blow your mind.

On Coot Island over the past day or two nothing maternal was ever mentioned to the elderly couple, and going by the way the agitated Wal had been restless on his perch one could tell, keeping just a simple secret was taking its toll on the blabbering Wal, he was really finding it hard to keep such an important joyful bit of news to himself, but appeared to be holding his own. Denzel, whilst in conversation, hadn't said anything more on the subject for fear of letting anything slip out in front of the two olduns. Clara, never got a sniff of Tootsy's condition, but the ageing broody hen was no fool when it came to knowing the two lads as she did "Something was going on" she had thought to herself, but for the life of her the old dear even with her motherly instincts, just couldn't fathom it out.

On the fifth day back together Denzel and Wal, decided it was time to swim around the whole perimeter of the lake in which they lived. Stepping from the island Denzel pushed off into the water, he was full grown now and as Aunt Clara put it to Clarence "that the little lad looked real handsome!" His majestic face and neck, which shone in the morning sun like an emerald. He had grown into a beautiful bird, and his distinguished Mallard markings were all there in the right places, and there was no doubt, that anyone who knew about such creatures could tell in an instant that he was a very well bred duck. Wally floating above could hardly wait to get going.

"What way Den?" he asked excitedly, as they both moved out into the lake further. Denzel told Wally that if they go left they can swim up towards the opposite side of the waterfall to where Treadwell's home was situated. On their way across the lake they met numerous friends and joyfully passed the time of day, they were just passing underneath the craggies on their way to the left hand side of the fierce crashing 'n' bashings they could hear in the distance. On passing they looked to see if there was any sign of Owen, knowing all the time there was very little chance of that at this time of day, for the old Wizard of the Willows would be well and truly in cloud cuckoo land at such an unearthly hour. The two lads were approaching the side of the waterfall, just below the place where they had their first ever meeting with Kenny's antics in the swallowing department. Denzel was enjoying every moment whilst he paddled on through the water, Wally was chirping away and appeared to be having a fair old time of it all, when all of a sudden they heard a terrible call for help coming from the waterfall area. At first, it wasn't easy for them to make out who or where, the cries were coming from but, as they came round a bend they saw quite a variety of mixed birds. At first Denzel thought it was just another gathering of friends enjoying the fresh morning air, but Wal, from his higher view point spotted the real reason for such a commotion, and what that boy saw terrified him There was a gathering of young birds of similar ages to themselves, some young males on the water, just out of reach of the dangerous down pour, which Uncle had warned them of on that first ever outing. The ones on the water seemed to be surrounding something that was floating on the water's surface, also a dozen or so young females on the sidelines were a-screaming in fright of something that had happened. Denzel saw at a glance that something was desperately wrong, so he and Wal hurried to the scene. Frantically, they moved nearer to the spot which was close to the bank at the left hand side of the waterfall. They couldn't believe their eyes, there in a mangled mess of broken bones and feathers, was a young male moorhen; the two lads could see at a glance that it was one of Aunt Clara's gossiping partners, Mini Moorhen's grandson, Melvin. Both gagged at the sight of their dear stupid friend, who hadn't taken a blind bit of notice of the advice and warnings given during the act of growing up.

No, Melvin unfortunately, now that it was courting time was doing his usual Jack the lad bit, by swimming so bravely, or so he thought, right underneath the evil pounding water, showing off to a bunch of giggly ecstatic girls, trying to get himself a wife. Yet through him not listening to his elders he had sadly lost his life. Denzel and Wal along with the rest of the gathering were devastated, and tears were streaming down faces of friends, and a dozen or so lookers on, who had witnessed the incident from the very start of the poor soul's plight. The two lad's immediately seeing there was nothing they could do returned to the island reporting their bad news. It was a very sad moment, especially when Clara had sent for Mini and gently broke the dreadful news, which caused a terrible upset in the moorhen family for months after.

All the time the duck had been enjoying himself, he had been unaware of courting time; but fortunately for him it hadn't escaped the old Wizard's attention; and whilst Denzel was getting up to all kinds of funny goings on about the place, Owen had been doing a crafty bit of match-making behind his Mallard friend's back. Ever since last autumn, when Owen first noticed that where Denzel was having so much fun with his pals, he had strayed from his natural path and hadn't been looking at the opposite sex It worried him at first; but he came to the conclusion that it was due to the lad's bad start in life. So without a word, he let Denzel carry on with his life style and was glad to see him grow into the intelligent good-looking bird he certainly was. However, one day he was on a return trip from visiting the king at Gracelands, over at one of the smaller lakes, and whilst on the way back his huge eyes had seen some families of Mallards having some fun and games together at the water's edge. But what really caught his eye was not so much the pleasantries going on, but the pretty female who was sitting on her own, who didn't seem interested in games. Owen dropped down, and settled nearby. She didn't see him at first, and then he spoke,

"Why aren't you out there enjoying yourself with the others, my lovely?"

"I don't like silly games!" she told him.

"My, you're a beautiful girl, you should be out there with the others having the time of your life, with looks like that!" he hooted again. "Have you any boyfriends?" At this question the dear girl burst into tears, explaining to Owen that there was only one boy she had set her heart on, and that he lived on the big Lake.

"Oh!" said Owen, "and what name would this young fella be having, and why do you like him, in particular?"

"I think his name is Denzel; I only met him once when I was small. He really is good looking though, and the bravest of all birds!" she recalled. Hearing this made old Owen's eyebrows turn up at the corners.

"Oh, I see!" he hooted. Then the cunning old Owl fell silent in one of his deep thinking moods. After plenty of thought Owen left the young lady and made his way over to where her parents were feeding and having a natter.

"Morning, Dan, and how are you and the missus then, eh?"

"Very well, thank you, Owen, and how's yourself?"

"Fine, fine!" He was still scheming... "Tell me now, your beautiful daughter; why is it that a girl with looks that would tear the heart from every young drake, who'd ever come in contact with her, and look at the sweet thing, she isn't paired off yet?"

"God only knows; I honestly can't make the girl out. It's not that she hasn't had any offers, in fact there were so many young drakes flapping 'n' posing around here in the autumn, I had to take a stick to them!" replied old Dan, sounding quite concerned for the daughter he rightfully idolised. At Owen's question Dandy, Dan's missus and the mother of the young beauty, soon put her quack in, and quickly came to her daughter's aid .

"I'll tell you what's the matter with the dear child, she's never been the same ever since returning from that trip with her Aunt Debbie, who took Daryl to the big lake early last summer. If my memory still serves me well, when she returned, all that anyone could get out of her, was that she had met the bravest, most good looking, most charming drake in the world!"

Hearing this, Owen knew in his mind that the two youngsters were made for each other, and all he had to do was come up with a plan so's they could meet one another. Once Owen's brain cogs ceased turning in his old wise head, he came up with a blinder.

"Right!" he hooted, "this is what I think we should do. Tomorrow morning after breakfast, I want you both to take the girl on an outing over to the big lake, I want you to take her to the small cove, you know, the one where that fibbing Rat hangs about!" The very respectful parents acknowledged that they knew the place he spoke of, and agreed to do as the wise one wished.

The old tawny told Dan and wife that after the youngsters introduction, and if all goes to plan, to leave them to find one another. He also went on to say, "Meet me at Coot Island mid-morning, I want you to meet Denzel's folks."

But before leaving he told them, "Whatever you do, don't tell your daughter anything!" Owen chuckled to himself... "I do believe we might just be able to work something out here, that will suit us all!" And before he left for the Craggies, he told the respected parents, "Mum's the word, let's keep our beaks crossed that some good will come out of this day's work, and if my hunch is right, I'm sure of that!"

The two lads had been out and about the lakes over the past week or so. They had kept well away from Treadwell's residence, letting the expectant parents have time to adjust, although they would have loved their cockney pal to be tagging along, but they were also old enough to know that he and Tootsy needed their own space, but today they decided to pay them a visit and see their amphibian pals; and both hoped, that Neddy would be about also. It was a glorious sunny morning, and after they had made up their minds to go and see the toads, Denzel, through being so eager, decided not to swim, but surprised Wally by challenging him to a race over to their friend's residence at the waterfall end of the lake.

"You're havin' a lark, ain't ya!" chirped Wally. The duck laughed, and told him that he should leave the island, as the crow flies, to another little island that was about the half-way mark. Wal gave it some excited thoughts and then... "On one condition!" the little rascal chirped.

"What is that?" asked Denzel.

"I can have a rest for ten minutes once I get there!" chirped Wal, in fits of excited laughter.

"Of course you can, Wally; I don't expect you to keep up with a bird of my size!"

The duck was laughing too, but once Denzel had agreed Wally took to the air and flew in steady little flits 'n' bursts out into the lake, heading in the direction of Toad's Terrace. He was in no rush at this stage, for Wal knew he would need all his strength for the last hundred 'n' fifty yards. He reached the very small island that was no more than twenty five feet by fifteen, and lacked vegetation, except for a few reeds that grew in patches around its perimeter. None of the locals could have fancied the little site to live on, otherwise it would have already been taken. There was an assortment of small bushes and a few thick clumps of grass, though not dense greenery with trees and foliage like most of the places already taken. But it didn't stop a couple of love-struck Water Rails snapping up the property a bit lively, and they were now in the process of tidying the place up ready to start their own family in the not-too-distant future. Wally when reaching the small island, settled himself on a branch of one of the trees available. The moment the excited Wal landed he turned to look back and saw Denzel talking to Aunt Clara; he also saw Uncle Clarence out on the feeding grounds ducking his head every few minutes nibbling at his favourite weed below. Whilst Wally was taking his allowed rest period, he was distracted by something rustling in the reeds below, and as he looked down he saw the two love-struck home-makers, who whilst doing their chores, kept stopping for a little cuddle 'n' peck at each other in passing. Wal smiled at the loving couple and admired the love that filled the air and dropped from his perch, flapping furiously and heading speedily towards Treadwell's neck of the Lake.

Yet with all his flits 'n' bursts the duck had taken flight and was gaining on Wally fast, knowing all the time that the little fella never stood a chance, even with the start he had. Flapping furiously Wally was going at it hammer 'n' tongs, but when he looked over his shoulder to see his pal in hot pursuit, Denzel was no-where to be seen, yet Wal wasn't giving up the race that easily and still carried on in case it was a trick the duck had played. Wally landed and before anything else, he turned to see what had happened to his mate, but there was no sign of him anywhere. He was starting to get worried, when Nuthouse Neddy spotted him and squealed to Toad close by...

"There's Wally!" It didn't take the toad long before he noticed an uncertain look come over the little bird's face.

"Cheer up, Wally me son! Wot's up then, eh?" Treadwell could see that he was looking out over the lake very agitatedly indeed.

"Er... I don't know really!" he chirped, and then went on to tell the two toads and Neddy all about their race and how he saw Denzel take to the air. "And that was the last I saw of him!" Wal told them nervously. All three amphibians shook their heads indicating that they hadn't seen a thing.

Denzel had seen Wally plotted up taking his given rest period at the half-way stage. While he waited he had given his wings a few flaps to warm up getting rid of the odd bit of stiffness seeing as he'd not long been out of the roost. Once Wally's time was up the duck had taken to the air in hot pursuit of his little partner's tail. He'd been very excited, with nothing on his mind except catching Wally up, when all of a sudden something made his heart beat even more quicker, and before he had the chance to get into top gear, he saw three of his own kind cross his flight path and drop down on the water over by the little cove where he'd first encountered Harry the Rat. Even at the speed he was going it didn't stop his eyes from almost springing from their sockets at the sight of the gorgeous chick among them. Well, that was it; at this sighting his wings just turned to jelly; even he never had an inkling as to what was happening to him. All thoughts and ideas of the race with Wal had gone from his head completely, and his mind was only on one thing: the little bit of fluff that had just gone by. Without the slightest bit of consideration for Wal, and unable to help himself, he did no more than follow his instincts, not even knowing what had hit him. Without any thought for his friends he'd unknowingly changed direction. It was as though for the first time in his life they had never even existed. Soon after the strangers had settled on the water just at the mouth of the small cove, when the love-struck duck came crashing down onto the water seemingly out of control. It was hardly surprising when the dear boy's knee caps and wings had failed him; it was oh so obvious that he had been bitten by a love bug, and believe me if you saw that same serene beauty he was looking at now, then you'd understand I'm sure. Being startled by Denzel's dodgy landing, the three Mallard strangers watched as they tried to get himself together as he quickly attempted to tidy his appearance.

"Why, good morning to you, young fella!" said the proud elder drake, whom Denzel had taken to be this lovely chick's father. At those few words, the poor lad was so nervous his heart started to pound so much, he felt it was playing a tune on his ribs, although he did manage a shaky hello, but never once took his eyes off the most attractive female he'd ever seen. She, at this time, was shyly smiling half hidden behind her doting parents. And what a smile; it was something her parents hadn't seen in months, and who in this world could blame him for his temporary forgetfulness regarding Wally? Well, let me tell you, if Aphrodite was the goddess of love, then you have seen nothing compared to what this chick oozed. No wonder the poor lad was besotted. Mum and Dad of course, when seeing Denzel's confused antics, knew exactly what his problem was and quickly broke the ice.

"And whom, do we have the pleasure of meeting?" enquired the elder female, whom Denzel had taken for mother.

"D...Denzel!" he spluttered, embarrassed, as he swam towards the smiling threesome.

"Is that so!" said the elder male. "This is my wife, Dandy, and this is my only daughter Daryl. Quite pretty too, don't you think son, umm?" Although Denzel nodded a dreamy sort of yes, going by what these strangers saw in the hapless duck's face, they didn't really need to be answered; they only had to look at Denzel's bloodshot eyes and stammering to see that the boy was completely beak-smacked, and was in dire straits in the love department. Under normal circumstances he would have been paired off back in the autumn, but through his earlier traumatic experience, followed by being raised by the caring coots, then his meeting with the leathery Londoner and Wal, coupled with all the exciting times they'd shared, he had never really thought about anything else. Fact was, he hadn't been doing what ordinary Mallards do at all. No, he, like any normal duck of his kind would pal up with their son, and do as Mallards do at the normal times, like finding their wives during the Autumn.

Soon after the meeting and introductions were made, the two grown-up conspirators made an excuse that they were hungry, and left the two lovebirds to themselves. Once left alone, Denzel asked Daryl if she would share some breakfast if they could find something suitable to eat, and when she gave a nodding yes, he smiled at her silent answer. At her agreeing nod, he turned and swam away, Daryl followed and together they swam around the edge of the cove in search of food. Denzel dearly hoped that whatever they found hadn't been eaten or housed by that dreadful Rat, Harry. Swimming slowly underneath the willows that hung over them, they found what was left of the water bailiff's lunch which he sometimes purposely left for any of the lake's residents, whoever came by the food first. The two love-birds shared their findings, and afterwards began chatting as though they were never strangers. It seemed that once Daryl's parents had left their company, the once shy beauty wasn't so shy. Only in the presence of her folks had she felt so shy and embarrassed. Only when they went out of sight did the dear girl come into her own; her shyness had completely subsided, and Denzel just couldn't believe the sudden change. Although the young beauty appeared shy at first, it couldn't have been further from the truth. He could tell she was not only a stunning female, but very intelligent as well. He also noticed that she had an air of confidence about her in the way she carried herself, and qualities he admired very much. He couldn't put his beak on it, yet he was sure he had seen this beautiful face before.

"Haven't we met somewhere before?" he asked.

"Y… yes we have!" she quacked. "But it was ages ago!"

"We have!" Denzel was astonished. Searching his mind, he tried to recall how or when this meeting could have been, yet curiosity got the better of him... "When?" he pleaded.

"Oh, it was back in the early summer of last year remember, when your tiny erratic friend, enticed you into the bravery contest against Charley the bravest of all coots, but he wasn't as brave as you!" she added, fluttering her eyes and causing Duck pimples to run up 'n' down the besotted drake's spine.

"Of course I remember now that you mention it, and the little rascal you call my friend, was Wally!" Yet even mentioning Wal's name didn't even register that he'd abandoned his best pal, leaving him high and dry, as he'd fallen in love with this bewitching beauty who had utterly stolen his heart.

"Daryl!" he exclaimed. "How on water could I have forgotten! Y... you were that girl in the crowd who quacked to me, and I asked you your name!" And before he could say another word the girl told him exactly what she wanted.

"Yes, that's right, and I've loved, and dreamt of you ever since!" she answered. Hearing the girl's statement, our boy's heart melted, for his own feelings, although recently stirred were likewise; and the only thing he wanted now was to spend the rest of his life with the beautiful girl with whom he'd hopelessly fallen in love.

"Have you any girlfriends?" she asked, hoping in her heart his answer would be no. But Denzel was so smitten he hardly let her finish.

"Er... no, but I do have lots of friends though!" hearing the answer she wanted to hear, Daryl had never felt so happy in her entire life, and the beauty didn't mince her words either. In her happy determined state of mind, she had waited quite long enough, and being a girl of the sixties never beat about the bush.

At this claim, Denzel could tell by the wonderful feelings that were running through his whole body, something was telling him that he and she were destined for one another. He did no more, but swam towards this girl who blatantly said that she loved him and pecked her gently on the cheek, knowing in his heart he at last had found what his own father had found in his mother, and that was the reality of true love; and from that day on the pair of them were inseparable. Well except when he has a day out with the chap's of course.

When leaving the cove Dan and the wife headed straight for Coot Island. They had planned to meet Owen there. And when telling Clara that the girl's parents were due at any time, she darted away to her mirror to give herself a little wash and preen up. When they arrived Owen was there already to greet them along with a pair of ageing coots whom they had never had the pleasure of meeting before. He was sitting on an old gnarled stump when he welcomed them aboard. Dan and wife were respectfully met at the water's edge, and once seated comfortably were shown much hospitality, which led to a good old chinwag for a couple of hours, although as you can imagine the main chatter was about the courting couple. The news that the old couple had unexpectedly received was wonderful, and both discussed the matter on several occasions knowing all the time the young lad should have been doing what he was doing at this very moment, way back in the autumn. Yet no one was more surprised when Owen, out of the blue had filled them in on the young beauty and the plan he'd prepared. Clarence was really chuffed at the news and listened to every detail of Owen's planning, shaking his old head at what he'd heard, then.

"You're a crafty old devil, Owen, but a very clever one, I'll give you that!"

"Oh, it was nothing really, it's what us owls call awareness. Oh, I knew all along that the boy was late in finding a wife, and when I saw that young girl sitting alone I did my calculations and came up with one 'n' one put together resulting in what you see now this very minute swimming towards us."

The small gathering on the island was interrupted by Wally's sudden appearance. He was just about to blab his beak about Denzel's disappearance. But then he saw Owen and the two strange Mallards talking to Clara and Clarence. His little heart almost stopped for he knew that any time the old Tawny was up and out of the roost at this hour it was usually a sign of bad times, or at least something of much importance. For a brief moment the little bird's thoughts were only of Denzel and what dreadful thing that could have happened to him.

"Where's Denzel?" he asked nervously, and going by the tone of his voice, and the worried look on his tiny face, the ever-caring Clara could see the little lad was in a right old state of affairs with worry. Knowing this, Clara almost immediately put him at ease.

"Come down here, ducks and sit by me!" Wally dropped from his high perch and settled on the branch of a small sapling right next to Clara, but facing inwards to the small circle of friends. He cocked his little head to one side and listened carefully to what she had to say. She was dreading it, knowing just how insecure he had been in the past; but even so, she began the task of explaining some of the facts of life, and how it was time for Denzel to settle down and start a family of his own. She introduced him to Dan and Dandy, then went on to tell of where and what Denzel was doing. Listening intently Wal was having trouble taking it all in, and was frantically biting his beak trying to fight the turmoil of hurtful feeling that tormented him inside. All he could get into his little head was that he'd never see his best mate again.

"And lost to a girl Duck too!" he sorrowfully thought to himself, though Clara's next word eased the terrible pain he felt right now.

"Don't go upsetting yourself now, little one, you'll still be able to see him!" she softly told him.

"When?" he chirped. And perked up a bit at what she said.

"Just be patient a little longer, lad, he'll be here soon enough!" chimed in old Uncle Clarence.

"What, and the girl duck too?" Wally had hardly got his question out when...

"Here they come now!" hooted Owen, who had been silently smiling to himself; for only minutes earlier he'd actually been watching the courting couple leaving the cove heading in their direction and, what he could see, if his eyes weren't playing tricks, was that his plan had worked a treat. Wal's little brain was scrambled; one half didn't at all like the girl duck's intrusion, but as they swam closer Wally saw her beauty, then the contentment on his best pal's face, he didn't know whether to laugh or cry; but Clara, and all were so delighted that the little lad chose the first choice and now was to-ing 'n' thro-ing absolutely alight with excitement. In fact he couldn't wait to meet the beauty with the wild eyes and the wonderful wicked, wicked smile. No one had to tell Wally anything anymore. Just looking at the approaching couple together made him feel like he'd never felt before, and it had occurred to him that he must be growing up, 'cause he wasn't getting any of those horrible hurt feelings like he used to. Well, not so much anyway. No, there he was completely the opposite, even at the thought of losing his best pal to a "blimmin' girl duck!" which, if the lad was to be truthful, did cross his little mind at first. Yet now the little bird's cheeky beak was full of smiles, especially after being assured by his lovely old aunt that he and Denzel would be able to see one another each day and still have good times together. She also reminded him, "Toad being married to Tootsy didn't stop you all being together as friends, and nor will it be with you and Denzel!" Aah, Clara did feel for the little rascal though, for she knew in her heart that the chances of him finding a girlie one of his own kind was very unlikely, and the old dear shook her head and raised her eyes to the heavens in the hope that something good would come of it all in the end; 'cause in truth the old girl knew her heart just couldn't take much more.

All but Owen rushed to the water's edge. He sat and watched the contented parent's wallow in their new-found happiness. As the love-birds swam across the lake, all could see the couple were getting on famously, side by side they were chatting happily together as they approached the reception of smiling faces that greeted them; so that in itself told them both that their choices were more than approved. Then, like a bolt out of the sky, Denzel saw Wally, and his first pangs of guilt shot through his veins like a firestick.

"Wally," he cried, "Oh Wally I… I'm so sorry, I… I set off after you in the race, and from there… Well, I just don't know really what happened!" Denzel felt uneasy not understanding what really did happen, but realized he'd been badly bitten by that bug that brings the love.

"Oh, that's all right, Den!" Then he surprised them all, by chirpily adding… "Well, aren't ya going to introduce us then?" Wal's cheeky face was now diverted to Daryl, who was thinking that very moment that being with Denzel, and part of what she saw of his family and friends, she was the happiest she had ever been in her life, and she hasn't even heard of the Cockney, yet Denzel couldn't believe his ears and eyes at the way Wally had taken it all so easily. He was confused at what he had done to Wal and found it hard to come to terms with himself, with so many wonderful things happening in such a short time; and not having to witness one of Wal's dodgy turns truly was a joyful bonus.

"Owen, Mum and Dad, and you Wal, I'd like you all to meet my beautiful intended wife Daryl!" Well, you should have seen the faces on the two olduns when hearing the lad refer to them as his Mum and Dad. The two elder females were sitting together with tears welled in their eyes. Clarence and old Dan were slapping their wings together in a manner which I've only seen in members of the human West Indian population. All were over the moon at the beautiful couple's news, and Wal, well, he just sat there in a little dream with smiles on board for sure, and Owen hadn't said a word. Oh he was more than pleased with the outcome, but did have a little chuckle to himself thinking he still hadn't lost his touch. On the other hand, whilst sitting on the water beside her Drake, Daryl looked so in love, and her beauty was such that it appeared to be held in the air by a radiant haze.

"Hello!" she confidently said, but never allowed herself to be too forward. Clara and Clarence ran their eyes over their future daughter-in-law and were more than contented in what they saw and after a quick smile in the old wizard's direction, they welcomed her into the fold with open wings. After a bit more excited chatter it was time for Dan and Dandy to leave and get back to their own territory, and after giving their daughter their blessings and a peck on the cheek, they left her in Denzel's charge. Just seeing that sparkle of love in both their eyes let them go away knowing at last their daughter's dreams had come true. They left word that they would be back in a few days to discuss and make plans for the wedding. Daryl had kissed her parents lovingly before they took off from the island heading for home. Whilst the company were engrossed in seeing them off, Clara still watching them fly off in the distance, and without moving her eyes, said to Owen,

"What a nice couple Daryl's parents are!" But did she get an answer? No. And when she looked over at the old instigator, he was fast asleep and snoring his head off. He had been very tired when returning from his night's hunting, but knowing his plan would be in action this very day, there was no chance of his missing the results of his handiwork for the world. But it seems once he was satisfied his plan had worked, he had fallen asleep without realising.

"Why don't you get yourself home, old bird? You look worn out!" said the concerned female.

"Agh, oh, umm, where am I er...?" The wizard was so tired he didn't know where he was for the moment. Then... "Did ya say something, old girl?"

"Asleep!" she reminded him.

"Who me? No, no, no, I was thinking, that's all!" the eccentric Tawny hooted. Clara smiled and looked at Daryl, then at the rest of the family, and they, like the old girl were smiling at his slippery recovery. After one or two long-drawn-out yawns, he told them that he was going home to get his head down, but not before telling the courting couple to come by the Craggies in a day or two for there was some matters he wanted to see them about, and after saying they would, they said their farewells and Owen took to the air and disappeared in the direction of his residence.

That night, once sleeping arrangements had been sorted out, the latest addition to the family had slept well on Coot Island, and after all the excitement of the day before, not a single member had over-lain. Clarence was the first to rise,

val so much that anyone watching them from a distance
have thought they were listening to a bit of live music.

the meantime, over at Toad's Terrace, Treadwell was
y concerned for his pal's sudden disappearance; and not
g any news by noon he was a very worried toad, and
iscussing it with his wife he decided he couldn't just sit
oing nothing, so he called on Shifty Swift, who had not
rived at the lakes from his winter migration. Treadwell
ked him if he would do him a favour, and after Shifty
f how important it was he agreed wholeheartedly to go.
asked to fly as swiftly as he could to Chislehurst pond,
l the Canadian Goose, Mac, to come to their lakes
y.

big goose arrived in just over the hour from when he
l the message, and had flown him and Tootsy straight
ld couple's island. The toads were surprised to see a
s girl duck, who was sitting talking to Clara and
e, but was soon introduced to Daryl as Denzel's young
en old Clarence took over by telling them where the
e now, and the reason why.

he first inkling who Daryl was, Tootsy, such a happy
n in her condition, leapt over to Daryl and kissed her,
r she welcomed her into the family, then instantly
talk in the language that young ladies do under such
ances.

l, I'll be blowed!" croaked the cockney; then as he
e looked into Daryl's wild eyes, he smiled to himself
eauty, and going by the way her 'n' his Toots were
p, he knew in his old cockney heart that the girl was

Stanley and the two lads left the island, they flew
cross land to the pasture to where daily sightings had
rted by Levy, who earlier had reckoned he'd actually
her. When they arrived they saw the main party of
at one end of the field by some trees that hung over a
ving Bunkhouse Bill and the old stager Champion at
where they were talking to a new face in the pasture.
ore interested in what he'd heard, had darted to the

exiting from the log at 6.30 a.m. followed by Denzel and Daryl who had taken up temporary roost in a thick bed of dried bulrush leaves that was among the dense new growth. And after saying their good mornings, one of Wally's eyes shot open at the sound of chatter and a bright new day which brought him wide awake. He now dropped down from his roost to join his friends below. Clara was the last to get up, but soon livened up and took charge of Daryl, wanting to get the dear child organised as soon as possible, to get her settled in so she would feel more at home.

"Would you like to freshen up before breakfast, dear?" fussed the old girl.

"Yes please, er…!" Daryl was so embarrassed, in all the unexpected excitement she had forgotten the lovely old lady's name.

"Clara, dear, you can call me Clara, if that's all right with you lass?"

"Oh thank you, Clara, I could do with it!" she laughed. Then… "Just look at the state of my feathers, I must look in a right old mess!" she quacked. The old hen Coot smiled at the young beauty and thought to herself…

"It wouldn't matter if the child was smothered in mud, nothing could hide that beauty!" Yet Clara recalled how she used to react when she had first met Clarence. "Come along ducks, let us leave these three rascals to get on with themselves!" The two females headed for Clara's puddle mirror so's to clean 'n' preen, powder their noses and talk as ladies do. Whilst the girls were fixing themselves up, old Clarence and the two lads did likewise, and by 7.15 a.m. all were washed, had breakfast and were now digesting their food in the sun. After an hour or so chatting to one another, Denzel suggested that he'd like to fly over to Treadwell's to fetch him and Tootsy back so he could introduce them to Daryl. He also wanted to see the faces of the two olduns' especially Clara's when being told the news of Tootsy's condition.

"Aye, if I had a lass like that, I'd want to show her to the world!" said the proud old Coot. "You run along now and fetch them, lad. The lass will be in good company here!"

Whilst Clarence was saying his bit Denzel, Daryl and the Dartford dodger were all looking at Clara, who was glaring at the old fella as he said it.

"Oh you would, would you?" fussed Clara, giving the eye to the three youngens.

"Nay lass, don't you go getting yourself all jealous now!" the old boy was grinning whilst giving as good as he got.

"Ha! Jealous am I now? What with you and your bad back 'n' piles I've got no worries in that department!" she taunted back at him. Daryl was in fits of laughter at all the comical carryings-on. And although she'd felt at home from the start, yet seeing with her own eyes the way the loving old couple were joking and larking about like they do, she loved living with her new family even more.

Then all of a sudden, Stanley fell from the sky, landing on a branch some eight feet above the company; but what he had to say made Denzel forget about his intended trip to fetch the Toads.

"Watcha, all!" he whistled and the company broke off from their conversation and looked up to where the not so narrow Starling was sitting. They could tell at a glance he'd put on even more weight; in fact it was noticed that the bough he was sitting on actually had a slight bend in it, and if he didn't watch out he'd go completely in the opposite direction to the proportions of his former self.

"Hey, it's Stanley!" greeted Denzel, leaving the rest to acknowledge him.

"What brings you this way lad? Anything in particular or have you just come to visit?" enquired the old Yorkshire Coot.

"As a matter of fact there is, Clarence, and it concerns young Wally boy there!" directing his beak in the Warblers direction.

"What's that then?" chirped Wal.

"Well, I was sitting on my ledge, you know, outside my place where we used to sit, Wal, when Moisha Goldfinch dropped by for a natter. Cor, flippin' 'ell, that boy can wave his wings about when he's talking. Blow him calling round in the future. He half sent me deaf, and... almost had me off the ledge a couple of times. Any-how a b[...] may have come out of it, from what I've [...] me that Levy the traveller had asked h[...] me at the stack.

He gave me a message, I didn't kno[...] in it, so I flew over there to see him ye[...] myself, and he told me there's been a lit[...] looks your age and he told me that s[...] pasture on and off over the past few day[...]

When Stanley had said his piece[...] diverted to Wally and not even a brea[...] showing signs of a bit of shyness, and [...] to say, in fact, he nervously started [...] upside down business like he do, and th[...]

"A little girl one of me...?" The[...] across Stanley's face as he nodded yes[...]

"Where is she then?" he nervously[...] make of it all. Stanley admitted he'd n[...] assured the little bird.

"Levy may be a gypsy, yet his i[...] doubtless!"

"Aren't you going to go and ha[...] ducks?" Clara's heart strings were dan[...] not heartache it's heartbreak!" she lovi[...]

"Come on Wally, let's go with St[...] go and find her for you!" Denzel, afte[...] when finding his own love was begin[...] little friend something, so he pro[...] warbler to go. Yet as fast as his shyn[...] curiosity got the better of him.

"You're not playing games are y[...] couldn't believe it possible for a [...] actually be in Dartford at the same ti[...] possibilities as folly, but it most ce[...] from wanting to go over to the pastur[...]

"Oh, I do hope so, Wally, it will b[...] Denzel?" quacked the beauty at his si[...] as for that Clarence and Clara, had be[...]

first patch of gorse that came into sight, for he knew that if a Dartford one was about, that was the kind of place he'd find her. The two big birds taxied in to land, but Stanley startled Levy, who swished his tail at the starling's cheeky landing on his rump. The big horse was also surprised at Denzel's sudden appearance, but was even more surprised when he turned to see his nit-picking partner prancing about on his hind quarters.

"Lord help us, my dear Stanley, you trashed me ta death ol' bruvver!" Then he started to think of that dreaded itch that was going on behind his ear, and hoped that the starling would oblige. He and his gypsy friends exchanged good mornings, then the huge stallion asked them where their little friend was.

"I'm up here!" chirped Wally. At Wal's little chirp Levy and the rest of the company looked up to see him. All could tell that the little chap had matured since they last saw him, and thought how smart he looked in his new shining rust-red waistcoat.

"Stanley bruv, that boy's grewed up ain' he moosh?" whinnied the ex-pit-pony. Stanley agreed, but his mind was on other things.

"Levy, since I saw you yesterday, 'as that young female warbler been back in the field?" At the starling's question Wally's heart quickened in the hope that the horse would say yes, but the little lad's hopes were dashed when the answer came back no. Denzel had intervened and asked them exactly when and where had she been seen, when Bubbles the bay, who'd been listening with all the rest, had nodded her old head towards another patch of gorse just along from them by the corner of the field. The instant Wally heard this, his eyes strayed and were now fixed on the little bit of dense greenery that was blowing lightly in the breeze; but neither he nor anyone else could see any signs of a Dartford girly one. Denzel and Stanley, along with the rest of the gang, took their eyes off the gorse and together looked up at the sorry sight of poor Wally being wound up in this way. Then from out of the morning air,

"He-har... he-har whack!" called Dinsdale the dopey donkey, who had found the little lady, and who better?

According to him he'd spent most of his working life up on the beaches of Blackpool, so he'd had enough experience at spotting the birds, especially the nice gul's on the beach. He had only been down this way a couple of months, after his Liverpudlian master sold him to some passing gypsy for one 'n' ninepence, although he didn't sound very valuable he was worth his weight in gold when it came to spotting the birds.

At the donkey's piercing call, Wally's old knee caps complaint started, but before they gave out on him altogether the little fella dropped from his perch and in short flits 'n' bursts headed towards the thicket of gorse where the long-eared lover from Liverpool was standing; and as he landed on the nearby gorse he asked the donkey.

"Where?" But as he did he just followed the now smiling carrot cruncher's gaze... And there, sitting on a broom of gorse, not one foot from the ground was the sweetest tiny thing you have ever seen, and even the rest were puzzled how so much delicate beauty could be contained in such a small face. Wally couldn't believe his eyes, and within moments he flew down onto the well chewed-grasses to make sure he wasn't dreaming. Well, he wasn't, the moment he hit the floor he was no more than three feet away and as he jerked his little head up in a surprised look, his head knocked the clock from a dandelion stalk, sending it drifting off into the pretty little thing's direction.

"Who are you, then?" chirped Wal. Just looking at him one could tell that he was knocked bandy by her pleasing pretty looks, let alone her courtly manner and style.

"Wanda," she replied shyly and like Wally was more shocked as well as pleased at last to have found one of her own kind.

At the sound of her tiny voice, all his insecure ways and carryings-on had died, bringing only the warmth of that feeling called love that rose within him, and the little fella felt whole for the first time in his life, since leaving his family all those days ago. Even she, when seeing the size of Wal's chest whilst he was out on that grass posing, the girl couldn't help but feel safe.

exiting from the log at 6.30 a.m. followed by Denzel and Daryl who had taken up temporary roost in a thick bed of dried bulrush leaves that was among the dense new growth. And after saying their good mornings, one of Wally's eyes shot open at the sound of chatter and a bright new day which brought him wide awake. He now dropped down from his roost to join his friends below. Clara was the last to get up, but soon livened up and took charge of Daryl, wanting to get the dear child organised as soon as possible, to get her settled in so she would feel more at home.

"Would you like to freshen up before breakfast, dear?" fussed the old girl.

"Yes please, er...!" Daryl was so embarrassed, in all the unexpected excitement she had forgotten the lovely old lady's name.

"Clara, dear, you can call me Clara, if that's all right with you lass?"

"Oh thank you, Clara, I could do with it!" she laughed. Then... "Just look at the state of my feathers, I must look in a right old mess!" she quacked. The old hen Coot smiled at the young beauty and thought to herself...

"It wouldn't matter if the child was smothered in mud, nothing could hide that beauty!" Yet Clara recalled how she used to react when she had first met Clarence. "Come along ducks, let us leave these three rascals to get on with themselves!" The two females headed for Clara's puddle mirror so's to clean 'n' preen, powder their noses and talk as ladies do. Whilst the girls were fixing themselves up, old Clarence and the two lads did likewise, and by 7.15 a.m. all were washed, had breakfast and were now digesting their food in the sun. After an hour or so chatting to one another, Denzel suggested that he'd like to fly over to Treadwell's to fetch him and Tootsy back so he could introduce them to Daryl. He also wanted to see the faces of the two olduns' especially Clara's when being told the news of Tootsy's condition.

"Aye, if I had a lass like that, I'd want to show her to the world!" said the proud old Coot. "You run along now and fetch them, lad. The lass will be in good company here!"

Whilst Clarence was saying his bit Denzel, Daryl and the Dartford dodger were all looking at Clara, who was glaring at the old fella as he said it.

"Oh you would, would you?" fussed Clara, giving the eye to the three youngens.

"Nay lass, don't you go getting yourself all jealous now!" the old boy was grinning whilst giving as good as he got.

"Ha! Jealous am I now? What with you and your bad back 'n' piles I've got no worries in that department!" she taunted back at him. Daryl was in fits of laughter at all the comical carryings-on. And although she'd felt at home from the start, yet seeing with her own eyes the way the loving old couple were joking and larking about like they do, she loved living with her new family even more.

Then all of a sudden, Stanley fell from the sky, landing on a branch some eight feet above the company; but what he had to say made Denzel forget about his intended trip to fetch the Toads.

"Watcha, all!" he whistled and the company broke off from their conversation and looked up to where the not so narrow Starling was sitting. They could tell at a glance he'd put on even more weight; in fact it was noticed that the bough he was sitting on actually had a slight bend in it, and if he didn't watch out he'd go completely in the opposite direction to the proportions of his former self.

"Hey, it's Stanley!" greeted Denzel, leaving the rest to acknowledge him.

"What brings you this way lad? Anything in particular or have you just come to visit?" enquired the old Yorkshire Coot.

"As a matter of fact there is, Clarence, and it concerns young Wally boy there!" directing his beak in the Warblers direction.

"What's that then?" chirped Wal.

"Well, I was sitting on my ledge, you know, outside my place where we used to sit, Wal, when Moisha Goldfinch dropped by for a natter. Cor, flippin' 'ell, that boy can wave his wings about when he's talking. Blow him calling round in the future. He half sent me deaf, and… almost had me off the ledge a couple of times. Any-how a bit of interesting news may have come out of it, from what I've been hearing. He told me that Levy the traveller had asked him to drop by and see me at the stack.

He gave me a message, I didn't know how much truth was in it, so I flew over there to see him yesterday to find out for myself, and he told me there's been a little female warbler who looks your age and he told me that she's been visiting the pasture on and off over the past few days!"

When Stanley had said his piece, the company's eyes diverted to Wally and not even a breath was heard. He was showing signs of a bit of shyness, and really didn't know what to say, in fact, he nervously started to do all that hanging upside down business like he do, and then the little lad chirped.

"A little girl one of me...?" Then a huge smile sprang across Stanley's face as he nodded yes without saying a word.

"Where is she then?" he nervously asked not sure what to make of it all. Stanley admitted he'd not actually seen her, but assured the little bird.

"Levy may be a gypsy, yet his integrity on that score is doubtless!"

"Aren't you going to go and have a look for yourself ducks?" Clara's heart strings were dangling on a thread. "If it's not heartache it's heartbreak!" she lovingly thought to herself.

"Come on Wally, let's go with Stanley and see if we can go and find her for you!" Denzel, after what he'd done to him when finding his own love was beginning to feel he owed his little friend something, so he prompted the half-hearted warbler to go. Yet as fast as his shyness had left him, the old curiosity got the better of him.

"You're not playing games are ya, Stan?" the little fella couldn't believe it possible for a female Dartford one to actually be in Dartford at the same time, no, he dismissed the possibilities as folly, but it most certainly didn't deter him from wanting to go over to the pasture to make sure.

"Oh, I do hope so, Wally, it will be lovely for you, won't it Denzel?" quacked the beauty at his side. Her drake agreed, and as for that Clarence and Clara, had been nodding their heads in approval so much that anyone watching them from a distance would have thought they were listening to a bit of live music.

In the meantime, over at Toad's Terrace, Treadwell was gravely concerned for his pal's sudden disappearance; and not hearing any news by noon he was a very worried toad, and after discussing it with his wife he decided he couldn't just sit there doing nothing, so he called on Shifty Swift, who had not long arrived at the lakes from his winter migration. Treadwell had asked him if he would do him a favour, and after Shifty heard of how important it was he agreed wholeheartedly to go. He was asked to fly as swiftly as he could to Chislehurst pond, and tell the Canadian Goose, Mac, to come to their lakes urgently.

The big goose arrived in just over the hour from when he received the message, and had flown him and Tootsy straight to the old couple's island. The toads were surprised to see a gorgeous girl duck, who was sitting talking to Clara and Clarence, but was soon introduced to Daryl as Denzel's young lady. Then old Clarence took over by telling them where the lads were now, and the reason why.

At the first inkling who Daryl was, Tootsy, such a happy soul even in her condition, leapt over to Daryl and kissed her, and after she welcomed her into the family, then instantly began to talk in the language that young ladies do under such circumstances.

"Well, I'll be blowed!" croaked the cockney; then as he turned, he looked into Daryl's wild eyes, he smiled to himself at her beauty, and going by the way her 'n' his Toots were shaping up, he knew in his old cockney heart that the girl was a blinder.

After Stanley and the two lads left the island, they flew directly across land to the pasture to where daily sightings had been reported by Levy, who earlier had reckoned he'd actually spoken to her. When they arrived they saw the main party of the herd at one end of the field by some trees that hung over a fence, leaving Bunkhouse Bill and the old stager Champion at the other, where they were talking to a new face in the pasture. Wally, more interested in what he'd heard, had darted to the first patch of gorse that came into sight, for he knew that if a Dartford one was about, that was the kind of place he'd find her. The two big birds taxied in to land, but Stanley startled Levy, who swished his tail at the starling's cheeky landing on his rump. The big horse was also surprised at Denzel's sudden appearance, but was even more surprised when he turned to see his nit-picking partner prancing about on his hind quarters.

"Lord help us, my dear Stanley, you trashed me ta death ol' bruvver!" Then he started to think of that dreaded itch that was going on behind his ear, and hoped that the starling would oblige. He and his gypsy friends exchanged good mornings, then the huge stallion asked them where their little friend was.

"I'm up here!" chirped Wally. At Wal's little chirp Levy and the rest of the company looked up to see him. All could tell that the little chap had matured since they last saw him, and thought how smart he looked in his new shining rust-red waistcoat.

"Stanley bruv, that boy's grewed up ain' he moosh?" whinnied the ex-pit-pony. Stanley agreed, but his mind was on other things.

"Levy, since I saw you yesterday, 'as that young female warbler been back in the field?" At the starling's question Wally's heart quickened in the hope that the horse would say yes, but the little lad's hopes were dashed when the answer came back no. Denzel had intervened and asked them exactly when and where had she been seen, when Bubbles the bay, who'd been listening with all the rest, had nodded her old head towards another patch of gorse just along from them by the corner of the field. The instant Wally heard this, his eyes strayed and were now fixed on the little bit of dense greenery that was blowing lightly in the breeze; but neither he nor anyone else could see any signs of a Dartford girly one. Denzel and Stanley, along with the rest of the gang, took their eyes off the gorse and together looked up at the sorry sight of poor Wally being wound up in this way. Then from out of the morning air,

"He-har... he-har whack!" called Dinsdale the dopey donkey, who had found the little lady, and who better?

According to him he'd spent most of his working life up on the beaches of Blackpool, so he'd had enough experience at spotting the birds, especially the nice gul's on the beach. He had only been down this way a couple of months, after his Liverpudlian master sold him to some passing gypsy for one 'n' ninepence, although he didn't sound very valuable he was worth his weight in gold when it came to spotting the birds.

At the donkey's piercing call, Wally's old knee caps complaint started, but before they gave out on him altogether the little fella dropped from his perch and in short flits 'n' bursts headed towards the thicket of gorse where the long-eared lover from Liverpool was standing; and as he landed on the nearby gorse he asked the donkey.

"Where?" But as he did he just followed the now smiling carrot cruncher's gaze... And there, sitting on a broom of gorse, not one foot from the ground was the sweetest tiny thing you have ever seen, and even the rest were puzzled how so much delicate beauty could be contained in such a small face. Wally couldn't believe his eyes, and within moments he flew down onto the well chewed-grasses to make sure he wasn't dreaming. Well, he wasn't, the moment he hit the floor he was no more than three feet away and as he jerked his little head up in a surprised look, his head knocked the clock from a dandelion stalk, sending it drifting off into the pretty little thing's direction.

"Who are you, then?" chirped Wal. Just looking at him one could tell that he was knocked bandy by her pleasing pretty looks, let alone her courtly manner and style.

"Wanda," she replied shyly and like Wally was more shocked as well as pleased at last to have found one of her own kind.

At the sound of her tiny voice, all his insecure ways and carryings-on had died, bringing only the warmth of that feeling called love that rose within him, and the little fella felt whole for the first time in his life, since leaving his family all those days ago. Even she, when seeing the size of Wal's chest whilst he was out on that grass posing, the girl couldn't help but feel safe.

"Cor, look at those pecks!" she said admiringly, and Wally now sporting a very large grin on his face, poked his little rib cage out even further.

"Do you like 'em?" asked Wal, tensing his shoulders up even more.

"Not you, silly, I mean the way that tubby starling's pecking at one of those horse's ears." Wally, pulling a bit of a face, turned and there was his old landlord up behind Bubbles the bay gelding's lughole having a right old root out, and the fair old cob had a smile for a while.

But Wal was deflated immediately, especially as the surrounding company absolutely roared up at the cheeky hussy, knowing full well that the Dartford dodger had found more than his match in the comical capers and winding up department. Well, the little girl decided there and then that this was the one for her. Even Denzel, at the time of Wal's first chat-up lines, couldn't help but laugh as he watched his little pal's chest-expanding exploits. He could have sworn Wal had been breathing in just at the time of Wanda's wind-up, yet all in all the duck was more than happy to see his bestest mate pull a bird. He began to think how strange it seemed to be having so much happening over such a short period of time; he could understand it happening to one of them, but both finding a female – he found it hard to accept, especially knowing the chances of another warbler coming on the manor. He began to wonder if this whole escapade of finding a Dartford female one had been instigated by Wal's ex-landlord Stanley and the elders back on the island. Yet never in a million years did he guess that his own destiny had been tilted just a little bit by a very wise old owl.

Once acquainted, at Wally's request, Wanda had decided to go back to Coot Island with him and Denzel, and after her being told of the caring coots, she could hardly wait to meet them. Just before they left Wally thanked all the travellers for making his good fortune in meeting Wanda possible. He and his two pals also wished them a good summer on the road, for they knew that soon these four-footed roamers would once again be pulling their heavy loads whilst taking their human gypsy owners across the length and breadth of the land and back, when their winter's rest would start all over again.

The four birds had left the pasture and were now just coming into land on the island when they saw a small gathering on the island. Not only were there the two coots, but they were surprised to see Mac the Canada Goose there; and as Denzel came skidding in on the water into the front edge of the island, he also saw the toads. Stanley and the two small love-birds had settled down in the branches above. Wanda was introduced to Clara and Clarence, Toad and Toots and then the Canadian Goose. The two olduns were filled with so much happiness in having their ever growing family around them. At this time both were thrilled to bits when seeing that young Wal had secured a helluva pretty mate; and after listening to her sweet little chirp and getting to know her personality, the pair of 'em couldn't have been happier, if every one of them was of their own blood. And of course Toad was chuffed in meeting Stanley for the first time, not at this time knowing just how much of a part that the starling had really played whilst he was in the kip. Once all introductions were over and all the excitement had calmed, Tootsy gave a little interrupting cough to attract attention, and when silence fell around her she began to croak.

"Clara dear, now you and Clarence have got over this excitement, there's something else!" At this Clara's eyes went wide, and you could tell the old dear was wondering what on earth and water it could be.

"Oh, and what's that ducks?" asked the very intrigued Clara, and even old Clarence's face lit up in wonderment. Daryl had immediately taken Wanda into her care, and in no time at all the two girls were getting on famously. She had already whispered to her about the good news that Tootsy was about to announce, which made the little one smile and whispered in Daryl's ear, "Ah, how lovely!" Then the two of 'em moved in closer to watch the joy on the two olduns' faces on hearing Toad's wonderful news.

"Or would you rather tell them, Treadwell?"

"Er… yers course I will sweetheart!" the leathery Londoner braced himself. "Me gel's expectin'!" he croaked. The ageing couple of coots were thrilled to bits.

"When are they due?" Clara asked eagerly.

"Around June time!" replied the expectant mum. Then the two olduns looked happily at one another and the looks on their faces was of real contentment. Soon after so many surprises the company took lunch together as one big happy family for the first time. After they had all stoked up their bellies, they got themselves comfortable so's to rest and digest like they do. Then, Denzel began to explain to Treadwell the things that had happened during the months that he and Tootsy slept. Telling him first of how Wally had blatantly refused to migrate, then he went on and told Toad of his winter stay at Stanley's stack. Treadwell had to have a chuckle on hearing of the gypsy horse episode and his eyes were real wide in sheer astonishment at some of the stories the duck had told. Whilst listening you could tell by the look on his face, that he wished he didn't have to sleep so long, missing out on all the fun 'n' all. Denzel had also mentioned the snow and ice, but left the fireworks till last, for there was something else he had to say.

"Treadwell, I… I should have told you this earlier, but I just didn't know how to begin!" Toad's eyes went even wider wondering what on earth 'n' water what his pal was about to say.

"What's up nah, my son?" croaked toad.

"Well, whilst you were sleeping the king almost died!" said the duck.

"Nearly d… died? Wot, d'ya mean, nearly braan bread, er… dead? 'ow dit 'appen?"

"One of those horrid fishermen's hooks got caught in the back of his throat, and Wally took it out and saved King Cyril's life!" Hearing this made the toad smile in real amazement. He was looking straight up at Wal perched up above.

"Blindin' Wal, blindin' me son!" the Londoner croaked. The little fella, as you can imagine, especially after hearing Denzel's account of his medical skills, had the old smile on board, and his tiny chest was sticking out so far the lower company could hardly see his little head, except Wanda of course, who was real made-up after hearing how proper clever her fiancé was.

Over the next couple of days much was happening in the camp. Daryl's parents had been over to make plans for the wedding, but when they arrived they didn't expect to find it was now decided by the youngsters that a double wedding was in the making. Just before dawn Owen, whilst returning from his nights hunting, had the surprise of his life when he saw not only the courting Mallards, whom he had asked to visit, but Wally and Wanda as well. The Owl was over the moon; when seeing the tiny angel at the cheeky chappy's side, he looked to the heavens and mumbled a few words to himself; and was thankful that, by some strange miracle, another little warbler wanderer had passed this way

"Especially a little girl one too!" he had craftily chuckled to himself. Whilst there the wizard had asked them to follow him, and when they reached the end of the ancient willows, Owen asked Denzel and Daryl if they would accept the tree for their future marital home. He told them it was a gift from him and his ancestors, who had resided there for more than a thousand years. Of course the couple were elated at Owen's kindness, and accepted with a nod and jubilant smile. Denzel after a moment's thought, came up with a name, and he whispered it in Daryl's ear, she was pleased at his idea to call it Craggies End; and when Denzel announced it to them all, he was glad to see the contented smile in the old wise one's face.

Wally, now he has found himself a lady, will start to build a number of nests, all of which will be poorly put together. These are called cocks' nests, though it doesn't really matter, because it's all in vain, for the female is the one who builds the family home, which is well thought out, then put together. The materials are usually of selected dried grasses, lined delicately with lush soft moss, unless the dear girl is choosy of course, and she isn't a lazy nest-wife, who likes a bit of home comforts 'n' class about the place. Then she'll probably drape the interior with a nice bit of soft comfortable silk from a spider's cocoon. These finest materials are spun and supplied by Sidney the well-spoken Spider and his long-legged web weaving wife Winnie, who both unsportingly get eaten for their hard labours. Unfortunately, spiders are one of the main food sources for the Warbler species, so you see Wally's firm really rely on the creepy crawlies for their every-day living, just as Owen the wise had taught him and Denzel about the foodchain of life.

Once news of the weddings had reached the king's ears, he had sent word that it would be his wish that they all get married on one very particular day, but no reasons why were ever given.

"If you all decide to choose that day, once joined in marriage, you will be entertained by the Kings 'n' Queens' of Kentish England!" Denzel, at the time, had asked what he had meant. The King just gave him a royal smile, winked, then asked the four of them if they would consider his proposal.

In no time at all, they made up their minds,
for the offer was too good to miss.
Denzel gave Cyril, their answer, yes,
Then turned and gave Daryl a kiss.
That day is the day when Kings 'n' Queens
From every lake in Kent.
Will come to dance so beautifuly
Like angels heaven-sent.

Once the date was fixed, messages of invitation were sent by every bird that had recently left to visit other waters, or by any welcomed visitors who had had their stay and were now returning to their own manors. These were asked to tell certain friends of the coming event. A message to the Chislehurst pond dwellers was relayed by Wesley the wandering woodcock, who was passing by that way whilst on his way to the lakes at Keston to visit his Uncle George, a regular flyer at the local aerodrome Biggin Hill. Woodcocks are very speedy birds and love to show off their skills in the air.

Actually, it is mentioned in local folklore, that many years before, George's great uncle Windthrop thought he was so good at flying, he had boasted to his pals that he could beat a Spitfire over a hundred yards. On the day of the race, quite a crowd had gathered on the sidelines to watch the woodcock's attempt. After they had waited for some time, a plane rolled out on the tarmac runway, the engine revved, and the plane started to taxi down the runway. When it got to the end, it turned and started to rev up, ready for take-off. But little did he know that the fighter ace in that plane was none other than the great Douglas Bader. But even after getting a tip off who the pilot was, Windthrop soon realised he'd never be able to leave this one standing. Yet he still wouldn't back down from the bet he'd laid, for this silly old bird persisted on his boastings that his opponent never stood a chance; and at this particular moment he was on the grass verge at the side of the runway, with his beak dead level with the Spitfire's nose. As the revs started to build up, the Woodcock's neck began to strain in anticipation, waiting for Mary the mistle-thrush to whistle the start.

"Well go!" she called, and what happened next according to what I've heard, is that the woodcock actually pulled away and had almost won his bet; but two inches from victory, as the Spitfire went by, it had sucked poor Windthrop into its slipstream and all that was seen was a cloud of singed feathers, and he was never seen again. (Strange story, but going by folklore, it was perfectly true.)

Well folks, the big day's arrived, and the goings on; my God, if you think there's been some carryings-on in the past on and about the manor, forget it! Activity! Let me tell you, that little plot at the Horton Kirby Lakes was so busy with incoming guests, it made Heathrow look like Biggin Hill in comparison. Not as noisy of course, mind you, with all the excited chatter 'n' screams of joyous laughter, but it wasn't far short, I'll wager. Mac was now on his second trip, he'd already brought in old Ted 'n' Tammy and a few of their smart relations from Chislehurst, and was now on his way to Dartford to pick up Trixy and Trevor along with one or two friends. Doves in their dozens above Coot Island were falling from the sky like snow-flakes. Swans, bringing even more whiteness to the sky, were seen coming in from every corner of Kent and were skidding in on the water from all angles.

Oh, everyone who was there knew what they had come for, and all were thrilled and longed to see the swans' surprise, although some of the older folk had earlier given some of the younger ones a bit of an insight of what was to come. Vast amounts of food like discarded bread, fruit and seeds, even a whole Dundee cake that was found, brought to the island and tarted up; and made into a wedding cake by Mini the Moorhen, so the grub was plentiful. Talking of coot's, they were well represented, and apart from the resident hosts, Charly chaperoned the new wife Chantelle, who were recently married at the Dartford Lakes, but for reasons of their own it was a quiet affair. Mini the Moorhen and her family settled in, and taking into account their recent family grief over the death of her nephew, appeared to be happy enough chatting away to one another excitedly, hardly able to wait for the wedding to begin. Tootsy had arrived without her hubby the night before, so she could be up with the brides and Clara at the crack of dawn, to help out in any way she could. Obviously Toots would be helping the girls get ready along with Aunt Clara, and Debbie the bride's mum The Brides were preparing themselves out of sight under some heavy foliage, getting ready to emerge from their seclusion and come out to meet their future husbands at 9.55 a.m. so they would be ready waiting for their grooms, although the actual wedding was scheduled for ten. As for those two, well five with Toad and Neddy, and would you believe old Yorky, who still thinks he's a teenager all over again, were all shacked up over at Toad's Terrace, where the cunning cockney had kept 'em out half the night for what he called a stag do. Toad's uncle Treadlightly was going to do the marrying, for he is a Toad of the Leather, which is equivalent in human terms to the Arch-bishop of Canterbury in the animal world, and does most of the marrying in his sector, South and East London, also this little plot at the Kirby; only because his nephew insisted, since his and

Tootsy's own wedding locally, so when Treadwell asked for him to marry his friends, and now that his sister's boy had set up home at the lakes, he decided to take it upon himself to do this service at Horton Kirby.

Victor and his furry family and one or two friends had arrived from the mainland with Cornelius, who since unintentionally ripping Vic's leg off and felt so guilty he had been doing his best to try and make up for it by helping this vole family, and at the moment was ferrying them back and forth to the Island. The deceased mother rabbit's family, whom the lads had befriended the day she was taken by man and his dreadful firestick, were brought from the mainland on a temporary raft of a bit of drift-wood that was towed across the lake by two proud Mallard Drakes. Lou the shrew turned up early with the wife and his ever-multiplying family. Kenny the clever kingfisher and his ageing wife Kate had arrived and had taken up a decent perch quite near to where the main party would be situated, and lucky they did, as the branches were being taken by the minute.

Clara, aided by Debbie, was busy putting the finishing touches to Wanda's headdress whilst Toots was trying to calm the little female down. She was ready, but not unlike Wally, was having a touch of the old nerves complaint; not too seriously, mind. Still Tootsy's croakings 'n' joking kept the little lady amused, and she was now ready to face the world.

"We all get butterflies in our tummies just before we get married, Wanda love!" croaked the female toad.

"Oh, so that's what it is making me feel as I do... I ate one this morning for breakfast!" chirped Wanda innocently. The other three females, who were just a yard or two away, had overheard the chattings, and now were rolling up in rapturous laughter, knowing full well that Tootsy had meant something else entirely. But what made 'em all smile was thinking that Wanda's tiny brain appeared to be much the same as Wal's when it came to being lakewise.

After being kept up half the night by Toad's tale telling, and reminiscing about his toadlet days on the banks of the

Quaggy in Lewisham, South East London. The rest of the company had fallen asleep where they had sat during Treadwell's marathon eight hour ear bashing, even though the cockney was on terribly good form and was so into his present yarn, he croaked on and on for at least another half 'n' hour before the old chap had tumbled it.

"Er... Y... you awake Denz?" he croaked utterly dismayed. But no answer came "Did ya like that story, Wal?" Again an answer never came. "Er... Wot abaat you two then?" he croaked. And as he looked over to where they were, Clarence was snoring his head off, and Neddy was beside him sound asleep.

"Cor, blimin' 'ell, wot an 'andy mob you lot are; look at yer's: lightweight's, that's wot you lot are! Oh well, I 'spose I'd better get me nut daan for 'alf hour, long ol' day tamorra!" he croaked to himself. Then the Londoner settled down and slept, not under his log, but most definitely like one going by the sounds coming from him.

Clarence was up early as usual, though after a late night decided to let the others have a lie-in, knowing the late night they'd endured, and even more than that, long tiring day ahead. He decided to call them at seven thirty, and when out of their roosts he ushered the wedding duo down to the water's edge so they could give themselves an extra good wash 'n' preen up. Even after the late night both of them were in a very jovial mood and there were no signs of any nervousness from either of them. Once they had washed and tidied themselves the sheen on both their feathers looked pucker; well according to Toad that is, and as they made their way back up onto Toad's Terrace. As they came Clarence watched over them proudly

"My, you two look grand!" he commented, and you could tell, by that look in his old eye, that he couldn't have been prouder if the pair of 'em had been his own.

"Yers... Proper dapper, don't ya fink, Neddy?" the cockney croaked as he admired his spruced up pals.

"Very tidy indeed!" squeaked the crinkled newt. "Are we going yet?" he called, getting very excited at the whole to-do; even more, he couldn't wait to go.

"Nay, lad, we mustn't be turning up at the island 'til ten. That's the time Treadlightly had fixed for the marrying. Don't you go getting too excited, lad; it'll soon come round!" the old boy assured him. To help pass the time Clarence had decided to tell Denzel about the day he had purposely pushed him into his first-ever flight, when he'd taken them on their maiden adventure to the river, which caused a few surprised laughs. Well, at last the time had arrived when they had to be on their way, and after having a few laughs 'n' giggles among the chaps, they left for the island knowing that this was the last trip they'd ever take as single birds.

As the five of them crossed the lake, Clarence had taken Treadwell and Neddy on board to fetch them across. Denzel would normally carry them, but owing to his and Wally's special day the old boy suggested he'd take them, so's they wouldn't ruffle the Mallards feathers and spoil the dear boy's attire; although Wally did cadge a lift from Denzel, after telling him he didn't want to fly 'cause he'd get all sweaty 'n' horribly smelly. Yet being so small the Duck knew he'd hardly make a mark.

With only a matter of minutes to go, the intended grooms and friends were rounding a bulrushed-covered bend, and into view of the island; they couldn't believe their eyes 'n' ears, when the little Island came into view. It was inundated with the happy smiling faces of the well-wishers and waiting guests. Wolf whistles were heard coming from every quarter of the island, as the over-excited relations and friends cheered as the lads swam towards the largest gathering of wildlife that any one on that lake had ever seen. Even Owen readily admitted he'd not seen such a gathering, and he doubted if there ever was; but I can assure you, that this that was happening now, made the animals at Chessington Zoo look like a hamster cage in comparison.

Now, at the same time, on the very same day in the human world, it was Cup Final Day 1965. Not that it made the slightest bit of difference to the animal world, for you'll never in all your life witness such comings 'n' goings. There were so many different birds on the Island, it was a twitcher's paradise, and who, should be out with his binoculars on this gorgeous sunny day? Why, Peregrine Crank from the Hall. Being the country gent he is, he didn't care too much for football. In fact it was one of his pet hates. No Peregrine would rather get his kicks spending the weekend strolling the lakes to do a spot of twitching. He had been out and about since early morning, although something to him seemed different and for the life of him he couldn't make out what it was, until he turned the next bend, that was. He was just about to pass some dense greenery when something sounding very odd reached his ears.

To his surprise there, on the small island which was at least one hundred and fifty yards out on the lake, he saw a spectacle that any member of the twitcher brigade would indeed give their right arm for. Immediately he knelt down out of sight concealing himself behind some leafy foliage just leaving his head protruding with his powerful field glasses, amazed at the sight he saw. Out on the little island and its immediate surrounding water was a gathering of mixed birds and animals of many kinds. He was so astounded at what he saw, he settled down, made himself comfortable and observed as the day unfolded.

As the grooms' entourage swam into the fold, not one of them could believe the sight before them. Denzel knew that Clara and ladies-in-waiting had something up their feathers with their secret giggling 'n' schemings earlier; but this, that was facing them now, was enchanting. The brides were sitting slap bang in the centre of the grass and mossy clearing at the front of the island; but oh, how different it was! They were immediately surrounded by the whiteness of at least two dozen swans sitting side by side facing inwards at the scene. They were in a line that stretched from the left side of the water's edge to the approaching grooms' view, that went in some thirty feet curving around the two brides, who were sitting either side of Treadlightly. Then the line went down the opposite side to the water's edge, making the shape of a horse-shoe, leaving the open end facing out onto the Lake and the approaching company. My, those girls looked a pretty picture! All Daryl wore was a small circlet of bluebells that dangled about her head, in the Cleopatra style, leaving her beauty to be admired; though Wanda being so small, settled for a little tiara of tiny pink chickweed flowers, which set off her exquisite cherubic face. The area between those swans was sensational: it was completely covered in petals that had been plucked from the many kinds of wild flowers that are found in the kingdom of Kent, and they were scattered everywhere in a thick carpet of multicoloured blooms. There was a beautiful circle of bluebells at least six feet in diameter, but only the pretty bells had been especially chosen and laid in the centre; and among this gorgeous blueness was an inner circle that was about a yard in diameter, decoratively interlaced with the pink blossom from the flowering cherry tree. All flower arrangements were gathered and supplied by Primrose the meadow pipit and her many relations, who were renowned for their arrangements and displays. She was known to have done this sort of work before, though reckons she only did it for a lark!

However, she and her fellow pipits certainly knew their game when it came to arranging a bloom or two. Branches from the higher trees, which hung over the Swans below, had doves perched at different levels all around the gorgeous setting. I must say every twig, let alone branches, had been taken by birds of every flight in life, not to mention by all types of land animals who were sitting inside the horseshoe on either side of a flower covered aisle that was made for the grooms when they left the water. Daryl sat on the soft pink bed of petals, whilst Wanda was sitting on a purpose-built perch that had been erected six inches above the gorgeous pinkness below. This was so that the tiny couple were raised just enough to be at talking level with the ducks, but mainly to be in better hearing distance of the half-deaf Treadlightly, and most probably up out of the way of his feet, going by what had accidentally happened to Tootsy, while he conducted his own nephew's wedding. The perch was knocked up very skilfully by two local head bangers the Yellowhammer twins: though Primrose wound a long daisy-chain decoratively around it to pretty it up.

All the food had been put at different parts of the Island for the guests to eat once the reception began, though a big cake had been especially put on display on a raised floral stand between the back of the wedding circle itself and the swans at the rear of them. Denzel and Clarence, with the chaps on board, swam to the edge of the Island at the mouth of this horseshoe of swans. The excited Wally, when spotting his bride-to-be, and the wonderful way she looked, darted from the duck's back, and was at his lovely's side on the perch and pecking her on the cheek, before you could say Jack Snipe. He was so eager to wed the catch he'd made, the excited little chap didn't even see the special aisle that had been laid on. Only when Wal was where he wanted to be, did he realise, when looking about him just how beautiful it all was; but just by looking at him, all could see the little soldier only had eyes for his pretty mate at his side.

It was one minute to ten when Denzel stepped from the water. He looked at his bride and surroundings, then at Wally and Wanda, which left him speechless with emotion, though he carried himself well as he made his way in a nice steady waddle up the aisle. He was smiling at the congregation as he went, and at the same time was thinking how gentle on the feet the soft coloured floor covering was, and then joined Daryl in the proper formal place at her side. Treadwell nodded silently as Denzel went by him before he sat next to the smiling beauty. Owen, when eyeing him up, had though he couldn't have looked more handsome, and so too did Wally, but he sure needed calming down a bit; the lovestruck lad could hardly keep his claws off the dear girl, though from what the whole of the congregation could see of it all they were so in love, they were both as bad as each other. All had gone according to plan so far, yet there was only one thing that could have spoilt it, and that was a single rain cloud that was drifting their way. Treadlightly shrugged his big rough shoulders and hoped it would drift over them; then raising his arms for all to be quiet he at last turned to the brides 'n' grooms. It as exactly 10 a.m. and time to start what he was there to do.

"Do you, Denzel Drake, take Daryl hen to be your lakeful wedded wife?" croaked the East Londoner. Denzel was quite shocked to hear how Treadlightly had refrained from using his usual mode of banter whilst conducting the ceremony, and was amazed he could croak posh when he wanted to.

"Yes!" replied Denzel, keeping it short and sweet.

"Do you, Daryl Hen, take Denzel Drake to be your lakeful husband?" The ageing Toad not only surprised Denzel, but was getting some reaction from many of the guests who were chatting among themselves and saying how well Treadlightly was doing, and can you imagine the little firm in the front row? Clara was sitting between Clarence and Tootsy, whilst Debs sat between Treadwell and old Dan, with Neddy sprawled out on the floral floor in front of them. There were a few tears coming from the two mums, and apart from one or two lumps in throats it was all going marvellously.

When he'd finished with the Mallards, Treadlightly was about to turn to marry the Warbler's, when a shower of rain fell upon them, and as all were about to grumble, a beautiful rainbow fell over the Island from one side to the other, which made this setting as near to perfection as one could only dream. The congregation, who had been just as mute as the swans, had hardly uttered a word since Treadlightly started, but now were all oohing 'n' cooing at the sight of the rainbow's appearance. The rain, which only lasted a few minutes, had stopped, and now it was Wally's and Wanda's turn. The old toad turned from looking at the rainbow in the sky, and just as he did, he had to have a giggle to himself when catching the excited Wal, who obviously wasn't ready yet, actually miming to Clara:

"We're next!" but soon pulled a little face when he saw the Toad of the Leather grinning at him.

"Now, Wally the Dartford Warbler, do you... take Wanda Hen, of the same species, to be your loving nestwife?" asked the now smiling toad.

"I do, I do!" chirped Wal almost bursting with love, and he was surprised at himself for not messing up his lines.

"Will you Wanda... Take Wally here, to be your ol' man, er... sorry abaat that, I forgot meself didn't I"... Lightly cleared his throat and attempted to start again, yet no one said a word or moved when hearing the dodgy cockney lingo accidentally slipping out during the wedding words; for all were amazed he could speak posh croakings at all, and it certainly put that Chislehurst lot's noses out of joint that's for sure.

"Yes, I most certainly will!" the tiny girl bird chirped.

"Lovely, my dear, you were just fine!" croaked the old Londoner. "I now pronounce both couples bird 'n' wife, you may kiss the brides!" And that was that! Although the wild life can put on a good do when it comes to celebrating weddings, they certainly don't hang about when it comes to the actual marrying. (And I've no doubt in my mind that if Lightly had been the character he was in human form, he'd have charged 'em) Well, the hoots, hollers 'n' whistles echoed around the lake in happy sounds of laughter, but it was nothing compared to the next step which was the cake-pecking department.

Immediately after the wedding it is traditional for the brides 'n' grooms to peck the cake. This tradition goes back to the beginning of time, and once pecked by the newly-weds, it meant all the others could tuck into the huge spread that was laid on. All four, plus Treadlightly who had got them surrounding the cake ready to take a peck each to mark the start of the wedding blow-out. Toad croaked for them to start, and as the four of 'em began to peck, all of a sudden Harry the Rat's bald head and wrinkled face came bursting from its top. He had done it again; and the cheeky rodent was grinning, displaying his custard coloured teeth at the surprised onlookers, then congratulated the wedding foursome.

It had made Denzel and Wally jump, but it caused frightened screams from the two brides, and some of the females in the pew, who most certainly weren't ready for H's sudden appearance.

On this particular day of each year the swans have what they call the Festival of Swans, which I gather is a yearly event, held at a different lake over a radius of thirty miles where the resident host's, the king 'n' queen of each individual lake, entertain their visiting counterparts, resulting in lavish gatherings. Both Denzel and Wally, along with their sweethearts, had agreed with the king's suggestion, apart from the swan's other surprise arrangements, for the entertainment had been made for the weddings of the year. And only wanting the best available, they called in Norman (The Throat) Nightingale. But this Norman was different, oh yes indeed, he sure was, and make no mistake! This was none other than the one... who actually 'n' truly sung in Berkley Square. Well, his time had come to entertain the wedding of the year, and I can tell you there was much excitement in the camp. Word had gone round that a very important celebrity had arrived from London. All the females were a screamin' 'n' dreaming to be serenaded by the most sought-after singer in the land. I'm referring of course, to nonchalant Norman, the Mr Cool himself. Norm, as known to his friends, wasn't just any old singing nightingale; no, most definitely not. Oh, he might have been that chap who sings in Berkeley Square, but he was originally bred 'n' born under the guttering of the Royal Festival Hall. It was there he, and his father before him, had learned, and nurtured their trade in the chirping 'n' chanting business.

Oh, how they loved to sing, whilst being backed below by such a beautiful harmonic orchestra. Even away from and out of hearing distance of the Hall, their voices were enhanced by their constant training, when singing along to the sound of harmony every time they played those instruments of heaven; and those sounds to this singing family of nightingales were priceless. It was a fact that his great-great-aunt Florence, according to local folklore, had had the most beautiful of voices of all the nightingale ancestry, well, until she got a frog in her throat that was. They say after her croaky mishap the poor girl couldn't sing a note. But it was said she soldiered on, and had nursed herself better: and when in the throes of making a comeback the following spring, the dear girl sang like a trouper.

And if you think in your tiny minds, that cockney sparrows can chant, or you like a blast from the old cock linnet, then you'll be thrilled to bits at this boy's performance; 'cause this entertainer's a bit special, and wouldn't be caught dead in any seedy joints. It was nearing the time when Norman had to start the job he was here to do at the Horton Kirby Lakes. The reception he got was ecstatic, which made him feel overwhelmed with emotion; and felt the proudest of all birds; present; because he was honoured to be chosen to entertain at such an important do.

"Royals in attendance too!" he silently sung to himself, whilst taking in the full extent of his huge audience below.

Weight-watcher Stanley, who since his landlord days had been putting the lard on by the day, had been chosen as master of ceremony, and after producing a very loud whistle, a silence fell about the place with incredible speed as the attention of all in attendance were fixed on the finest singing performer in the land, and a few other lands come to that. He, with such throaty talents, gets invited to all the upmarket 'n' posh do's. Funnily enough, it was Norman's father, Norman senior, who once said to have entertained Walter, the wasteful pigeon, when he threw a bash, at his penthouse loft in Kensington. This of course took place long before alcohol had stolen the poor chap's brain. He was said to have held the most lavish parties, and quite frequently too, so my informant hastened to tell me.

Norman was up there on the tip of the highest branches. He gave a chirpy cough to clear his tuneful tonsils, and the last was directed at the centre, to where the brides 'n' grooms and the main party were situated. The sight he saw appeared to him like heaven here on earth, as he gazed at the sight 'n' happy faces, which now confronted him. The adrenalin in his veins brought about a strength in his body he had never experienced before, a feeling of ecstasy, love and understanding, at the sight of such a gathering. His lungs began to fill with sweet fresh air, and the exuberance was so much, that the dear fellow began to think they never would, but once they were full to bursting point, it, my friends, was all worth waiting for. And sing! I've never heard the likes, and I've gotta speak as I find;

and as for the Italian contingent of these times, you know, that there Pavarotti and co, they most definitely wouldn't have stood a chance; and I must say the boy was blinding! Once that very first enchanted note shot out of Florence's great-great-nephew's trap, every creature at that ceremony were charmed at what they heard; and by the end of his third number, just as the formal part of the wedding was over, many of the guests, whether furry, feathered or skin, started to sing along to the songs the boy from London was singing. They clapped, whistled 'n' cheered, and Norman was in his element up there, blasting his little brains out, fetching gaiety to the ears 'n' hearts of every single one in attendance.

You should have seen 'em all; they were a dancing 'n' singing, jumping 'n' bumping, and screams of laughing pleasure were heard in every quarter. Can you imagine how that boy felt sitting up there? Being in the position he was now in, regarding the chirping department, he loved being constantly in demand by the highest order in the land. Half-way through his fifth song, Norman had to smile at his own thoughts, thinking "I've not done too bad for myself, considering when I first started out, I was even lower than the gutter!" During his performance Clara had leaned forward from where she and Clarence were seated, saying to Tootsy how lovely Norman could sing, then the old dear sighed and raised her ageing eyes, and finished by saying,

"I still love to hear my Wally singing, and I think if he had the same training as Norman, he'd be just as good!" Tootsy was grinning at her words, knowing only too well the old hen was only looking after her own, being so caring 'n' all. Well, the partying went on all morning, during which time Norman gave two half 'n' hour sessions, and it was obvious, going by the sounds of 'em all, he couldn't have gone down any better if he'd have been a meal in a French restaurant.

Treadwell's family and friends seemed to be making the most of the festivities, for it's not every day, or every year come to that, where such a gathering occurs. But the amphibians took full advantage of such a beautiful and exciting day. Oh, it was wonderful to watch; they were a jumping 'n' leaping, croaking 'n' joking, and enjoying themselves to the max. Treadwell and his Uncle Treadlightly were in fine form in making the others merry, and were having the time of their life. But, for safety reasons, they had to decline the dancing frolics, for fear of doing damage to any of the family, especially the juniors who might accidentally hop under their feet. (If you get my drift. I mean, can you imagine the damage, that could have been done by four of those plates of meat flying about that island at the same time?) The two sisters-in-law Tootsy 'n' Trixy, got on famously together, and being in the prime of their lives, were really making the most of the occasion. They were the life 'n' soul of the amphibian entourage; and apart from the odd short rest, so's to take refreshments and powder their noses, they had rarely left the dance floor. Even during Norman's rest periods, they had been cutting loose to the sounds of an up-tempo linnet, who had travelled down from Bow in the East End of London. Apparently he was actually a good pal of Treadlightly's, and only a week or so previously, they had met and discussed the coming event; and whilst in cockney conversation, the singer had offered his services to sing during the interlude, whilst Norman took a bite to eat and rested. Though the East Londoner readily admits he;s not 'alf as good as Norm, whom he'd always looked upon as his idol, yet in his own right he was a master at cheering the guests.

> He came to these lakes via Bexley,
> And flew over that old cuckoo's nest.
> And when settling down on the island,
> Breathing heavy 'n' needing a rest.
> Now Lenny was chanting a number,
> That made 'em all hop 'n' leap,
> Tread tapped his plates to his singing,
> And Lightly was snoring in sleep.

By noon the party goers were in full swing, and you should have seen the shenanigans taking place; the once peaceful Coot Island was completely the opposite. And if you think it was packed that day when the little Warbler returned from Crank's Hall, forget it. It was so over-crowded, that Owen, in jest, said to the king when spotting uncle 'n' nephew's earlier foot tapping exploits on the side-lines,

"That if their feet had been of normal size, at least four other members of the Toad family could have attended." This caused a deep belly laugh to erupt from the King of Dartford, who agreed entirely, with the old owl's observations. Though at the time zzzs were coming from the ageing Treadlightly's nostrils, who was a bit too old for this game, and had to snatch a wee cat nap. However, all in all, going by the grins on both cockney toads' faces, even though one was a-kip, you could tell they were alight with happiness at the way the day had gone so far.

After so much fun Treadwell, with Tootsy, who had left the main party soon after the wedding to join the amphibian's in their dancing frolics, had now decided to leave those of their own kind, and do their friendly bit by going around on the Island saying hello to every one they met, making sure everyone was happy, or maybe needed anything. But, at the same time were heading in the main party's direction to get themselves settled at the water's edge with their closest friends in time for the big surprise of the day. Yet, little did they know that close on their heels, and not too far behind them, was another character following them, and every time the Toads stopped for a natter, the pursuer stopped as well. It was about Toad's fourth stop 'n' natter to guests, and he was now listening to Dougy the dazzling dragonfly and his dainty wife Diane, who was having a right old laugh whilst telling Treadwell how he'd stung a human last Sat'dy week.

Well, if the Toad hadn't been so quick, he'd have missed the flicker which caught the cockney's eye. This wasn't the first time he thought he'd seen something odd going on behind, but now with his suspicion confirmed, and after pushing Tootsy gently out of sight, he also ducked behind Mac, the Canada Goose, who was talking to his own in-laws, old Ted and Tammy, and a couple of young poseurs from Chislehurst. All the while Toad was hiding, he wondered who it could possibly be following them. Well it was only a few seconds before Treadwell faintly heard skittering coming his way. All of a sudden...

"Gotcha! Gawd help us, Neddy, it's you! Nah wot's all this following me abaat caper then, eh?" croaked Toad.

"Aagh!" the little newt screamed "Treadwell, y...you, frightened me to death! I... I don't like dancing!" he said meekly "And Tread, I... I really want to come with you and meet Denzel and Wally's new wives, 'cause I haven't even seen 'em yet, let alone met 'em!" Neddy sounded so sad the tricky Toad laughed at his request and envited him to tag along. They made their way to where the main party were sitting, Neddy was so excited he could hardly wait, and as they approached the company they were greeted by much fun 'n' laughter coming from the happy brides and grooms, who at this moment were surrounded by what must have been the best part of the island's inhabitants, and as I say, many guests from other parts. There were so many, the lesser-known dwellers were watching it all from the tree tops at a distance while all the party revellers had settled down for the coming surprise that Cyril had promised. Norman had finished his spot, and so had the cock linnet, leaving all the eager reveller's sitting facing out onto the Lake. The main party were seated at the water's edge surrounded by the multitude of guests who had just about covered every place there was to sit or perch on.

"Here they come!" squealed Neddy, who had plotted himself up right in front of the married couples. Also Stanley's sharp eyes had caught the first sign of movement; as the Festival of Swans came out into view, he gave an almighty blast as he whistled in excitement. As the spectators watched, four and twenty mute swans came into view. The commotion that followed coming from the rapturous audience was astounding, but did cease immediately as the King of Dartford led the entourage of royal performers out onto the lake. They were in single file where each cob had his pen, directly behind him, leaving the lovely Grace as hostess to bring up the rear, until they came within twenty or so yards of the front of the Island's edge. Reaching this spot, suddenly Cyril began to

277

swim in a full circle still being followed by the rest of the royal swans. Then, just as he was about to complete the most perfect ring, by swimming up behind Grace at the tail end, at this perfect timing Grace 'n' Cyril broke off and each swam to the centre, leaving King George from the lakes at Hever paddling to catch up the rear of Bella the Queen of Bewl Water, completing the circle once more, leaving the two resident monarchs facing each other in the middle. Only Owen and one or two of the older folk had ever been lucky enough to have seen the likes before, leaving the rest never having the pleasure. And ever since Stanley's signal the noise on that Island erupted so much, at first Peregrine had thought a goal had been scored at the other meeting. He began to get very agitated and his frustration started to say,

"Where in God's name are all the fishermen? Every blithering time I've been here before there have been anglers by the score, and today of all days there's not a damn living soul for miles!" was heard coming from his hiding place. Then, "That blasted Warbler episode was embarrassing enough, but how in God's name can I explain this magical moment to anyone who's sane?"

Since his first sighting he had been running all over the place searching for some-one to tell. It was then, he saw the beautiful white birds heading towards the island. Poor Mr Crank was in an helluva state over all he'd seen so far; and as he hadn't been able to contain himself any longer, he was out of breath because the dear man had been galloping around those lakes trying to find a fisherman, or at least someone to back his claim to what he'd seen, and not finding a soul returned to his hiding place rather than miss any more of the most beautiful sight he had seen in his life. Just before he left in search of another soul as his witness, he had noticed that the singing 'n' dancing, appeared to be coming to an end, and he could even have sworn he spotted a foot-tapping toad, if his eyes did not deceive him. Swans, who had created the horse-shoe for the wedding scene earlier, had left for Gracelands to ready themselves for the festival, and were now swimming in single file heading once again towards the island gathering, which he also knew had never been recorded, although he did admit to himself it was a very unusual sight indeed. What really puzzled him was the way the island gathering was all seated facing out over the water. It appeared to him that the whole assembly seemed to be waiting for something else to happen, especially by the way they were all facing the water, let alone the humdrum mixture of noises coming from what must have been, in his calculations, the best part of the local residents, and a few more from other parts, he excitedly thought to himself. Peregrine was more than happy at what he saw and settled a bit more comfortably, to watch in true amazement; but he didn't realise what was to come.

Once the circle was formed each of the queens turned and faced their respective kings; at this sight the assembly on and about that island were quieter than the local nunnery and as we know there's a few funny black 'n' white birds there also.

Also at this time Clara couldn't help but notice, and remarked how well Cyril looked since the hook episode.

"Commence!" hissed the king. At his command the circle of beautiful white birds, as graceful as heaven itself having been treading water in their readiness, began to swim weaving in and out of one another bowing their long necks to each other as they passed, in a bow to the left, a bow to the right movement in synchronised perfection. In the centre of the circle a yard apart sat Grace and Cyril. They were facing each other, as the remainder of them swam round 'n' around the resident monarchs out in the middle, and were bowing to one another in a side-to-side movement.

This ritual only lasted for twenty five minutes, and is mainly performed so that each king and queen can individually show one another respect and love for their own species and the titles they held. The spectacle was extraordinary, and I can confirm without doubt there wasn't a dry eye on the plot, it was as though the angels had come calling displaying their heavenly dance. As for the audience, mesmerised wasn't the word. They, like myself were as enchanted, completely absorbed by this pageant so remarkably performed. It was more wonderful than each one present could ever wish to see in a life-time; unless a traveller of course. But I can most definitely vouch that once witnessed, the memory of it all is enough to last me, and no doubt everyone else who saw it, a dozen lifetimes.

Once the swans had ended their marvellous display they all made their way onto the island, and they were greeted and cheered as they came. Earlier, even Norman, whilst watching their performance when sitting in the wings with Lenny the Linnet who's eyes 'n' ears were fixed on his idol, absorbing the nightingale's every word, although he was the star turn at the big do, the swans had stolen the show. Denzel, and the main party were full of smiles as they greeted the swans on board.

"Well, was it all worth waiting for?" the king asked the happy married couples.

"Apart from my wife Daryl, it was the most beautiful sight I have ever seen," replied Denzel. Well, the singing and dancing went on for quite some time afterwards and most of the guests after expressing their joy and said their goodbyes, were leaving by the minute. Especially the ones who had travelled from far-off manors, having had to be home before darkness set in. By 6 p.m. that evening the main party had gone, and apart from a few close friends who had stayed to help Clara and the girls to clear up it seemed dead in comparison. The Yellow Hammer twins stayed on a bit to knock down the wedding perch, that they had earlier erected, and got rid of the sticks. Primrose, and her vast flock of relations were busy clearing away the floral setting and arrangements, even though old Clarence kept telling her, not to worry and leave it 'till the morning, but Primrose insisted that it wouldn't take her and her army a couple of hours, and later the dear girl who'd done 'em proud wasn't proved wrong. It was almost 8 p.m. before the majority of clearing up had been done, and the worker birds had left to go home.

Clara and Clarence's family of four, plus Stanley, had enjoyed it all so bloomin' much that they didn't want to go home. Treadwell and Tootsy stayed so they could help out the following day, which pleased the very excited Nuthouse

Neddy who at this time was tired but was more than pleased to stay over with the friends he loved so dear.

Peregrine stayed at his post until he had seen almost every visitor leave the island; and according to my information the way he began to talk to himself, the poor man was beginning to sound somewhat disturbed by the funny sights he'd seen. The wedding and the swans' dancing had blown his mind, but toads climbing on the backs of geese and taking off had just about destroyed any hope of sanity the mixed-up chappy was suffering. I'm afraid to report that Mr Crank vacated those Lakes in a very different manner from that in which he came; in fact you would have thought he was a young boy again, and run! The man was like a whippet chasing a bunny; and when he got to the perimeter fence leading out of the lakes he sprang over a stile in one almighty leap and headed straight for the village pub. From here, I can only go by the landlady's account.

Alice's account.

I was bottling up behind the bar, getting ready for the celebrating football fans, when I heard someone come crashing through the door, I turned and saw Mr Crank from the Hall. He was in a shocking state of extreme excitement, and before I got a chance to pull him his usual pint he started blabbering incoherently, so I decided not to serve him any more of what he appeared to have had too much of already. It was then I realised and became aware that it wasn't the booze at all; but something of what he was saying, and going by the nervous twitch he had, every time he opened his mouth, I began to think he must have hit his head or something. He kept on blabbering something about swans dancing over at the lake, toads being chauffeured about the place on geese's backs, and gawd knows what else the poor man was coming out with next. But when he dropped the second treble brandy and port over me new carpeted floor, that's when I rang 'em."

"Rang who?" I enquired.

"The men in white coats: from that funny house on the hill!"

From 'the men in white coats', I gathered she meant the place that the cockney linnet flew over at Bexley. Even up at the hospital, whilst telling what he'd seen, not a living soul believed him. Fact was, all respect that the locals had for him in the past had gone. They now looked upon him as a bit of an Walter Mitty; in lake lingo, or just another Harry the Rat. Alice finished her tale, but did add,

"They only kept him in for observation!" Well I ask ya? All the poor man did was tell what he'd observed, and there he was in a room at the funny farm being observed!

A day or two after the wedding Coot Island was back to normal, and looking at it now one would never know that such a huge gathering and festivities had actually ever occurred at all. It was early in the morning and the sun was just visible as it rose in the east, when a small company of early-birds set out from the Island. They were on their way to meet Owen at Craggies End, for this was the day that Denzel and Daryl will move into their new home that the old fella had given them to live and raise a family. It was a fine residence and was situated at the opposite end of the ancient row of willows to where the old wise guy lived. Yet at this moment in time the newly-weds, along with Wally and Wanda and the caring coots, were very excited as they made their way across the lake heading for the Craggies.

Yet Clara's exhaustion because the past few week's excitement with all the goings on and preparing for the weddings, had taken its toll. The old dear had much moaning from her ever worrying spouse Clarence, who had tried to persuade her not to make this trip even though it wasn't very far. But she had made her mind up and was adamant to be at the Craggies when Owen handed over the property to her adopted family. In fact the company all knew that wild horses wouldn't keep her from going to see Denzel and Daryl move into their very impressive abode. As the four big birds swam along they nattered 'n' chattered in excitement, whilst the two smaller ones floated above them enjoying and joining in the laughter that surrounded them as they went. The willows came into view and all saw Owen sitting on a low bough at the foot of the ancient tree, that the duck had earlier named Craggies End. He had been waiting for them as arranged before the wedding. He had agreed to meet them at such an early hour because he didn't want to miss showing them around their new dwelling, but the old rascal didn't want to lose any more kip than he had to either. So he thought if they met early he could settle them in, dearly hoping not to miss out on anymore sleep.

"Good morning to one and all!" Owen hooted to the approaching group. All returned their individual compliments of the day as the company came together. Immediately the old owl flew up and landed on a thick branch near the hole in the huge craggy trunk. Wally and his little wife flew into the branches and settled on the opposite side of the hole to where the wise one was perched. Leaving the four bigger birds settled on the water underneath the old tree, each looking up at the Tawny.

"Come on up, and I'll show you the place!"

Denzel and Daryl, with large smiles on board their young faces did not need to be told a second time and were up beside the owl in no time at all leaving Clara and Clarence sitting on the water's smooth surface as contented as can be, looking up at the smiling couple, who were now up there listening to Owen's every word.

"Well, go on then!" the wise one hooted. The newly-wed Mallard's looked straight at one another and Denzel, like the gentleman he is, gestured for Daryl to be the one to inspect the inside of their new residence to see what she thought. Not being able to contain herself any longer the dear girl was off her perch and indoors before Owen, or the others come to that, blinked, and once inside she was in no hurry to come out until she'd looked over every bit of her new home. Whilst at the same time on the outside, Denzel looked across at Owen, who had a look on his face wondering what on earth could the sweet girl be doing in there for such a long time. Then he looked down to the water to see Clara and Clarence's necks stretched 'n' strained hoping they wouldn't miss too much of what was going on just ten feet above. The two warblers were toing 'n' frroing impatiently unable to keep still for one moment, as they couldn't wait to see Daryl's face emerge from the threshold of her own front doorway. But still there was no sign of her. Half 'n' hour had elapsed now and Owen, who thought it would be a two minute job began to get a bit moody 'n' restless, started to tread up and down getting very impatient indeed.

"What ever is that girl doing in there?" retorted Owen. "Has she fallen asleep ma, boy?" Just as Owen's beak had closed Daryl exited from the hole looking even more lovlier than when she went in, and that look told them all that she was more than thrilled with their new home now she had thoroughly inspected it.

"Did you find everything suitable and to your liking my dear?" asked Owen a wee bit sarcastically. All present detected this in the old owl, but all knew only too well that him missing out on his sleep was making him a little grumpy.

"Oh Owen, thank you, I just love it! And I cannot wait to start spring cleaning and get it ready for our coming family."

At the same time that Daryl was stressing this, she was pushing her husband into the hole for him to have a look and see what he thought. Unbeknowings to her Denzel could tell the Owl was a bit grumpy through sheer tiredness, and no sooner had he gone in that hole he was out again in seconds expressing how wonderful it was inside the trunk. Whilst below down on the water's surface the two olduns were as chuffed as anything seeing that their daughter in-law was not only a good looker, but showing obvious signs of a good nest-wife and mother to her coming ducklings. In fact all present were happy in what they saw in the two Mallard's faces, and, as anyone could clearly see, there was love and contentment from their beaks, all the way down to their webbed feet. Well, the inspection was over and smiling faces were on board everywhere, even Owen, as tired as the old boy was, managed a smile now that it was all over, but excused himself immediately afterwards and flew straight for his end of the willows, before he fell off his present perch altogether. Clara and Clarence returned to Coot Island alone after telling the two couples that they will be alright, and for them not to be too long in visiting them once they got settled into their new homes.

Soon, Wally and Wanda after seeing their best friends move into their new dwelling, returned to their own territory hidden in a thick covering of gorse, where at the moment they were just roosting among the tiny yellow buds bursting from its dark green branches. They had only recently found this place for themselves; not too far from the Craggies, and quite close to the back of Coot Island. Another two weeks had passed, and Wanda, just like all female Dartford Warblers, selected the spot in the place they had chosen, and single-handedly constructed the family home. She had more or less built this without her hubby's knowledge, for he was too busy knocking up; and offering her several of those silly fragile cock's nests that those male Dartford ones do. After many attempts and getting loads 'n' loads of knock backs; the little scout as one can imagine found it hard to accept his loved ones refusals. Even though it's quite natural for the male to build and offer such poor residences.

However the lady Dartford ones always have the final say in the matter, and that's that! But once she showed him the comfortable silky interior he realised she was a far better home-maker than he was and accepted that fact whole-heartedly; which made the tiny chap love her all the more. And after his feelings of rejection had subsided he had to admit he adored what the female had created. Soon after this episode the young couple were already talking of starting a family of their own, just as Denzel and Daryl were planning Also their toad friends who were already expecting a new family of their first ever young ones; so now as they had settled into their new abode both knew it was time for them to lovingly create their own.

One month later after the home-making had ceased, the two females were each sitting on a clutch of eggs, Daryl seven, and Wanda five. The two girls hardly saw one another over this period, for both were spending long hours on their nests, only leaving to feed, and on some days never leaving at all. On those times the doting male would return with food they had collected, so's the females could eat without having to leave the nest and the warm live eggs beneath them. Sometimes the male woud take turns to give the girls a break for this was the only chance to catch up on each other's progress before the infants arrived. It was on one of these breaks Daryl and Wanda were having a little discussion...

"Are you getting excited Da'l? I am." chirped Wanda smiling to herself.

"Excited! I'm over the moon, and my Denzel's been so wonderful!" sighed the beautiful girl.

"And so has my Wally too!" the wee girl insisted. "I know he drove me mad the other week with those silly cock's nests of his, but he's certainly made up for it now!" Daryl couldn't help but laugh at her tiny best friends chirpings of sticking up for her adorable hubby. After this conversation both females returned and had taken over their positions on each ones respective nests.

Daryl, once settled began to tear feathers from her breast and firmly, but carefully placed them about herself to keep her brood at the correct temperature.

At the same time over at Toads Terrace, the cockney and his once again slender wife, were proudly gazing down over the water at what was a thousand 'n' one tadpoles. They were not particularly happy at this time, for they were seeing their huge family getting less 'n' less each and every day since they were born. All manner of fish were eating 'em, birds and small animals were taking them for natural food. But alas, there was nothing that could be done, except sit by and watch their multitude dwindle. Yet as frustrating as it appears both parents knew it all was all part of nature and the Foodchain of Life. So naturally both had a deep down in built knowledge of such happenings, and had been warned by their elders of the heartache. Though it didn't stop the two over-seeing parents worrying of just how many would be left to bring up, and enjoy. At the very moment as they were watching over their youngsters, another shoal of fish were swallowing many of the remaining tadpoles, and the leathery Londoner was raving, and did he have the hump!! He was leaping about winding himself up, knowing there wasn't a single thing he could do other than let nature, as cruel as it can be at times, take its natural course.

"Toots, gel, it's all wrong mate! It's aht ov order, that's wot it is!" Tootsy just sat there unable to look any longer with tears streaming down her lovely face, when seeing even more of her babies disappear from the scene, not in the mood to even answer her despaired husbands frustrations.

The weeks had passed and after so much perseverance from the two expectant mums, and helpful dads-to-be, time was drawing near where both couples were getting very excited indeed. Why, only yesterday the two females during one of their rest periods whilst out on the lake were heard to be saying,

"That they can even hear the youngsters stirring inside their shells!"

Well if what I heard is true the eggs should be ready to crack at any moment. And going by Denzel and the little fella's antics it wouldn't surprise me, if one or two of 'em had broken out into the world already the way those two have been shaping up! It was the last Wednesday in April; Denzel was standing guard over his loving Daryl, whilst she performed her task of motherhood, he was very nervous at this time and was swimming up and down below in great expectations of their very first young to arrive at any moment. Not too far from him was the Dartford dodger, who as one can imagine was in bits over the whole to do. He was darting everywhere toing 'n' froing from twig to bough outside the family home and forever looking at Wanda to see if anything below her was happening yet!! And every five minutes or so kept nipping over to Denzel from time to time asking if he'd had any movement in the camp; he was in a right old two 'n' eight; as the cockney would say. Well, by noon on that fine sunny day in April Daryl reported the good news that the first of the eggs had hatched, and before it got dark that evening Daryl was sitting at the nest-holes entrance, looking at the doting dad perched on a thick craggie branch only inches from her. Both proud parents had large smiles in board as they watched over their brood of seven healthy ducklings, five girls and two boys, who were clambering all over them for love and affection. And knowing the parents as we do, that is one thing that this family will never go short of. During all the excitement at Craggies End Denzel was so busy with his lot, he hadn't noticed Wal's absence, and going by the look of him at this moment in time he appeared to be in another world entirely.

At ten past six in the morning, on the very same day over at Gorse Green Wanda gave Wally the wonderful news that the first of their young had hatched, and similar to their Mallard friends by the end of the day all had hatched into the world, except one!! The ones that had hatched were all girls, and although the parents were absolutely thrilled to bits both were anxious for the fifth but nothing came. Wally was sitting at nest-side and from time to time giving his devoted wife a little peck on the cheek; whilst this was going on she had noticed a slight hint of worry on his face. Night came and both went to roost in hope that the last of the brood would arrive. During the night Wanda had realised what had been eating at Wally. it came to her in a flash,

"Of course there are no boys!"

NOT LONG NOW STEAKY ME SON

It was a lovely time of the year, when after a long hard winter, spring had arrived and it was time for all of nature's life to go forth and multiply, keeping the balance of all God's creatures and plant life as it should be. It's such a shame that Humans with all their so called advanced brains have to let the side down by upsetting this balance of nature in our world.

The cause! Greed and uncaring ways and attitudes towards their own kind, and all other less fortunate species in a world that belongs to all.

EPILOGUE

(Three months later)

I think we'll leave our friends and relations to get on and enjoy their lives and thrive at the lakes. So for the time being Denzel and Daryl are happy living with their new family of seven, five girls and two boys at Craggies End. Owen's wedding gift, that wasn't too far from the ever caring coots, who incidentally are in their element having all the ducklings running amok all over the island, let alone Wally's lively littlen's. As for the Dartford Dodger Wal, he and Wanda and the four girls and a boy, whom he'd named after Stanley his landlord, were contented as can be with their life at present, skittering over and under the place they'd made their home at Gorse Green which was a thick cover of gorse on a bank, quite close to Denzel and the loveable Coots. As for the Cockney Toad, well, he's cushty, he and Tootsy and the cotchel of tads are doing pretty well for themselves. Their hoard of infants whom had changed from their tadpole stage were now happy toadlets who, appear to be enjoying life, whilst swimming 'n' leaping about the place having the times of their young lives below their overseeing parents. Giving Mum 'n' Dad five minutes to themselves to have a cuddle up on the Terrace outside the family home. Oh, he just wants a word wiv ya...

"Cushty it is? Me 'n' my gel Toots plotted up 'ere relaxin' 'n' all lookin' daan over our dustbin lids, yers, proper pukka! It is, gawd bless ya's. From me 'n all."

Why, that slippery toad! See what I mean about that cunning cockney; he's tried to nick the book not only from Denzel, but from the author too. Well, I ask ya, I can see in future I'll have to keep an eye on him!!

GLOSSARY

Irish Duck (The Shoveller)

Be Jasus	Jesus
Oi	I
Oi'll	I'll
Tought	Thought
Ya	You
Fink	Think
Dabs	Feet
Loif	Life
Dats	That's
Em	Them
Oi've	I've
Jig	Dance
Foin	Fine
Tree	Three
De	The
Meeten	Meeting
Moils	Miles
Dare	There
Troly	Truly
Roight	Right
Ja's	You's
Egit	Idiot
Ting	Thing
Ta's	To
Wid	With
Flutter	Gamble
Shufty	Look
Orf	Off
Tumped	Thumped

Cockney Toad

GG	Horse
Gander	Look
Cushty	Good
Yorn	Yours
Two 'n' eight	State
Sproggs	Children
Daan	Down
Aht	Out
Nah	Now
Good Gawd	Good God

Gypsy Horses

Gry	Horse
Dikeye/Dik	Look
Chavvie	Man
Grewd	Grown
Trashed	Frightened